YEAR *of the* SHEEP

A Novel of the Highland Clearances

James Y. Bartlett

For Susan
with undying gratitude to the many people of Scotland
who have made this traveler welcome over the many years

*Mo thruaighe ort a thir, tha'n caoraich mhor a'
teachd*

Woe to thee, oh land, the Great Sheep is coming

For Susan
with undying gratitude to the many people of Scotland
who have made this traveler welcome over the many years

*Mo thruaighe ort a thir, tha'n caoraich mhor a'
teachd*

Woe to thee, oh land, the Great Sheep is coming

PROLOGUE

The STORY WAS TOLD IN THE crofts of Glencullen for years afterwards. On a cold winter night, the people of the village would gather in one or another of the rude mud and wattle huts, where a warm fire in the center of the large central room would send its peaty smoke rising to the hole in the thatched roof. The women would gather on one side, knitting, sewing, mending and catching up on gossip, while the men sat on the other side of the fire, smoking their pipes and discussing the weather. At one end of the long narrow croft, the cows and sheep and chickens would make themselves comfortable in the straw, glad for a chance to be out of the cold wind that howled down from the snowy heights of Ben Cullen and rifled through the river valley. On the other side of the croft, the children would play quietly in the sleeping quarters, or climb up into the rafters, beneath the thatched roof, waiting for the music and the stories to begin.

There was never a schedule. After the gossip had been exchanged and the smokers' pipes emptied and filled again, someone would haul out a battered old fiddle and begin to play. The mournful notes would help drown out the sounds of the wind outside, and fill the croft with ageless melodies they all knew. Perhaps someone would hum along, or one of the women with a nice voice might begin to sing the words, telling of lost love, long journeys, or the heroic battles of days long gone by.

And when the fiddler had put down his instrument and picked up his pipe again, one of the old men would clear his throat and beckon the children to gather near. It was time for the story of the blind bard and the soldiers at the Battle of Culloden Moor, when the warriors of the Highlands had met their final defeat just fifty years ago at the hands of the Butcher of Cumberland, the hated brother of the English King.

Every teller of the tale had his own version. He would add his own personal dramatic flourishes to add emphasis to the story and hold his listeners' interest. But it was not necessary to exaggerate the facts of the tale. The women would quietly work at their mending, their fingers moving deftly as they listened. The children would be wide-eyed, hanging on every word. Even the animals seemed to listen to the story, the cows gently chewing their cuds, their large black eyes limpid and wide with interest.

This is how the story went.

The air was cold at Culloden Moor that day, when the men of the Highlands gathered to stop the English army and protect our Bonnie Prince. No Highlander ever shrank from his duty to God and his Prince because of a wee bit of rain or snow, and they did not on this day either. The MacDonalds held the left, Monaltrie and Lady MacIntosh's regiments the center and Lord Lovat and Lochiel's men were on the right flank.

But our brave troops were tired and hungry and cold. They had marched all the way to Nairn the night before, close enough to Cumberland's camp to hear the officers snoring in their tents. But our generals decided not to press the attack, and the men turned and marched all the way back to Drumossie before the dawn. They had not had so much as a piece of bread to eat for two long days.

But when the English troops arrived on the field of battle at the noon hour, our brave Highlanders were ready. They were singing of victory and glory and thinking that once they had put that Butcher Cumberland to route, sending him back to his brother the King, they would return in freedom to the glens and mountains. They would be welcomed as heroes in the arms of their families, their wives and their children. They would prepare to take the cattle to the summer shieling and plant the spring crops of barley and wheat. The days would pass as they always do, bringing good tidings and bad. And they would dwell in peace once again, with the memories of this final battle to keep them warm when the winter wind turned cold.

Now one of our own was there that day. Iain Ban Mackay, born of this very village, had gone to join the army of the Bonnie Prince when the call had come the year before. He was then in his eightieth year and had been blind since birth, but he was no less brave than a man of twenty with both his eyes. Iain Ban had taken with him his granddaughter Margaret to help him in the camp of the army. She cooked his meals and prepared his bed and helped him get where he needed to go. And Iain Ban was a great comfort to the clansmen. He recited the ancient poems and sang the songs of battle at night round the campfire. He reminded the brave men of their duty and told them the tales of the heroic warriors who had battled before and gone to the summerlands of heaven laughing in the face of death. Iain Ban was known throughout the army of the Prince as the keeper of the stories of old and the singer of the songs of death. It is said even Prince Charlie himself heard of the bard's fame and came one night to hear his poetry and his songs.

Now as the two armies prepared to fight on the cold and snowy fields of Culloden Moor, Iain Ban felt the presence of death in the cold rain and the sleet that came down. He took Margaret and hid her in a thick patch of gorse at the rear of the battlefield and told her to stay there and make not a word nor sound no matter what might happen. And then he stood nearby, singing of the victorious battles of old, and calling on the forefathers to protect the clans on this day and bring victory to Scotland once again.

Then the English began to fire their cannons, of which there were many. Oh, so many. From the left and the right, the big guns roared and roared, pouring out smoke and fire and sending ball after ball across the treeless plain. Oh, the bloodshed was piteous to behold! Our brave men stood in their formations, brother next to brother, father next to son, silent and strong. And many died where they stood. A young McLeod holding the reins of the Prince's white steed was laughing at the sound of the cannons until his own head was removed from its shoulders.

He was just one of many who went home to their fathers that day. The English cannonade was relentless, and it went on for what seemed like hours. And one of the balls found its way to the place where Iain Ban was standing and singing his songs and it took off his very leg at the knee. Margaret, watching from the darkness of her thorny shelter within the gorse cried out to him, but he motioned her to stay where she was, and he sat painfully down against a rock and continued to sing of the glory to come, in this life or the next.

It was as if the loss of Iain Ban's leg was the signal to advance. For the generals finally gave the word to the Highlanders, and with a shout that must have startled the Blessed Virgin in Heaven, they charged across the moor, swords drawn, shields at the ready.

Alas, alas. It was a sad day. The saddest that has ever been in fair Scotland. Where before the English bastards had turned and run at the first sight of our brave and glorious warriors, on this day they stood and fought. Their muskets cut *down the first wave of men, and then they used their bayonets on the next, and the next, and the next after that.*

The bodies of our brave men piled up, one upon another. The MacDonalds and the Grants and the Campbells and the Colquohons. Died all. The ground ran red with blood that froze into red ice. There are still old men alive who can remember the day the ice turned red with the blood of Scotland's finest.

Iain Ban was not killed by the cannon ball which removed his leg. Oh, no. He was a strong man, even in his eightieth year. He sat back against a rock, just next to the patch of gorse wherein Margaret huddled, weeping silently as she watched her grandfather bleeding upon the same cold ground. He spoke to her calmly, telling her that his day of death had arrived, as it must for all men. He was happy that the Father in Heaven had allowed him to die on the field of battle. It was honorable to die in this way. While the battle raged, he told her many things that he had not before. She spoke not a word in reply. Had he not told her to remain silent no matter what? She wept, in fear and fright and sadness; but she wept silently, making no noise.

The battle was as short as it was fierce. When the last wave had come to naught against the English bayonets, and the English reinforcements came up from the rear with freshly loaded muskets, the Highlanders left alive knew the day was lost, and they turned and ran for their lives. The English cavalry began attacking from the flanks, chasing after the fleeing Highlanders and cutting them down without mercy. And the other English troops began to march across the blood-red field, finishing off the wounded of our men without mercy. There was no mercy that cold, cold day on Culloden Moor.

Soon, a troop arrived at the spot where Iain Ban sat, his life slowly ebbing away. He made no sign and asked no quarter. Iain Ban knew his earthly life was over, and he began to sing of the glories of the next life. He heard the men coming and he uttered a prayer—some say a curse, others say an incantation of magic—that his little granddaughter Margaret might remain silent as the English came.

The captain of the troop ordered one of his men to finish off the man singing his dirge against the rock. The soldier unsheathed his sword and prepared to kill the old man. Then he leaned down and took a closer look.

"Captain!" the man cried out. "This bloody bastard is blind! And as old as these hills! And he's bloody mad—he's singing!"

"We haven't got all day, soldier!" the captain cried. "Get on with it!"

The soldier shrugged and did his duty, running his sword through the chest of Iain Ban Mackay. May his name be remembered as long as there are people in this valley and as long as Scotland remains one nation and one people.

But the soldier stopped after doing his merciless deed. "Did you hear something?" he asked. He looked around. There was no one else near at hand. Just a thicket of gorse, dark with shadow. He took his bloody sword and stabbed once, twice, into the thicket. And he was about to stick his head inside the branches, when the captain called out to him again.

"Come on then," the captain said, irritated. "We've got them on the run. We can't stay here and chase after every ghost. Move out!"

And so the soldiers left. There were more, of course, who followed. The army of the Highlands was routed and the English began the chase to find the stragglers that has not stopped to this very day.

Day passed into night and night into day again. And all that time, the young girl named Margaret huddled inside the thicket of gorse, wrapped in her tartan. But her wool was now red with her own blood. The soldier had caught a part of her arm with one of his thrusts and sliced the skin from elbow to *wrist. It was not a deep wound, but the girl's blood ran free for quite a while. She was glad to see the blood and feel the hurt, for it matched the pain in her heart. She would peer out from time to time and look at the body of her grandfather, and begin to weep again. But she stayed in her hidden place for three days and nights, until she heard friendly voices, Scottish voices again. The townspeople from Nairn and Inverness had finally come to remove the dead from the field of death, and when Margaret was sure that the soldiers had gone, she crawled out from the thicket, and stood up on her shaky legs.*

She leaned over and kissed the forehead of Iain Ban and she reached inside his cloak and took out a small leathern bag which she knew he carried with him always. He had told her of the secrets it held and the powerful spells, and he had taught her the songs and poems. He had known that she, too, had the gift of second sight and the power of the spirit world, and he had taken her on his journey to death so he could teach her more of the things that he knew. And he knew that Margaret Mackay of Glencullen would one day become a greater bard than even he had been. He had known these things from the very day of her birth.

And when the teller of the tale was finished, the croft was silent as the grave, and the sound of the cold north wind could be heard pushing at the door and the roof. And finally one of the children would ask, "But what happened to Margaret? Did she become a famous bard?"

And the story teller would smile, and wink at the other adults gathered around the warm smoky fire. *Aye,* he would say. *She had the gift. She somehow managed to make the journey back to the Highlands, despite the roadblocks and the soldiers who flooded through all of Scotland. searching for those who had served in the army of the Bonnie Prince. Those were dark, dark days, children, when many a man and woman were killed, or beaten, or arrested. Margaret was just a wee lass, but she was as strong as Iain Ban and had his red Scottish blood in her veins.*

But from the moment she came forth from the thicket of gorse after that terrible day, she never spoke another word. She returned to this very village and she lives here yet today. You know her as Mute Meg, who lives in the rude hut beside the River Cullen. She is now almost as old as Iain Ban on the day he died.

Mute Meg? The children gasped, even though they had heard this tale a hundred times before. *But she's a witch!* they would say.

Nae, the storyteller would shake his head. *Mute Meg has the second sight and knows the recipes to ward off sickness and cast out the evil fairies. But she is nae a witch. She may not speak, but her wisdom is deep, deeper than that of any man. I will hear no words against Mute Meg, granddaughter of Iain Ban Mackay, bard of Glencullen and martyr of Scotland.*

The children would think...Mute Meg? That tiny old white-haired crone lived by herself at the edge of the River Cullen. The children were full of stories about Mute Meg and the spells she could cast. They knew to give her a wide berth, even though she rarely ventured outside of her small dusty yard. People came to her often with their troubles and maladies, hoping she would have some tincture or balm to ease their pain, help their disease. Mute Meg the Witch? It was not possible that she had once been the granddaughter of the teller of tales and singer of songs.

But that was the story that the men of Glencullen told, night after night, year after year. So it must be true.

BOOK I

1

London - February 1804

It had been the busiest of days for the staff of Cleveland House on Queens Walk Park. Lord and Lady Stafford were entertaining that night. That was not unusual—almost every night someone of high station arrived to dinner. His Lordship, one of the richest men in Britain, if not all of Europe, had no dearth of friends, or those who wanted to be counted among his favorites.

Still, Mr. Gunn, the head butler, had spent the entire day making sure all the arrangements were in place and the staff prepared. Her Ladyship, the Countess of Sutherland, had been specific in her instructions that no detail was to be overlooked. The people coming for dinner that night were her peers, if it was possible to compare anyone to her own exalted position. The invited guests, lairds and landowners, fellow owners of vast tracts of land in Scotland, were all neighbors, distant relatives and even friends of the Countess.

Most of them still held the title of "chief" of their ancient clans, as did the Countess, Elizabeth Gordon, the 19th chief of Clan Sutherland. In other times, these men would have met in some empty mountain strath, far from the comforts of any city. They would have parleyed around a huge fire, dined on the juicy meat of a freshly slaughtered cow, drunk freely from kegs of *aqua vitae* that had been distilled nearby and danced the night away to the music of the fiddle and the pipe. It would have been a meeting that lasted many days and nights; with many roasted steers and emptied kegs, many songs and poems, and probably, many drunken fights.

But now the descendants of all those valiant and hardy men, whose bits of dust had long been reclaimed by their native soil, mostly lived in the comfort and splendor of London, as did the Countess and her wealthy English husband. They dressed in fine French silks instead of rough, warm tartan plaids. They ate from the finest English china instead of with fingers and dirk, and while they may have drunk with the same gusto as their ancestors, they tended to prefer a fine claret or port served in a crystal goblet.

Late in the afternoon, the Countess came downstairs to preview the settings. The rooms had been swept, dusted and polished, the table laid in a glittering array of crystal, china and silver, a huge spray of flowers set in the entrance lobby. The Countess looked at the flowers and frowned, her delicate features momentarily dark. Mr. Gunn noticed—he noticed everything when he was in the presence of the Countess—and he in turn raised his eyebrows a notch. *Shall I change them?* was his silent query. The Countess thought for a moment, and then made a barely perceptible shake of her head. *No…it's just that Lord Stafford, despite being the richest man in Europe, still watches the expenditures like a hawk.* Mr. Gunn relaxed.

The Countess double checked to make sure there were extra candelabras set out throughout the public rooms. Lord Stafford did not like dark rooms; he even insisted that candles burn throughout the night in his bedroom as he slept. His eyesight had been a trouble to him since his boyhood, and he much preferred bright light to shadowy darkness. The Countess did not bother going below stairs to check on progress in the kitchen. She knew that Mrs. Murray would have the dinner well in hand.

Like Mr. Gunn, Mrs. Murray had been with the Countess for decades now. Neither of the two senior servants required extra supervision.

"I expect our guests will arrive at seven," she now told Mr. Gunn. "Do you have the whiskey ready?"

"Yes, m'Lady," Gunn said. "And a number of bottles of his Lordship's finest claret."

She nodded, pleased. "After the dinner, we will move into the library," she said. "Mister Loch will be joining us there." Gunn nodded. Lord Stafford's business superintendant was not of the exalted class permitted to dine with the others. Gunn knew that Loch bitterly resented the slight, but understood there was nothing he could do. Like Gunn, he was a hired hand, not one born to his station.

The Countess went back to her chambers to dress, a process that would take several hours. Mr. Gunn made one more round, his practiced eye looking for anything out of place. It would not do if his Lordship had to interrupt his important evening to reprimand the staff for any miscue, large or small. Not do at all.

Mr. Gunn had begun working for Lady Stafford more than forty years ago, when he was barely a teenaged lad, and long before the lady had married her husband. His parents had been poor farmers and, like the rest of the people living in the rugged Highlands, could barely scrape together enough food to feed themselves and their seven children. When both parents had died during one particularly harsh winter, Mr. Gunn's relations had offered him in service to the Countess, the ultimate chief of the clan. It was either that or send him to join the Sutherland Fencibles, which would have meant a lifetime of fighting in America, Africa or now, against Bonaparte in Europe. Put to work as a gardener on the Dunrobin Castle estate near Dornoch, Mr. Gunn had worked his way upward over the years, first to a position in house, and eventually to that of head of house. The

Countess, an orphan herself since childhood, always had a soft place in her heart for those likewise afflicted by life. She had insisted on his coming with her to London when she had married Lord Stafford.

Mr. Gunn allowed himself a brief, secret smile when he remembered that event. It had been a party for the ages, worthy of celebrating the conjunction of two of the greatest houses in all of Britain. George Grenville Levenson-Gower was at the time the second Earl of Gower and stood to inherit all the wealth, property and titles of his father. The family owned vast estates in Staffordshire, at Trentham and Lilleshall. And, Mr. Gunn remembered, a reputation as a family of little distinction apart from the ability to marry into wealth. Which, of course, his Lordship had done when he married the Countess of Sutherland.

The marriage had been arranged by Lord Stafford's paternal uncle, the Duke of Bridgewater. That great man, unsuccessful in matters of love and marriage himself, had turned his energies into building things. His crowning achievement had been the construction of the Bridgewater Canals, which linked the busy mines and manufactures of Manchester and Birmingham with the seaport at Liverpool. With groaning barges moving non-stop up and down his canals, the Duke had become immensely wealthy. And when he died, just a few years earlier, the childless Duke had bequeathed his entire estate to his nephew. Lord Stafford's father had followed his brother to the grave shortly afterwards, and so Levenson-Gower, who was also Earl of Ellsmere, Viscount Trentham, and Baronet of Sittenham, now controlled all the wealth, property and power of the vast estates of Bridgewater, Stafford and Sutherland. He was easily the richest man in Britain, the King included, and was said to have an income greater than even the Pope himself.

When before his death the Duke of Bridgewater had begun to think about a suitable partner for his nephew, someone who could add to the financial depth of the family, the Countess of

Sutherland was first on his list of candidates. Elizabeth Gordon had been orphaned as an infant, and after a nasty and long legal battle with a grasping uncle, ably defended by an army of lawyers and solicitors, finally had her rights to her title affirmed in the House of Lords when she was barely ten. Growing up with family in London, the orphaned child had no idea that as Countess of Sutherland and chief of the clan of that name, she had inherited the family's one million acres of land in Scotland's far North. The Sutherland estates were the largest contiguous holding in all of Britain. The Duke of Bridgewater thought that adding that vast tract of mountains, lochs, rivers and glens to his family's own rich Midlands holdings would make his nephew and the family secure and comfortable for generations to come. And so the marriage had been arranged.

Outwardly, the wedding had been the grandest of affairs. The Prince of Wales had been the honored guest, and most of the Court had been in attendance. It was, all had agreed, the most lavish party of the year in London. Champagne had poured from the lips of statues and a pair of white muted swans paddled placidly in a special pool constructed for the occasion. The Archbishop of Canterbury had presided over the vows at the grand altar in St. Pauls, and afterwards there had been dining and dancing that had lasted all night long. Later, the couple had traveled to the North and received the blessings of the people of Sutherland. Although officially banned after the Rising of '45, the wailing of the bagpipes had greeted the Countess and her new husband at their palace near Dornoch, along with free-flowing drink and dancing into the wee hours.

Surprisingly enough, and contrary to all expectations including those of the participants, the marriage had been a success. The young Countess was considered one of the most beautiful girls in London, with her long black curls framing an attractive pale face from which her clear blue eyes sparkled with life. Her figure was slender, she danced divinely and she had read widely. George Granville Levenson-Gower, on the other hand, was anything but an attractive man. He had an odd-shaped head, a very large hooked nose and, because of his poor eyesight, had a habit of blinking rapidly and starting as if surprised that people were actually addressing him. The Countess, however, found him to be charming in a certain way. Perhaps wishing to make the best of the situation, she soon found herself growing fond of him. They had four children: George, the Ladies Charlotte and Elizabeth, and Francis, known as Gower.

Stafford, of course, considered himself fortunate indeed to have taken such a prized, not to mention wealthy, beauty as his wife. Together, buoyed by the hundreds of thousands of pounds flowing into their coffers from their canals and estates, the Stafford's had thrown themselves energetically into London society, entertaining lavishly, attending the latest plays and operas, and occasionally traveling to visit one or another of their holdings. Lord Stafford had long been a regular at the auctions at Christie's and had soon acquired one of the finest collections of European art in all of Britain, much of which now hung in the elegant rooms at Cleveland House. And he had his eye on an even grander house just a few streets away and within sight of Buckingham Palace, that boasted even more wall space for his growing collection.

Mr. Gunn straightened the frame on one such painting. All in all, he thought to himself, he had been lucky to have served in this household for so many years. Now that Lord Stafford had consolidated the other parts of his vast wealth, he had announced his intentions to concentrate on her Ladyship's Scottish estates. That was the purpose of the meeting this evening, and why the other Scottish grandees and chieftans had been invited. Mr. Gunn hoped that meant they would be spending more time at Dunrobin Castle near Dornoch in the Scottish North. He much preferred the brisk Scottish air to the foul smell and constant noise of London.

2

The CONVERSATION AT DINNER IN THE brightly lit dining room at Cleveland House was spirited. Bonaparte was threatening to blockade the British Isles and everyone in London suspected that he was planning an invasion. The gentlemen assembled at the table debated where the French general would launch his attack.

"The question, gentlemen, is whether the Scottish people will rise to support that French bastard," said Lord Reay of Caithness. "They've done it before, after all."

"Sir," protested Lady Stafford, "My people are loyal to the Crown. It was sixty years ago when the last rebellion was put down. And neither my grandfather nor any of his kinsmen joined with the Jacobites. Napolean offers nothing but subjugation to the people, and is related by family to no Scotsman. What possible reason would the people have for rebellion today?"

Lord Reay, a callow youth of twenty-five years, turned to address the Countess.

"Poverty and hunger, madam," he said, swirling the wine around in his goblet. "It is the engine of every rebellion. It drove those ungrateful wretches in the Colonies. It is what killed Louis in France. That and the secret desire, I fear, that still burns in the heart of every poor bastard in Scotland to yet see a Popish king on our throne."

"My dear Lord Reay," said Sir John Sinclair, the laird of Ulbster. "You are quite correct about the poverty of the people in the countryside. But I can assure you that those unfortunate creatures do not care about politics. If the King asks them to fight against the French, the Russians or the Austrians, they will fight—it's the only thing they know how to do well. And it may be the only way for them to put food in their bellies."

They began a debate as Mr. Gunn refilled their wine goblets. Lady Stafford thought back to the first time she had seen her vast Scottish estates, since leaving as an infant. She had been just a girl of seventeen. Her parents had died when she was a baby and she had been brought up by her uncle. She had lived her entire life in London or Edinburgh until that summer when her uncle told her it was time for her to see her Scottish home and meet her people.

Her people. How that phrase always caused her to shudder. Elizabeth Gordon had always been a shy girl. Although her cousins had been kind to her, she always felt different from them and all the other people in her circles. She could never quite define the feeling, other than knowing it was a sense of apartness. They all had something she did not: a family. She had always preferred to keep to herself. Now her uncle was informing her that she owned a vast number of square miles of countryside in the cold and forbidding mountains of Scotland, and that all the people who lived therein—*thousands upon thousands!*—were "her people" and looked upon her as though she were their leader and savior.

She had been frightened into rigidity when, after a long ocean voyage from London, she and her uncle had landed at Dornoch Ferry. There had been hundreds of people standing around the pier when she arrived and they began waving and shouting in a gruff, guttural language she did not recognize.

Her uncle, seeing her fright and confusion, had smiled at her and leaned down. "They are bidding you welcome, m'dear, and showing how delighted they are to greet the chief of Clan Sutherland," he had said. "Try to smile and wave if you can."

She managed to raise one hand to shoulder height and gave it a trembling shake. She hoped what felt like rictus on her face would be received as the smile she intended. She made it through the greeting ceremony with a bow here, a shake of the hand there and the occasional nod of her head. She remembered none of the names of the rough-clad, long haired, heavily beard-ed dignitaries who had come to greet her, and understood not a single word of the Gaelic in which they made their fine speeches. Finally, she was able to collapse in a nervous heap inside the large carriage her uncle had arranged. The crowd of people continued to mill around, shouting huzzahs and waving their woolen caps. To Elizabeth, they had looked half-starved, unwashed and hideous.

"Why do they carry on so?" she asked her uncle. "They do not know me at all."

He patted her hand reassuringly. "It is not just you they are cheering for, my dear," he said. "It is what you represent. You are the personification of the clan, a family that goes back eight or nine hundred years. You are the 19th Earl of Sutherland. Since your poor father died—God rest his soul—the people have waited to see you, to know that there is someone, a real living person, who cares for them, will care *about* them."

She had buried her head in her hands, trying not to weep. "But I am just a girl," she had cried. "I am no chief, and I am certainly no Earl. How can I pretend to be what they want me to be?"

Her uncle smiled at her kindly. "You do not have to be anything other than what you are," he said. "They already re-spect you and will do what you say. You are their chief, their leader."

"But I don't want to lead anyone!" she cried. "I don't know how to lead!." She was almost wailing. She could not imagine being the leader of anything, much less an entire shire of strange and frightful people.

"You will learn," her uncle had said. "One way or another, you will learn. It is your destiny."

The carriage had entered Dornoch after a short drive up from the port. There were more people gathered on the streets, still cheering at the sight of their long-awaited leader. Elizabeth had peered out at the rude houses of the village. To one who had lived most of her life in London, Dornoch did not appear to be much of city. The road was rutted and filled with puddle holes. The grandest building seemed to be the red-bricked Tolbooth, or local gaol, and it did not seem to be in very good repair. The carriage drew to a stop in front of the entrance to the churchyard. Looking out of the carriage window, Elizabeth saw a gravel path running through the gravestones, and leading to the steps of the blackened ruins of the Dornoch Cathedral, a limestone structure which seemed to have suffered greatly from a recent fire. A dour-looking minister, dressed in a severe black suit, stood at attention, surrounded by other worthies of the town dressed in their Sunday-best suits and hats.

"Now what?" she had asked her uncle, somewhat petulantly.

"You are to greet Mr. Grant and the presbytery and attend a service of welcome and thanksgiving," her uncle said. "Then we will go on to Dunrobin Castle, which is your ancestral home."

Elizabeth Gordon, the 19th chief of the Clan of Sutherland, and, until just a few moments earlier an uncertain and frightened teenage girl, frowned and shook her head.

"I will greet the man," she said, "But I will not enter his kirk. Pray tell him I am weary from my journey, anxious to see my new home and cannot stop to pray."

Her uncle had looked at her, amused. "Yes ma'am," he had said. "I believe your natural inclinations to leadership have already begun to show themselves."

As the dinner drew to a close, Lord Stafford looked around the table. Some of the gentlemen dining with him were known to him, either through general acquaintance in London society, or through his work in Parliament, where he had, from time to time, represented a constituency in Staffordshire. But others were strangers. His wife had filled in some details for him, but his man Loch had characteristically provided Lord Stafford with detailed dossiers on each of them.

Sitting to his left was the young Lord Reay, who owned vast tracks in Caithness, the county to the north of Sutherland. The unmarried Reay was a regular guest at London's most elegant soirees. Hostesses admired his youthful passions, his chiseled good looks and his ability to hold forth on almost any subject with energy. Still, everyone knew that after the dinners and the dances were over, Reay would head for the brothels near Covent Garden, where he was equally well-known and popular. According to Loch's dossier, Reay was running dangerously low on funds, was said to have borrowed heavily to support his gambling habits and might well be a candidate for selling some of his Caithness holdings if push came to shove. *Perhaps we can do something to provide that shove,* Stafford thought to himself.

Next to him were Sir Hector Munro of Novar and his cousin, Sir William Munro of Culcairn. Sir Hector had been a Colonel in the Black Watch and had spent most of the last twenty years in India. He was now well into his 70s and Stafford suspected he was not much interested in his Scottish farms. Sir William, on the other hand, depended on his holdings for his income, which was small but steady.

Across the table, Sir John Sinclair of Ulbster was deep in conversation with Sir Charles Ross of Balnagowan. Sinclair had been actively trying to modernize his estate, Stafford knew, and would likely be open to some of the ideas that would be presented this evening. Ross had purchased his lands when the previous laird of Balnagowan had been executed for joining the uprising of '45. Loch's dossier said that he rarely visited his holdings, much preferring the convivial atmosphere of Edinburgh to the cold and damp of Cromarty. The lairds of Foulis and Tulloch looked uncomfortable in the rarified air of Cleveland House; they were both minor landowners within the Sutherland estates and were distant relations of the Countess, but Stafford knew it was important that they were kept informed. His grand plan demanded that the countryside be united in agreement.

The servants began to take away the dishes. Stafford rose to his feet, blinking rapidly.

"Gentlemen, a toast," he said, holding up his glass of claret. "To Scotland, a land with a sad and barbaric past, but a land ripe with opportunity for the future."

"To Scotland!" they all replied in unison, and they drank.

Stafford led the group into the large library, where the servants had lit a roaring fire and brought in as many candles as safety would permit. Even so, the towering shelves filled with row after row of musty volumes made the room seem dark and gloomy. The gentlemen were served glasses of port or whiskey, as they desired, and they took seats arranged around the large stone fireplace. Lady Stafford slipped into the room quietly and took an unobtrusive chair near the door. Mr. Gunn circulated with the decanter of port and made sure everyone's glass was full. He melted back into the shadows of the room and stood there as motionless as marble, seeing all and hearing nothing.

Stafford emptied his glass and stood facing his fellow landowners.

"Sirs," he said, bowing politely, "I have asked you here tonight to talk about the future of our holdings in Scotland. I do so with some hesitation, in that I am not myself a native-born Scot, but have instead been fortunate enough to marry into the country." He nodded in the direction of his wife. "Nevertheless, while most of you carry within the bloodlines of Scotland, I believe you share with me a desire to see the country pulled up from its current lowly position. After all, if we can work together to bring prosperity to our country and its people, that will in turn reward us with, I am convinced, an increase in income for ourselves and our families in the years to come."

He nodded toward a thin, dour man standing against the wall at the back of the room. "I have asked my estate's commissioner, Mr. James Loch, to join us this evening to discuss ways of making our holdings better suited for modern commerce," Stafford paused while the group of lairds turned to look at Loch. His face was sharp and intelligent, with cool gray eyes peering out from behind a pair of thin spectacles. He met the gazes of the lairds with a barely perceptible nod of his head.

"Mister Loch has, at my request, spent a great deal of time in the last six months visiting our estates and holdings in Sutherland," Stafford continued. "He has visited every corner of the Countess' estates and most likely has called on most of you as well. We are both gratified for the hospitality you have provided. As a result of his travels and his observations, Mr. Loch has drawn up a series of recommendations for our consideration. It is my hope that once you have heard his ideas, you will consider joining with me in forming the Highlands Improvement Society. It is my wish that we, the lairds and landlords of these vast and ancient lands, begin to cooperate with each other in a series of much-needed improvements. It is my considered belief that our lands have been ignored for far too long, and that we, as rightful owners and lairds, have a duty to do what we can to bring more advantageous commerce and prosperity to the land."

Sir Hector Munro shifted uncomfortably in his chair, trying to ease the discomfort of his gouty left leg. "My dear Lord Stafford," he said, "While I thank you, and your lovely Lady, most kindly for your gracious hospitality here tonight, I am afraid you are trying to improve a part of the Kingdom which beggars improvement in any form. We in this room are unfortunate enough to own some of the worst land in Christendom. By location it is far removed from the rest of the kingdom and to the greatest extent impassable to all but the most determined. By its nature and its weather it is almost totally unsuited for any kind of agriculture. And the people…" He paused and shook his head sadly. "They are barely savages, the lot of them. They do not speak our native tongue, they live happily in the worst kind of squalor, they believe in superstitions and black magic, and they are the laziest creatures God has ever seen fit to create. If they are not stealing our cattle and poaching our deer, they are constantly drunk, whoring or sleeping. Improvement? The only way I can see to improve this lot is to put it all to the fire and hope something better grows from the ashes."

Stafford smiled to himself. Loch's report had mentioned that Sir Hector thought poorly of his holdings in the North; luckily for him, his Army pension and other East Indian investments provided more than enough income for his family.

"Sir," Stafford said, nodding at the older man. "You have quite concisely identified the problems we all face with our holdings in the North. It is indeed a remote and harsh land, difficult to farm and peopled with a citizenry lacking in modern skills. But rather than abandon the entire North as a hopeless mess, I see these conditions instead as an opportunity for improvement. I believe that when you hear what Mister Loch has prepared, you will be quite impressed."

The lairds looked at one another doubtfully, but no one spoke.

James Loch took up a large portfolio of papers and came to stand next to Lord Stafford in front of the fireplace. He bowed to Stafford, then turned and repeated his bow to the room. He opened his portfolio, adjusted his spectacles, coughed once into his hand and began to speak.

"Honored gentlemen and M'Lady," he said. "Lord Stafford has, over the last numbers of years, been involved in the process of improving his own states in Shropshire and Staffordshire. Under the influence of his late uncle, the Duke of Bridgewater, and his late father, he has undertaken to improve these properties in a modern and systematic way, taking advantage of new knowledge that was not available to previous generations of gentlemen. Change, especially on a large and outwardly unwieldy estate, is never an easy task. But with careful planning and considered implementation, it is possible to achieve excellent results."

He shuffled his papers. "My Lord Munro has eloquently pointed out one of the main obstacles to change in the North—the people. They live unhappy lives. They are not gainfully employed in any kind of modern commerce. Indeed, they live in the same manner as their forebears have for generations and they appear to have little or no interest in joining with the rest of the modern world. They do not have the modern implements of agriculture at their disposal, and they adhere to their traditional methods and ways; thus they barely grow enough to feed themselves. Their livestock is generally sickly and undependable. And as you all know, in every third year, their pitiful crops will fail due to mildew or frost and they must throw themselves on the mercy of their lairds."

"By Jehovah, that is right!" exclaimed Sir Charles Ross. "I was made to lay out nearly ten thousand pounds in the last year to keep these ruffians from starving to death. And they still stole my cattle and poached my deer without shame!"

The others nodded and murmured in agreement. Saving the people from starvation was indeed a costly business.

"Still, the people, by and large, are quite affectionate towards their homelands," Loch continued, peering out at the group. "Some of the young men are taken into the service of the King's armies, and others go to find suitable employment in the manufactures of Edinburgh and Glasgow. Still others have emigrated to the Americas. But the vast majority of the people prefer to remain in their lowly places, struggling to grow grains and potatoes, hoping to keep a few cattle alive long enough to sell at the market. I have seen these farms, if you could call them that. The squalor of their living conditions is shameful—they sleep side by side with their cattle, their sheep, their pigs and their dogs. They themselves breed without care or forethought to the need for supporting their children or even feeding them. They apportion the best land to those with the closest connections to the tacksman, and their attempts at raising crops would be laughable if not so pitiful."

Loch shook his head and reached into his portfolio and withdrew a map of the Sutherland estates, which ran from the North Sea across the breadth of Scotland to the Atlantic coast in the north and west. He placed the map on an easel so all could see.

"His Lordship and I have come to the conclusion that it is only by offering the people an alternative to their current unsustainable conditions that we shall be able to make headway in our plans for improvement," Loch said. He began pointing to dots on the map along the North Sea coastline north of Dornoch, the main city of Sutherlandshire. "Here, at Helmsdale, His Lordship intends to improve the harbor and instigate a fishing fleet to produce herring. Here, at Golspie, we have learned there is an excellent prospect for coal mining. Here, at Brora, there will be salt pans which, with the proper management, could develop into a prosperous business.. To the west, here at Tongue, there are prospects for more fisheries, and the people can also be put to good employment gathering kelp from the beaches, to be exported as fertilizer to the farms in the rest of the Kingdom.

"All of these new industries will have needs for strong workers, so that the people who now dwell in unhappy poverty in the straths and glens may be encouraged to relocate themselves and provide steady and profitable employment for their families."

"And what, pray, do you intend to do with the land they leave behind?" It was Sir John Sinclair. He sounded doubtful.

Loch turned to look at the man. "Sir, in a word, we propose to replace the people in the interior with sheep."

"Sheep!" This time it was Sir William Munro, who almost leapt from his chair. "Sir, you must be mad! There are no sheep that can survive in Scotland's winter! It's been tried many times, to the regret of all, including myself. While a strath full of sheep would be an improvement over the human wretches that live there now, it is impossible!"

"Sir," Loch said calmly, "I am happy to report that you are mistaken. In fact, farmers in the shires of the Borders and the North of England have already produced some fine new live-stock varieties that have not only survived but thrived in harsh conditions in the Cheviot Hills and elsewhere."

He rummaged in his leather satchel once again. "I have here a letter from Thomas Kinkaid, a sheep farmer in Northumbria." Loch pushed his spectacles up on his nose and read from the paper. "In the winter last, which those hereabouts considered one of the harshest in recent memory, with frosts lasting from November until March and unrelenting snow, I can report that of our initial flock of one thousand ewes and two dozen rams, there were but seven fatalities among the sheep. This loss is of the same rate, or indeed less, than that suffered by farmers in more benevolent climes."

Loch looked around the room. "Kinkaid's results have been duplicated in other areas," he said. "The Cheviot breed is made to order for the North country and may indeed be the answer to our prayers. Where now the land lies bare and useless, we can introduce great sheep walks. In the winters, the herders will bring their flocks down to the straths, where there is ample water and grass to survive a harsh winter. In the spring, the lambs will be plentiful. Some will be sold to the market for meat, and we will harvest the wool to send to the mills. In the summer, the flocks will find a virtually endless supply of deer hair in the mountain machrie."

Loch looked around the room. "Gentlemen, the economics are astounding. Where we are all lucky to receive a few shillings per acre today in rents from ouir tenants, we can almost guarantee that same land returning nearly two pounds per acre under sheep."

There were a few gasps around the room as the lairds began mentally calculating their profits. *Two pounds an acre?* Their excitement grew as they looked at each other. Then Sir John Sinclair stood up, a frown encasing his red face.

"But will the people remove themselves from the interior?" he asked. "You have mentioned that they seem unnaturally attached to their poor circumstances. In my view, it is not unnatural at all. These lands are their home and have been for all time they can remember. Will they leave?"

Loch smiled as the other lairds nodded in agreement. All of them had seen how the families living on their estates had demonstrated their love of the land, even as poor as they were.

"Sir," he said. "It will be up to us—our agents, our ministers and even ourselves—to make the case that a better way of life exists for them along the coastal regions. We will build the docks for the fishing boats, invest in the mines, clear the lands for new houses and gardens. When the people understand that a better life awaits them and their children away from the unfriendly struggles of the interior, they will gladly relocate."

"And if they won't go?" Sinclair was not convinced.

Loch stared at the man coldly. "The law, sir, is quite clear. The owners of the land have full authority to do with it what they will. If the lairds decide the people must go, then the people must go, willingly or not."

His words filled the library and hung there amid the crowded shelves of books and portraits of famous men of old hanging on the walls. The lairds knew what he said was true, but they all thought of the consequences of forced removals of their people. They knew it would not be an easy thing if it came to that.

"My people trust me," said the Countess, sitting quietly at the back of the room. "They will do what I say, in the end."

"I hope madam, for your sake, that what you say is true," Sinclair said.

3

Dornoch - March 1808

In the late afternoon, the Countess heard a soft knock on the door of her antechamber at Dunrobin, the castle that had been the home of the chiefs of Clan Sutherland since the 13th century..

"Enter," she said.

Mr. Gunn came in, closed the door behind him, and bowed. "The dinner list, ma'am" he said, holding out a paper. She motioned at him impatiently to read the names aloud.

"In addition to his Lordship and yourself, ma'am, the guests at table tonight will include Mr. Young, His Eminence Mr. Kirkwell, their ladies, and Mrs. Anna Kenton," Gunn said. The Countess nodded at the names of her factor, Young, and Kirkwell, the new minister of the kirk she was restoring in Dornoch. But she raised her eyebrows in question at the last name. Gunn, attuned as always, caught the gesture

"Mrs. Kenton is the niece of His Lordship, ma'am," he said in explanation. "She arrived this afternoon. I believe she wishes to …"

"Yes, yes," the Countess interrupted. "I recall now. She wants to go live with Mr. Fraser in Glencullen and start a public school for the children in that strath."

"Indeed, ma'am," Mr. Gunn said. He kept both his facial expression and the tone of his voice noncommittal.

"For the life of me, I don't know where these young people get such ideas!" the Countess exclaimed. "Teaching the scalawags to read? Very well, very well. Does she know when we dine? Gower does not like his evening meal to be late."

Mr. Gunn assured the Countess that all the arrangements had been made. She waved him out of the room. She recalled the letter that her husband had received several weeks ago from the young woman. She was the youngest child of Stafford's third sister. The girl had been married off to a suitable young man, Captain Kenton, a rising officer in the army and a member of a respectable family in Staffordshire. But that young man had gotten himself killed in the war against the forces of Napolean on the Continent, and, soon after, both Stafford's sister and then her husband had been carried off by the influenza. So the young Mrs. Kenton was now both an orphan and a widow. Her letter had stated that rather than remain in Staffordshire and spend her life in idle mourning, she felt herself still young and able enough to do something worthwhile in the world. She had been corresponding with the Reverend Mr. Fraser, the minister assigned to the kirk and district of Glencullen, and together they had devised the concept of a school to teach letters and numbers to the children. Mr. Fraser and his wife had apparently extended an invitation to Mrs. Kenton to reside at The Manse with them, and the good reverend had offered both the use of the small Glencullen Chapel and his assistance in convincing the people of the strath to provide their children for the purpose of being educated. A society for the propagation of education in Scotland had been investing in educational programs across the country, and Mr. Fraser had been impertinent enough to independently obtain some funding to allow Mrs. Kenton to begin her school. But the Countess suspected that, in the end, she would be the one asked to pay the bills for this unconventional scheme. She had already been asked to provide funds for new schools in several larger towns in Sutherland. And she had been made aware of several other "dame schools," as they were called, that had sprung up here and there, some with the kirk's blessings.

Normally, the Countess would have been quite in favor of such a plan. She believed in education, even for the poorest of her subjects. And as regards Mrs. Kenton, the Countess always had a soft spot in her heart for orphans, as she was one herself. In reading the letter, she had felt a connection between this young girl and her own feelings when she was the same age—the desire to be of some use to the world. But she knew that her husband and Mr. Young, the chief superintendant of the Sutherland Estates, had plans to remove the people of Glencullen within the next year or two, to continue with the plan of improvements to her land. The program had begun soon after that long-ago meeting in London, in coordination with the other nearby landowners.

The Countess looked out her window at the gray and icy sea that lay beyond the castle's extensive gardens. The program to remove the people from the interior of her county and relocate them to the coastal areas had been slow in implementation. It had not been easy, nor without controversy. One of the first areas to be cleared had been the parishes located along the River Naver to the northwest. Mr. Young's ambitious assistant, Patrick Sellar, had been in charge of the removals, and although he tried to give the residents of the strath nearly a year's notice, and had showed them the new areas for housing she had set aside at the river's mouth at Torrisdale, the people had shown no enthusiasm for relocating themselves, and, in the end, had simply refused to leave their homes.

There was nothing for it but for Mr. Sellar to physically remove them. He had unfortunately accomplished his task with an enthusiastic zeal. The Countess frowned as she remembered those times, a few years earlier. Sellar and his men had entered the people's hovels and thrown their worldly goods out into the rain, set fire to the thatch on the roofs, pulled down what rafters they could, and flung open the gates that contained the people's precious black cattle. Some of the villagers had managed to save the timbers from their homes from the fires but most lost all their possessions. Worse, some of the elderly residents of the strath who had been sick abed had not been properly cared for, and after exposure to the elements during the removals, two or three had died.

There had been a great hue and cry after the removal of the people from Strathnaver, and the incident had even been reported in the newspapers back in London, to the Countess' great mortification. She had had to write several letters to some of her friends in London explaining that while she herself had never authorized any manner of brutal treatment on her own people, the law was clear that she had the right to relocate them for their own and her estate's benefit. The Procurator Fiscal in Inverness had even brought a charge of manslaughter against Sellar. But, thankfully, a jury assembled in Inverness to hear the case had returned a not-guilty verdict.

But after that incident, Lord Stafford had decided to move more cautiously in his plan to introduce more sheepwalks throughout Sutherland. He had spent thousands to build new housing sites for the people along the coasts both east and west. He had helped finance overseas transportation costs for those who decided to emigrate to Canada. Indeed many residents of the interior had elected to move away and start their lives anew in the New World. But the process had been slow and contentious, and an element of fear and distrust rose between the Countess and her people.

And, the Countess knew, Glencullen was scheduled for removals in the near future. Mr. Young had outlined a schedule, arranged leases for the new sheep farmers, and the Sheriff had reported on the likelihood of resistance in the glen, which he thought not to be great. The people there were poor, ill and il-literate, and they were used to doing what they were told to do. The Countess did not know whether she should tell this young woman what the future held, because, sooner rather than lat-er, even Mr. Fraser himself would be asked to leave Glencullen. With no communicants left in the strath, there would be no need for a minister.

The Countess sighed, deeply. She did not like forcing peo-ple to leave their homes, even if those homes were nothing more than hovels and rude mud huts set against the rain and wind. But she believed, as did her husband, that the people would be the better for the change, as his grand plan continued to press forward new types of industries and opportunities for the people along the coasts. Already, the herring fishery Stafford had set up in Helmsdale was reporting good profits. Coal was being mined near Brora. And, though prices were dropping rapidly every year, even the kelp works in Tongue was still making money. Still, with the wars in Europe continuing to drag on and on, the need for uniforms for the soldiers had driven the prices for wool and mutton sky-high. The quicker the Sutherland Estates could be turned over to sheep, the richer the entire county would soon become. It was thus not only sensible to remove the people from the straths, it was quite necessary for the survival of all. The Countess only wanted the best for her people; a chance at a rea-sonably happy future. She did not understand why they resisted the obvious.

"My sister was a woman of little education," Stafford was saying at dinner later that evening. He nodded at his niece, who sat mid-way down the broad mahogany table. The large, drafty room was paneled in golden oak and crowned with a plastered, beamed ceiling. A coal fire in the marble hearth fought against the chill, as did the banks of candelabra on the table and set at the four corners of the room. Portraits of the Sutherland ancestors posing with their favorite dogs peered down from their gilt frames. "You are to be commended for obtaining one. But I do not understand what purpose you propose to do with it."

"I wish to help others gain their own education," Anna Kenton replied. "To whatever purpose they themselves can determine."

Lord Stafford blinked at the girl. She was a pale, skinny young thing, with long, dark hair that framed an oval face. Her features were sharp and intelligent, and her dark eyes glistened with spirit. Now that her proscribed year of mourning had expired, she wore a modest gown in a muted green, with lace decorations at the cuffs and bodice. He knew she had had a difficult life, growing up in his sister's drab, unsophisticated household before both her parents had been lost to sickness and her husband to war. But she did not appear to be in the least cowed or beaten by the difficulties she had faced in her life; indeed, her spirited eyes almost dared him to challenge her, looking forward to engaging him in debate. It was a most unusual attitude for a woman, he thought to himself. But in a way, he found himself admiring her, as he almost always admired men he met who burned with the desire to achieve something in the world. Lord Stafford had learned that if there were profits to be made in a thing, it was best to give that thing over to a man who was most desirous of seeing it succeed.

Anna, in turn, studied her uncle, resplendent in his golden coat, with ruffled lace cuffs and silk cravat tucked into his paisley waistcoat, blinking at her myopically despite the bright light of the candle-lit room. During her childhood, she had only encountered the great man during the holidays, at one or another of the festive balls that marked the season. And as a child and a female, those encounters had been limited to a brief curtsy and a nod. She remembered that her parents had resented Stafford for his high position and great wealth and especially the fact that he seemed totally disinterested in sharing any of it with them. Oh, there had been a small annual allowance and her father had been allowed to supervise a small group of tenant farmers in Shropshire. But that enterprise had been deliberately small in scale, and there had never been any invitation for her father to join in the vast empire of the House of Stafford, a world reserved for the first-born son and his own children. While Stafford had enjoyed the most exuberant life in London and Edinburgh, serving in government and enjoying the many fine properties scattered around the country, her own parents had been left to lead the quiet yet unfulfilling life of a country squire and his family.

She had often overheard her parents arguing about Stafford. Her father, who had married into the family, was resentful that he had not been given more responsibility. Her mother had loyally defended her elder brother, and worried that if they made any complaints about their station, that which they had might be taken from them. So they had endured, quietly, resentfully, until death finally came and carried them away.

Anna knew that her uncle was one of the richest men in all of Britain, but to her he looked quite ordinary: myopic, stiffly polite, a man with very little capacity for small talk. To her, he seemed a prisoner, hemmed in on all sides by his responsibilities, unable to have a human relationship that did not involve either the giving or taking of money. During most of the dinner, he had sat silently at the end of the table while Mr. Young, his chief factor, had recited endless lists of figures and estimates, discussing rents and arrears, taxes and prospects until her head, try as she had done to follow the conversation, began to spin.

"You do understand, m'dear," Stafford continued, "That the people where you propose to go live do not have our ways. They live in the rudest of shelters, in conditions of squalor and filth, and can barely manage to feed themselves one meal a day, if you can consider a bowl of boiled oats and some cow's blood a meal."

"All the more reason to do something to help them rise above their poverty," Anna responded calmly. "If they can read and write and do sums, perhaps they can find more lucrative employment and begin to better themselves."

"Very few of them even speak our language!" The Countess chimed in from her end of the long table. "How in the world will you even be able to teach them?"

Anna turned to look at her aunt, the Countess, who stared at her in amazement, her cheeks glowing red in the bright light, her beautiful ringlets of hair framing her lovely face. Her silk gown of the lightest pink almost glowed in the candlelight. Although Anna's own marriage had been both arranged and brief in tenure, she had been able to experience a small measure of the happiness in her companionship with Captain Kenton. She missed, above all, the conversations they had held in front of their own hearthfire at night. Her husband, free of the need to project the image of the military man, had relaxed when they were alone, and confided in her his own worries and thoughts about his future, and she had tried to comfort and support him. It had lasted all too short a time, a mere three months, before he went off to war, and to his death in battle. But Anna wondered if the Countess enjoyed such times, such conversations, with her own husband, the cool, quiet and seemingly reticent Lord Stafford.

"I have begun to learn the rudiments of the Gaelic tongue," she replied calmly. "My abigail, Mrs. Ross, is a native of Glencullen and has their language. She has been teaching me the grammar. And Mr. Fraser, who does have the language, has said he will continue to teach me enough to be able to communicate with the people in the glen. We shall learn each other's language together."

The Countess tossed her head in frustration and turned to look imploringly at the young Mr. Kirkwell, the minister and chief elder of the Dornoch kirk. He had been silently listening to the conversation while picking at his plate, his small, black eyes following the parties as they spoke. Now, seeing the Countess' appeal, he took off his small round spectacles, carefully wiped each lens clean and replaced them on his nose.

"There is certainly a great deal of Godliness in the idea of education," he began carefully, nodding at the girl. "How else, after all, can one become truly familiar with the teaching of the Scriptures unless one reads and studies them?" From the corner of his eyes he caught a frown from the Countess. "But Her Ladyship is correct to question the efficacy of the idea of teaching the very poor to read," he continued quickly. "After all, what use will there be for education amongst the lowest class? Certainly, they do not have books. In their Sunday services, does not the minister read aloud the pertinent passages from Holy Scripture, and explain it to them? They do not need letters in order to farm or raise livestock..." This time it was Lord Stafford who shot a sharp look across the table. "...Nor will they need book learning when they move to the coasts to become fishermen or coal miners," he quickly added. "No, I think it is fair to say that God's plan for these people is to remain in their places and let the higher classes do the reading."

"I would remind you, Mr. Kirkwell, that the church once felt the same way about people like us," Anna said, her cheeks reddening slightly. "Only the priests were allowed the pleasures of the Bible, and the rest of us had to wait for them to read it to us. Surely you do not believe that only a certain privileged few should have access to the Lord's word?"

"That was the Roman church, madam," Kirkwell said calmly. "The Scottish kirk has always believed in the spread of literacy to the people."

"Then all I am proposing is to do the kirk's work among the people of Glencullen," Anna said, a small smile playing about her lips. "Is it not true that the church supports the efforts of the Society in Scotland for Propagating Christian Education? Mr. Fraser tells me that he has obtained a modest grant for our proposed school, and he has volunteered the wee kirk in Glencullen in which to hold our classes. And because there is no man to hire as schoolmaster, there is no requirement for a salary of any kind. Although I do hope that I may convince the Society to increase its support after the first year, as I do not feel it is just that Mr. Fraser be asked to subsidize me without compensation."

Kirkwell glanced helplessly at the Countess and fell silent. *You argue with her*, his eyes said.

"I am worried about your safety," the Countess began next. "Who will protect you out in the glen, a young woman alone?"

Anna smiled to herself. "I will hardly be alone, madam, whilst living in The Manse with Mr. Fraser and his lady. My servant, Mrs. Ross, being of those parts, will help introduce me to the people and assure them of my good intentions. And Mr. Fraser has written that the people in Glencullen are generally peaceful and orderly," she said. "Certainly, neither my uncle nor yourself would permit any kind of lawlessness or ill behavior to exist in your domain?"

Until now, the corpulent form of William Young, the superintendent, had been silent in his corner of the table. With his napkin tucked over his cravat to keep stray missiles of food and gravy from staining his brown coat, he had been calmly and methodically dissecting with knife and fork the meat from the Cornish game hen on his plate and shoveling each morsel into the gaping maw of his mouth, stopping only for gulps from his wine goblet. He now erupted in a loud guffaw. "By Jove, M'Lady," he said, slapping the tabletop with a meaty hand, "I believe she's got you there!"

Both Stafford and his wife glared at the man, whose wig was as usual slightly off-center, and whose prominent jowls jiggled obscenely as he laughed again. "Methinks the young woman has made the better arguments," he said, "By Jove, I do believe she has. Madam, Sir? I think she was won the right to go to Gl-encullen and see what she can do with the ruffians there. I wager she'll be back here at Dunrobin in a fortnight's time. Fraser will look after her, mark my words. He's a crazy old coot, but he'll not let her come to harm. And once she sees what she's up against, she'll be back here for a hot bath, a warm meal and a quick passage back to Shropshire."

He turned now to look at the girl, his eyes narrowed and serious. "Mark my words, young lady. This is a brutal and foreign land, Scotland is. The people who live here have been hardened by God to deal with the cold and the rain and the snow and the wind; with the drought and the starvation; with the daily threat of death and the knowledge that life is hard and bleak and unforgiving. These people are interested in finding food to eat, shelter from the rain and snow and living through the night. They care not for the Lord's words, nor those of Shakespeare. But I can see that nothing we say at this table tonight will convince you of this. So go! Be off with you! Go to Glencullen and try living with Fraser, that madman, and see if you can teach letters to the most misbegotten, slovenly, lazy, and dirty creatures on the face of the earth."

The Countess looked like she was about the say something, but Stafford rose, nodded all around and announced that he and the gentlemen were to retire to the library for cigars and a glass of port.

4

The Countess led the ladies into her study, where a cheerful fire had been set against the chill trying to seep in from the one large window to the east. The wind blowing in off the North Sea was rattling against the panes. Mrs. Young, the factor's wife, was almost as round as he, with cheeks red as apples, drooping jowls and thin wisps of white hair escaping from beneath her black evening bonnet. Mrs. Kirkwell, in contrast, was thin and pale, dressed in black from head to toe and draped in a fringed shawl that she clutched tightly about her shoulders as if it was protection against the sins of the world. While the Countess, from her chair next to the hearth, poured each of them a steaming cup of chocolate from the silver salver the maid had left on the table for them, Anna stood for a moment looking out the window. The steady winds had blown away the layer of clouds, leaving a starry sky and diffuse light from the half moon rising in the North.

"Come, Anna my dear," the Countess said. "Sit by me. It's warm here."

Anna obeyed, and gratefully accepted the delicate china cup filled with hot cocoa.

Mrs. Young sniffed at her own cup and sighed aloud. "Ooo, there is something about a cup of chocolate at night," she said, closing her eyes in mock exultation. "I hope, Mrs. Kirkwell, that the pleasures of the cup may not be counted as sinful in the eyes of the Lord!"

She was being jolly, but the minister's wife was implacable. "The taking of sustenance to maintain the health and well being of the person is blessed in the sight of the Lord," she said sternly. "But sinfulness walks the earth everywhere and with great stealth. The differences between that which is pleasurable to us and that which displeases the Lord are very often difficult to discern. We must always be prayerful and ever vigilant."

Mrs. Young did not know what to say to that, so remained silent. But she did take a healthy draught of her chocolate, and smiled.

The Countess reached across the table and took up a little silver bell, which she waved back and forth. Answering the cue, the door to the study opened and three children entered, followed by their grey-clad nanny. The two oldest were girls dressed in their neatest muslin frocks, while the youngest boy looked to be about ten or twelve years old, his hair askew, his clothes a wrinkled mess. He grinned at Anna with unabashed friendliness, while the two girls merely curtsied politely and stayed silent, while their dark eyes darted around the room, taking note of the women in attendance. The nanny, after a final fierce glance at her charges, melted into the shadows of the room, against a wall, and stood there silently.

"My dears," the Countess said to the children. "Allow me to introduce you to your cousin, Mrs. Kenton of Shropshire. She is pausing here at Dunrobin on her way to Glencullen, where she will be assisting the good reverend Fraser with his work."

"Oh," exclaimed the boy, his face creasing with a huge smile of delight. "Mister Fraser has the *best* collection of frogs in the kingdom! I've seen them myself! They're dead, of course, but he keeps them under a glass and they are wonderful!"

"Francis!" The Countess' voice was sharp with displeasure. "Where have your manners gone? I do not believe I heard anyone address a question to you."

The child, embarrassed, mumbled what sounded like a kind of apology and fell back into line with his silent sisters. Anna smiled at him, trying to put him at ease.

"Mrs. Kenton, may I present my two youngest daughters," the Countess continued. "This is Sophia and Mary. Their older brother George is currently away at his studies in London."

The girls curtsied again. The oldest, Sophia, looked to be in her late teens. She was pretty, with dark hair and a rosy complexion. Her sister, some years younger, was at that ugly duckling stage of childhood, where she was no longer a child, really, but neither had she grown into full womanhood. She fidgeted constantly, trying to smooth out the wrinkles in her pinafore and tuck a stray tendril of her hair back inside her lace bonnet. Her eyes darted about, not daring to alight on anyone or anything for very long in fear that someone might actually ask her to speak.

The Countess poured out three small demitasse cups of warm chocolate and nodded at the children, who stepped forward to take them from the table. Francis reached for a biscuit as well, before he caught his mother's disapproving glance, and pulled his hand back quickly.

"It is a pleasure to meet my kin," Anna said, nodding at her cousins. "And I am grateful for your hospitality for my visit."

"How long are we to enjoy your company, madam?" asked Sophia shyly.

"I'm afraid I am traveling on to Glencullen on the morrow," Anna said. "Mr Fraser has asked me to come as soon as possible. We have plans to open a school for the children of the glen, to teach them to read and write and do ciphers."

Sophia wrinkled her nose. "Mr. Fraser is a very learned man," she said. "He would be quite excellent as a school master. However, my brother is correct," the girl said, laying an affectionate hand on the shoulder of the young boy, who was still hungrily eyeing the biscuits on the table. "Mr. Fraser has over the years gathered quite a remarkable collection of creatures common to the strath. Although I am not sure I understand the reason why he finds it necessary to keep them all displayed on the tables and shelves of his study."

"It is the scientific method." The voice was that of Mary, the shy little girl half-hiding behind her older sister, but she had deepened it in imitation of something she had obviously heard the reverend say many times before. All three children giggled and even their mother smiled. She nodded at Francis and he grabbed for his sugar biscuit.

"I am sure there is a great deal we can learn about our world by studying the creatures of Nature," Anna said. "Even the lowly frogs." She smiled again at Francis, who was nodding his head in agreement while he devoured his biscuit and gulped his chocolate.

"Oh, yes," he said. "Perhaps you should try kissing one, to see if it will become a handsome prince, like in the stories!"

"That's quite enough," the Countess rapped on her table. "We will have no talk of kissing frogs in this household. Bid your cousin and the ladies adieu, children, and be off to bed."

The children obeyed, placing their empty cups on the table and, one after the other, coming up to curtsy to Mrs. Young and Mrs. Kirkwell, and then to kiss first Anna and then their mother goodnight. Francis, the last, couldn't resist giving his cousin a hug. She stroked his tousled hair and smiled down at him. "Good night, dear boy," she whispered to him. "Pleasant dreams."

Their nanny escorted the children away and left the older women alone again.

"They seem lovely children," Anna told the Countess. "Very bright and friendly. You must be proud."

The Countess waved her hand in dismissive acknowledgment. "Children can be a burden, yet they are a source of happiness as well," she said. "And happiness is a quality that must never be discounted, especially in this house."

She sounded wistful and Anna wondered what she meant. Was she referring to her marriage? Or the House of Sutherland, which went back into history for eighteen generations and more? The Countess saw the cloud pass across Anna's face and stirred in her chair. She stood, crossed to the fireplace, poked at the coals glowering in the grate.

"Forgive me, my dear," the Countess said, turning. "The spirit of melancholy descended upon me for a moment. I was a mere babe when my own parents died and never had a family I could call my own. Until now, of course. I am, of course, thankful to the Almighty for his blessings." She nodded in the direction of Mrs. Kirkwell, as if that lady, clutching her shawl tightly around her shoulders, were the conduit through which one sent messages to heaven. "Still, there are echoes of unhappiness in this place, and I find I must often step carefully to avoid them as best I can."

Anna understood. She knew the story of the Countess' childhood. Her father, William Gordon, the 18th Earl of Sutherland and chief of his clan, had married Mary Maxwell, a fine woman from a good family, and brought her to live in Dunrobin Castle. They had been blessed with the birth of their first child, Catherine, who had quickly been followed by their second, Elizabeth, and it seemed that many more would certainly follow. But then came that day when Catherine was not quite three, and her sister still a mere baby. No one could remember, or perhaps wouldn't say, what had happened that day, shortly after the New Year. The Earl had been playing with his wee girls. It was said he doted upon his daughters, loved to play games with them: hide and seek, cock and chicks, gruff nanny goat and the rest. The halls of Dunrobin were often filled with the sounds of laughter and screams of the young girls' delight. But on that fateful January day, something had gone terribly amiss. Perhaps the Earl tripped on a corner of the rug, or slipped on a wet spot on the marble stairs. No one could, or would, recall. But the baby Catherine had fallen, somehow, fallen from the warm and happy clasp of her father's arms, onto the cold and hard marble of the grand stairs at Dunrobin. The child hit her head, lost consciousness, and soon was dead. A mantle of grief descended upon the house of Sutherland.

The baby Elizabeth had been sent with her nurse and nanny to Edinburgh, to her maternal grandmother, the Lady Alva. Her parents, desperate to escape their grief, had travelled to Bath in the south of England to take the soothing waters and try to wash away their memories and the sense of guilt that could not be denied. Weakened, wracked by sadness and the weight of responsibility for his daughter's death, the Earl of Sutherland had developed a fever and taken to his bed. His devoted wife stayed at his side, bathing his forehead in cold cloths, trying to get him to eat, drink; something, *anything*, to keep him alive. The doctors called it the putrid fever. It was as though the Earl's body was rotting away before he died. The doctors did not hold out much hope for his recovery. A death watch began. Urgent letters were sent, to London and to the North. And then, without warning, the Earl's wife also fell ill. Had she breathed in the corrupting vapors of her husband's sickness? Or had she decided she no longer wanted to live in a world without him, and without her daughter? Whatever the reason, she was dead within two days. The Earl followed her into eternity a week later. They were buried together on the grounds at Holyrood in Edinburgh, along with their little daughter Catherine. Elizabeth, now the inheritor of the name and possessions of the House of Sutherland, the 19th chief of the clan, the owner of more than a million acres of heath and mountain, glen and town, played with her dolls at the feet of her grandmother in her grand house in Edinburgh.

The little girl was orphaned, and soon she would be attacked. One of her uncles, later joined by a distant cousin, soon filed a legal claim against Elizabeth's title and inheritance. Lady Alva, who was not without resources, marshaled an impressive legal team for the wee Countess, including Lord Monboddo and Boswell of Auchinleck, It took nearly ten years, with endless hearings in the London Courts and sessions before the House of Lords before that distinguished body finally voted in favor of Elizabeth's claim to her title.

Now, with her own familial losses fresh in her mind, Anna felt a rush of pity for the woman beside her. "I understand, madam," she said, reaching over to lay a hand on the Countess' arm. "It is one of the reasons why I decided to leave Stittenham. It is a place with good memories for me, but there are places where I cannot help but confront the ghosts of the past and reminders of those I have lost."

The Countess smiled her thanks for the young woman's understanding. Then she shook herself. It would not do to wallow in sentimentality. The world was a cold and harsh place, the Countess knew, and dwelling on the past and all its sadnesses was not the proper way to live in it. One must forge always ahead, always thinking of the future. The past could not be changed. The future, its possibilities, could sometimes be bent to one's will and desires.

"Is that why you wish to locate at Glencullen?" the Countess asked. "I must confess, I am not sure I understand your reasons, despite your defense of them at dinner tonight."

Anna paused for a moment to gather her thoughts. The other ladies waited, curious.

"I ... I suppose that is part of it," Anna said finally. "I do not see a great deal of possibilities for a person in a small country village."

"Nor will you find many in a place like Glencullen," Mrs. Young said with a chuckle. "I should think all possibilities left that strath many a year ago!"

"Amen," said Mrs. Kirkwell, nodding.

Anna smiled. "I am quite sure you are all quite correct that Glencullen is a far cry from civilized society," she said. "I am not expecting to find life there will resemble even my own little village of Stittenham. I am hopeful that the work Mr Fraser has in mind for me will be interesting and fulfilling."

"But…" the Countess was interested, her head tilted, eyes raised.

Anna felt herself blushing. "You may find this a bit silly, perhaps," she said. "But the nanny my parents employed when I was a girl, her name is Mary Ross, was born in Glencullen. I remember we would take long walks through the countryside and she would tell me stories about Glencullen. How the mountains are bathed in pink clouds at sunset, how the wind tries to blow all the houses down, how the people gather at night to sing and dance and tell wonderful stories about the past." She paused, remembering. "She made it sound like a magical place, Mary Ross did. I made her promise to take me there one day. I wanted to see the magic for myself."

Anna stopped and sipped some chocolate. The other three ladies were staring at her, rapt. "Now, instead, it is I who is taking Mary Ross there, rather than the reverse. She has been a loyal lady's maid to me, and I am looking forward to seeing the strath where all her wonderful stories originated. I have never stopped wanting to see it for myself. So when Mr. Fraser wrote to me, asking me to come and teach the children, I took it as a sign. Perhaps the Lord has a plan for me there. But I felt that I had to go."

"Or perhaps a young girls' fancy has overtaken good sense and devotion to duty," snapped Mrs Kirkwell. She did not like talk about signs and omens from another world. That way led to evil and sinfulness.

"Now, now, Mrs Kirkwell," the Countess intervened. "None of us really know what the Lord intends for our time on earth. It is just as likely He wants Mrs. Kenton in Glencullen as in Stittenham. If her instinct is to go to Glencullen, then we should respect that. Mr Fraser and his lady will look after her, I am sure of that. And as Mr. Young said at table, if she finds she does not like the place after all, she can come back here and we'll help her find another path to follow."

Now that she understood the young woman's feelings, the Countess was somewhat relieved. Especially since she knew that the girl's time in Glencullen would be limited no matter what she discovered there. The Countess knew that her husband and his factor had plans to remove the people from the strath at Glencullen, and all others as far south as Lairg. It would not be more than a year, two at the most, before the strath would be empty of people and full of sheep. Stafford and Young had already received offers from two or three gentlemen who wished to lease the strath for sheepwalks, once the people had been removed. It was only a matter of finding the right time.

5

The next morning, Anna made her way down to the court-yard in front of Dunrobin Castle before the sun had risen. William Young had made arrangements for a carriage to take her to Glencullen. "My assistant, MacCray, has some business to attend to in the strath," Young had told her. "He will drop you off at the Manse. Be ready at dawn. It's a good day's journey."

Anna had one small carpetbag to hold all her worldly possessions, which included her clothing, toiletries, her Bible in which was folded the last letter she had received from her husband from Spain, and her well-thumbed copy of Lowth's *Grammar*.

The day was overcast and cool, but at least it was not raining. In the forecourt, she found an open carriage and a large dusty horse waiting, but no sign of MacCray. She placed her bag near the carriage and returned to the entrance hall inside the large oak doors to the castle. An elaborate, carved marble fireplace took up one wall of the hall, and a warming fire crackled in the hearth. She sat on a bench in front of the fire and waited, keeping an eye on the horse and carriage through the large windows on the opposite side of the hall.

Mary Ross came bustling in several minutes later, her face

reddened by the chill of the day. Mary was not that much older than her charge. She had a pleasant, plump figure, and wisps of her reddish, curly hair drifted down from her traditional mutch, or muslin cap. Her muslin dress was plain and gray and she had a warm woolen shawl wrapped around her shoulders. She came and stood next to the warm fire, trying to rub some of the heat into her reddened hands.

"Och, you should see the gardens on the terrace down below, Anna," Mary said. "Looks like bloody Versailles, it does. Statues and pathways and fountains … the whole lot! Must take an army of gardeners to keep it."

Anna smiled. Mary Ross had always had an active imagination. It was one of the things she most loved about her. The woman had never been to Versailles, indeed, she had never been outside of Britain. But she knew enough to compare the Countess' formal gardens – Anna had seen them from her bedroom window—to the fabled gardens of the French royals.

"Where's our driver?" Mary asked. "I thought we were leaving at the break of dawn?"

"I don't know," Anna answered. "I believe that is our conveyance, but there is no sign of Mister MacCray. You might as well sit down with me and wait."

It was a long wait, the better part of an hour, before a side door was flung open and into the hall strode a young man whom Anna assumed was MacCray. He was tall, dressed in a dark coat, breeches and black leather boots that came nearly to his knees. He was clean shaven, his features sharp, eyes black. His long black hair was pulled back and fastened at the rear. In one hand he held a basket covered with a cloth; the other arm was snaked familiarly around one of the housemaids, who was blushing furiously yet looking at the man with lively and bright eyes, a half-smile playing on her red lips. The two of them stopped short when they saw Anna Mary Ross, and they jumped quickly apart.

"You must be Mrs. Kenton," MacCray said, his voice low with the hint of a menacing rasp.

"I was told to be ready at first light," she replied coolly. "That was some time ago."

"Had to get my victuals," he said, nodding at the basket he still held. "Hannah here is as slow as molasses." He turned and gave the housemaid a curt nod. "Thank ye, m'love. I will see you when I return."

"Maybe," said the girl flirtatiously, "Or maybe not." She edged past him, or, it seemed to Anna, deliberately close to him, tossed her head and disappeared back through the doorway, closing it behind her.

MacCray smiled at the door for a moment, and then turned again to regard Anna. She returned his look, refusing to look away. "Right," he said, "Are you ready?"

"As I have been for the last hour or more," she said evenly.

MacCray did not reply, but led them outside into the court-yard where he tucked his basket under the bench seat of the carriage. He assisted the two women as they climbed onto the open carriage, Anna in the front and Mrs. Ross onto the bench seat behind, and secured their two small bags onto the back platform.

"Traveling light," he said. "Unusual for a woman." Anna chose not to respond. He nodded to himself. "And not talkative either. Also unusual. Suits me, though. I have no patience for the usual caterwauling of womenfolk."

"Oh, if it's talking you want, I can provide all ye need," Mary Ross snapped at him.

"How long is the journey, do you think?" Anna asked, pulling a woolen blanket around her knees.

"To Glencullen? Best part of the day," he said. He walked forward and inspected the horse and livery, then came back and hoisted himself up onto the seat effortlessly. "Long as the roads haven't washed out. Which they do after almost every hard rain." He pulled a long buggy whip from its holder, grasped up the reins and with a flick of his wrist cracked the whip sharply against the horse's flank. The sound made both the horse and Anna start in surprise, and the carriage began to move smartly down the long avenue of trees that led away from the castle. Anna turned to look back as the morning mists closed in on the castle's turrets and the limbs of the overhanging trees blocked the castle from view.

MacCray turned the horse to the south on the main road leading down to Dornoch. But soon he turned again on a much narrower track to the west. This road, barely more than twin ruts carving through the grass, followed a river running swiftly to the sea. Gentle treeless hills rose up on both sides of the river's banks. From time to time the valley broadened and they passed small farm homesteads where the rich black alluvial soil in the fields held the yellowed remnants of the crops that had recently been harvested and stored away for the winter. For the most part, the land was empty and silent save for the occasional squawking of birds unnerved by the sight of the passing carriage.

"Do you visit Glencullen often?" Anna asked, turning to look at the man next to her on the bench.

MacCray shrugged. "A few times a year," he said. "The minister will sometimes order supplies for his collection. Boxes and jars for the dead animals and birds he shoots. And, of course, I go to collect the rents twice a year." He shook his head. "That's usually a wasted trip, since the beggars at Glencullen always claim they have no money. His Lordship had to send four bolls of grain to keep them through the winter last. My life will be much easier once we remove the folk to the seaside at Golspie."

"When, pray, is that event to occur?" Anna asked. She had heard the gentlemen at Dunrobin discussing the improvements planned for the inland areas of the shire.

MacCray shrugged again. "Whenever his Lordship and Mr. Young decide," he said. "They've started building new lots near the colliery at Golspie already. Once they are ready, I expect I'll get the order to move the people without delay."

"Do they want to go?" Anna asked.

MacCray laughed. "What do they know?" he asked. "They are a miserable collection of souls. Can't support themselves with their livestock nor the few bits of crops they can coax out of the ground. They can neither read nor write. All they do is breed and eat. Eat and breed. Not good for much else besides. Long past time for his Lordship to move them out and put his land to good use."

"These are human souls," Anna said, "Whom you discuss without much in the way of charity."

"Wasted," MacCray snapped. "All human charity and benevolence is wasted on such as these. Lazy, drunk, they are lawbreakers of the worst sort. Time to be rid of them, says I."

"I am sure there are some qualities the people of Glencullen possess that speak well of them," the young woman offered.

MacCray laughed. "If you find any, by the throne of Peter I hope you tell me," he said. "I've traveled to Glencullen and everywhere else is this forsaken land, and I've yet to find one you could bring back to civilized folk."

"Where are ye from, Robert?" asked Mrs. Ross. She had been quietly listening to the conversation.

He flicked his whip at the horse. "I grew up near Helensburgh," he said. "Not far from Loch Lomond. My father was a lumber merchant. He found a position for me in Inverness, and there it was I met Mr. Young. 'Twas three years ago, I first began working for The Countess."

"I see," Mrs. Ross said. "Would you say the people of Helensburgh are all fine and upstanding citizens?"

"Well …" MacCray started to respond.

"None of them drunkards? No layabouts there near Loch Lomond? Every man gainfully employed and raising families of well-fed and highly educated children, are they?"

MacCray snorted. "I see what …"

"No, sir, I do not think you do see," Mary Ross said, her voice suddenly filled with anger. "You apparently do not see that the people of Glencullen are exactly like the people of Helensburgh. They are Christian sinners in both places, sir, trying to live the best they can. A man in one place may have more money than a man in the other; a woman in one may have better finery than a woman in the other. But they are both precious in God's sight. Precious and worthy of our respect as much as they are respected by God above. You would do well to remember that, and to hold your tongue, sir."

MacCray's face turned red, but he did not answer. He flicked his whip angrily at the horse and they rode on.

As the morning passed, the clouds began to draw apart and the sun broke through in concentrated beams streaming down onto the landscape. Soon, the river had turned into a rocky, swift-running torrent, swollen with snowmelt, angry and black and filled with ancient boulders worn almost smooth. In places, as they continued to the west, the forest came down to the river's banks, tall dark pines crowding against the shore. When the road passed through, even the sound of the nearby running stream was silenced in the dark gloom that descended and their carriage squeezed past the massive trunks while even the sound of the horse's hooves was muted against the layers of pine needles that covered the forest floor.

Anna pulled the blanket higher against her with a shiver. MacCray noticed and chuckled.

"Tis no wonder the people in these parts still believe in ghosts and fairies," he said with a sneer. "You can get lost in an instant wandering through these woods, and then the hobbeldy goblins will come out and get you. Tear you limb from limb and drink your blood for tea."

Anna said nothing. She knew that MacCray was trying to

frighten her, hoping that she would move closer to him for protection on the narrow bench. She had no intention of allowing herself to be frightened and certainly not to get any closer to such an odious person.

"There were once two men who lived on the slopes of Ben Lomond, in that district from whence you came, sir," Mary Ross said. "One night, they were returning to their home, each carrying a small barrel of whisky upon their backs. As they passed along the road, they heard music and then saw lights coming from within a *brugh*, or hill hollow. Curious, they went inside and there, in bright candlelight, they saw dancers and musicians and all forms of merriment.

"Now one of the men, wise to the ways of the faeries, stuck his dagger in the frame of the doorway. The other man began to dance with the others, a frantic reel to a tune that almost commanded his feet to move. After a time, the first man was able to leave the brugh, because he had used metal to prop open the door. But the other man continued to dance, even with his whisky barrel still strapped to his back, and would not, or could not stop.

"The first man went to his home, and told no one what he had seen. But he went back the next morning to find his companion. Yet he could not locate the brugh, search high and low as he did. Indeed, there were many in his village who thought he had done evil to the other man, and some wanted to try him for murder.

"But the village elders waited. And exactly twelvemonth later, on the very same night, the man retraced his steps along that road, and once again encountered the brugh, the music and the candlelit dancers within. Again, he propped open the door with his dagger and entered. And there, still dancing with them, was his friend, still with the whisky upon his back. He took his hand and led him outside, and once out from the spell within, his friend appeared weak and exhausted and nearly dead from a year of dancing with the faeries. But he lived and told his tale to his children and grandchildren and all generations to come."

MacCray laughed. "Superstitious twaddle," he said derisively. "Utter nonsense. A man cannot dance unstopping for a year without food nor drink. Nonsense."

"A man cannot," Mary Ross said, nodding wisely. "But a faerie can."

EVENTUALLY, THE ROAD came out of the forest, still with the raging creek on their left, and began to climb. At the crest of the hill, the landscape changed again, and Anna caught her breath. Lying in front of them, from the north to south, was an unending vista of treeless land. Far off to the north, Anna could see the ragged saw-toothed peaks of several mountainous crags, black and wet, with blankets of snow cascading down between the mountain tops like spilled milk. Straight ahead, to the west, the land was flat and the wind, unimpeded by any natural barrier, blew straight at them like a cold, damp fist. More mountains rose again to the south, looming purple in the distance and also daubed in the blinding white of snowfall.

"How beautiful it is!" Anna exclaimed. "It's like we're riding off to the very ends of the earth!"

"Hah!" MacCray spat off to his side. "If Glencullen isn't the end of the earth, you can damn well see it from there!" He cracked the whip again, asking the horse to move quicker against the strong headwinds. The horse shook its head and continued at the same pace. "I would nae call this land beautiful, miss," he continued. "Harsh? Yes. Dangerous? It is indeed. Not fit for man nor beast, I'd say. Forsaken by God, if you want to know the truth."

"Now why would the Lord God want to forsake this particular part of his Creation?" Anna said. "It must serve His purpose in some way."

MacCray shook his head. "Well, Miss, if you find out what

it is, I'd be happy to know it. I see a land where the Lord tries to kill a man with the cold and the snow and the thunder and the hail. And if that don't work, He's got the biggest collection of ruffians and ne'er-do-wells ever seen on Earth who'll steal a man blind, poach his Lordship's deer and, if you don't keep a close eye on 'em, they'll lie about drinking their poteen and get up to no good, no good at all." He shook his head. "Nae, Miss, there be not much beauty here."

"Some would say there is naught else but beauty here, sir," Mary Ross said, tossing her head. "It is a beauty where Nature is in control and man and woman have their place. It is a beauty where the cold snows of winter are followed by the warm sun of spring, the bleating of a newborn lamb, the colorful faces of the daffodil and the crocus. It is the beauty of the proud roebuck and the soaring eagle. Oh, there is beauty to behold in this land, sir, if one would just look and see it."

As in her previous discussion with MacCray, he could not think of a thing to say after that, and so he drove on.

By the noon hour, they had reached the village of Lairg, perched at the intersection of another road that followed the River Dornoch down to the sea and the shore of Loch Shin, a black and broad lake on which the relentless wind had churned up waves frosted white with foam. MacCray steered the carriage behind the town's alehouse, found some hay for the horse and told Anna they would stop for lunch. "You can get some bread and cheese from the publican," he said. "And warm yourself by the fire for a bit. It's about three hours journey to the north afore we reach Glencullen." He took his basket and disappeared around the corner.

Inside, Anna and Mary found a chairs by the fire and a dour woman who brought them food and drink. The bread was warm and fresh and the small plate of cheese that came with it was soft and flavorful. The only other customers in the place were two old farmers enjoying large mugs of beer and idle conversation. They each wore tattered coats and stained caps that looked like they'd spent many a year in the elements, and each sported an unkempt beard and long, graying hair. The farmers looked with interest at the new arrivals, nodding and pulling at their caps' brims.

"Look, Donald," said one. "Visitors. I wonder where's they're headed."

"What's that?" the other cried. "What did you say?"

Anna smiled. "we're traveling to Glencullen," she said. "With Mr MacCray of Dunrobin Castle."

"Ah, Glencullen," the first old man said, nodding. "Donald, she's heading for Glencullen."

"What?" the second gent said. "Where?"

"Glencullen," the first man said, speaking loudly and directly into his friend's ear. "She's going to Glencullen."

"Now why would she want to do a thing like that?" Donald said. "There's little prospect in Glencullen. Why, I hear that Her Ladyship is going to remove all the people there and give it over to a sheep walk."

"Aye, I've heard that myself," said the first man, drinking a bit of his ale. "Just like she did with those poor bastards in Strathnaver. A bad business that was, very bad."

"Who is mad?" Donald said. "Mad about what?"

Anna finished her lunch and went outside for some air, leaving Mary to rest by the fire. The town of Lairg was surrounded by low hills that sloped down to the banks of the loch, but in the distance she could see mountains rising into the gray skies. The wind was still fresh, but it seemed to have lessened a bit.

She heard a sharp whistle and, turning, saw MacCray on the bench of the wagon, a new horse in the livery, pawing at the road a short distance up the hill. He was waving at her.

"Come, Mrs Kenton, come!" he shouted at her. "We must leave at once!"

Anna went inside to fetch Mary and together they climbed

the hill where the carriage waited. MacCray jumped down to help them up.

"I've had a report," he said to her, almost breathless in excitement. "It's that bastard Billy Hanks. He's been seen near Glencullen." He came around the wagon and climbed up, grabbing the reins and flicking the whip sharply at the horse, who started and then began to move forward.

"I'm sorry," Anna said, grabbing for the rail of her seat to steady herself. "I do not understand."

"It's Hanks…that damned Billy Hanks." MacCray cracked his whip again and managed to get the horse trotting, which set the wagon to bouncing as it hit the ruts and stones in the narrow roadway. Anna grabbed the side rail to prevent being flung out of her seat. "We've been after him for nearly two years," he continued, his eyes sharp and his mouth pulled back in a grim smile. "Lord Stafford has offered a bounty of ten pounds to the man who can bring him in, dead or alive."

"My goodness!" Mary Ross exclaimed. "That's a goodly sum. Whatever has the man done?"

"Hah!" MacCray exclaimed. "The better question would be: what hasn't he done? He is an outlaw, a criminal. He has poached his Lordship's deer, and even helped himself to His Lordship's cattle. Worse, he has rebelled against His Lordship's authority and helped many a man escape the law. He has agitated the people against their chief, tells them not to pay their lawful rents."

"Gracious!" Anna said, hanging on as she rocked sideways on the bench. "Why do you not have him arrested?"

"If we could find the bastard, we would, I assure you, madam," he said. "But he's like a ghost, Billy Hanks. Some even say he *is* a ghost. He's a master of disguise, he usually travels by night, knows where to hide out in the wilderness where no man can track him. No dog, either. We'll hear that he's been seen in this village or that glen, and by the time we get there, with the Sheriff and his deputies, he's vanished. And, of course, the people cover for him. 'Never seen him, Governor' they'll say. 'There's not been such a man here' they'll say. Oh, he's a thorn, he is, Billy Hanks. But we will find him one day. And if we're quick enough getting to Glencullen, we may find him this very day!"

THREE HOURS LATER, they entered the valley known as Glencullen. Here and there Anna could see groups of mud-and-thatch houses sprawled haphazardly up the steep hillsides that rose on both sides of the River Cullen. Smoke from those houses swirled in the air before being swept away by the wind. The houses were surrounded by small patchworks of fields, and Anna could see black cattle grazing near the bothys.

The road from Lairg had climbed at first for some miles until they reached an upland moor that was mostly flat and tree-less. The river snaked calmly through the bottom of the glen, while the mountains rose dramatically to the east and west. Long rocky arms swept downwards towards the valley floor from time to time, and Anna could see long white tails of waterfalls spilling down the mountainsides on the way to the river.

The journey from Lairg had been a mostly silent one. Mac-Cray was intent on keeping the horse moving as fast as possible, given the conditions, and the poor horse was wet with sweat and sounded winded. They had stopped briefly to let the horse rest, but MacCray had quickly pushed on again. Anna noted the in-tensity of his expression, and thought it best not to interrupt the man with idle conversation.

Mary Ross had been mostly silent on the latter part of their journey, but as they approached the settlement she point-ed out the parish church, a small, lime-washed rectangle with a slanted tin roof rusted to red and a tiny steeple at one end, perched on a high bluff overlooking the river, surrounded by its churchyard and a grove of pines.

"I learned my letters there," she said. "Like most in the strath, we never had much in the way of possessions, but our mums and das made sure we knew our letters."

There was a narrow wood bridge carrying the roadway over a small burn spilling down off the hill to the right. Over the bridge, a blacksmith's shop sat beneath some large trees, still bare of leaves in the early spring. And a few yards away, next to the rushing stream, a gristmill stood, its large wooden wheel turning slowly, spilling water over the weir.

"Where is everyone?" Anna wondered out loud. Despite the buildings, she could see no people.

"Tis the time to prepare the fields," Mary Ross said. "Manure to be carried and spread. Plowing will being when the weather clears. Potatoes go in first. The grains must wait until May for planting."

"More likely they're all drunk and sleeping," MacCray growled, his eyes scanning the hills. Mary Ross looked at him, eyes angry, but said nothing. He guided the horse over the narrow bridge and pulled to a stop beneath one of the trees. He peered up the road, which climbed a short hill and disappeared around a bend. Then he jumped down from the wagon and pushed his head in the door of the blacksmith's shop.

"Empty," he said, coming back out. "Fire's not going. Looks like its been unused for quite a while."

"Well," Anna said. "Perhaps you can take me to Mr Fraser's. He is expecting me, I trust."

"Aye." MacCray walked back to the wagon and prepared to jump back onto the seat.

Just then, a young girl came around the corner of the road, leading a grizzled donkey who was pulling a small flat wagon piled high with straw. The girl could not have been more than twelve or thirteen years of age and was wearing a tattered long dress and the traditional white snood, under which she had pinned her bright red hair. She held a thin switch in one hand which she occasionally flicked against the side of the old mule. She saw the two strangers outside the blacksmith's shop, but continued down the dusty road, speaking a few words softly to the donkey.

MacCray watched her with narrowed eyes until she reached the clearing.

"Where are you going?" he demanded loudly, holding up one hand.

The girl looked at him with curiosity, then looked up at Anna on the wagon seat. She looked puzzled.

"*I gcás ina bhfuil tú ag dul?*" Mary Ross said to the girl in Gaelic. Where are you going?

The girl smiled. "*Tá mé ag dul go dtí mo theach,*" she said. I am going to my house. She pointed back down the road to indicate where her house was. Mary translated for MacCray.

"And who in the hell is that?" MacCray looked into the bed of the wagon and was pointing to the figure of an old woman, lying in the straw in the back of the wagon. She was wrapped in layers of blankets from head to toe, and had pulled her tartan plaid cloak around herself, with just a bit of her forehead and closed eyes visible. He poked the woman with the butt end of his whip, and they all heard a mournful sigh as the old woman moaned in response.

"*Is é sin mo sheanmháthair,*" the girl said, "*Tá sí an-tinn leis an fiabhras.*" That is my grandmother. She is very ill with the fever."

When MacCray heard the translation, he stepped back quickly from the side of the wagon. "Move on," he almost shouted, waving the girl on, "And the devil take your pestilence with you."

The girl flicked her switch and the donkey plodded forward with a shake of its head. The girl ignored MacCray, who glared as she walked past, but she looked up at Anna and Mary Ross and smiled. As the rickety wagon passed by, Anna looked down at the grandmother, swaddled in the straw. She noticed that the woman's feet were clad in pair of sturdy leather boots. Men's boots.

MacCray swung himself angrily up onto the bench seat and cracked his whip over the horse's head. "I'll take you to Fraser," he said. "Then I need to find Duncan Gordon, milady's tacksman. He's supposed to know what's going on around here."

As the wagon started forward, Anna glanced back at the girl, the donkey and the wagon, creaking slowly across the bridge and down the dusty road towards the river.

6

Billy Hanks waited until the cart was well out of sight of the clearing by the bridge. When he was sure that MacCray was not following, he threw off his cloak and unwrapped himself from the layers of woolen blankets. He sat up and smiled at the girl leading the donkey cart.

"Nicely done, Fionna," he said. "Your 'grandmother' is in your debt."

The girl chuckled softly. "He is always so angry when he comes to the glen," she said, nodding in the direction that MacCray had gone. "Him with his whip and his angry voice. Why does he hate us so?"

Hanks brushed the straw off his clothing and out of his unruly shock of black hair. He leaped from the cart gracefully. Billy Hanks was about forty years old, though still strong and sinewy, with hands the size of anvils. He was not a tall man, but his broad shoulders and narrow waist gave him a lean and hungry look. His eyes, however, were those of a man who has seen too much of the world. They were wary, alert, constantly scanning; the eyes of a man who fully expected the worst. He gave himself a last shake.

"Och, don't fret about MacCray," he said. "He just follows orders from Lord Stafford. He's probably angry all the time because he knows that he'll never beat us."

The girl thought about that, then nodded and flicked her stick at the donkey. They started down the road again.

"Will ye be at Mute Meg's this evening, then?" Billy Hanks called after her.

"Aye," the girl said, and walked on.

He watched her go. They'll never beat us, he thought, because of people like her. A simple girl, hard working, honest, loyal always to kith and kin. Like everyone who lived in this glen, and countless others in the shire, she just wanted to be left alone, to live and love on this land as her parents had, and her grandparents and generations going back hundreds of years. Yes, it was a hard life. But it was the only life they knew. They knew how to handle the hard years and how to enjoy the good ones. They asked little from the outside world. Just a fair price for their cattle, fair weather for their crops and the peace to follow their ways. They would do almost anything that the Countess asked of them. She was their chief, their leader, their connection to the centuries that had gone before. She had asked the young men of the glen to volunteer for the war in Europe against Bonaparte, and the young men had gone, willingly, arm-in-arm and singing songs of bravery, battle and death. But the people of the glen would not willingly just pack up and go, leaving behind forever their glen, the wind rushing down from the peaks of Ben Cullen, the wildflowers on the moor, the roebucks and the grouse, the salmon in the river. They would not leave all that, especially not to go live in a small hut near the ocean, where they would be expected to become fishermen, colliers or gatherers of the kelp. Or, worse, to do nothing at all.

"Not if I can help it," Billy Hanks said to himself as the girl and her donkey and cart disappeared around a corner. He turned and headed toward the river. There was a hidden pathway near the water which followed the bank upstream, covered in most places by the overarching brush and small trees. He walked this path for about a mile up the glen until he came to the rocky point where the home of Mute Meg stood. The light of the day was beginning to fade. Wisps of smoke trickled from the central hole in the roof of the house, instantly swept away by the breeze. Billy Hanks paused for a bit, still under cover, listening and watching the hut and its clearing, alert for the presence of any others that might be watching. Once he was satisfied that the coast was clear, he headed for the door.

He ducked into the low doorway, past the woolen blanket that had been hung to keep the drafts out. The fire crackled cheerily in the central hearth and Billy could smell the stew that was bubbling away in its clay pot at the side of the fire. A dog, its sleep disturbed by Billy's entrance, raised its head and looked at the newcomer. Its tail thumped fitfully in greeting before the dog lowered its head and closed its eyes again. Good thing I'm not MacCray, Billy thought to himself before leaning down to give the dog's ears a brief scratch, This old dog's days as a watcher were long past.

"Billy Hanks!" cried a woman's voice. "All in one piece, I see. Thanks be to heaven for that!"

Catty Greer appeared from the shadows of the hut and gave Billy a big hug. She was middle aged, round and red-faced, her smile full of welcome.

"Catty," Billy said, nodding at her. "How's Meg getting along?"

"She's well, Billy," Catty said, pulling up a three-legged stool next to the fire and motioning at Billy to sit. "Her body may be old and weary, but her mind's still as sharp as a knife." She glanced towards the sleeping quarters at one end of the hut, across which more tartan blankets had been hung for privacy and quiet. "She's been having a bit of a wee nap, but should be up and about soon."

"Good, good," Billy said, sitting and stretching out his long legs before the fire. "Let the old woman sleep."

Catty brought him a mug of cool water, which he gratefully drank. "Are ye hungry, Billy?" she asked. "The stew's about done, I think. The girls brought me some nice plump rabbits this morning, to go with the tatties and curran."

"Smells good," Billy said. "I can wait a wee bit to eat, thanks."

Catty suddenly made a small sound, turned and disappeared behind the woolen wall. Billy smiled to himself. The women who dwelled in this house seemed to communicate with each other in ways no mortal man could understand. Mute Meg, who had not spoken a word aloud since that terrible day on Culloden Moor nearly seventy years ago, had always had women living with her who somehow understood her unspoken wishes and commands. Some in the glen said they all had the second sight, and spoke to each other in the language of the fairies. Billy, who did not believe in superstitions and fantasies, nevertheless could not explain how they communicated with each other. Nor did he, or any of the others who lived in the glen, know where some of these household helpers came from: They usually just appeared in their midst, coming from places far and wide to live with and help care for Mute Meg. Catty Greer was perhaps the fourth or fifth such caregiver who had appeared in Glencullen to live for a time in the rude hut beside the river, helping Meg nurture her garden of herbs and mysterious medicinal plants. Some said Catty had escaped from a brutal husband in Edinburgh; others claimed she was a foundling orphan who had been raised by a kindly family in Argyll. But nobody knew for sure; she had just appeared one day and settled in as Mute Meg's caretaker. All the people of the glen knew was that if they were ill, they went to see Mute Meg. Catty, or one of the others, would ask a few questions. Then Meg, with a wise look and perhaps a brief touch of the patient with her wizened old hands, would gather up a packet of herbs or roots, or mash together some salve or poultice. One of the helpers would provide instructions on how to use it. And the people knew that if Mute Meg sent them away without one of her emetics or potions, it was time to make themselves right with their Maker, because death was certain to be coming soon.

The curtain was pulled back and Catty helped a frail woman cross the room to sit in an old rocking chair next to the hearth. The woman was of undetermined years, white haired, skinny, wrinkled, pale and pink. She walked slowly and carefully, yet with a straight back and her head held high. And, once seated, she peered out at Billy with bright eyes that still shone with life. She smiled at him and reached out to grasp his hand. Her hands were cool in his; her skin felt like delicate paper, as if he could rub it gently away leaving nothing but her ancient bones.

"Greetings to you, mother," Billy said formally. "I trust you are well?"

Mute Meg smiled and nodded.

"She would like to know where you have traveled and what you have seen and heard," Catty said, fussing around the old woman, making sure her shawl covered the frail shoulders, and that her favorite pillow was placed behind her back.

Billy stared into the fire before answering. His journeys had troubled him, and he knew they would trouble the old woman sitting next to him.

"I've been to the north," he said. "I've spoken to Lord Sinclair himself, as you suggested, Mother. But he cannot, or will not, help. He himself is preparing to remove a goodly portion of his people to the seashore."

Billy saw the old woman's face clouded to reflect the disappointment of his news. She had sent Billy to Sir James Sinclair of Ulbster, having heard that the man might have some land available in his own straths and glens for her people. It would have been a bitter blow to the people of Glencullen to pack up and move themselves far to the North, to the unfamiliar lands of the shire of Caithness, but at least they might have stayed together and been able to continue in their familiar ways of life.

"The landlords throughout Scotland are turning to the sheep," Billy Hanks continued. "I've stopped in to see for myself. Reay, Munro, even Ross of Balnagowan. They're all letting tracts to the sheep farmers. They've all overwintered flocks of the new Cheviot and when they see how the beasties survive the snow and the ice, well, they start adding up their profits. It's only a matter of time. The people will be moved out, and the sheep moved in."

A gloomy silence took over the room. Catty brought Billy a bowl of the stew and a crust of freshly baked bread, still warm from the hearth oven. He set to eating with hungry enthusiasm. The old woman stared into the fire, deep in thought. After a time, she glanced at Catty.

"Well then," Catty said, "We'll just have to stop them."

"What is MacCray doing in the glen?" Billy asked.

Catty and Mute Meg exchanged a glance and Billy Hanks noticed a smile playing at Meg's lips. "He's a-chasing you, Billy," Cattie said with a chuckle. "Someone in Lairg said they'd seen you strolling down the road in the middle of the day."

Billy Hanks shook his head and frowned. "I haven't been in Lairg," he said. "I came home from the north. Walking mostly at night."

Catty laughed. "Of course you weren't in Lairg," she said. "But Lord Stafford has offered ten guineas to the man who turns you in. For that kind of money, a man will swear he's seen you standing in the doorway, plain as day."

Billy wasn't amused. "Where is the bloody bastard now?"

"He's at Captain Gordon's place," Catty said. "We'll find out tonight what they're talking about. Jenny and Sam will he here later."

Hanks nodded. Captain Duncan Gordon was cousin to the Countess and her tacksman in the glen. In the old times, he would have ruled his kinsmen with an iron hand, distributing the best farmland and the choicest cattle to those in his family, collecting rents and keeping law and order in the name of the Clan Chieftan in Dornoch. But the old times were no more, and Capt. Gordon was mostly a figurehead to the rest of the people in the glen. He owned and ran his own large holdings along the River Cullen and otherwise kept to himself. The Countess' authority was now in the hands of her estate agent, MacCray, and her superintendant, William Young, who rarely left the comforts of Dornoch. And MacCray was an outlander and not one to be trusted. But Capt. Gordon still employed a small domestic staff, including Sam and Jenny Ross who both had been born, raised and married in the glen. They would attend that evening's *ceilidh* and bring whatever news they could glean from Gordon's meeting with MacCray that afternoon.

Billy Hanks went back to his stew, deep in thought.

Mute Meg shifted in her chair, turning her head to look at Catty with eyebrows raised. Catty nodded back at her.

"Mother says they may be planning to move on the glen," Catty said to Billy.

He mopped up the last of his stew with the bread and popped it into his mouth. Sighing with satisfaction, he handed the empty bowl to Catty.

"I thought the plan was to wait until next year to begin evictions," he said. "Isn't that what our man at Dunrobin told us?" One of the servants at the castle in Dornoch had been born and raised in Glencullen and had reported back things he had overheard being discussed by Lord Stafford and his managers. After the bad publicity that had resulted from the vicious evictions that had been undertaken by Patrick Sellar in Strath Naver a few years earlier, Lady Stafford had insisted on a delay in her husband's plans to enforce similar removals across Sutherland.

The timetable had been adjusted and Glencullen's turn had been forestalled until the next year, they had been assured.

Catty nodded. "He did," she said. "But if Lord Stafford has a tenant at the ready, well, that man has never turned down the chance to make more money, may the Good Lord see fit to send him to Hell and damnation!"

Mute Meg nodded, and waved her hand at Billy.

"She says that if Lord Stafford thinks the people of the glen are harboring the notorious criminal Billy Hanks, he would feel justified the more to remove them all to the sea, sooner rather than later," she said with a frown. Mute Meg reached over and grasped Billy's hand. "She says you are not to blame yourself, of course, Billy," Catty said. "It's just an excuse for doing what he's planning to do to us already."

Billy Hanks nodded, and gave the old lady's hand a reassuring squeeze. "I know it, I do," he said. "Perhaps we can come up with another way to change the old bastard's mind."

7

The Manse, the cottage allocated to the minister of the glen, stood on a gentle hillside above the whitewashed church. It was surrounded by its own well-tended acres, the glebe, which the people of the glen kept for their spiritual leader. Beyond the dark flood of the River Cullen, the ground rose dramatically in the distance to rocky peaks extending to the ever-higher ground to the north. Behind the Manse, further up the hillside, a thick forest of pines grew like a dark green blanket tossed over the rocky ground.

When MacCray pulled his wagon up to the door, three young girls came bustling out of the doorway, their ruddy faces wreathed in smiles. They were quickly followed by the Reverend Fraser, dressed in his black clerical garb. His face was covered by his long white beard, and the hair on his head blew in the breezes cascading down the hillside.

"Welcome, welcome!" he cried, clapping his hands in delight. "Girls…help the ladies with their bags. Look lively now!"

The three girls, all giggles and blushes, rushed to collect the bags from the carriage and carry them into the house. Mary Ross climbed down from her seat and followed the girls inside while Fraser held out a hand to help Anna from the carriage's bench. Once she was down, he held her hand and shook it energetically. "Welcome to Glencullen, dear lady," he said. "We are so happy to welcome you at last!"

Anna could not help but smile and thanked him.

Fraser turned and looked up at MacCray. "Robert," he said. "Are you coming in? The girls have the teapot ready and I think there's a bit of cake. Can you come in and visit?"

"Nay, sir," MacCray said, pulling at the rim of his hat. "I have business at Colonel Gordon's."

"Aye," Fraser said. "I understand. Go on then. I hope you can stop in again when you have the time."

MacCray nodded and cracked his whip. The horse started up and they drove away.

Fraser led his guest into the Manse. "I am so happy that you have arrived," he said. He ushered her into the parlor, a small but sunny room with windows looking down the glen, the river spilling down its rocky banks and the mountains rising majestically in the distance. A cheerful, small fire sputtered in the stone hearth.

A small woman dressed in severe black raiment sat next to a small table upon which rested a tea pot and several china cups and saucers. She wore a black bonnet that almost hid her face in its shadows. "My dear," Fraser said, "Mrs Kenton has arrived. Mrs Kenton, may I present my wife?"

The woman tilted her head upwards, allowing the visitor a clearer view of her face, tucked away in the depths of her bonnet. Her face was careworn, almost skeletal, her gray eyes redrimmed and rheumy. Her expression barely changed as she gazed upon the visitor, but she nodded ever so slightly and extended a narrow and bony hand. Anna shook the hand and murmured a greeting. The older woman's hand was cold as ice and quickly withdrawn and hidden again in the depths of her black shawl. Her head returned to its former position and her face once again fell deeply into the shadows, obscured and largely invisible.

"May we get you some tea?" Fraser, excited to have a guest, was full of restless energy. "Mary!" he called out, rubbing his hands together. "Tea! Cakes!" He turned to Anna with concern. "How was your journey, m'dear?" he said. "I trust the journey from Dornoch was not too taxing. The roads can be very difficult this time of the year. How did you find the Countess? I trust she is well? Mary! Katharine! Eliza!"

One of the girls came in, wearing a starched white apron over her gingham dress. Her red hair was pinned high on her head, showing off her bright red cheeks and glistening blue eyes. She made a curtsy, smiled broadly at the guest, and began to pour out the hot tea.

"Thank you, Mary," the reverend said when he was handed a cup and saucer. "Didn't I smell one of Katharine's spice cakes baking?"

Another of the girls that had greeted Anna on her arrival at the Manse came into the parlor bearing a silver tray with slices of a warm brown cake slathered with butter. Fraser took a slice and popped it whole into his mouth.

"Ah," he said, eyes closed in delight as he chewed. "Katharine, your spice cake is one of the earthly reminders of the Almighty's benefice."

"Ta, sir," the girl said, blushing a bit at the compliment. "Ma'am?" She held the plate out towards Anna, who took a slice and laid it on her saucer while she took a small sip of the steaming tea. Katharine placed the plate of cake down on the table next to Mrs Fraser, who did not move a muscle either to take a slice of cake, or to pick up her cup. The girl curtsied again and left the parlor, followed by Mary.

Fraser placed his saucer down with a rattle of bone china. "Right then," he said, "May I show you my study? I have been making some notes about our proposed school. Why, just last week…"

"Let the poor woman enjoy her tea, husband." The voice came from the wraith from deep within her black shadows.

"Of course, of course," Fraser said, flustered. "My apologies, my dear Mrs. Kenton. I am perhaps a bit over excited to begin our work together. Of course you must have time to get settled in." He forced himself to sit down in a wooden side chair and folded his hands. "So, I trust the journey from Dornoch was uneventful?"

Anna, too, set her saucer down and smiled. "Yes, Mr Fraser, quite uneventful, thank you," she said. "Although the last leg from Lairg was a bit faster than the rest. Mr MacCray was apparently in pursuit of some miscreant he seemed very anxious to find and arrest."

"Really?" Fraser said. "Who would that be?"

"He said it was someone he called Billy Hanks," she said. "Have you heard of him? Mr MacCray seemed to believe he was quite a dangerous criminal."

Mrs Fraser gasped audibly and her hands flew up to her throat. Fraser himself leaped to his feet. He strode over to his wife and touched her shoulder reassuringly.

"There, there Martha," he said to his wife. "I'm sure it will be fine. MacCray and Captain Gordon know what to do." He turned to Anna and began stroking his long white beard nervously.

"This Hanks fellow is a well known outlaw in the county," he said to Anna. "His Lordship has laid quite a bounty upon the fellow's head. It doesn't seem to matter much to the ordinary people—they seem to look upon the man as something of a folk hero—but I am quite certain the Sheriff Depute and whatever patrols of soldiers from Fort William are in the vicinity are looking for the man."

"What is it he has done?" Anna wondered.

"He is wanted in the main for his activities in poaching and stealing from His Lordship," the old minister said. "But he is also suspected of stoking the fires of rebellion among the people against Lord and Lady Stafford and their plans for improvements upon the shire. The former crime, alas, is quite common, especially when the people are hungry. I suspect it is the latter which offends His Lordship the most."

"I have heard of the plans to remove the people to the seashore," Anna said. "I can imagine there might be some resistance from the people. They have lived in these glens for centuries."

"'Tis so, 'tis so," Fraser nodded in agreement. "But Providence has decreed that this is the time for improvements in the county and has designated His Lordship to carry them out. It is the duty of his people to obey and trust that this is the Lord's will for them."

"Amen," said Mrs Fraser, the voice coming from deep inside her bonnet.

"What do you know about this rogue, this Billy Hanks?" Anna asked, sipping at her tea. She was quite interested in this story. She thought she might have seen the outlaw earlier, hidden in the donkey cart, and that gave her a frisson of excitement. She supposed she should say something about what she had seen, but something held her back from speaking. He is probably long gone, she thought to herself. And I don't even know if it was this Billy Hanks I saw hidden in the cart. Perhaps that girl's grandmother, who happened to wear men's boots, was indeed ill with fever. Or, the blanketed figure Anna saw in the straw wagon might have been that young girl's father, or brother, or even her lover.

Fraser sat down again, casting a wary eye upon his wife. "Billy Hanks is said to actually be a son of Glencullen," he said, stroking his beard thoughtfully. "But nobody can confirm or deny that as fact. They say his parents were carried off with the fever when he was just a lad. I believe he was raised by relatives and educated by Mute Meg, who lives by the river."

"That witch!" said the voice from the bonnet. "Saints preserve us from her evil magick!"

"As soon as he was old enough—indeed probably before he was old enough—he was sent off to the army," Fraser continued, ignoring his wife's outburst. "We heard that he served bravely in the Americas before he was kidnapped by the red savages of that land and forced to become one of them. He learned their ways, living in the forests among the wild animals. They say he learned how to walk as silent as a ghost and how to disappear into Nature without leaving a trace behind. They say he can follow a man through bog or mountain only by the scent the man leaves behind." He stroked his beard again. "But as with all fairy stories and children's tales, I am sure there is a great deal of exaggeration, both in the details of his history and the extent of his abilities. He is a man like any other, and one day he will be called before his God to answer for his sins."

"Amen!" Mrs Fraser spoke again.

Katherine returned to the parlor with a silver tray to begin collecting the tea things.

"Well," Anna said, "I am quite sure this Billy Hanks will be caught one day soon. No man can hide from the law forever."

"Och," Katherine piped up, "I wouldna be so sure upon that, Miss. They've been searching for Billy Hanks for near on a year now, since he returned from Canada, and they've not seen hide nor hair of him yet! 'Tis said he's seen here, he's seen there. There must be ten Billy Hanks running free in the shire, if ye believe the stories. But all are shadows and dreams. None has yet to catch the man!"

"Ten Billy Hanks! Ten?" The voice from within the bonnet shook with emotion and could say no more.

"Now, now, Martha," said Fraser, reaching over to pat his wife's arm, concern in his voice. "Think not on't, dear woman. We're safe enough here in our own home. There's no reason for Billy Hanks to come here."

Anna sought to change the subject for the poor woman's sake.

"Is it in this house that we shall begin the school, sir?" she asked Fraser.

He shot her a look of gratitude, and then shook his head.

"Nae, nae," he said. "The children will gather at the kirk. It is most central to all in the strath and familiar to the people. We shall merely rearrange the seats somewhat and it will serve quite admirably as a schoolhouse. In addition, I can then petition the presbytery to advance some money to our cause, if the parish's own facilities are being used for educational purposes. We shall go tomorrow to look at the church so we can begin preparations that classes may begin soon."

Katharine finished collecting the tea cups and plates and stood for a minute. Catching Fraser's eye, she curtsied.

"Begging your pardon, sir," she said. "But there is a ceildhe tonight. I thought Mrs. Kenton and her lady might enjoy coming along with us. She can meet some of the folk and listen to our music. It might be interesting for her. And she can begin to meet some of the women of the strath and talk up her school a bit to them."

Anna sat up, excited. Mary Ross had told her stories about the ceildhe, the gathering of the people of an evening to share gossip and news. The men would smoke their pipes and talk and the women would knit or crochet and talk and sooner or later someone would bring out a fiddle and then the singing and dancing would begin, and often last well into the night.

"What a wonderful idea!" she cried. Turning to Fraser, she remembered her place and made herself calm down. "If you think it wise, sir," she added, eyes downcast demurely.

Fraser paused, thinking. He had hoped that he and Anna might spend her first night in the glen in his study, discussing educational theory and going over the ideas that consumed him. But there was plenty of time for beginning that later. And Katherine was right—Anna would probably enjoy the experience of

meeting the local people, and they meeting their new schoolmis-
tress.

"If Mrs. Kenton is not too tired after her long journey..."
He paused.

"Oh, no sir," she said. "I would very much enjoy meeting
some of my new neighbors!"

"Very well," the old man said with a smile. "But I want
you all home at a reasonable hour. We must commence with the
work first thing in the morning!"

"Oh, thank you, sir!" said Anna, and she and Katherine
exchanged a secret and victorious glance.

8

*M*any *years ago, in the times that can no longer be recalled by any living man, there once lived in this strath
a man known as Connell the Piper."*
The speaker was an old man, his ruddy face mostly hidden behind a fluffy white beard that descended almost to his
belly. He was sitting upon a stool next to the warm fire in Mute
Meg's small but cozy cottage. Smoke from the fire rose lazily up
from the central pit on the floor and drifted away into the rainy
night through the gap in the thatch above. About a dozen wom-
en had drawn up their chairs and stools in a rough circle around
the fire, and most of them were working on a piece of knitting
or fussing over repairs to a garment with needle and thread. The
men, and there were just four or five present that night, mostly stood by the entrance door, smoking their pipes and passing
around a flask. There were children there, too, the youngest
playing on the earthen floor at their mother's feet, while some of
the older ones had gathered in the byre, to the left of the central room, where two cows, an old horse, a few pigs and a dozen
chickens had settled in for the night on their beds of fresh straw.
Some of the older girls had woven together garlands of straw and
flowers for the cows, which patiently allowed themselves to be
crowned. But even the animals' dark, limpid eyes seemed to be

focused on the old man, as he began weaving his tale. He wore leathern breeches and a tattered woolen coat, and he held his stained, knitted cap in one of his gnarled hands, using the other to paint the air for emphasis.

Now Piobroch Connell was known far and wide throughout Glencullen as the best piper ever to have lived and played in these parts, or any other. No wedding feast was considered complete until Connell had been summoned to make his piobroch skirl and drone until every last soul was up and dancing. No chief could be laid to rest until the pipes played the coronach to ease the way to the summerlands where the forefathers dwell.

One day, Connell the Piper was summoned to a distant village, beyond the arms of Ben Cullen, to play for a wedding feast. It was a long journey, through the bog lands and across the treeless heath, but Connell was ever ready to do his duty and he kissed his lovely bride and his many lovely bairns farewell and set off, promising to return in two days' time.

They say that never before had Connell played with such power and dexterity as he did at that wedding feast. It is said that he played near the night through, and the dancing was as joyful and wild as had ever been witnessed, here or anywhere in Albion. But finally, just before the breaking of the dawn, Connell made ready to leave to return to his home here in Glencullen. He took a mighty draught of the deoch-an-doruis, the door drink, bid his hosts good-bye and set off for home.

His wife expected him the next afternoon, but Connell did not arrive. She prepared his dinner, but he did not come. She put their bairns to bed and tried to wait up for him through the long night, but finally fell to sleep. He was not there the next morning. Worried, she asked her neighbors to look for him, and they began to search far and wide, scouring the banks of the lochs and the river, climbing into the mountains to peer into caves and behind boulders, and creeping through the mists of the boglands that lay along the way. But there was no sign of Connell on that day, or any other.

There were many who tried to guess at what fate had befallen Connell the Piper. Some say he had become lost and was still wandering through the Highlands, searching for a way back to his home. Others said the drink had gotten to him, and he had fallen into a bog, nevermore to be seen. Still others wondered if some other piper, jealous of Connell's superior skill and talents, had acted against him with violence.

But the older ones in the strath, who had seen and heard of many strange things, looked at one another knowing that Connell the Piper had been taken away by the fairies who dwell below the land and above the clouds, had been taken to their great halls and drinking places, where he would play his piobroch *for their entertainment until that Day when the Lord returns in his Glory."*

The old man paused. He was handed some water. He took a draught, and handed it back, and continued to tell his story.

Now Cullen's wife—her name was Maud, but all knew her as Bean-Mhath, *the good woman—was deeply saddened by her husband's disappearance. Every night for six months, she kept a candle burning near the door of the poor hut where she had lived with Connell the Piper, hoping that he would see the light wherever he might be, and follow its warm and hopeful beams back to her side.*

But after six months passed and Connell had still not returned, the good pastor of the parish took Maud aside and said she must ask him to perform the services for the dead. It was, he said, the only way to ensure that poor Connell's spirit would be released to its heavenly home. But the Bean-Mhath resisted. As she did when the elder of the strath, an old man of nearly one hundred years, told her that Connell was likely dwelling with the fairies and would not return to the land of the living.

"Now Maud the Bean-Mhath had long been a midwife in the strath, and had helped many a woman through the pangs and troubles of childbirth. Her skill and calmness during the crisis of birth had served her, and her patients, well and her reputation and expertise was known throughout the strath and even far beyond.

So she was not surprised, one dark wintry night many months after her husband had disappeared, to hear a knock at her door. There she found a little man dressed all in green, carrying in his hands a bow and some arrows that seemed to be made of silver.

'A good evening to you, Bean-Mhath,' the wee man said, doffing his cap. 'It is following me you will do, for my wife is in travail and has sore need of you.'

Maud understood at once that it was one of the fairies who stood before her. She had seen in the embers of her hearthfire a sign that predicted his arrival at her door. She tried to refuse her services to the little man ... once, twice, even a third time. But at last she consented to accompany him, even when he insisted that he wrap one of his green cloaks about her eyes and that she follow where he led.

For an hour, then two, then yet another, she was led by him unseeing. She felt the mists of the bogs against her face, and felt the winds of the mountains disturbing her hair. Finally, she heard the sound of distant music—someone playing the pipes—and then her blindfold was removed.

She was standing in a magnificent underground grotto, the stone floor covered in sumptuous carpets and thickly strewn, sweet-smelling straw; the walls covered in tapestries more elaborate than those to be found in the greatest houses of Europe; magnificent brass candelabras everywhere, bathing the grotto in golden light and warmth. And the grotto was filled with little men and little women, all dressed in green. And most were dancing furiously to the skirling sounds of the piobroch. Bean-Mhath, in wonder, was led by her host toward the far end of the grotto, where she could see the Fairy Queen on her velvet couch, in the throes of that black passage of childbirth.

As she made her way through the throngs of dancing fairies, the piper turned as he played, and Bean-Mhath saw the visage of her husband, Connell the Piper. His face was haggard and worn, his hair had turned nearly all to gray, and his shoulders were stooped and weary. Yet he played as beautifully as ever, his clear notes echoing through the grotto and playing about the rocky pinnacles that hung from the dark reaches of the cave above.

Bean-Mhath could not speak to him then; she had business to attend with the Queen. The labor was long and hard, but eventually, with Bean-Mhath's help, the Fairy Queen arrived at the green land of joy that is childbirth, and a squalling heir was laid upon her breast. At once, all the faeries in the grotto, dancing or not, began to cheer and clap. As Bean-Mhath was led back towards the cave's entrance, she was besieged with ecstatic shouts of thanks, and many of the little people tried to thrust food or gold coins or trinkets and jewels into her hands.

But Bean-Mhath was not the least interested in these treasures. Instead, she made her way straight toward the piper, who was still pacing and still playing his clear, ringing notes.

'Is it coming home with me you are, Connell, my good husband?' she asked. 'Your children have missed their father these long months and I, too, wish to have him back in my home, and in my bed.'

'Soon, soon,' he said to her, turning away. 'I just have one more melody to play. I promised my friends one more song, and that is a promise I must keep!'

'You have been gone long these many months,' said she. 'I think you have played for them enough. Come home with me, husband.'

He looked at her, and in his eyes she could see that there was a veil between them, a veil as strong and impenetrable as a wall of brick. 'You are mistaken, woman,' said he. 'It has been just one night, and I have but one more song to play.'" He turned away and began again to play the notes of his song, clear and loud and ringing.

The faeries led Bean-Mhath to the entrance of the grotto, and bade her farewell. There, the smiling faery who had come for her was waiting to lead her back to her home again. He prepared to wrap her eyes in his green cloak once again, in order to make sure the pathway to the faery grotto would remain unknown. 'Wait, wait' Bean-Mhath said, 'I must first tie my boot.' And she bent down to pretend to tie her laces. But she slipped a clew of thread from her apron pocket, strong black thread that she always used to tie off the cord of the newborn babe, and quickly looped it around the base of a small tree at the entrance to the grotto.

Then, she allowed herself to be led sightless back to the strath, back to her own warm hearthside. The string between her fingers played out and out as she followed her guide, and finally she was forced to drop the end.

Soon thereafter, the faery guide unwrapped her eyes as they stood at the threshold of her own modest house, and she could see that the dawn was just beginning to rise and that the long night was at an end. She turned to bid farewell to her guide, but he had disappeared in a blink, and there was no one there.

"She woke and fed her children, and then returned to the path to search for the end of her thread. After a bit, she found it, tangled in a bush near the River Cullen, and, winding it carefully in her fingers again, she began to follow it back into the strath, up the nearby mountains, across the boggy plains, through the rocky heathlands and finally to a hillock rising near a placid lake. There she found the end of her string tied to the roots of a small rowan tree. She searched and searched for an way inside to the faery grotto, but could find nary an opening, a crack, or a fissure that might lead into the spacious interior of the home of the little people.

Bean-Mhath returned to her home that day, but she spoke to the old crone of the strath, who knew things of faeries and spells and healing properties, and a few days later, she retraced her steps down the strath and up the nearby mountains, across the boggy plains and through the rocky highlands and found again the small lake and the rocky hillock where her husband must still be playing his pipes.

Following the instructions she had been given, she walked around the hillock: once, twice, thrice. Then she laid upon the ground a cross made of branches of the yew, with a garland of oak and ivy at the center. In the four spaces of the cross, she laid the fins of a haddock, the comb of a black rooster, the mane of a horse, and the skin of a snake. Then, she repeated aloud the words of a duanag or ditty that the old crone had taught her.

No sooner had she finished her spell than she heard the drone of the piobroch, loud and clear and resonant, and stepping out from behind a rock came her beloved, Connell the Piper. When he saw his wife, he laid his pipes down upon the ground and took her up in his arms and time stood still while their embrace filled, each the other, with the warm and nurturing sustenance of love.

The couple returned to the strath of Glencullen and lived together for many happy years thereafter. But first, as the crone had warned them to do, they fortified themselves against the faeries. They put a strong wooden door at the front of their house, and every night, Bean-Mhath was careful to leave a bowl of warm milk on the threshold outside the door as an offering to the little people. And there were other spells and incantations that they used to protect themselves and their children from the visitors of the night air.

But the crone had warned Bean-Mhath, and one morning, after some thirty years had passed, she awoke to find that Connell, her husband, had again disappeared. At once, she retraced her steps to the faery grotto in the hillside, but again, there was no sign of what lay within. She listened with all her ears, but could hear no music, no sounds, no piping. And she never heard the music, nor ever saw her beloved husband ever again, from that day to this. As the crone had warned, there was something inside of him that, when the faeries beckoned, he would have to answer, and return to that magnificent cave and its golden warmth, where he would play and play for days, months and years without end. He is likely still there today, perhaps playing the tune 'I am away from Assynt' and he will likely be there forever, until the Lord returns in all His Glory to save the faithful and cast the sinners into the pits of Hell.

Crùbach, or Lame John, an old man with a bushy white beard and a pronounced limp from a childhood broken bone that gave him his name, cleared his throat in the silence that enveloped the warm cottage where the people of the strath had been listening to Old Malcolm's story, one they had all heard many times before.

"He probably tired of Maud's constant nagging and decided to go back to a place where he had but one demand—to play the bloody *piobroch*," he said, pulling at his beard, his eyes alight with a devilish glow.

The men guffawed. The women harrumphed.

"I notice that Bean-Mhath didn't chase after her man the second time he disapperared," said Agnes one of the women in the circle around the hearth. "Perhaps she thought she was finally well rid of him." This time, the women all laughed merrily.

An old fiddle appeared in the hands of one of the other men, Old Malcolm, and after a bit of tuning, he took up his bow and began to play the notes of a lament that they all knew.

"Careful, old man," his wife called out from across the room, her white hair bobbing up and down as she spoke. "Play too well and the faeries may take you off to their grotto as we find our way home this very night."

Old Malcolm continued to play, his notes drifting out into the night. "I'm not afeared of that," he said to no one in particular. "My fingers are old and my memory is spotty. I'm sure the faeries can find another soul to play the music for them, and one who is better."

But, as if to disprove his statement, he launched into a new tune, a lively reel this time, his fingers dancing up and down the fingerboard with the sudden dexterity of a man a third his age. At once, the room was filled with his fast moving lilt accompanied by the thumping beat of a dozen feet. In the byre, two young girls began to dance in the straw under the uninterested gaze of the dozing cows. Soon, an old man and his wife began to dance as well. While they went through the pattern of steps in the dance, their bodies revealed themselves as timeworn: their steps were hesitant and truncated, their aged, painful joints almost audibly creaked. But in the eyes of the old couple one could still see the fire of youth, as they remembered that night so many years ago when they had been courting under the disapproving stares of their parents. They had danced this same dance, to this same music, perhaps even played by the same man. And had looked at each other with the intoxicating mixture of excitement and desire and animal wildness and had felt the sense of eternal possibilities lurking in the shadows and corners of their lives.

Anna Kenton saw that look in the old couples' eyes as she watched them dance. She smiled to herself in recognition, remembering the way she had felt herself one night, long ago, when Captain Kenton had taken her to a village dance and they had exhausted themselves by dancing for hours as if they were the only two people in the world, and the orchestra was playing solely for their pleasure.

When Anna and Mary Ross had first arrived at the cottage, she was introduced to Mute Meg and Catty Greer, Meg's companion and helper. The old woman peered up at Anna with her clear, ice-blue eyes and patted her on the arm. Next to her, Catty drew in a sharp breath.

"This is the one?" Catty said, her voice surprised. "Are you sure, Mother?"

The old woman nodded. Anna began to ask what she meant, but some others from the strath arrived at the moment, with a show of hugs and kisses to one and all, and she never did find out.

The others in the cottage now began to dance, too. Because there were few men present that night, the women paired off and danced with one another. The steps were complicated and involved lots of twirls and dips along the way, and Old Malcolm played each verse in a tempo slightly faster than the last, so that soon, the floor was alive with motion and the rhythmic sounds of the dancers' feet threatened to shake the thatch from the roof. With a peal of laughter, Mary Ross broke away from the dancing group and came to stand next to Anna, her face flushed with happiness, her hair broken free of its restraints and cascading down onto her shoulders. Looking at her, Anna could not repress her own giggles.

"Och, m'lady," Mary Ross said, pushing her hair back and straightening her dress which had twisted around as she twirled in the dance. "I canna recall the last time I danced such a reel as that. Tis hard to keep still with music such as that."

"Tis, indeed," Anna said, nodding in agreement. She felt a pang of loneliness rise in her breast, and wished, as she did almost every day, that her husband was there to share in the fun, to grab her hand and whirl her out into the dancing.

Mary Ross saw the shadow pass across her charge's face.

"It is too bad there are not more menfolk here tonight," she said, raising her voice against the shrieking sounds of the fiddle as Old Malcolm sawed away. "But so many are away at the war, I am told. It is a hardship for many of the womenfolk here. They must rely on old men and young boys to do the hard work of their farms. But at least they can dance with each other."

Anna smiled at her friend. Mary Ross, looking over Anna's shoulder, leaned in closer.

"Now there's a braw laddie, just come in," she said in a conspiratorial whisper, nodding at the man. "Perhaps he would be willing to dance…"

Anna turned to glance at the tall and she thought rather handsome man standing nearby, leaning back against a post. She had not noticed him come into the cottage. But there he stood, hat in hand, overcoat glistening with the misty rain that was falling outside. In a glance, she took in his dark hair, broad shoulders and hands that looked rough and reddened from hard work. She saw that he, too, had been watching the old couple dance, and she noticed, or thought she saw, a look of longing in his eyes. She hoped so, in any case.

She grabbed a platter of sweetmeats that someone had brought to the gathering and, walking boldly across the cottage, held them out to the man with a smile. He nodded his thanks and took one. His eyes were pale and gray, watchful and wary.

"You are the new school teacher, are you not?" he asked her. "Staying with the Reverend Fraser I believe?"

She nodded. "Yes, I hope to begin classes next week," she said. "I hope the people will send their children. It would be good for them to learn their letters, and more."

"It would indeed," he said. "Do not be discouraged if students are slow in appearing. People in the strath are always suspicious of new ideas. But if Fraser approves, that will help a great deal. And you're being here tonight is good, too. Once the people…especially the mothers…know you better, they will send their bairns, along."

She nodded. She had been worrying about how the people of Glen Cullen would respond to her and her plans for their children. She was relieved to hear that someone else understood. She turned to speak again, but the man was looking at the dancers as they joyfully pranced about in the small cramped space of the cottage. She watched his eyes as they followed the old couple, still dancing to their own internal rhythms.

"They look to have danced to this tune before," Anna said.

The man smiled, eyes never leaving the dancers. "I've watched them dancing like this since the day I was born, it seems," he replied.

"You were born here in the strath, then?"

He turned now to look at her. "Aye," he said. "In a cottage not unlike this one, perhaps half a league upstream."

She gestured at the room. "Are any of these your people?"

He smiled again. "My people, yes," he said. "But none are my relations. My family are all dead and gone, long ago. Whilst I was away."

When he smiled, she felt her heart miss a beat. A drift of black hair fell across his eyes, and she watched as he brushed it back. She could see that look of longing again. It made her want to reach out and touch him, but she did not. "Away?" she asked, gently.

"Aye," he said, his eyes turning cold and hard. "To the colonies. I was kidnapped in Inverness when I was just a lad of thirteen. They called it volunteering for His Majesty's service. I was hogtied and constrained in the hold of a sailing vessel for more than a month. Fed moldering bread, which I shared with the rats that crawled over my body at night when I slept. I did not see the light of the day again until we arrived in Halifax. I was then sent, in chains, on to Quebec City where I was handed over to the 7th Regiment of Foot. After a couple years of that, I walked away."

"You abandoned your Regiment?" Anna said, her voice betraying her disapproval.

He shrugged. "They never asked me if I wanted to serve His Majesty, so I never asked permission to leave. I wandered through the wilderness until I was captured by a tribe of the Algonquins. They usually tortured and killed any white man they found, but the chief of the tribe seemed to like me. I don't know why. He made me one of his sons, gave me one of his daughters as a wife, and taught me the ways of his people."

He paused as Old Malcolm came to the end of his tune, and the dancing stopped amid clapping and calls for another. The fiddler took a draught from a flask of whiskey that was pressed into his hand, and then began to play again, a tune just as frenetic as the one he had just finished. Hands began to clap and more of the people rose to dance around the small room.

"We hunted and fished for our food," he continued, his own toe tapping along with the music. "They taught me much about their ways. I taught them something about planting and growing the grain. My wife and I had two fine sons. They were good boys. Then one night, a party of soldiers came out of the trees. Bloody efficient killers, they were. They killed every man, woman and child in the village. But me, they spared. I was a white man, after all. Not a day has gone by that I do not think back to that night, see in my mind the dead faces of my boys, my wife, and wish they had slit my throat as well."

This time, Anna could not stop herself. She reached out and grasped one of his hands. She said nothing. The words, if she had been able to conjure them up, would not have made it through the constricted passage of her throat.

"I pretended to be happy that they had saved me," he continued. "I was taken back to the civilized world. I saw Philadelphia and New York and Boston and eventually managed to get back here to Scotland. My real family was long dead and gone, I learned. But Mute Meg took me in. She understands the deepest parts of a person's soul and how to help it heal. And she gave me a new purpose: to fight for my people against the injustice being done to them."

He stopped suddenly and turned his head, as if listening for something. A lad, he looked to be in his teens, appeared at the door to the cottage, poking his head through the heavy woolen blanket that covered the entrance. He looked at the man standing next to Anna and whistled, a single sharp note, nodding.

Anna turned her eyes from the lad at the door to the man who stood beside her. But he was gone. In the instant of that whistle, he had disappeared. Startled, she looked around, but he was nowhere to be seen inside the cottage. He was gone. No one else seemed to notice the sudden disappearance. The music never stopped and the people continued to dance, hands clapping and toes tapping. Mary Ross had returned to the dancing, while the three servant girls from the Fraser house were happily gossiping with some other young women in a corner near the kitchen.

Suddenly, the doorway blanket was pushed aside and four men burst into the cottage, all dressed in long black coats glistening from the evening rain. The first, a tall man with a bushy red beard beneath a pair of fiery, angry eyes, held the coat collar of the young lad who had whistled just moments before. The lad was struggling to get away, but the man cuffed his ear and threw him aside, in the general direction of the byre.

The music died, and the dancing people stopped and stared. Old Malcolm pulled himself wearily to his feet, holding his fiddle and bow, and nodded at the man with the red beard.

"Captain Gordon," he said. "You are welcome to this humble home. We are honored with your presence. Please come in and warm yourself by the fire, along with your friends."

"Be silent, you old fool," Captain Gordon growled, his voice dripping with menace. "Where is he? Where is the outlaw Billy Hanks?"

Old Malcolm sighed. "Billy Hanks?" he said, shaking his head. "Why, he has not been seen in these parts in many a year. We had heard that he was taken to America to serve in His Majesty's Army, but..."

"Quiet!" thundered Gordon. He turned to the other men with him and muttered commands at them. "Search the house. If anyone gets in your way, burn it to the ground."

Two of the black-coated men began riffling through the cottage. There was not much to search, as Mute Meg's cottage was small and basically one large room, with byre and sleeping quarters leading off the main room, and a smallish cooking area to the rear. One of the men took a look there and reported back: "There's a window out the back," he said.

"Go! Go!" Gordon shouted, and the two men disappeared out the doorway.

The fourth man slowly removed his cap and folded his coat collar down on his shoulders. He went over to Anna and bowed.

"Mrs. Kenton," said Robert MacCray, a small smile playing at his lips. "We meet again."

"What is the meaning of this interruption, Sir?" Anna said, trying to keep her voice even. "Is there something amiss that you should stop these people from their evening enjoyments?"

"We were told that Billy Hanks would be here this very night," MacCray said, glancing around the cottage. "There are warrants outstanding. His Lordship would very much like to take him into custody to face the law's wrath. I don't suppose you have seen him here?"

"I have not made the acquaintance of such a gentleman," she said. "I am quite sure that no outlaw has been here this evening, nor any other."

"Gentleman?" MacCray laughed to himself softly. "I can assure you, madam, that Billy Hanks is no gentleman. I would call him a savage, perhaps, possibly a murderer. But a gentleman? Nay, that word does not apply to such the likes of Billy Hanks."

He turned, suddenly, and made two strides toward the fire. He grabbed Old Malcolm by the front of his shirt and slapped the old man, twice. The dull thuds echoed in the now deadly silent cottage. Thirty pairs of eyes stared, then turned downwards to focus on the floor.

"Where is he, you insolent bastard?" he said. "Where has he gone?"

Old Malcolm sat down heavily on his stool, nearly toppled over but managed to catch himself and remain seated. His old rheumy eyes stared balefully at MacCray for an instant, then they, too, dropped to the floor. He remained silent.

MacCray stared at the old man with undisguised contempt. He turned and looked at the others in the cottage. "Hear me!" he said. "Hear me and pay heed. We will find the outlaw Hanks, if not tonight, then soon. And when we do, any man, woman or child who has helped him in his criminal ways will be charged as well with the same crimes. Billy Hanks will be hanged by the neck, and anyone here who tries to help him escape will be hanged alongside of him. I swear this by authority of the King and by that of the Lady Sutherland. Mark me well."

He turned to leave, drawing the collar of his great coat up to shelter his neck from the rain falling outside the doorway of the warm and cozy cottage. As he turned, he locked eyes with a small boy, perhaps five years, who was staring back at him with wide, terrified eyes.

MacCray stooped down so his own eyes were level with those of the boy.

"Have you seen the outlaw, this Billy Hanks?" he asked, his voice stern.

The little boy, frightened beyond all sense, nodded.

"You have?" MacCray said, a small note of triumph in his voice. "And was he here this night?"

The boy nodded again.

MacCray looked around the room. All the people stood frozen, eyes cast downward, faces immobile.

"Where did he go? Tell the truth, lad."

The little boy paused, blinked and swallowed. "He disappeared," he said, his voice high-pitched and clear. "Like a ghost. He is gone."

MacCray raised his hand as if to strike the boy. Anna moved, quickly, and grabbed the boy, crushing him against her side, pulling his face into her skirts.

"Mister MacCray," she said, her voice a tightly controlled hiss. "Control yourself, sir! There were no ghosts here this night, nor outlaws of any kind. I bid you good night, sir."

MacCray stood for a long moment, his hand still raised in the air, staring at Anna, and then at the others who stared back. Then, he dropped his hand, pulled his coat tight around himself, and strode out into the dark night. Captain Gordon followed.

Anna released the boy, who ran to his mother. She felt a wave of emotion, her face hot. She wanted to weep, but would not allow herself to do so. The others in the small room stood in place, shocked, for a moment. Then, all at once, several of the woman came to Anna's side. One embraced her, and the others murmured words of sympathy and understanding.

"Ta, ma'am," one said, patting her hand. "That man is a beast."

The ceildhe was at an end. Children were gathered, hats and coats donned and by small groups, the people began to leave. Anna looked around for Mary Ross. She found her in the cooking area, deep in conversation with Catty, Mute Meg's companion. Mary turned to look at Anna, her face white, her eyes wide with shock.

"What is it, Mary?" Anna asked.

"It's Billy...Billy Hanks," the woman said, shaking her head in disbelief.

"What about him?"

"It turns out that he is my brother!"

9

MacCray, Gordon and the two men from Gordon's holdings spent more than an hour searching up and down the banks of the River Cullen, but could find no trace of Billy Hanks. They swept though Mute Meg's chicken coop, but found nothing but fowl protesting loudly at this unusual night-time activity. There was a pile of fresh hay, into which one of Gordon's men repeatedly thrust a pitchfork. But there was nothing hiding within the heap. Not even Gordon's prized hound was able to find a scent that went more than 20 feet before it died out, leaving the dog furiously turning this way and that, yelping with frustration. It was, MacCray thought to himself, as if the man had taken three or four large running steps and then had disappeared into thin air. Like a ghost. MacCray thought of the young boy in Mute Meg's warm cottage and his fist clenched again. *Damn these savages*, he thought, *When will they learn to obey their betters?*

They called off the search when the steady drizzle turned into a constant hard rain, and the wind came up, cold and harsh, blowing the rain underneath their coats and into the tops of their boots. MacCray whistled the men back and when they assembled, told them to return to their horses.

"He's long gone," MacCray said. "I've sent word to Lairg to check on all traffic coming out of the glen on the morrow. We'll look again come the morning."

"Begging the Governor's pardon," said one of Gordon's men, "But we don't know for sure if he was ever really here. And watching the road will do ye no good … tis well known that Billy Hanks moves like a wraith, in the shadows. They say he's lived among the red Indians in the Colonies, learned their ways. They say he can move as silently as the wind, stride across the land at night as if it were as bright as day, and can cut a man's throat before the man even knows he's there."

"Enough!" MacCray said, his voice low with anger. "He's just a man, same as any other. He may know a few hunting tricks, but no tricks of infidels and savages can for long withstand the resolve of the Christian man. We'll find him, and soon, and that will be the end to it."

The other man fell silent, and the four walked back to the clearing beside Mute Meg's cottage and recovered their horses, swinging up into their saddles and heading downstream to Captain Gordon's farm. Riding in the cold rain, MacCray pulled his greatcoat tighter around his neck, thinking about a cold steel blade slicing across his throat. Like the others, he rode in silence, watching not only the road ahead where the horses were walking, but the bushes and trees that lined both sides, alert for any movement that might be an attack by the bloodthirsty savage Hanks. But the roadway was silent in the rain, the only sound that of raindrops falling against the trees and rocks and the clomping of the horses' hooves as they picked their way slowly home in the cold, wet night.

The search party arrived at Captain Gordon's holdings after a mile or two. Here, the River Cullen made a sharp turn to the left and dropped over a rocky ledge before continuing on its sinuous path down the glen. A wooden bridge spanned the dark waters and the path led uphill on the far bank to an elevated plateau where Gordon had constructed a fine stone and masonry home. The windows on the first floor glowed from the candlelight within, and MacCray imagined the dry warmth and cheerful company to be found inside by the hearth, and the warm dry bed that awaited. Behind the house and spilling down in terraces toward the river were the fields and pastures of Gordon's farm, and the riders made for a solid wooden barn set apart from the stone house. Fresh hay filled the stalls for the men's horses, and they worked to remove the saddles and brush down their horses under the watchful eyes of a small herd of dairy cows, lying in their own straw-filled byre.

As he dried and brushed his horse, hanging the saddle on a wooden rail and making sure there was fresh water in the trough, MacCray thought about Anna Kenton and the scene they had just played at Mute Meg's. He replayed it all in his mind. Surely, she could understand that the boy had been cheeky, speaking back to his superior. Surely, she would not be one to take the side of these common peasants, ill-dressed, uneducated, lazy and dirty. She, after all, was a member of Lord Stafford's own family. How could she defend such rude behavior? He had almost convinced himself that she could not, but he kept recalling the look on her face when she had intervened to save the boy from his well-deserved cuffing. It was a look of surprise and hurt, of scorn and derision, and even, if he was to be honest, a look of *hatred*. He was not used to being hated. Oh, he knew that few of the tenants of the Sutherland estate looked upon him with affection. Being feared and disliked by the tenants was part of his job. He understood that, and was reconciled to it. Being hated by a peasant from one of these Godforsaken glens was nothing for a man of his position to be upset about.

But Anna Kenton was of his own station, perhaps even slightly higher than his own. He had found her attractive in many ways, and had considered that a matrimonial connection would help solidify his position with the Staffords. It could lead to his own sinecure and a productive holding like this one of Captain Gordon, one that could ensure his own financial stability in the years to come. All of this had occurred to him during the day's travel from Dunrobin, though tucked away in his mind while he performed his other, necessary duties of the day. But he had thought of it, and the thought was not unpleasant. Which is why that look of hatred on Anna's face when he was about to strike that insolent bairn took him so aback. In his brief but pleasant reveries, he had never considered the possibility that she might not want to marry him. A young widow, going off to the wilds of Glencullen to teach a group of uncouth urchins ... how could she not see how marriage to the likes of Robert MacCray would be an immense upward movement in the world? No, she would come to understand that he represented salvation from a cold, unfeeling and lonely world. How could she not? But there was that look on her face, as she sheltered the boy from his upraised hand.

"Come gentlemen," said Captain Gordon, breaking Mac-Cray's reverie. "A late supper awaits, and some excellent port. After a good night's sleep, we shall begin our hunt for that outlaw, the devil take him." He led them across the yard and into the waiting warmth of his stone house.

BILLY HANKS WATCHED the men searching for him from an aerie well hidden near the top of a towering elm on the banks of the River Cullen just across from Mute Meg's cottage. Escaping was like child's play to him. He never went anywhere without first formulating a plan that would allow him to disappear quickly and quietly if the need arose. It was a strategy for survival he had learned from his brothers in the tribe of the Haudenosaunees where he had lived in the American wilderness. He had long ago devised several escape routes from Mute Meg's, and, as was his usual practice, had assigned a boy to keep watch outside. When that boy had whistled the approach of MacCray and the others, it had been a simple matter to slip out the back window of the cottage. There was a stout length of rope, painted black, tied to a tree behind the cottage. The other end of the rope was securely fastened to the trunk of the elm where he now perched. He had looped several handholds in the rope, and made a series of thick knots, to give himself secure grips in case of wet weather, and tonight he was glad he had done so. Still, it was an easy matter to swing on the rope across the dark waters of the River Cullen, catch a branch of the tree on the opposite bank, and climb swiftly up to his well hidden perch, pulling the rope up after him. There, he made himself as comfortable as possible in the rainy drizzle while he watched the men stomp through Mute Meg's fowl coop, and stumble in the darkness up and down the riverbank for several hundred yards in both directions. Billy knew that the tracking dogs would not be able to find him, nor would the men be able to see him in the darkness, even if they had thought to look upwards into the tree. He had a crust of bread in one pocket of his coat, and a flask of whiskey in another, so he knew he could hide easily, if not entirely comfortably, through the night if need be. But he suspected that the men would call off their search when they got wet and when they could find no trace of him, and he was, of course, correct.

He waited for some time after they left. He watched as Catty came out behind the cottage and looked around for him. He smiled, but kept silent. It was always possible that one of MacCray's men might yet be hiding under cover somewhere nearby, waiting for Billy Hanks to show himself again. Suspicion and caution had kept him alive many times in the past.

He munched on his crust of bread while he thought about the events of the night. He had enjoyed talking to the English woman, the schoolteacher. They had not been formally introduced, but he was sure she knew his true identity. There was something about her, a look in her eyes perhaps, which convinced him that she would never tell MacCray or anyone else about him. He thought about this while he ate, wondering if it was true, or if he just *wanted* it to be true. Billy Hanks was no stranger to deceit, and usually trusted no one—neither man nor woman—completely. But his intuition told him that this woman, in particular, was worth trusting. He did not know why, but he had always listened to his intuition, and it had never led him astray. *Not yet, anyway*, he thought to himself.

But there was something else about his conversation with the woman that bothered him, picked at the corners of his consciousness. He tried to ignore it, but it would not go away. He tried to concentrate on his current situation, sitting in the top of a tree in a cold rain, trying to stay warm. And of the morrow, and what plans must be laid, what steps needed to be taken. But her face kept appearing in his mind, the light in her eyes, her hair, the touch of her hand on his, the warm scent of her body. It was no good trying to force his emotions away, not to pay attention. Those feelings were still there, and, he knew, they were too powerful to ignore. She was a woman, and he was a man, and they had connected that night on that most basic of levels. He tried to repress those feelings by invoking the memories of his Haudenosaunee wife, Oheo, now many years dead, and his two boys: Wahta, a bright lad of ten years, and Onas, who had been six when the Long Knives had attacked the camp and killed them all, his family, his life. Their faces played across his memory again: the boys at gleeful play, his wife smiling up at him, her eyes full of invitation and pride. He shook his head and returned his thoughts to the present, sitting on a wet branch in the cold, raining night. His old life was over, he reminded himself. He had lived through several 'old lives' already in his forty years of life. He had once been a boy in this glen, but that life had ended when he had been kidnapped by the soldiers. He had once been a soldier in the Colonies, but that life had ended when he walked away into the endless woods of Canada. He had once been a prisoner and then a productive member of a tribe, and that life had ended when the Long Knives came. His new life, the life he was leading right now, was the only one that was important.

He had work to do, people who depended on him for leadership and strength. He could not allow himself to falter now, because of some woman. He told himself to banish all thoughts of the English woman, and they went away. For now, anyway, he told himself.

Billy Hanks waited another hour before climbing back down the tree, stowing the rope he had used to escape, and heading up the hill to the deep forest on the upper slopes high above the river. There were several caves atop the high ridges and a few old cattleman's sheds in the high grounds as well. He would be able to find a dry, if not warm, place to sleep this night. And tomorrow?

We'll deal with tomorrow when it arrives, he thought.

ANNA, MARY ROSS and the three servant girls had made it safely back to The Manse in the dark and wet and, mindful of not awakening Fraser or his wife, had tip-toed inside and amid quiet whispers and giggles, bid each other good night and crept off to bed.

Anna and Mary Ross shared a small bedroom tucked in the rafters of the old frame house, and with the dim light of a single candle, they undressed and prepared for sleep.

"How did you find out about your brother?" Anna asked Mary as she combed Anna's unpinned hair.

"Mute Meg knows all the secrets of the strath," Mary Ross said, running her brush through Anna's long tresses. "She has lived long enough and knows and remembers things. She remembered when my parents died of the sickness, one following the other within a few sad days. I was just a wee girl, perhaps ten years of age. I was sent off to live with some relations who had gone to live in Glasgow. All I was told as a girl was that I was orphaned. No one ever mentioned that I might have family, save for distant relations who might still live here in Glencullen."

She finished brushing and helped Anna pin her hair up and tuck it beneath her sleeping cap.

"But they told me tonight that I had an older brother. His name then was Donal. He was five or six when our parents died. It was Archy Hanks who took him in, raised him. Archy was himself a widower with no bairns of his own, so having a young lad to help about the farm was a good thing. He called him Billy after his own Da, so that became his name. Young Billy had driven Archy's cattle to sell in Inverness that year, and was making his way back home again when the soldiers took him off to the Colonies."

She paused, helped Anna climb into her bed.

"They said Archy Hanks died of a broken heart when he learned that Billy was gone. And then no one heard a thing about him until the day just a few years ago when he came back to the glen."

Anna listened to the story, engrossed.

"And did Billy know about you? That he had, or has, a sister?"

Mary Ross shook her head sadly. "Nae, nae," she said. "Mute Meg did not know if I was dead or alive. My own journey had taken me away from Scotland and into service for Lord Stafford, where I met you, of course. So not a soul knew anything about me, at least until I returned to the glen this very day. Mute Meg says that when I walked into her house this night, she knew who I was. She has the second sight, you know. She knows things that others do not."

Anna shivered. "To think that you are the sister of such a man!" she said, shaking her head. "An outlaw!"

Mary Ross stood suddenly, her chin thrust outwards defiantly.

"You talked to him," she said, her voice quivering with emotion. "You touched his hand. You looked into his eyes. Can you tell me that he is a bad man? An outlaw as you say? From what the others in the glen tell me, he is a good man. He is trying to help the people stay in their homeland. They tell me of all the good things he does."

"But they say he is an outlaw, a poacher, a …"

"They!" Mary Ross was indignant. "Who is it who makes such claims? That devil MacCray? His lordship? What do they know of Billy Hanks and his heart? You talked to the man. Did you perceive evil in his heart?"

Anna was silent. *No*, she thought to herself. *I did not.*

Mary Ross quickly undressed herself, climbed into her own bed and blew out the candle. But sleep would not come to Anna. She lay there in the dark, listening to the wind pushing against her windows and the occasional patter of rain.

At first, she could not help but think about the confrontation with MacCray, that horrible, evil man. She did not know why she had stood up to him when he first burst into the dancing party at Mute Meg's. The rudeness shown by MacCray and Captain Gordon when they first arrived could explain her own reaction, but she did understand that MacCray's job was to manage the tenancy of the estate, and to do the bidding of Lord Stafford and his lady. But the group that had gathered that night at Mute Meg's was hardly a raucous gathering. Indeed, it was old men, some children and mostly womenfolk. Nobody there was any kind of threat to Lord Stafford and his millions.

But, of course, they had been looking for Billy Hanks. The very man she had been talking with. The very man who now inhabited her thoughts. She recalled his looks of longing at the old dancing couple. She recalled his sad story of love and loss in the vast forest wilderness of the Americas. She recalled the shank of his dark hair spilling down over his eyes, his broad shoulders, his dark and defensive eyes. She could even recall the way he smelled, a heady mixture of leather and pine. And his voice, deep and somehow calm.

What are you doing? she asked herself, biting hard on her lip. *He's an outlaw. Wanted by His Lordship, hunted throughout the shire. If they catch him…* when *they catch him, he will hang. That's the future for Billy Hanks, and there is no part of that suitable for Mrs. Anna Kenton.* She tried to recall the face of her late husband, his boyish grin and reddened cheeks. But his face would not appear in her mind's eye. All she could conjure up was the colors of his uniform, the one he was wearing when he and his regiment marched away the last time she ever saw him. She supposed she should cry. Cry that he was dead. Cry that he was gone. Cry that she could barely remember what he looked like, remember the sound of his voice, or remember the touch of his hand.

But she didn't cry. Couldn't cry. All she could do was lie there in the dark, and remember the words Billy Hanks had spoken to her that night. And how he looked when he spoke them. And that's what she was thinking when she finally drifted off to sleep.

10.

Anna Kenton wasted no time. The morning after the *ceildhe*, she was up early, along with Mary Ross, and as soon as they had breakfasted, she asked to be taken to the local kirk to view for herself the facility that would house her new school.

The Reverend Fraser, who had also arisen early, was more than happy to accommodate her. Together they set out to make the short walk from the Manse to the small, white church about a half mile away. A gravel path led from the road down a short hill to the churchyard, inside a waist-high stone rubble wall, where old, moss-covered headstones tilted defiantly against the wind. A half-circle of evergreens inside the wall, their lower boughs spread out like welcoming arms, seemed to protect the churchyard, a facade of greenery shielding the church from the outside world. The wind sighed as it moved through the boughs, and their branches cut off some of the light of the day, creating an atmosphere of a protected, set-apart place in the world. In that quiet, darkened place, the small church itself sat, its mullioned windows crossed with a latticework of cast iron and a short bell tower set on the northern roofline, reaching toward heaven.

Fraser led the way inside, which was dark and cold. Beneath the open beams, a plain wooden communion table sat between the windows, topped with white lace altar cloths and a simple gold cross. There was no pulpit to speak of, just a simple wooden lectern to one side of the altar. A second, matching lectern to the other side held the Holy Gospel. A large wooden chair was reserved at the front for the reverend, while the nave was filled with a few low wooden benches: most of the worshippers would stand throughout the services.

"I thought we could rearrange the benches for the children," Fraser said, motioning. "And if the Presbytery approves, we can order a slateboard to be placed here for the lessons."

Anna blushed slightly. "I took the liberty, Sir, to order a slate from Edinburgh," she said. "It was not that dear in price. I have been told it should arrive any day now. I hope you don't mind."

"Good, good, my dear," the reverend said, smiling. "'So whoever knows the right thing to do and fails to do it, for him it is sin.' James, I believe."

"How many children do you think will come?" Anna asked. She had been worried about this for many weeks. Would there be any interest in a school from the people of the glen? She had no idea.

"I believe I can say with some authority that there are ten or twelve children who will come at once," Fraser said. "Once you get established and the word begins to spread, that number may well double. There may be some in the glen who will resist, but I don't think it is many. All the mothers I have spoken to seem excited at the prospect that their children will be educated, be able to read and write and cipher. I do not think you need to worry about that."

"Oh, Sir!" Anna was relieved. "That would be an excellent start. I hope to go visit all children in the glen as soon as I can, and explain to them and their parents what we hope to accomplish here."

"Fine, fine," Fraser said, nodding his approval. "Let's first get the sanctuary in order. We will, of course, need to restore it for Sunday services, but I'm sure that the children will be willing to help move the furniture around as required."

They worked together silently for the next hour or so, putting things in order, deciding how to set up the small sanctuary as a schoolroom. Finally, satisfied, they prepared to return to the Manse for the midday meal.

Fraser closed the church door and followed Anna up the hill to the main road down the glen. He stopped, and looked up and down the glen for a moment.

"I think we should stop in to visit with Jenny MacLeod," he said. "She has two wee bairns that might be interested in some schooling. And if we can convince Jenny to send us her students, then many others in the glen will do the same."

Anna nodded her approval for this idea, and Fraser set out down the road. After a few hundred yards, he turned to the right and began to climb the hillside filled with bracken and clumps of long grass. There was a bare pathway, mostly trodden down vegetation and some bare earth. They climbed until they had almost reached the timber line, where tall, narrow trunked pines grew closely together in an almost impenetrable wall. Tucked in a sheltered plateau in the hillside, guarded by some large boulders, was a smallish cabin made of logs with mud and grass caulking and a flattish roof of pine boughs and bracken, held down against the wind with a netting of stout ropes. Smoke trickled lazily from the open hole in the middle of the roof, proof that within lay a fire and someone to tend it.

There was a narrow front entrance to the house, no more than three feet high and covered with a woolen blanket. Fraser stood outside this doorway and called out. "Halloo!" he called. "Are ye at home Jenny? It is the pastor calling. Halloo!"

After a brief wait, the woolen door was swept to one side and a woman's face appeared, dirty with soot, eyes peering out cautiously, her hair covered in the traditional white linen kertch of the married woman. Almost at the same time, two children, a boy of perhaps ten years and a girl a year or two younger, both with heads full of curly hair, came running around the corner of the cabin. They had heard the Reverend's calls, and come running to see what this unusual visit meant.

"Halloo, Halloo," the reverend said, doffing his hat at the woman in the doorway, greeting her in Gaelic. "I hope you are well, Jenny. This is Mrs. Kenton, who is to be our new school mistress. We would like to come in and talk about Willie and Jane, if that is permissible."

The woman's eyes looked Fraser up and down, then shifted and looked Anna up and down, lingering perhaps a bit longer on the woman. The head withdrew from sight as the curtain dropped back to cover the doorway, but was quickly swept back out of the way so that the entire doorway was open.

"*Thig a-steach, thig a-steach,*" the woman called out. Come in, come in.

Fraser motioned for Anna to go first, and she ducked down and squeezed her way inside the low, narrow doorway and pulled herself inside. It was quite dark in the cabin, as there were no windows, but the fire crackling in the hearth on the floor in the center of the one room threw off a bit of light. And Jenny was busy lighting the wick on a candle, something reserved only for important occasions and company. There were three or four three-legged stools set around the firepit, and a metal tripod that held a large cast iron cooking pot over the flames. The floor was bare earth, covered in boughs of heather and fir. With the fire and the protection from wind and weather, it was quite cozy and warm.

Reverend Fraser managed to fold his large frame in through the small doorway, and he stood next to Anna and bowed to the lady of the house. The two children also ducked inside. The boy, Willie, stood next to his mother, his eyes locked warily on the strangers. The girl, Jane, went to the side of a third child, this one a baby of perhaps two years of age, who was sitting on the earthen floor, happily tormenting two chickens who were trying to peck among the scattered boughs in hopes of finding something to eat.

"*Failte*," the woman said, motioning for Anna to sit on one of the stools next to the fire. Welcome. Anna smiled and took a seat.

"*Taing*," Anna replied. "*Ur clann a tha modhail.*" Thanks. Your children are well behaved.

Jenny MacLeod smiled and nodded. She rummaged through a nearby box and came up with a flask. She opened it and poured a bit into a glass, which she handed to Anna.

"*Failte*," she said, motioning at Anna to drink it. "*Slainte!*"

Anna sipped at the amber liquid and felt its warm fire spreading down her throat and into her stomach. It was the *aqua vitae* that had been brewed in the glen the same way for hundreds of years. Sharing it was a sign of hospitality and welcome. Anna smiled her thanks, and was glad she did not need to say anything more. The whiskey had momentarily taken her tongue and she was not sure that any words would come out, even if she had tried to speak.

Reverend Fraser, perhaps understanding, spoke instead, again in the native tongue of the glen, translating his words for Anna, and Jenny's replies.

"Mrs. Kenton has arrived in the strath and intends to begin a school in the church," he told the woman. "We think your two oldest children might like to attend. They will learn to read and write and perhaps learn their sums. We are hopeful that you and the others in the strath will come and see. We plan to begin classes next week."

Jenny MacLeod looked down at her lap, wringing her hands together. She seemed distressed.

"I have no money," she said. "I have no way to pay."

"Oh, no," Anna said, her throat now clear again. "There

is no cost to you. Reverend Fraser and the parish will bear whatever cost there is. We simply wish to help your children learn to read and write their names."

Jenny poured a glass of water for the Reverend, who nodded his thanks. She then looked at Anna across the fire.

"You are not a local," she said. "You are not one of us. How do I know you will not try to steal my children? How do I know this?"

"I wish only to help your children," Anna replied coolly. "I wish them to know how to read, and write, so they can better themselves in the world. I wish no harm for them. And you are most welcome to come to the kirk yourself and listen and watch and see what it is we will do."

Jenny nodded, though she did not appear to be entirely convinced.

"I am a man of God, Jenny MacLeod," Reverend Fraser said. "I have never lied to you. Mrs. Kenton is a good woman. She wants to help the children of Glencullen. Nothing more."

Jenny nodded, but did not look convinced. The baby tottered over to its mother and began to whine, pulling at her dress. Jenny swept the baby up in her arms, unfastened the buttons in the front of her dress, and began to nurse.

"I...I will wait outside, Mrs. Kenton," Reverend Fraser said, his face turning red. "Willie...come show me your cattle. Mrs. Kenton, we shall return to the Manse when your conversation is completed."

He ducked down and scrunched his frame though the doorway. Willie followed after.

"Where is your husband?" Jenny's question, spoken in English, was abrupt and took Anna somewhat by surprise. On the other hand, she realized, it was a question that made some sense. She had arrived in the strath out of nowhere, and nobody here knew her story.

"My husband was killed in the wars, in Portugal, fighting against Napoleon," she said calmly. "Almost two years ago. I understand your husband is also in the army, is that not correct?"

Jenny nodded, slowly. "Yes," she said. "He serves with the 93rd Regiment of Foot. The Sutherland Highlanders. All the men of the strath are in the Regiment. They are fighting in a place far away. Pre…" She fumbled with the word. "Pre…tor…"

"Pretoria," Anna said. "It is in South Africa. It is a long way from Scotland, to be sure."

"I pray the Lord keeps him safe and returns him to Glencullen soon," Anna said.

Jenny's eyes filled with tears and she could only nod her appreciation. She poured herself some water.

"We have heard that the Countess wishes us to move to the seaside," Jenny said as the baby moved from one breast to the other. "Will you bring your school to the seaside as well?"

Anna paused before answering. "I have not heard anything more about the plans the Countess may have for Glencullen than you have," she said carefully. "I can tell you that Her Ladyship and her husband are both aware that I am here. Neither of them mentioned to me any plans for removing the people of this strath. Perhaps that means the rumors are untrue. Or perhaps will not happen for many years yet to come. I do not know. But, yes, I would move with you, if that sad occurrence were to take place. I wish to teach the children. I do not care where the children are."

Jenny MacLeod listened to Anna carefully, watching her face as she spoke. When she finished, Jenny nodded, as if to answer a question only she could hear.

"I will send Willie and Jane to your school," she said finally. "Willie may be needed for the spring planting soon, however. And you should know that most of us will be going to the shieling, come the summer."

"The shieling?"

Jenny smiled. "Most of us in the glen, but especially the women, take our cattle to the high ground on Ben Cullen in the summer months," she said. "The grass and forage there is better for the cattle, and we all enjoy spending a few weeks on the mountainside. You will find you have no students left during that time. Unless, of course, you come with us." She reached out and touched Anna's arm. "Please do! You would enjoy the shieling. I know you would!"

Anna smiled. "I will, Missus MacLeod. Thank you!" she said. "I look forward to it. And I look forward to having your children in the school Monday next."

11

It was a week after the *ceildhe* at Mute Meg's when all the households of Glencullen received word that Captain Gordon, their tacksman, wished to see all lease holders at his steading. On the appointed day, they began arriving late in the morning, in ones and twos, some from their farms several miles upriver, others from their holdings adjacent to that of Gordon and further downstream. Most of the farmers came on foot, as few of the tenants could afford to keep horses. Most who arrived at Gordon's farm were old men, as the young men of the strath, for the most part, had been asked to volunteer for the British military. About ten women also made the journey to Gordon's farm, representing their family, as there were no men of legal age residing in their households.

By noon, the entire group of some 30 tenants had gathered in the courtyard between Gordon's large stone house. They talked among themselves, exchanged news on their recent harvests, talked about plans for this year's crops and asked each other if anyone knew why they had been summoned. No one did. No one cared to speculate, but they all feared the news that was to come.

Gordon kept them waiting for another half hour before the back door to his house flew open and the Captain strode out.

He wore knee-high leather boots and a long black greatcoat over his breeches. He held a sheaf of papers in one hand, and a riding crop in the other. Behind him came Robert MacCray, a smile playing on his lips as he surveyed the householders gathered in the courtyard. Gordon and MacCray stood in the middle of the yard, and the group of men and women shuffled into a half circle around them.

"What is it, Gordon, that you want with us? Do you not know we all have work to do?" The speaker was Old Ross, a man of some seventy years, who had three acres, two cows and whose three sons were all fighting in the wars in Spain.

Gordon stared at the man. "Is that a proper way to address your tacksman?" he asked the man.

Old Ross stared back, and then spat in the dirt nearly hitting one of Gordon's well polished boots. "Ye may be our tacksman in name and by the law," he said. "But no man here looks to you as did our fathers and grandfathers to your forebears. Once, we could rely on Gordon of Glencullen to defend his people and protect all those who dwelled in the strath. Once, we were all joined by bonds of family or friendship or by the memories of our service to the King. But we have no tacksman like that today. There is no one to look out for us, to defend our lands and our way of life. Just you. To collect our rents and apply the extra burdens of our life that the Lady Stafford decrees. So I address you properly indeed, landlord." He spat again. "Now tell us what you want."

For a moment, it looked like Gordon was going to strike the man with his riding crop. His face turned dangerously red and he took a step towards the old man. But he managed to check himself. He glanced down at his papers, cleared his throat and began to read.

"Her Ladyship, the 19th Chief of Clan Sutherland, has decreed the following Summons of Removal. The leases on all farms to the north of Craigach Bridge shall be terminated effective on the first day of Lammas term hence. All lessors and their families will remove themselves and their households and furnishings from this property at that time. Her Ladyship has graciously made available land in the amount of one acre per household in Golspie Parish and she has ordered that employment in the herring fisheries there be offered to any man, woman or child from Glencullen. This decision is final and cannot be appealed."

Gordon stopped reading and looked up. The silence in the courtyard was absolute. This was the news each man had long been dreading, yet none was prepared for it. They had just been ordered to leave their homes and their livelihoods behind, forever, and locate themselves to the unknown provinces near the sea.

"Do you all understand what this order means?" Gordon said.

"Aye," said Willie MacKay, a round man with a full red beard and wild-looking red hair bursting out from beneath his woolen tam. "It means that after MacKays and Gordons and Rosses have lived in this valley for some two thousand years; where generation after generation have lived and loved and worked and worshiped; where countless men have bravely fought and died for the honor of Clan Sutherland and through it, for the Crown itself ... after all that, Lady Stafford has decided to cast us out and throw us away. Aye, we understand all that, Gordon. That is what your papers mean. But we will not do it. Not for you, not for her Ladyship, not for Almighty God himself. And it will take the Devil himself to get us to go, and The Horned One better be prepared for a good fight."

There were murmurs of agreement from the other men in the half circle, which edged closer together as if to demonstrate their unity.

MacCray stepped forward, a grin on his face. "Under the laws of the Crown, Her Ladyship is free to do with her land what she will," he said. "If she says you must leave this place, then you had better make your plans to go. I can assure you that all the force that the Law can muster will be brought to bear to eject you, willing or no." He paused, and his grin grew wider. "And it will be my very great pleasure to enforce the laws of Her Lady-ship and see the back of all of you from this Glen. If you resist this lawful order, it will make my work all the more enjoyable."

The men in the half circle stared at MacCray. But no one spoke. They did not need to speak. The hatred on each of the faces of the men and women from the glen was plainly there for anyone to see. Words were not required.

"Now, now," Robert Gordon held up a hand. "There's no need to speak of violence," he said. "Most of you are my rela-tions, and I know you all to be men of honor, sworn to obey your chief. These orders..." he held up the sheaf of papers so that all could see ... "These are the orders of your chief. Lady Stafford wishes no harm to befall you and your kin. That is why she has set aside land in Golspie for you to inhabit. She is not abandoning you. She is merely moving you to another part of her shire, which is in her interests, and legal ability, to do. You men have never failed to obey your chief's lawful commands, not in the thousand-year history of this clan. I know you will obey this one."

"Have you seen the lots in Golspie to which we are to re-move?" Willie MacKay growled. "I have. The land is not suited for habitation, which is why there is no one living there now. It is too sandy for cropping, and there is no room for our cattle. How, then, will we live? The herring fishery? There's not a man here knows shite about herring, nor fishing. Not a man here has ever set afoot upon a boat in his life. Are you going to send Jack...or Angus...or Old Charlie..." he pointed to the white-haired men he named ..."Are ye going to put them on a vessel and send them over the deep? You might as well kill them now and have done w'it."

The half circle of men growled in assent.

"Her Ladyship would never ask her loyal subjects to do something of which they are incapable," Gordon said. "And she believes the allotments which she has set aside for your use will be more than adequate to your needs. Are there any other questions?"

"Lammas term is just a few months from now," MacKay said, shaking his head. "Our crops, our corn and our potatoes, will not be ready for harvest by then. How does Her Ladyship expect us to survive the winter without food? Even in Golspie, our bairns must eat."

Gordon rattled the papers in his hand. "Under the terms of the removal, you may take with you any harvested crops," he said. "By the terms, however, anything left growing in the earth is considered property of Her Ladyship and must be left behind. I think that is fair —"

"Fair!" Willie MacKay practically exploded. "We will have prepared the land, planted the crops and will nurture them for several long months of labor. Fair? To deforce us of our food? Fair? Next you will tell us that up is down, east is west. Fair!"

MacCray put a hand on Gordon's arm. "There might be a way to extend the date for the removal," he said. Captain Gordon looked at him as if he had suddenly gone mad. "I might be able to convince Her Ladyship to postpone the removal date until the crops are in and the harvest completed. But it would take a concession on your part as well."

"And what would that be?" Willie MacKay sounded dubious.

"Give me Billy Hanks," MacCray said, grinning again. "Tell me where he is, and, once captured, I'll beg Lady Stafford for a delay of a few months. You can reap your corn and move to Golspie in October."

The men stood silent. A crow flew overhead, his loud, raucous cries echoing off the tall hillsides that loomed on either side of the river.

"I-I don't know where he is," Willie said, shaking his head and looking down at the dirt.

"Nor I," said the man standing next to him. All the men shook their heads, murmuring in the negative.

MacCray's smile disappeared and his eyes narrowed.

"Then you will begone of Glencullen by the moon at Lammas term. See to it." He turned on his heel and walked away.

One of the women, weeping, began to utter loud, mournful cries. Two of the other women rushed to her side. But the weeping woman struggled free from their grasp, tore at her hair and loosed a string of Gaelic words, shaking her fist at Captain Gordon. The men stood impassively, listening, while she screamed at the man.

"What is the witch saying?" MacCray asked, finally.

No one spoke. The screaming, the incantations, went on and on.

"She is cursing the Gordon name," Old Ross said. "She is calling on the Spirits of Disease and Sickness to descend upon this house and all who dwell in it. She is praying that all your cattle may fall ill and die, that your crops may wither, that you and your family suffer pestilence and illness and that the male line of your family die childless."

Captain Gordon crossed himself quickly and muttered a prayer of his own. The woman continued to wail. "Begone," he said, and turned to go back inside his manse.

A younger girl, daughter of one of the women who had come to the meeting, stopped him with a hand to his arm.

"Who will live in the strath once we are gone?" she asked. "Will there be people no more upon the banks of the River Cullen?"

Gordon looked down on the girl. "Lady Stafford has leased this land to Mister Knowles and Mister Reid, both of them businessman from Moray," he said. "They are to place sheep here. Thousands of them. There will be a few shepherds in Glencullen, but there will mostly be sheep. It is the same throughout Sutherlandshire. The people are going. The sheep are coming."

The young girl nodded.

"Then we must curse the sheep as well," she said.

GORDON RETURNED TO his house, slamming the door behind him. MacCray saddled his horse and rode off at a gallop down the valley towards Lairg. He planned to be back at Dornoch by nightfall to report to Lord Stafford and to William Young, the factor. The tenants looked at each other sadly and began their journeys home, walking in groups of two or three.

Willie McKay and Old Ross, along with two women, both also of the Ross name whose steadings were near those of the two men, began to follow the rough road upstream, the black rushing waters of the River Cullen to their left. They walked in silence for the first mile, each lost in thought. Willie McKay, whose face was now as red as his hair and beard, finally broke the silence.

"I'll not do it," he said, his voice trembling with rage. "I'll not leave the home where I was born, and my father before me, and his father before him. I'll not leave the home of my own children. They cannot make me leave this place. Nae, nae, the Sheriff can come with a thousand men, General Wellington himself leading his cavalry and cannon. I'll not move an inch."

Old Ross shook his head. "The same has been said throughout the shire," he said sadly. "In Cromarty, in Tongue, in Strathnaver, the men promised to stand and fight. And what happened? They came with men, with dogs, with brands of fire. They tossed men and women, old and young, out of their homes and put those homes to the torch. They tore down the timbers of the roof, murdered the livestock, fired the barns, trampled the corn in the fields. They put sick old women out in the rain and cold and left them to die. Nae, Willie, if Lady Stafford has decided to put us out and bring in the sheep, there is no hope. We shall have to leave."

"I wouldn't be so sure of that."

Both men jumped, startled, stopped and turned as one to look behind them on the road where the voice had come. Billy Hanks had looped an arm with that of the two women who had been walking behind Old Ross and Willie and now was grinning at the two old men.

"Where in the bloody hell did you come from, Billy?" Old Ross asked, shaking his head in amazement. "I swear, I think it must be true what they say about ye, that ye are a bloody spirit and no man."

Willie McKay whooped aloud and pounded Billy Hanks on the back in welcome. "Billy, ya right silent bastard," he said with a grin. "What do y'mean, ye wouldn't be so sure, eh? Sounds like ye've been cookin' up a plan, ye have."

Billy smiled and led the group to some boulders on the side of the road. He sat down on one and motioned to the others to do the same. He reached under his woolen cape and pulled out a flask, which he opened and passed around. When it came back to him, he took a drink, capped it and put it away again.

"Old Ross is correct" he said. "If Lady Stafford and her rich husband wish to eject the people of Glencullen, there is not much we can do to prevent it." He paused and looked up at the rolling hills above them, where the first shoots of the growing machair painted the fields in the lightest of greens. "In the end, they will win. But we can make life unpleasant for them," he continued. "Buy some time. Cost that old bastard some money. Make him squeal a little. He'll know he's messed with the men of Glencullen when he's finished, I can tell ye that."

"Sounds good to me, Billy Hanks," Willie McKay said. "Tell us what we have to do."

Billy looked around at the group, making eye contact with each of them.

"We're now on a war footing," he said. "The enemy has declared their intentions. Our job is to deny them progress. Failing that, to delay it. We shall fight them, but only at the time and place of our choosing. This is our strath, our home, and that is to our advantage. We know every rock and tree in this place. They do not."

Willie McKay stood up, shaking his head. "But Billy, they will come with deputies, wagon loads of them to expel us," he said. "Lord Stafford may well send down to Fort George for a battalion or two of the Black Watch. They will have guns, and swords and bayonets. And what do we have? About a dozen men too old to serve in the Regiment of Foot along with their sons and brothers. About a dozen boys too young to steal for the Royal Navy. We're outmanned, Billy Hanks. Outmanned and outgunned and outnumbered. That bastard MacCray would gladly kill us all if he could. He as much as said so not an hour ago."

Billy Hanks nodded. "Ye speak the truth, Willie," he said. "We are outmanned and outgunned. But we have a secret weapon that they do not."

" And what is that?" McKay sounded dubious.

"Us." It was Mhairi McKinnon who spoke, the single word spoken harshly from beneath the white kertch which covered most of her face. She stood and pulled her bonnet back to look the men in the eyes. "We have me, and Rosie here next to me, and the other women and girls who live up and down the breadth of Glencullen. D'ye think it is only men who will mourn the loss of our homes? D'ye think it is only men who want to fight this injustice? I will fight. Rosie will fight. Agatha Ross will fight. Betty Gordon will fight. Your wife Elizabeth will fight, Willie McKay."

"Womenfolk?" Willie McKay sneered. "Is that your plan, Billy Hanks? To go to war with Lord Stafford with womenfolk?"

Mhairi turned to face the man. "Willie McKay, who do you think runs the farms in this strath, but womenfolk?" she said. "My man is off in Spain marching against that man Bonaparte.

Who is it, do you suppose, who is planting the corn, milking the cows, feeding the chickens? Who keeps the fire burning in the hearth, bakes the daily bread, fetches the water, sweeps the floor and wipes the arse of the wee bairns? It is the womenfolk, that's who. And do ye not think we can fight for our homes as well? Ach, *luinnseach mhor*!"

Willie laughed aloud. "Oh, I may be a clumsy lump, Mhairi," he said, standing in front of her, hands out wide. "But I can fight better than a thousand women. And it would take a thousand thousand to stand up to the likes of Robert MacCray. There is no way ..."

Rosie McFie, who had been sitting quietly listening to the argument, stirred. In a movement that was so quick that none could later describe how she did it, Rosie stood and moved behind Willie McKay. In her hand appeared a knife, withdrawn suddenly from deep within the folds of her dress. And that knife was pressed, firmly and inerrantly, against the neckbone of the unfortunate Willie. Her movement had been fast, silent and firm. Willie could feel the sharpened blade pressing against his skin. His heart pounded, but he kept still. Very, very still.

"What are ye doing, Rosie McFie?" he croaked. "Be very careful now. That blade feels sharp."

"It is indeed, Willie McKay," Rosie said. "And it is only because you are my neighbor and your wife is my friend that I will not make her a widow. I could if I wanted. Or I could make you a gelding. It would be just as easy for me to do either one."

Billy Hanks burst out laughing. "Do ye not see, Willie?" he said. "Of course a man can defeat a woman in a fair fight. That is obvious to all. But the womenfolk have other ways about them that serve them well. They have stealth and wiles. They can sneak up on an unsuspecting man, as Rosie just did with you. They can get him to lower his guard. Oh, we have our secret weapons, here in Glencullen all right. And we will use them, every one."

Still laughing, he nodded at Rosie, who took her knife away from the throat of Willie McKay. He slumped down on a rock, rubbing his neck. Billy Hanks handed him the flask, and never did a man need a wee dram more than Willie at that moment. He glanced over at Rosie McFie, shuddered, and took a long draught before handing the flask back to Billy Hanks.

"Right then," Billy said. "We've got plans to make. Let's get to it."

12

Dornoch - Dunrobin Castle

Lady Elizabeth listened carefully to Robert MacCray's report on his visit to Glencullen, scowling as he explained that Billy Hanks remained at large. She sat in an uncomfortable Louis XIV chair next to the peat fire in the marble hearth of the drawing room at Dunrobin Castle. Her husband, Lord Stafford, and their factor, William Young, stood nearby, listening with blank faces as MacCray described the reports that had placed the outlaw Hanks in the strath, but admitted that he and Captain Gordon had been unsuccessful in finding any trace of the man.

"It seems improbable that one man could so thoroughly elude capture in so small a place as Glencullen," she said when MacCray was finished.

"With all due respect, Milady, Glencullen is anything but a small place," MacCray said, bowing respectfully in her direction. "Though the number of residents in the strath is not so large, there are vast tracks of mountains and moors in all directions. A single man can easily hide in that vastness, especially one who knows how to live away from civilization, as this Hanks apparently does."

"I would concur with that," said the rotund Young, sniffing into a handkerchief which he then stuffed into the cuff of his silk coat. "While the people of the glen reside mostly alongside the river, the parish boundary extends northwards a dozen or more miles to the slopes of Ben Cullen and at least as far to the east and west of the River Cullen, and I daresay there are places in the higher reaches that have not been visited by a human since the days of the Norsemen."

Lord Stafford stirred, blinking rapidly against the harsh light pouring in from the windows which faced east to the sea. "I don't understand the fuss," he said. "This man is an outlaw, and while he may be damned hard to find, does anyone believe that he will not be discovered soon and brought to face justice?" He noticed his wife, sitting a few feet away, straighten herself and begin to protest, and quickly cut her off.

"I know, I know," he said, waving a hand dismissively in her direction. "He is a poacher and a thief, and has become something of a local celebrity. But he is just a man, like any other, and must one day stand to account for his actions. What harm can he do to our plans? I certainly want him captured, but I do not see the reason why we should overturn heaven and earth to accomplish that which, in due time, is certain to occur."

The face of the Countess darkened, and the red spots of rouge on her cheeks expanded as her anger grew.

"My dear Sir," she said, struggling to keep her voice from wavering with emotion. Her husband did not like outward displays of emotion. "This outlaw, this Billy Hanks, is dangerous because he has the people on his side. They protect him, lie for him, provide him shelter and sustenance. It is a form of rebellion, against me, against you and against the King's own law. If we allow him to continue to roam freely through the strath, there is no telling where this rebellion will end."

MacCray bowed again. "Your Ladyship is quite correct," he said. "The people are on his side, and that has the potential to be troublesome. Especially in light of the coming removals."

Lady Elizabeth nodded her approval of this statement and turned again to face her husband and Young. "You see?" she said. "There is potential for trouble with this man. You promised me that there would be no more trouble with your program of removals. I need not remind you of the scandals we suffered as a result of the incidents at Strathnaver."

The three men winced inwardly at the mention of the name. *Strathnaver*. That had been one of the first of the removals of the people from their ancestral grounds in favor of the new generation of sheep farmers that Lord Stafford was planning to import to his estates. That particular job had been turned over to Patrick Sellar, another of William Young's assistants, and it had been a disaster. Sellar had been utterly ruthless in his execution of the removal of the people. The tenants of the strath had been given short notice to move themselves and their possessions down the River Naver to the small sandy lots at the seashore, and Sellar, who was himself one of the new tenants planning to replace the people and their homes with flocks of the new Cheviot sheep, had moved quickly and without mercy to eject them from their homes. Hiring a band of ruffians, Sellar had moved in on a cold and rainy day, throwing people's belongings out of their rude huts, tearing down the roof timbers, setting fire to the thatch. In the course of that single day, all the settlements in Strathnaver had been destroyed, and the people turned out into the harsh weather. There had been physical violence and several of the older and infirm inhabitants had suffered and one old woman had died. It had been an ugly and brutal affair.

Worst of all, it had been publicized. Some of the Strathnaver residents had written accounts of the brutality, the firing of their possessions, the death of the elderly left out in the cold rain. And those accounts had made their way into the newspapers in Edinburgh and, worse, London. Inquiries had been made. Members of Parliament had harrumphed. Sellar had been charged with manslaughter for his actions, but the case, tried in

Inverness, had been overturned by a jury convinced that Lady Stafford had both a legitimate and a legal right to determine who could live on her lands. Sellar had returned to Strathnaver and continued to oversee his sheep farm there. Still, the affair had left a black mark on the Sutherland family and Lady Elizabeth had noticed a new coolness among some of her friends in London society. As a result, she had demanded of her husband and his factor that any future removals be accomplished without undue hardship to the people.

Robert MacCray tried to address the problem. "Milady," he said, "You should not fear a repeat of the mistakes that were made at Strathnaver. In that unfortunate instance, Mr. Sellar was deemed to be an outsider, not one of the native people. In this case, Captain Gordon, a close relation of yourself, is himself resident in the strath and is respected and admired by the people there. He will see to it that the people come along with the plans and that the removal will be orderly and peaceful."

The other two men nodded in agreement. They expected no problems from the people of Glencullen. Captain Gordon, the traditional tacksman of the glen, would see to that.

Lady Elizabeth was not convinced. She shook her head.

"Nae, nae, you underestimate this fellow, this Billy Hanks," she said. "I have seen what can happen when the temper of the people is aroused by scoundrels and rabble-rousers. A peaceful and obedient populace can turn into a raving and dangerous mob in an instant. My Lord Stafford and I lived in Paris when that sad country was in revolt. I have not forgotten the horror of those days, and I never shall."

"My dear lady," Stafford said haltingly. "I, too, will never forget those terrible events. But I can assure you that this situation has nothing in common with those long past circumstances. That was another country, in another time. Such things cannot happen here, especially in a backward place like Glencullen. No, I am confident that Mr. Young and MacCray here, working closely with Captain Gordon, will be able to pacify the people and enact our plans without problems. And this Hanks fellow will soon be caught and hanged. Of that I am certain."

Lady Stafford said no more about the matter, feeling she had pressed as far as she dared. Sutherland was, of course, *her* estate, as opposed to her husband's land in Staffordshire, and his vast network of commercial canals and manufactures that belched smoke into the skies of England. As a dutiful wife, she of course deferred to his wisdom and advice when it came to the administration of her estates. At the same time, both of them understood and implicitly agreed that as the hereditary countess of Sutherland, it was, in the end, her decisions that were final.

So she kept her thoughts to herself. The men moved on to a discussion about the progress being made at the colliery in Helmsdale and the new herring fishery at Golspie. These and other projects were continuing on as planned, creating jobs and living places for the now land-bound workers in Glencullen and the other Highland straths and valleys who would soon be removed. Lady Elizabeth understood and approved of these plans. It was clear to all who cared to look that the old way, the subsistence farming of the past, was no longer beneficial to either her tenants, or to herself. The land ... *her land* ... must be put to its best and highest use. And that meant moving people out of the glens and into the new towns growing on the coasts. And moving the sheep men in.

That much was rather obvious, she thought to herself as the men continued to drone on around her. But Lady Elizabeth feared that enacting those plans was not going to be as easy as her husband and his associates seemed to believe. Lord Stafford had been appointed His Majesty's Ambassador to France at the worst of that unhappy country's Revolutionary times more than ten years earlier, and Lady Elizabeth had witnessed for herself the ugliness and danger loosed in a society when law, order and tradition broke down. She shuddered, inwardly, to remember those days of riots and unrest. She had seen men and women hung mercilessly from lamp posts and bridges. She had avoided the Place de la Louis XV, which the rebels had renamed the Place de la Revolution and where they set up their horrible killing machine that had eventually beheaded their own King and Queen. She had herself felt physical danger. She knew that, here in her own castle, surrounded by her own servants and protected, at least nominally, by the people, *her people*, who lived around her, that she was safe. But she also knew that if those people, those servants, those destitute people living in the straths and glens of her land; if all those people ever decided to turn on her, their beloved clan chief, there was nothing or nobody who would stop them. Could stop them.

After dinner that night, while the men smoked cigars and enjoyed their port in the drawing room, Lady Elizabeth begged off, pleading tiredness and a headache, and retired to her suite of rooms. Mr. Gunn brought her a small glass of sherry. She sat at her writing desk and pulled out a sheet of paper, dipped her pen in the inkwell and began to write. The letter was addressed to General the Viscount Cathcart, commander of the British troops garrisoned at Fort George near Inverness. Cathcart had served with distinction in the Americas, Russia, the Low Countries and Germany, and had been a frequent guest at her lavish parties at Cleveland House in London.

"My dear General," she wrote. "I wish to bring your attention to the troubling possibility of popular discord and revolt of the people of Sutherland to the expressed wishes of my husband and myself; and to request the disposition of a squadron of well-armed dragoons in sufficient numbers with which to maintain the peace which has been threatened."

She would post her letter in the morning, she thought. She considered asking the General to keep the matter between themselves, but knew that was hopeless. He would write back with dispatch, and things would be set in motion. Lord Stafford and his factors would soon learn of what she had done. They would not be pleased. *No matter,* she thought, *I must preserve order in my lands. It is my duty.*

13

Glencullen - May 1808

William Knowles pulled his cloak tighter around his shoulders and ducked his head to one side to allow the rain to spill off the broad leather brim of his hat. He was most uncomfortable as the rain pelted down and a cold wind tried to drive the icy droplets up under his clothing. He was on horseback, as he had been for three long days now, ever since he left his comfortable farm in Morayshire, driving the large herd of Cheviot sheep northwards to their new steading in Glencullen. Three other men from his farm in Findhorn were riding with him, positioned before and behind the slow-moving herd; another six boys were on foot, using their sticks and a dozen or so yelping dogs to keep the sheep moving in a relatively compact mass. The boys and dogs would chase after the individual animals which wandered off, attracted by the occasional patch of rich green grass or a freshet of water sluicing down from the surrounding hills, and push them back into the slowly moving sea of white wool creeping ever northwards.

They were close now to their final destination at Glencullen. Captain Gordon had signed a lease with Knowles for a large steading at the entrance to the glen, about two miles south of Gordon's own farm and another two miles or so from the settlements of Glencullen.

"You'll be the first to bring sheep into the Glen," Gordon had told Knowles when they signed the papers in Inverness some weeks ago. "I'll have my own steading ready for animals by the end of summer, and by fall the rest of the people will be gone. Next spring, after the lambing, you'll have two or three new neighbors to the north, in the higher reaches. And there are at least a dozen farms, probably more, between Glencullen and the Cromarty Firth where the sheep have been introduced. It is the way of the future."

Knowles was satisfied with the arrangement. Down at the entrance to Glencullen strath, the fields were broad, well drained by the fast-flowing river, and situated for excellent grazing. He would have to invest in some fences and build some lambing pens, but the rocky cliffs that defined the hills as they began to rise steeply on both sides of the valley would provide a natural barrier against most wandering sheep. Knowles would need but two or three experienced shepherds to keep his flock in line. By next spring, the rams would have done their work and the flock would increase in size. Some of the lambs would be sold for meat, others would join the thousands grazing in his fields, turning grass into the wool which would fetch excellent prices at the markets in Inverness and Edinburgh. The great British armies were on the march in Spain and the Low Countries, in India, Africa and the Americas, and they all needed uniforms and blankets. When he thought of the profits that were sure to come his way, Knowles could forget, briefly anyway, his cold discomfort as he rode through the rain.

The flock stopped moving. At least, it no longer seemed to be moving forward up the road. The huge central mass of animals stopped, bleating piteously, while those on the fringes darted into the underbrush where they could. Knowles spurred his horse forward, pushing and scattering sheep out of the way. It took several minutes of this kind of slow progress before he could see the reason for the holdup.

The road, really nothing more than a narrow dirt track, followed the path of the River Cullen, but on higher ground, well above the rocks that were scattered along the river's edges. But as Knowles pushed his horse forward through the sea of dirty white wool, he saw the place ahead where the road narrowed as it rose up a long and slight incline and passed between two broad and tall rocky pillars, placed as though a giant had been building a gate. Knowles had learned, when he had first visited the strath, that the locals called this natural formation the *Bodsgate*, using the Gaelic word for phallus, or sometimes the *Geata Diabhail*, or the Devil's Gate. It had made Knowles smile, thinking how apt the term was, as the two rocky pillars did indeed resemble male sex organs, and the pillars were large enough that it was easy to envision them as the organs of the Horned One. He had wondered what the women of the strath thought of the term, just one of hundreds of place-names the local people assigned to the terrain in the strath: It seemed there was a name assigned to every rock, large tree, hillock, pooling of the river and more. *Strange people, these Irish*, he thought.

While the flock would have slowed anyway as it passed through this natural gateway, it had been completely stopped by an unnatural impediment: ten men blocking the roadway at this narrow entrance with cut tree limbs and trunks. The nervous sheep had been forced to stop, forced to reverse against its inexorable forward momentum.

Knowles kicked his horse forward up the incline and forced it through the turbulent eddy of the sheep massed at the rocky gate. The men waiting there formed a semi-circle across the roadway, arms crossed, some holding wooden cudgels. Knowles swung his horse broadside to the men.

"What is the meaning of this?" he cried. "Remove those timbers at once."

"We canna do that, cap'n," said one of the men. He didn't

nod or doff his woolen cap. "Your beasties are no' allowed in the strath. Ye must return to where ye came from."

"Don't be ridiculous," Knowles snapped. He turned and rummaged in a bag tied to his saddle, pulling out a cylinder of papers tied with a ribbon. "This is my lease for the farm known as Carsewood. Signed by Captain Gordon. If you have a problem, I suggest you take it up with him. Now let me pass!"

Another man, hatless with his long black locks tied at the back of his head, stepped forward and took the roll of papers from Knowles' hand. He untied the ribbon, unfurled the sheaf and studied the writing, reading it slowly and carefully. Then, he looked up at Knowles with a grin, and slowly and carefully ripped the papers asunder and handed them back. Then he turned and nodded at the men standing beside him. They started forward, waving their arms and shouting. Startled, the sea of sheep turned and began retreating back down the road from whence they had just come. Their nervous and confused bleating grew in loudness and echoed off the rocky gate.

Two of Knowles's men pushed their horses through the flood of sheep into the clearing beyond the rocky gates. Moving swiftly, the waiting men grabbed their halters as well as Knowles' and the three men from Moray were pulled roughly off their mounts.

Knowles knew immediately what was happening. The movement of sheep into the Highland districts of the north was well known throughout the land, as was the grumbling of the inhabitants there who knew what this woolly invasion meant. In his stops the previous few nights, dining in the public houses of Dingwall and Beauly, Knowles had sensed the displeasure of the local populace: he heard their muttering, saw their dark looks in his direction. He had been warned to expect some kind of trouble along the way.

He signaled to his men to remain calm. Three of the group which had been waiting for them at the rocky gate leaped upon the horses and began driving the mass of sheep southward back down the road with loud shouts. The sheep slowly managed to reverse direction and within a few minutes, the herd was moving again. But they were now heading south, back in the direction of Lairg. Once the flock had been turned around, the tall man with long black hair, the one who had spoken and had ripped the lease papers in two, turned to Knowles with a smile.

"You are welcome to follow your flock home again," he said. "We mean no harm to you nor your beasties."

"What is your intention?" Knowles asked.

The tall man shrugged. "We shall collect all the sheep from the district and send them back whence they came," he said. "If we can, we'll drive them all the way to Inverness. I'm sure you can find your way back to Findhorn from there."

So, Knowles thought to himself, *this savage brute can actually read. He saw my name on that damned lease.* He filed that information away.

"What is your name, Sir?" he asked, with a short bow.

The man laughed, head thrown back, teeth bared. "I have no name," he said. "I am a ghost."

"I think not, Sir" Knowles said. "For I can see and hear you as plain as any man."

They did not speak again. Knowles and his three shepherds walked side by side, following along as the men of Glencullen drove his sheep back down the river road. The half dozen boys and their dogs who had been helping to drive the flock one way, now helped drive it the other. The man with the black hair walked behind Knowles and his men, now grasping a thick wooden stick in one hand, polished to a glistening sheen, wrapped near the top with strips of leather. From time to time as they walked, one of the men on horseback would ride back and have a brief whispered conversation with the black-haired man, before wheeling the horse around and heading back down the river road after the slowly moving mass of sheep.

"I suspect the Sheriff Depute will soon be informed of this infamy," Knowles said to the black-haired man as they walked along. "I suspect you will become a hunted man."

"I suspect you are correct, Sir," the man said calmly. "But I have been hunted by one sort or another most of my life. Having one more after me will not burden my sleep."

"Do you really think you can get away with this?" Knowles pressed. "Chasing me and my sheep out of your glen is not going to stop others from coming behind me. They will have sheep, too, many thousands of them. Do you intend to chase them all away?"

The black-haired man was silent for a while. "The people of Glencullen do not want to leave their homes so the sheep may take them," he said. "Nor do the people of all the other glens and straths where this is happening. We are defending our homes from invasion. We have that right, no matter if the invaders are Bonaparte's men, or your bloody sheep."

Knowles shook his head sadly. But he said no more.

In a few hours, the woolly procession reached the outskirts of Lairg, where the townsfolk came out to watch the slow parade move through the streets. There were calls of encouragement as the bleating sheep were herded down the High Street and southeast toward the Firth of Dornoch. Just south of the town, another sea of sheep was seen moving down the burnside from Glen Grudie to the west. This flock, too, was being driven by a handful of local men from that strath, waving their sticks and boughs to keep the woolly sea flowing. Soon, the two flocks had become one, stretching almost as far as the eye could see. Another two or three hours later, they met up with yet another flock being driven from Culrain, and still later, a large flock from the strath at Dounie.

As the afternoon began to deepen into evening, the huge flock reached the outskirts of Ardgay, crossing the fords at the River Shin. The men from the straths herded the mass of sheep into the grassy fields alongside the river, set the first watch, and prepared to bed down for the night. Raging fires were lit and bread and other victuals were passed around. Not a single beast was slaughtered for food. Instead, the townsfolk of Ardgay came out of their homes and distributed what food they had to share with the men gathered in the fields. The sheep settled in peacefully, glad of the chance to stop walking for the first time all day, and the drovers too began to relax. They gathered in groups around the crackling fire pits to laugh and talk while they passed around flasks of whiskey.

Billy Hanks, the black-haired man from Glencullen, did not join the other Highland men who were gathering around the roaring fires, talking excitedly about the events of the day, passing the flasks back and forth. He first made sure that sentries were posted all around the fields where the sheep now lay in small groups, some asleep, some chewing peacefully on the bits of grass. Next, he sent other men out to scout the surrounding hills and down along the firth, looking for signs of official response that he was sure would soon come. Only when that was done did he allow himself to return to the fire made by the Glencullen men. There, he squatted next to the warming flames and pulled a crust of bread out of his rucksack. One of the other men offered him the flask, but Billy Hanks waved it away.

"Nae, nae," he said with a slight smile. "I must keep my wits about me. We have poked the lairds in the eye this day and they will soon be poking back. There will be time for drinking and song, but this night is not that time."

But Billy Hanks was almost alone of all the men in his determination to remain sober and alert. The whiskey was flowing freely, and men from the various glens and straths began to wander between the fires, greeting one another and exchanging congratulations on a successful day. Several men had brought their fiddles, others their pipes and flutes and soon there was music and singing around the fires.

The showers of the day had passed, giving way to a brisk wind sweeping down from the western hills and pushing out toward the sea. The flames in the fires jumped and crackled as they were brushed by the breezes, and the men pulled their tartans tighter around their shoulders and reached again for a flask to help warm their insides.

Three men entered the circle of light around the fire of the men of Glencullen, where Billy Hanks still crouched, staring into the flames. The tallest of the men had a head of long, stringy red hair and a massive beard to match. He was broad-shouldered, his legs thick and powerful, his hands large as skillets. His two companions looked like they could be his brothers, in both size and countenance.

"Hanks!" the large one called out as they neared the fire. "Billy Hanks!"

Slowly, unfolding himself from his crouch, Billy Hanks stood and faced the large red-haired man. "I am the one called Hanks," he said quietly.

"Dougal Ross," the man said, extending his arm. Billy Hanks took the man's huge hand in his own. "These are my kinsmen, Jacob and John," Dougal said, and the men nodded greetings. Willie Gordon, a man of Glencullen, came and stood next to Billy, and Willie extended his hand holding a silver flask of whiskey toward the red-haired giant and his two kinsman.

The big man took the flask, threw back his head and drank deeply. Done, he wiped his mouth with the back of his hand, passed it to John, and looked around approvingly.

"Tis a fine day's work ye've done here, Billy," he said. "The laird of Glen Grudie will be annoyed when he learns his sheep have been driven away from his steading. Most annoyed. As will your Lady away in her keep at Dunrobin, I expect."

He took another long pull from the flask. Billy Hanks stood silently.

"What is the plan for the morrow?" the giant said.

"We start at dawn," Billy Hanks said. "We'll drive the flocks southeast, through the pass at Kildermorie, then down through Wester Ross to Dingwall. There's an old drover's trail to follow through the heights. We will overnight at Lord Munro's property outside of that town. There's plenty of room in his fields, even if his Lordship won't make us a proper welcome. We should make it to Inverness the following afternoon, if all goes well."

"Be easier to take the road along the coast," Dougal said, nodding to the east.

"But longer," Billy said, shaking his head. "And that way takes us close to Tain. There is a sheriff there. Best if we can avoid sheriffs."

Dougal Ross nodded to himself thoughtfully and exchanged a glance with his two kinsmen. "Tis true, 'tis true," he said. "But I dunna fancy climbing up to the pass at Kildermorie with a thousand sheep to look after. Perhaps I'll take my men and our flocks and go 'round the seaside road. We can meet at Dingwall."

"Nae, Dougal," Billy Hanks said, looking the man straight in the eyes. "It would be a mistake to split up the flock, and the few men we have to drive them. We all agreed to do this together. If we begin to split apart, the lairds will be able to pick us off, one by one. If you go your way, Sheriff MacLeod will be waiting for you with two dozen men. Believe me, the word has gone out to the lairds, and they will be scrambling to stop us as soon as they can."

Dougal Ross took one final pull from the flask and handed it back to Willie Gordon.

"Ye may be right, Billy Hanks," he said. "But it has been a hundred years and more since a Ross of Glen Grudie has followed the lead of anyone, much less a man from Glencullen. I'm taking the sea road, and that's an end to it."

Billy Hanks stood facing the man for a moment, staring into his eyes. Dougal Ross smiled back at him, cracking his knuckles.

He stood at least a head taller than Billy and outweighed him by several stone. Billy Hanks had been expecting something like this. Highland men were proud, and they were warriors. The entire history of the clans was a fairly simple and brutal story of contests of strength, bare-knuckle battles for domination, and changing alliances. He knew that his leadership would be challenged at some point, and that if he was going to continue to lead, he would have to act.

What happened next was a blur. But in the blink of an eye, Dougal Ross was lying flat on his back, his long, unruly hair spilling dangerously close to the snapping flames of the fire. Billy Hanks had a knee firmly planted on the large man's chest and he held the long blade of a knife, which had appeared seemingly out of nowhere, pointed at the man's eyes.

"Now, Dougal," he said calmly, moving the knife's point back and forth between the large man's two eyes, which tracked its movement closely. "That won't do. It won't do at all. We agreed to do this together. We agreed that by working as one, we would better get our point across to the lairds. We agreed that if we allowed ourselves to go our own ways, they would find a way to separate us, and then defeat us. So we will not let that happen, Dougal. When the sun rises in the morning, you and the other men of Glen Grudie will climb with us to the pass at Kildermorie, and then down the far side to Dingwall. Are we quite clear about that?"

Dougal Ross nodded his head slowly. Billy Hanks stood up and then reached down with a hand, offering to help the man stand. After the briefest of hesitations, Dougal Ross reached up and took Hanks' hand. By the time he was back on his feet, the knife had disappeared and Billy Hanks wore a broad smile.

"Good," he said. "Have you eaten? We seem to have some bread and cheese as well as some fine Glencullen oatcakes. It's not much, but it's food. Come join us."

Dougal Ross brushed himself off, shrugged at his brothers and followed Willie Gordon over to the clutch of the other men of Glencullen, who were laughing and passing around a loaf of bread. They welcomed the Rosses of Grudie will claps on the back, broad smiles and knowing looks.

"He's a fast bastard, is our Billy Hanks," said one of the older men, grinning at Dougal. "Learned his tricks from the savages in the Americas when he lived among them. Moves like the wind. Appears out of nowhere. Silent as the grave, he is. But he's a good lad. When Billy Hanks says he'll do a thing, you can count on him doing it."

Dougal and his brothers joined the feasting and the laughing and the drinking and the singing that went on late into the night. But Dougal kept glancing over at the black-haired man squatting near the fire, staring into the flames, not moving. And he wondered what sort of man this Billy Hanks really was.

14

The next morning, while the combined flocks of black-faced sheep were driven up the old drover's trail, used for generations of Highlanders to bring their black cattle to the autumn tryst at Inverness, towards the mountain pass at Kildermorie with the brothers Ross of Grudie taking the position of honor at the front, a cold panic had set in along the dusty streets of Dingwall, a town on the Cromarty Firth midway between Inverness and Tain. The Sheriff-Depute, Robert MacLeod, called to order at about ten o'clock an extraordinary meeting of some two dozen landowning lairds from the surrounding area. The Sheriff immediately deferred to Sir Hugo Munro of Foulis, the chief of his clan and wealthiest landowner in Rosshire. Most of the other men in attendance were related to Sir Hugo either through family or business, and they all owned large agricultural estates in the district, most including large flocks of sheep.

"Report, please," Sir Hugo barked at the Sheriff when the group had settled down in the meeting room of the Courthouse, a stone-and-brick edifice on the High Street, with a central tower topped by a round wooden spire.

"Sir Hugo, gentlemen," MacLeod began, nodding at the men gathered around the table. "My sources tell me that there could be as many as four hundred men driving the sheep out of Sutherland and Wester Ross. There have been reports of disturbances and tumultuous behaviors in several townships these seditious rebels have passed through. I have a report, unconfirmed as yet, that Lairg has been put to flames. These men are said to be armed with muskets, sidearms and swords."

"And artillery!" cried one of the assembled. "They are said to have cannons. Imagine if they set up south of Kildermorie and begin firing upon our town! The blood will run through the gutters of Dingwall if we do not stop them!"

Excited jabbering filled the hall as the lairds discussed this horrible news. MacLeod waited until the conversation died down, holding up his hand.

"My dear Sir," he said, addressing the man who had last spoken, Alexander Cameron of Lochaber. "I have received no intelligence that indicates this rebel group has had access to artillery of any kind. Think, man! Where in the world would they obtain access to such things? How would they transport artillery through the glens and straths without a huge force of troops? They would need horses…oxen…hundreds of men! I pray you, Sir, and all the rest of you, do not fall victim to panicked thoughts or listen to wild rumors. This event appears to be a rather simple rebellion against the coming of the sheep to the counties. We do not know what these ruffians intend, but there is no evidence that they plan to commit widespread bloodshed against their own countrymen."

More excited hubbub filled the hall with echoes as the gentlemen expressed their opinions for and against this statement. Sir Hugo stood, and the room fell silent again.

"I agree with the Sheriff," he said. "There are more rumors than facts abroad in the streets this morning. Let us first agree to remain calm until we learn more about what is going on." He turned to the Sheriff. "When do you anticipate having more intelligence on these rebels, where they are and what they want?"

MacLeod smiled to himself. He knew that Sir Hugo, who had served with the Army in India some twenty years ago, would remain calm under pressure. He was glad to have the man act as a brake against the uncontrolled panic that seemed to have infected all the others.

"I am awaiting reports from the Sheriff-Depute in Tain, who is watching the coastal road," MacLeod said. "I have also sent some men to Ardross and beyond in case the rebels attempt an overland route."

One of the lairds, Captain Cameron, the brother of Alexander, rose to his feet, face red and furious. "And if they come through the pass at Kildermorie, they could be here by tea time, and this town and all the farms within twenty miles, could be put to the fire by nightfall. I think, Sir, your defense of our homes and lives is sadly lacking. We demand something be done!"

There were strong murmurs of agreement among the gathered lairds, who drummed their feet on the wooden floor to signal their agreement with Cameron's outburst. The Sheriff held up a hand, and the drumming sound stopped.

"Finally," he said, as if he hadn't been interrupted, "I sent a message yesterday to General Cathcart at Fort George, asking him to send three companies of the Black Watch to help us keep order if necessary."

"*If necessary!*" Rising again to his feet as if pulled by an invisible wire, Captain Cameron was apoplectic. "More than four hundred savages are marching on our farms and towns, stealing our property and threatening our very lives. If such a circumstance does not warrant an armed response, I cannot conceive of one that will!"

"In the meantime, m'Lord," MacLeod continued evenly, keeping his voice and countenance calm, "I suggest that we distribute what weapons we can find to the menfolk of the farms represented by the assembled lairds here today, and have them posted outside the town limits to help slow the progress of these rebels, if indeed they come this way."

Sir Hugo nodded, and made a note to himself in a small book.

Captain Cameron was not pleased.

"That is your solution?" his voice trembled with rage. "To pass out muskets to thirty or forty men of Ross and send them out to face four hundred heavily armed Highland lunatics? Have you lost all sense, Sir?"

"No, Captain," MacLeod shot back, his voice sharp. The hall fell silent. "I have maintained my sense of reason, unlike some others in this room. I would remind you, Sir, that those who are promoting this rebellion, if that is what this is, are fellow countrymen. Many of them are our relations, many others our friends of long standing. Again, the only information we have at hand is that this group is driving the sheep out of their straths and glens. Beyond that, we do not know who they are, where they are, nor what they want. Until we know that, I cannot recommend further actions."

This time, the Sheriff's words earned the drumming feet of approval from the assembled. Cameron sat down, unhappy but, for the moment, outvoted.

"Thank you, Sheriff," Sir Hugo said. "I agree with your summarization of the circumstances we face. Our response should be cautious and reasoned. Let us each nominate some men to set up a defense of the town and send others out into the country for the purpose of gathering intelligence as to this rebellion. I will send my own dispatch to the Commander, Lord Cathcart, at Fort George, as well as to the Lord Advocate in Edinburgh, and redouble our request for troops to be sent to our aid. But I think any response to these ruffians should await the arrival of the Black Watch. If a military action is indeed required, I would prefer to allow the military to undertake it."

"I concur, Sir Hugo…a very wise policy, indeed." The voice crackled through the meeting room and all heads at the table swiveled to look at the doorway from whence it came. Standing there was a major in the Black Watch, resplendent in his red coat, leather sash, tartan waistcoat and white breeches that disappeared into his highly polished, knee-high boots. The major removed his feathered black bonnet and bowed deeply to the assembled gentry in the room.

"Sir Hugo, gentlemen," he said, his deep voice continuing its sharp-edged tone, "I am Major Charles Darnell of His Majesty's 42nd Regiment of Foot. My troops have been dispatched by order of the Governor General to put down a rebellion against the public order. I am now in command."

His boots rang as he strode across the floor to stand next to Sir Hugo's chair. The major was a man of medium height, round of body, and his short hair was flecked with streaks of gray. He moved with a military bearing, back ramrod straight, and eyes scanning constantly all around. He removed his leather gloves as he glanced around the table, taking the measure of the men gathered there. His gaze came to rest on Robert MacLeod.

"You are the Sheriff, are you not?" Major Darnell said, his eyes measuring the man while a small smile played on his lips.

"I am, Sir," MacLeod bowed slightly. "Robert MacLeod at your service."

"I see. By order of the Lord Advocate for Scotland, Sir Robert Dundas, I am now in command of the response to the rebels."

"And are you also in command of ensuring and maintaining the peace of the county as well, Major Darnell?" MacLeod knew better than to try and counterman a direct order of the Lord Advocate in Edinburgh, especially one who was also the nephew of the powerful Home Secretary in London, but the major's arrogance was troubling.

Darnell's eyes narrowed as he again cast his eyes over MacLeod.

"When an army of Highland jackals is rampaging through the countryside, stealing property and disrupting the public order, I do not see much peace that can be maintained, Sir." He turned to address Sir Hugo Munro at the center of the table.

"What is the latest intelligence on the mob, Sir Hugo?" he asked.

Lord Munro smiled and nodded at MacLeod. "Tell him," he said.

MacLeod grabbed a map of the area and unfurled it in front of Major Darnell. He pointed out the main coastal road that ran north by northeast from Inverness along the Cromarty Firth up to Tain on the southern shore of the Dornoch Firth.

"Last night, they stopped outside Ardgay, south of the River Dornoch, here…" He pointed to the spot on the map. "There are two possible routes they could be taking today. One is the main coastal road. I have men stationed at Tain and other places along this way, and if they are coming, we will know soon."

He pointed next to the interior portions of Wester Ross. "I believe, however, they will travel overland today, aiming for the Pass at Kildermorie. There's an old drover's route through the mountains. It's steeper and more difficult to traverse, but it's far shorter, and although they must negotiate the lower slopes of Beinn Tharsuinn, I believe they will come that way."

"And do you have scouts posted on that possibility?" Darnell said, probing.

MacLeod felt his face growing red, and wished he could stop it. He hated showing weakness or uncertainty. "I have a man in Alness who is sending a party into Strath Rusdale this morning," he said. "I expected to hear from him by now, but …"

"But you haven't," the major finished, voice dripping with sarcasm. "Indeed."

He paused for a moment, studying the map.

"This is no time for hesitancy," he said finally. "We must act. We shall march at once for Alness and make our camp there tonight. From there, we can intercept the rebels no matter which direction they choose. Corporal!" He turned to the doorway, where his factotum stood at attention. "Tell the men to replenish their water and foodstuffs. We march in an hour for Alness."

The Corporal snapped off a salute and disappeared.

"Hear, hear," said a relieved Cameron, mostly to himself.

"Any of you gentlemen who wish to accompany us are welcome," the major continued. "We may see action, but I assure you it will be short and bloody, and entirely upon the side of the rebels. I would only request that you remain safely at the rear when we begin our attack."

The room quickly emptied as the gentlemen of Ross ran for their horses and weapons. What had just an hour earlier been an event fraught with fear and danger had been turned into an adventuresome lark which promised violence and bloodshed, but at someone else's expense.

Soon, the only men left in the cavernous room were Sir Hugo, the Major and the sheriff.

"Is there anything else you require, Sir?" Munro asked the major, who nodded thoughtfully, looking at the sheriff.

"I am interested in what you know of this man they call Billy Hanks," he said.

"Hanks?" Sir Hugo said, scratching his chin. "Billy Hanks? I confess that I have not heard that name. I am sorry."

"Sheriff?"

"He is an elusive, yet well-known criminal," MacLeod said, wondering why this Army officer might be interested. "He is mainly a problem of Sutherlandshire. But I have heard of him paying visits to the farms and steadings in Ross as well. Why do you ask?"

Major Darnell smiled, showing a row of pointy teeth. "I am familiar with the man," he said. "He served under me in the Canadian provinces. Many of my troops are late of Glencullen and other straths in the country, and they have heard stories from their relations. I keep an ear out for such things, any good commander of men would do the same. He is quite famous among the people. Or infamous, I should say."

"Well then Sheriff, you should find and arrest this Hanks!" Sir Hugo said with an exhalation.

MacLeod bowed to Sir Hugo, but managed to keep his face impassive. He wanted to laugh out loud. "I can assure you, Sir Hugo, that I shall make every effort to apprehend this man, and shall remain in close communication with my counterpart in Tain as well."

"Good, good," Sir Hugo said, satisfied to have accomplished another task. "Well, I shall saddle my pony and accompany you gentlemen at least as far as Alness. I'm afraid I'm a bit too old for combat, however. I shall leave that to you younger men."

He heaved himself out of his chair and waddled toward the door. Before he exited, he turned and looked at MacLeod.

"Sheriff," he said, brows beetling up and down atop his florid face. "You should ride with Major Darnell. Fill him in on your knowledge of the county. Help him do his job. Together, we should quickly bring an end to whatever this action is and restore peace to the countryside."

Both the Sheriff and the Major bowed as Sir Hugo strode away.

AN HOUR LATER, Darnell and MacLeod watched from atop their mounts as the first company of the Black Watch marched out of the town, to the cheers of the populace. Small boys armed with wooden sticks pretending to march alongside the impressive lines of red-coated soldiers followed along, women waved their handkerchiefs and dozens of dogs ran to and fro, barking furiously at the excitement. Once the first company had passed, the

Major, the sheriff and a half-dozen other officers on horseback fell in behind, followed by the last two companies in formation and, finally, the undisciplined collection of landowners and their tacksmen.

It was, MacLeod thought to himself as he glanced around at the scene, quite the parade. He let some time pass before he nudged his horse to bring it even with that of the Major.

"I am interested in your previous relations with this Hanks fellow," he said. "I believe you said you served with him in the Americas?"

Major Darnell was silent. Silent for so long that MacLeod began to think he was being ignored. A flash of anger coursed through his body, but he pushed it down. If the Major, obviously a man of some status and station, did not wish to communicate with a mere sheriff from an insignificant Highland shire, there was not much he could do about it. He was about to rein in his horse and return to his place in the formation, when Darnell spoke.

"Hanks was a good soldier," Darnell said. "Our division was assigned to the Upper Canada province following the war in the Colonies. While most of the residents there were loyal to the King, and many others fled north during and after the Rebellion, there were still rumblings of rebellion among the populace here and there. We were there to maintain the public order and ensure that His Majesty's Canadian holdings were not lost as well."

"So you did not see combat?" MacLeod asked.

"Not there, no," Darnell said, shaking his head. "Our duty was maintaining law and order, protecting the townships against attacks and raids from the native savages and ensuring that allegiance to the King was maintained. Our work involved a great deal of intelligence gathering. If we heard that a township had held a public meeting for the purpose of organizing a political movement of one kind or another, we would send a company of

lancers or foot into the area to maintain order. Arrest a few leaders, burn a barn or two, that kind of thing."

"I see," MacLeod said, thinking that such activity sounded more like occupational duty than peace-keeping. "And this
Billy Hanks was good at that?"

"He was a soldier," Darnell said again. "He had come to us
quite young, I believe, and like many of the Scottish breed, he
was made for soldiering. He followed orders, did what he was told
promptly, did not fraternize with the native populations, kept
himself in an upright and moral condition at all times. It is well
known that His Majesty's Scottish troops are well disciplined. I
cannot recall the last time we've had to hang one of the buggers
for thievery or lying or being late to roll call."

"The legend about the man says he lived for some time
among the wild savages," MacLeod said. "Is that true?"

"Oh, indeed," Darnell said. "He deserted his post one day
and walked into the woods. That was the last I'd heard of him
since the events of these recent days."

The men rode in silence for some time.

"Forgive me, Major," MacLeod said, "But that does not
make sense. You have noted, and rightly I should think, that His
Majesty's troops from these shires are notably loyal and disciplined. Yet this Hanks fellow just walks off into the woods one
day? Why would he do such a thing?"

"We had been stationed near Ancaster," Darnell said.
"That was close to the Townships of the Six Nations on the Grand
River, where the Governor General had tried to encourage the
native savages to settle. Naturally, there were constant problems
between the savages and their Christian neighbors, the savages
being Godless heathen who do not subscribe to the normal rules
of civilization.

"One day, I adjudicated a case in which a local boy had
been caught stealing a pail of milk from one of our cows. He

said his mother was ill and needed it. He was found guilty of the crime and was executed per the law."

"A boy?"

"It matters not, Sir, that he was but ten years. Boys grow into men and if they are allowed to steal the property of others as boys, they will surely continue to do so when they are older."

"So you hanged him."

"I did indeed, Sir, and would do so again," Darnell said hotly.

"And Hanks was there?" MacLeod asked.

"Part of the execution squadron," Darnell said. "That night, he was missing from roll call. In his tent we found his uniform, neatly folded, and his weapons. He simply vanished."

"Did you search for him?"

"Of course we did, Sir," the major snapped. "One cannot let the enlisted men simply decide one day to up and leave His Majesty's service! That would be sheer anarchy! I sent the Lancers out to every village in the Territory, but there was no sign of him. He apparently made his way south instead, crossed over into the colony of New York and disappeared in the woods there. We assumed he was dead. By that time, the natives of that region were known to kill any white man on sight."

"And yet, here he is," MacLeod said. "Fully alive, and apparently fighting in a new cause."

"Not for long, Sir," the major said grimly. "Not for long."

15

Mother? Mother McAdie? Are ye awake?"

The eastern sky was just beginning to brighten above the low hills that spilled gently down into the bowl-shaped valley of Strath Rusdale. The slightly larger hills to the west of the valley were still and silent in the last vestiges of the night. Billy Hanks and the brothers Ross from Glen Grudie stood outside the modest hut of the widow McAdie at the edge of the valley, built just above the narrow, rock-filled stream of the River Rusdale which cut a series of S-curves in the valley floor as it flowed easterly toward the Firth of Cromarty and the sea. The strath here was broad and open, treeless and grassy, mostly dry except for the occasional boggy spot. And it was now filled with several thousand black-faced sheep, all mostly now asleep after their long march through the Kildermorie Pass the night before. With so many sheep to control, their progress had been slower than any of them had predicted, so they had only reached the valley after midnight.

"W-w-ho's there?" came an uncertain, frightened voice from within the hut.

"It's Billy Hanks, Mother," he said, "And Dougal and Willie Ross of Glen Grudie. Can ye come outside?"

"A minute," the old woman called. An old mongrel dog came limping out into the dawn, tail wagging hopefully as he studied the men standing in the courtyard. He was soon followed by Mother McAdie, tucking the last wisps of white hair beneath her bonnet. Billy watched, amused but understanding that a proper Scottish woman would never appear in public without the expected dress and decorum. Her dress was plain and home-spun, but it was clean and in good repair. Even out here at the edge of the civilized world, she was too proud to allow her stan-dards to fall.

"I thought you were one of the fairie folk, come to drag me off to the underworld," the old woman said, her voice waver-ing with age and relief. "What is it you want, Billy Hanks, before the day has properly begun?"

"We wanted to warn you, Mother," Billy said. "The sol-diers will be coming this morning. You need to be prepared."

"Soldiers?" Her voice cracked again. "And why in the name of all that's Holy would there be soldiers coming to the house of James McAdie, may God have mercy on his soul? Is that vagabond Bonaparte hiding in my wee barn?"

Dougal and his brother laughed aloud, which earned them a glance as sharp as a dagger from the old woman.

"Nae, Mother," Billy said, his voice even and calm. "They will be coming for the sheep."

"The sheep? What nonsense are you on about, Billy Hanks?" the old woman said. "I have a milk cow and two goats here. That is all I can care for. I have no sheep."

"Oh, but I think you do," said Dougal Ross. He gestured out towards the bowl-shaped valley floor of the broad glen. Mother McAdie followed his gesture, and gasped. Nearly half the broad valley was filled with animals, most sleeping, some grazing. There were thousands of them.

"Mary, Mother of God," the old woman said, crossing her-self furiously as she beheld the sight. "What have you done, Billy Hanks?"

"We have decided to rid ourselves of these beasts, which are being used to force the people out from their homes in the glens and valleys throughout the country," Billy said. "Dougal, Willie and I have been busy collecting these beasties and driving them back to Inverness."

The old woman turned to look at Billy. "This is not Inverness, Billy Hanks," she said. "This is Strath Rusdale. Have you gone mad?"

He smiled at her and patted her on the arm.

"Nae, Mother, I am not mad," he said. "But we have run out of time. The government has heard of our plans and sent the soldiers to arrest us and recover these beasties. The boys and I must go now, else we'll be spending some time in gaol or be placed upon a ship bound for Botany Bay."

"I should think so!" Mother McAdie said with a cackle. "The lairds who own these sheep must be furious that someone has stolen their animals."

"Returned," said Dougal Ross. "We didn't steal a one of them. We were just returning them from whence they came."

She regarded the young man with a steely gaze. "So you say," she said. "I daresay Lord Munro, Lady Sutherland and their friends might have a different opinion."

"Indeed they do," said Billy Hanks. "Which is why we are leaving them here for the soldiers. We must go now, before they arrive. They'll be looking for us."

"Where are you going?" the old woman wanted to know.

Billy Hanks smiled and shook his head.

"We canna tell you that, old woman," he said. "So that when they ask, you may truthfully say you do not know. But fear not, the boys and I know the country fairly well, and we'll do our best to keep out of their way."

"Do you have time for some porridge and a bit of bread?" she asked. "It won't take long to make ready."

"Thank you kindly, Mother," Billy Hanks said with a bow. "But we'd best get underway. I suspect the Black Watch left Alness an hour ago. They'll be here before the sun is half-high."

"Then Godspeed, Billy Hanks," the old woman said. "Godspeed to you."

IN FACT, THE three columns of soldiers, all protesting under their breath about the lack of sleep after the previous day's long march, had left Alness shortly after the dawn, and were making their way up the narrow road that followed the twists and turns of the rocky River Rusdale as it spilled out of the hills. It was slow going, slower than Major Darnell would have liked, but the road, a mere path really, would not allow the men to march at the same speed as they could on a wider highway.

Sheriff MacLeod had received word the night before, when the party staggered into the small town of Alness, that the sheep had arrived in the broad valley at Boath, deep in the broad glen of Strath Rusdale. Since the invading party coming down from the moors on the higher ground had only begun reaching the valley floor late at night, there had been no good intelligence on how many men were driving the sheep, nor what arms they bore. Hearing this, Major Darnell had ordered his men armed with muskets and ball, bayonets at the ready. Carrying the bulky weapons had slowed the party down even more.

So it was about the noon hour when the first scouts breached the last hill and saw the broad, open bowl of the valley floor, now filled with several thousands of white-backed sheep, placidly munching the tender shoots of grass and wildflower. Yet, strangely, these first scouts could see no human forms among or around the sheep. Dutifully, they sent word back.

Within the hour, Darnell and MacLeod rode up. Quickly, the major dispatched troops to begin searching for the miscreants who had driven the beasts to this desolate place. Squadrons of the red coats were sent up the banks of the river, and into the forests that rose on the gentle hills that surrounded the valley.

"It seems the rebel army has deserted," MacLeod said. "Perhaps their artillery is bogged down on the mountain passes."

Major Darnell was in no mood for sarcasm. He pointed to the collection of huts, barns and fences that defined the only human habitation within sight. All else was nature, sky and mountain. "Bring me those people," he ordered with a bark. "They must have seen *something*."

More soldiers were pouring into the glen from the river path. Their sergeants directed them to sit and wait, orders which they gratefully obeyed. Some began to clean their weapons, while others merely laid down and fell fast asleep.

A group of red coats approached, pushing before them two old, white-haired men and the old woman who had spoken to Billy Hanks earlier in the morning. She alone walked with her head held high, while the old men fell on their knees before the major and implored him, in Gaelic, for mercy.

"Silence!" he said. "Sheriff, as I do not have the tongue of these ruffians, ask them when the sheep arrived and where the men driving them have gone."

MacLeod spoke to the two men, reassuring them. They responded eagerly to him, their heads bowed and eyes downcast, pointing to the sheep in the glen.

MacLeod turned to Darnell.

"They have no idea where the sheep came from," he said. "They said they woke this morning to find the glen filled with beasts. They are afraid you will charge them with thievery. They say they saw nothing, heard nothing in the night."

"Arrest them," Darnell said, his mouth drawn tight with anger. "Perhaps a few nights in the gaol will freshen their memories." He turned to look at the old woman.

"What about you?" he said. "What did you hear in the night?"

Mother MacAdie put her hands on her hips and looked Major Darnell in the face. In Gaelic, she began to speak and continued to do so for some time, gesturing from time to time as she spoke. When she was finished, Darnell turned to MacLeod.

"She says that many years ago, when she was still just a wee girl, a religious man came to this strath," he said. "She says he was old, and dressed in rags, but that he had the second sight. He was a seer, a fortune-teller. At that time, many families lived in this glen, men, women and children, raising cattle, raising crops, going off to war when their chiefs asked them. But this seer, this teller of the future, he warned the people that their time was drawing to an end. The sheep, he said, the sheep were coming. O woe to the land, he said, the Great Sheep are coming! He was dressed in rags, this man, and so no one paid him much mind. She says the people laughed and chased him away. But then the people began to leave the glen. Their chiefs turned their back on the people. Some were driven off, some left on their own. And now look, she said. The strath is full of sheep and empty of their clan. She said that the seer was right. The land is cursed, cursed by the sheep, and all is woe among her people."

"I do not have the time for such nonsense," Darnell exploded. "Did she see anything?"

MacLeod said a few words; Mother MacAdie responded.

"She says she heard and saw nothing. She said, 'the Great Sheep have come, as it was foretold. It is the Year of the Sheep.'"

THE SQUADRONS AND patrols returned within the hour. They had eight men in custody. They had found the men asleep in the forest, or wandering near the river. Most of the men were of the Clan Ross, which was prevalent in the area. None of them admitted to knowing anything at all about the sheep. Or the men who had driven them here to Strath Rusdale.

"We shall take them all back to Dingwall and let your justice see what it can do to loosen their tongues," the major decided. "Sheriff, please organize the men who have followed us here to drive the herds back to Dingwall as well. We'll let Lord Munro sort out the next steps."

"The thieves are probably hightailing it back across the Kildermorie pass," the sheriff said. "If you had horses, a cavalry, you could probably catch them."

"But I don't," the major said darkly. "So their apprehension will have to wait for another day."

At that moment, high on the slopes of Kildermorie, where the streams began that would form into the north-flowing River Carron, Billy Hanks bid farewell to the brothers Ross and the men of Glen Grudie.

"You're not returning to Glencullen, then?" Dougal Ross asked as they clasped each other's hands.

"Nae, not yet," Billy Hanks replied. "I have business to attend to in Dingwall first."

"Dingwall!" Dougal was surprised. "The bloody Black Watch will go back to Dingwall. The soldiers will be all over."

"Aye, tis true," Billy said. "But some of our brothers will be there as well, locked away in the sheriff's gaol. I must attend to them. And it will be possible for a body to learn something of what Lord Munro and the others have planned next for us, if that body is on the streets of Dingwall with his ears wide open."

Dougal Ross chuckled as the cool wind of the mountain plateau ruffled through his long red hair and beard. Low clouds were blowing over the rocky peaks above them and a mist began to creep down the slopes. "You are a cipher, Billy Hanks," he said.

"Aye, that I am," Billy agreed. "Now take care, Dougal. The lairds will strike back against what we have done these last days. They will send someone to Glen Grudie to find and arrest you and your men. It may be the Black Watch who come, or the sheriff with a crowd of men behind him. But they will come for you before the summer is half done. Keep your watch in place, have a plan to escape to higher ground when they approach. They may come soon, they may come later, but come they will. Be ready."

"Aye, we will," Dougal said. "We'll take our cattle to the high grounds for the summer. No one will follow us there."

"Be ready." Billy Hanks repeated his warning. "I know this Darnell who commands the Black Watch," he said. "He is a brutal man. If his blood is up, there is no man, woman or child who's life will be safe. He is a monster."

"And he will be a dead monster if he ventures into Glen Grudie," Dougal Ross said. "I swear it on the names of my forefathers!"

The men clasped their hands again. Billy Hanks turned and began walking swiftly in the direction they had just come. Dougal Ross and the men of Grudie watched until he disappeared into the swirling mountain mists, and then they turned for home.

BOOK II

16

Paris: June 1791

The carriage carrying Sir George Granville Leveson-Gower, His Majesty's Ambassador Plenipotentiary to the Court of the Most Christian Majesties of France, Louis XVI and his wife Marie Antoinette, proceeded slowly through the crowded streets of Paris. The Earl of Gower had left his expansive home on the rue de Faubourg Sainte-Honore late in the morning to travel to the British embassy, located on the rue Jacob on the left bank of the Seine, in the St Germain des Pres district. But, like every day, the streets were crowded with people wearing their jaunty red caps, most with the tricolor ribbons, symbols of the Revolutionary fervor that had taken over the capital city. In some of the city's many squares and parks, a politician or an ordinary citizen belonging to one faction or another mounted a bench or a stool or a plain wooden box, and began to harangue anyone who would listen about the issues of the day. If the speech-making was particularly forceful and colorful in language, a crowd would assemble to listen, nod, applaud, and cheer. If the points being made were done so with patriotic feeling that aroused the emotions of the crowd, they might respond with a spontaneous march to some nearby government building, there to demand reform of one kind or another from whatever hapless functionary they could confront. Sometimes, if the bloodlust was up in the crowd, they would storm inside and pluck some poor unfortunate bureaucrat out of his office to face rough justice on the street outside. Likewise, if the speech-making turned out poorly, and the growing crowds of listeners disapproved of the sentiments being expressed, the rough justice of the people listening *towards the speaker* could be immediate and harsh.

Earl Gower did not pay much attention to these daily public debates going on throughout the districts of Paris. His carriage avoided the Place de la Revolution, formerly known as the Place Louis XV, where the dreaded guillotine had been set up on its central wooden stage, and was busy every day reducing the numbers of enemies to the state. The carriage in which he rode was old, sagging at the springs, and in need of a coat of paint. That was deliberate, as the Earl had been warned when he arrived in France the previous year to avoid all outwardly ostentatious demonstrations of wealth and power. Those could prove to be fatal, as many an aristocrat had discovered at the hands of the newly empowered and armed plebian classes. So he rode through the noisome streets in his old, squeaking carriage, pulled by a single old gray horse, and only the presence of his two Swiss bodyguards, riding on the rear platform, gave the slightest indication that a man of power might be riding within. And even his bodyguards were dressed not in fine livery, but in dusty old overcoats that seemed in desperate need of repair.

Gower did not bother looking outside his carriage at what might be going on in the crowded streets. For one thing, his myopia was bad enough that he could barely focus on anything more than five feet away. But he was deep in thought as he rode, remembering that afternoon a year and more since when he had been given his instructions.

"MILORD: THE RIGHT Honorable Earl of Gower, sir."

Gower had been ushered into the presence of William Pitt the Younger, the Prime Minister, in his expansive Whitehall offices, with huge windows overlooking the busy scene below on the River Thames. The day had been blustery and cold, with clouds hiding and unveiling bursting rays of sun, like shining a torch around a dark room, illuminating this building, now that neighborhood, now this section of the waterfront.

Pitt sat behind a desk whose polished surface seemed to cover an acre in space. Two fully uniformed, red-coated military guards framed the doorway, holding ceremonial pikes of highly polished steel set atop long round wooden handles. At least, Gower *hoped* they were merely ceremonial.

The Prime Minister was a young man, barely over the age of 30, and had an aura of youthful vigor about him, in the way he moved and carried himself. His eyes were sharp and clear and Gower felt them take in the man standing before him. Gower bowed, deeply, then stood erect and waited for a command.

"Come, George, sit," the Prime Minister said, gesturing towards a chair set beside his monstrous desk. "How is your beautiful bride? I so enjoyed the dinner of Tuesday last. I must have you and Elizabeth to dine with me at Downing Street. You would enjoy seeing some of the changes I have made to the place to make it a less awkward place to live."

Gower smiled and nodded. He did not know the Prime Minister well, although they were former colleagues in the Commons. And, being of the same general age, Gower being a few years the older, they were considered by many in government to be leaders of the future. Gower. nephew to the Duke of Bridgewater and his wife, the inheritor of nearly a million acres of land in Scotland's far northern Sutherlandshire, were firmly ensconced in London's bustling social scene, entertaining and being entertained almost nightly. Their circles of friends and acquaintances included all the major players of society, including, of course, the Prime Minister himself.

"George," the Prime Minister ended the small talk and went straight to the point. "Lord Grenville and I have decided to appoint you to represent His Majesty to the Court at Versailles," Pitt said.

"I?" Gower had repeated, unable to keep the incredulity out his voice. "Ambassador? To France? Do you think that is wise? I have no experience in the foreign service. Very little in politics, for that matter"

Pitt smiled and nodded. "Exactly," he said. "I don't have to tell you how dicey things are in Paris these days. After the tragedy of America, it appears that the French are thinking of upending their country next."

"Forgive me for interrupting," Gower said, interrupting. "But would not that indicate the need for the appointment of, er, a more *experienced* gentleman than myself?"

Pitt nodded, as if expecting Gower's objection. "Yes, George, it would," he said. "And therein lies the problem. I could appoint the Duke of something or other to go over the Paris and remonstrate with the unruly crowds, and the even more unruly representatives of their National Assembly, but no one would listen to him. In fact, they might do something a whole lot worse. Dukes are treated with great suspicion in France at the moment, especially British Dukes. No, George, I need a dependable and wise pair of eyes and ears on the ground in Paris, someone who won't be easily recognizable, someone who won't raise suspicions, someone who is not objectionable to anyone due to his position in life."

"And that would be someone like me," Gower said. "I'm not sure if I should be honored or insulted, Prime Minister."

William Pitt threw back his head and laughed, delighted.

"Quite so, George, quite so," he chuckled. "I hope you will eventually come to consider this appointment to be the honor it is intended to be. Foreign Minister Grenville and I spent a great deal of time considering various candidates for this job, and you were far and away the most felicitous choice. It is quite likely that almost no one in France has ever heard of you. You will be a clean slate, George, perfect for our purposes. Yet, of course, you are a loyal member of the party. And, inasmuch as you will one day soon stand to inherit your uncle the Duke of Bridgewater's rather extensive holdings, I am certain you are willing to help preserve our kingdom and way of life."

Gower, embarrassed at this rather plainspoken assessment of his future prospects, accurate as they were, could only nod.

"And I must add: this will be a dangerous appointment," the Prime Minister continued. "We will, of course, do everything in our power to protect and defend you in your assignment, but you should be fully aware that if civil society in France breaks down completely, and the indications are plain to see by anyone that such a thing is not without possibility, and indeed becomes more likely by the day, then you may be left to protect and defend yourself as best you can."

"What about Elizabeth?" Gower asked. "Is it safe for her to accompany me?"

Pitt frowned. "I would strongly recommend that you do not take her with you to Paris," he said. "It is no place for a woman these days. Or children. Especially a British woman. Especially a rich British woman."

"She is Scottish by birth," Gower said.

Pitt was shaking his head. "It is up to you, sir. But my recommendation in the matter remains strongly in the negative."

"What would you have me do there?"

Pitt nodded again, as if he had been expecting the question. Gower hoped the expectation was approving.

"The usual," he said, picking up and glancing at a sheet of paper on his desk. We need to be kept abreast of the goings-on inside Louis' court. Who advises the king, who supports him, who opposes him ... things of that nature. I really don't give a whistle for whichever party or faction eventually rises to the top of the heap over there—as far as His Majesty's government is concerned, the French can spend the next hundred years arguing over new Constitutions and oaths and citizenship, arresting damned priests and corrupt aristocrats and all the rest. I am more concerned with our other European alliances. There is talk of the Austrians invading France to protect and defend the Queen, Marie Antoinette; perhaps in league with the Swedes and maybe even the Russians. That would upset the apple cart that I have spent the last five years rather carefully building. His Majesty would not like that to happen. Nor would I."

"Nor I," Gower quickly added.

Pitt went on as if he had heard nothing.

"We especially need to know about the state of French arms," he said. "Right now, it appears that only Monsieur de Lafayette controls what can accurately be called an army, and those troops are all concentrated in Paris to keep control of what passes for the public order. There may be smaller groups of men under arms in other parts of the country, and if they ever are brought together under one command, there will certainly be trouble. In France and in all of Europe. And I have heard whisperings that the French intend to rebuild their navy. That would be important news for us to know."

"So I am to become a spy for Britain," Gower said, frowning.

"Only in part," the Prime Minister said. "Most of your duties will involve attending social events at the Court. Parties, dinners, dances. They are big on that sort of stuff, the French," he said. "Even now, when the whole thing threatens to come crashing down around their heads. Information flows freer where the wine is poured with a liberal hand. But your other duties are those more typical of a British ambassador: you will intercede on behalf of any of our citizens and their commerce that might be caught up in any of the troubles going on. You will protect British financial obligations and investments, such as are made or administered in France or elsewhere in Europe. You will be asked, from time to time, to make council with the King of France or his appointed officials to discuss various policy or military concerns our own King may have."

Gower paused. Then he spoke. "I am honored, Sir, to be considered for such an important position," he said. "But I cannot believe I am the most qualified candidate to undertake this assignment. Surely ..."

Pitt waved his hand in dismissal. "No, George," he said, staring across the desktop. "You are the perfect candidate. You are young, rich and unknown. You are also intelligent. And you are a loyal subject of the King. And the Party. You know what we need, and I'm certain you will find a way to provide it. And you won't be alone – we have good people in Paris, very good. Lord Grenville and the Foreign Office will brief you on all the details. You will be an important cog in the machine, George, but there will be many people to provide assistance along the way. You may count on that."

"You leave me little choice, Prime Minister," Gower began...

"Good man," Pitt said, jumping to his feet and coming around the desk to pump Gower's hand. "Capital! Now, please return here tomorrow morning at eleven. Lord Grenville will be here and we shall visit Windsor to see the King. Eleven sharp, George!"

THINGS HAD PROCEEDED in a whirlwind after that, Gower recalled in his jostling carriage as it passed over the Pont de Neuf, the grayish waters of the Seine flowing turgidly on to the sea. There had been the meeting with George III, recently recovered from a lengthy bout of the madness that had led to lengthy debates in both houses of Parliament over the appointment of a regent. Gower had found His Majesty to be quite mentally acute, and the king had participated in a spirited discussion with Prime Minister Pitt and his foreign secretary, Lord Grenville, over the potential issues that might arise in France.

It had been the King who decided the issue of whether or not to allow Elizabeth Gordon of Sutherland to accompany her husband to Paris.

"Of course she must go with you," the King had cried. "Of course she must. A man in a position of such importance must always have the wise counsel and gentle influence of his beloved wife. Unthinkable to leave her behind for a year or more, unthinkable! Besides, she will be an asset to you in Louis' Court. I hear that fat bastard has an eye for a good looking woman. Perhaps some of the other members of the Court will as well. And they say Louis' Austrian whore has his ear. Perhaps your wife can get close to the Queen, find out something, eh?"

The three politicians, understanding that royalty is alone free to gossip about other royals, let the King's salty observations pass without comment. But all three immediately saw that the King was right: it would be helpful to Gower's mission to use his wife to build relationships in the French court. It is often easier for a man to be honest and straightforward with an interested, encouraging woman.

And, as it turned out, the King had been correct. Elizabeth had immediately ingratiated herself, both with the French King and especially with his wife the Queen. Marie Antoinette had taken to Elizabeth almost from first sight, and they were soon close and constant companions at the Court.

And Pitt had also been right in his assessment of the embassy staff on the rue Jacob. Sir Jeremy Decker, the Chargés d'Affaires, was the quintessential professional diplomat. Although Decker was a large, ruddy and somewhat boisterous man by nature, he was also shrewd, strategic and knowledgeable about French politics and society. And Sir Jeremy seemed to know everyone in Paris. More importantly, he seemed to know everyone's secrets. Earl Gower had long stopped being amazed at the things Decker knew; had long ago learned to trust the man and follow his instructions to the letter. They had become an excellent, formidable, and efficient team and Gower's dispatches back to Whitehall, which incorporated Decker's excellent sources and advice, had been praised for their insight and wisdom.

Thomas Thackerey, chief Consular Officer, was another asset in the embassy. Because his mother was French, Thackerey had spent a great deal of his childhood in the nation and was fluent in the language. He had married a French woman, the sister of some landowning Count from the Languedoc region. The unfortunate Count had long since been taken to his appointment with La Guillotine in the Place de la Revolution, which had only reinforced Madame Thackerey's determination to help her husband's efforts on behalf of the British nation. She had proved very helpful in her connections inside the court of Louis XVI, providing a steady stream of excellent gossip and inside information.

Sir Jeremy was in total command of the rest of the staff at the embassy. The various assistants, secretaries, attachés and other staffers were completely loyal to him, and obeyed his every command without question. Everyone on the embassy staff understood the dangers of living in Paris at this time, especially for representatives of a foreign nation never well-loved by the French. In this hair-trigger environment, when the passions of the crowd might erupt into bloody conflagration at any time, the British subjects understood that they walked a narrow and dangerous path every time they ventured outside the doors of what the locals called the *Hôtel d'Angleterre*.

Surprising even himself, Gower had found himself fitting neatly into the day-to-day operations of the embassy and its work. He was smart enough to understand that there was a great deal he did not know about diplomacy and how it operated, especially in such fraught conditions as existed in Paris during these days of upheaval. So he let Sir Jeremy handle most of that, and concentrated mainly on fulfilling his role as spelled out by Lord Grenville the Foreign Secretary and the Prime Minister. Once the staff of the embassy understood that, unlike previous tenants of the office of the ambassador, the Earl of Gower had no intentions of trying to control every aspect of their operations, they accepted him without condition. Gower was certain that many secrets were kept from him, but he decided not to worry about that, and instead concentrate on doing his job, task by task, day by day. So far, this approach seemed to be working quite well.

When his carriage arrived at the embassy on the rue du Jacob, Gower waited for his two shabbily dressed bodyguards to descend from their postilion, clear the way in front of the embassy door of passersby and visitors waiting in line to come inside, and finally signal with a curt nod that the ambassador could descend. He quickly made his way through the marble halls into his private suite of offices on the second floor and waited for the familiar rotund shape of Sir Jeremy to join him.

"Milord," said Sir Jeremy as he eased himself into a chair before the Earl's desk. "I trust you passed the night comfortably."

Gower blinked at the man, and rewarded him with a wry smile. "As well as can be expected with the usual marching and singing and banging of pots and pans going on in the streets outside until nearly dawn," he said.

"Indeed, milord," Sir Jeremy said. "It seems that, having thrown off the yoke of the oppressive governance of both the Church of Rome and the ancient aristocracy, the people have France have decided to use their new freedoms to avoid sleeping at all costs."

Gower, never a man to appreciate a jest, merely held out his hand. Sir Jeremy, thinking to himself, not for the first time, that the ambassador was perhaps the most humorless man he had ever met, passed over a slew of papers. Gower, with a frown, peered closely at each one.

"'Tis the usual collection of irrelevant things that need a signature from the ambassador," Sir Jeremy said. "Nothing of great import."

"Fine," Gower said, taking up his quill pen and preparing to dip it into the ink well. He glanced up at Sir Jeremy, who continued to sit calmly and peer across the desk. "Is there something else?"

"Yes, milord, there is," Sir Jeremy said, tapping his fingers on the arms of his chair. "I have taken the liberty of arranging a meeting for you this evening."

Gower had begun affixing his signature to the many papers that Decker had handed him. "Mmmm?" he said as he signed. "A meeting with whom?"

"Mr. Quentin Craufurd, milord," the other man said. "He wishes to discuss certain financial matters with you."

Gower paused and looked up at Decker. "Craufurd?" he said, raising an eyebrow. "The banker and art dealer?"

Sir Jeremy smiled. "Quite so, milord," he said. "He wishes to meet with you privately this evening. He asked that just the two of you might dine together. I have taken the liberty of reserving a private room at the Grande Taverne on the rue de Richelieu. You know the place, I assume?"

Gower nodded. He also knew Craufurd, and had purchased several fine paintings from the man for his growing collection back in London. Though Craufurd was known as a financial dealmaker, he had a side business in the buying and selling of fine art. Indeed, in many cases, the two avocations went hand in hand. "What does he want? I have no need at present for any of his pictures."

"That, milord, he was not at liberty to divulge to your humble servant," Sir Jeremy said. "But I do not believe his request for your company has anything to do with the gentleman's extensive collection of fine art. Mr. Craufurd is known to be well connected to the financial accounts of the King and the government. I suspect that the royal personage may be thinking of the future and hoping to preserve something of the royal fortune in the event that, shall we say, future events do not portend to continue said personage's position. Do you understand?"

Gower frowned again. He had little patience for diplomatic jargon, preferring to speak plainly and to the point. "Yes," he said. "The King of France wants to invest his fortune, or what's left of it, somewhere where the people can't take it away from him."

Sir Jeremy chuckled softly. "Quite so, milord, quite so," he said.

"Is our government prepared to assist the King in this endeavor?" Gower asked.

Decker's fingers began tapping nervously on the chair arms again.

"That quite depends, sir, on what the proposal may or may not entail," he said carefully.

Gower continued frowning. More jargon. More diplomatic evasion. "So I suppose I must go to dinner with this Craufurd fellow tonight and find out what he wants," Gower said, taking up his pen again.

"Milord." Sir Jeremy stood and prepared to leave the office. "I will have a briefing paper for your review before you leave. I'll arrange the carriage to depart here at half past seven." He was nearly out the door, when a cough from Gower halted him in his tracks.

"I should inform my wife that I will not be dining at home tonight," Gower said. "Where is she this afternoon?"

Sir Jeremy bowed. "I believe she is with Her Majesty the Queen at the Tuileries," he said. "I will have a note sent at once."

Gower nodded silently, picked up the pen and began signing his name again.

THE COUNTESS GOWER, who thought of herself merely as Elizabeth Gordon, although she was also the 19th Chief of Clan Sutherland in her native Scotland as well as the wife of Earl Gower, sat in the shade of a plane tree in the Gardens of the Tuileries Palace and watched her son, George, playing with a phalanx of tin soldiers and the Dauphin of France, Louis-Charles. The two boys, like any other four year olds, were totally engrossed in their battle, to which they added their high-pitched sounds of cannonades exploding and horses screaming in fear. The boys were so caught up in the imagination of their game that they paid no heed either to the Countess, the half-dozen real and fully armed soldiers of the National Guard who formed a rough protective perimeter around the shaded grove, the several dozen citizens of Paris who stood nearby gaping at the scene, nor the center of that attention, the elegant and regal person of Her Most Christian Majesty, Marie Antoinette the Queen.

Even with the presence of the Guardsmen, Elizabeth could not help but keep glancing over at the motley collection of citizens that stood nearby watching their Queen and the Dauphin. While some of the women in the crowd were smiling and tried to catch the Queen's eye with a wave of a handkerchief, the men who stood there looked at the Queen's party with stern, disapproving countenances and arms folded against their chests. Elizabeth watched as three men came in from the Grand Carrousal and joined the group of citizens: these new arrivals wore the clothes of peasants, the *sans-culottes*, with the now-traditional red woolen cap festooned at the top with a tricolor ribbon. The cap and the ribbon and the pants were the new symbols of the Revolution, worn by all who believed in its goals, whatever those might be.

The three new arrivals spoke with some of the other royal watchers, and pointed at the Queen.

"Behold the whore of Austria," one of them called out, his voice harsh. "Her filth infects our royal family! Death to the whore!"

"Death to the whore…death to the whore!" The other two peasants took up the cry and repeated it, over and over. The other citizens standing there looked surprised at the new arrivals, but soon, they, too, were repeating the cry.

"Death to the whore! Death to the whore of Austria!"

The sergeant of the Guardsman spoke to another solider, who in turn nodded at some of his men, and they began to sidle over to where the citizens were gathered.

"That's enough," one of the soldiers growled. "Move along, citizens, move along."

Four of the soldiers in the guard made a barrier with their long rifles affixed with sharp bayonets, and they began to push the group of citizens away from the Queen's party and toward the entranceway to the Gardens. There were shouts of protest and some pushing, along with more catcalls and accusations, but eventually, the crowd dispersed and quiet returned to the gardens.

Elizabeth watched the Queen watch the boys at play. While the people were calling vile things to her, the Queen had remained calm and unresponsive. She was used, now, to the mobs of Paris, and the calumny tossed her way. She had learned to ignore it all, at least outwardly, although Elizabeth knew that the name-calling and the harsh feelings expressed by the people hurt the Queen deeply. Raised from girlhood in Austria to the royal station, Marie Antoinette believed that the people were, in a real sense, her children, as much as the young boy born of her blood who was playing at soldiers beneath the tree next to her. She did not understand why the people suddenly hated her so. But they did. That was the new reality.

Elizabeth saw the Queen smile to herself as the boys organized a flanking attack on what seemed to be an impregnable castle; heard her laugh aloud as the attack caused grievous damage, resulting in the overturning of large numbers of unfortunate tin soldiers to the delighted huzzahs of the two young generals.

"Maman, maman!" cried the Dauphin, "We have captured the fortress! The enemy has surrendered! Monsieur George and I have won the day!"

"Bravo, bravo, my brave little men," the Queen answered, clapping her hands in delight. "Would *mon generales* perhaps be interested in a bit of cake? I believe Madame Campan has thoughtfully brought some to us in her basket."

The Queen's lady in waiting brought forth the basket and the boys came running for their treats. The Queen insisted that they thank Madam Campan, as etiquette demanded, and then they all sprawled out on the grassy lawn, basking in the warm sunshine and the pride of their military prowess. The Queen watched them a bit longer, and sighed.

"It is strange, Madame Countess, isn't it? That our boys play at games of war, with the attacking and the killing and the destruction; yet at the end they have some cake and nothing is real. Yet all around us are real men of war, and real feelings of anger and hatred, and the real destruction they can create is all very real. What is it that Monsieur Moliere wrote? 'The world is a strange affair,' no?"

Elizabeth was not sure how to respond. Certainly, she could not dispute the truth of the Queen's observations. The Queen had experienced the hatred herself, personally, some eighteen months earlier when a mob of women from the city had marched out to Versailles to petition the Court for food. One thing had led to another and the vicious mob, reinforced by angry men with pikes and swords and long knives, had attacked, killing her bodyguards and threatening her very life. She had fled to the safety of her husband the King's chambers and, later that day, the Royal family had been driven to Paris and installed in their new quarters in the old, dilapidated Tuileries, a three hundred year-old palace that had seen better days. The King, his Queen and their children, the twelve-year-old Marie-Therese and the four-year-old Dauphin, were not exactly prisoners of the National Assembly; yet neither were they exactly free to go where they would. Their status in the city and the world was not exactly clear to anyone. The King was allowed the freedom to hunt, an activity he enjoyed perhaps more than any other, and the royal family had been allowed to decamp to the cooler and more elegant surroundings of their palace at Saint Cloud the previous summer. But now they were required to stay within the musty halls of the Tuileries, save for the occasional Holy Mass or an appearance at some public event approved by the National Assembly. They were under the protection of General Lafayette and his Guardsmen, but their every move was closely watched. The Queen's own suite of rooms was on the ground floor, and she had been forced to install heavy curtains on the windows because of all the people of Paris who came to stare at her through her windows, night and day. It was a strange existence, being prisoners, but not in prison. Guarded, yet still considered royal. The Queen had noticed that her hair, one of her proudest and most luxurious possessions, had begun to turn gray in places even though she was but halfway through her third decade of life.

"The world, Majesty, is always quite mad," Elizabeth finally said as they watched the boys laughing to themselves. "But the dreams of young boys are perfectly sensible ... to themselves at least."

The Queen smiled and nodded her approval. "Yes," she said. "That is so. I am so thankful that you bring your little George here for Louis-Charles. He enjoys his company so much, and it is a needed diversion from the reality of his life."

"All boys, even future kings, should have friends to play with," Elizabeth said, smiling back. "Queens, too, I should think."

Marie Antoinette laughed aloud. Elizabeth was glad to hear the sound: the Queen rarely laughed these days. "I will set up the soldier men in a row, and you shall knock them down," the Queen said, "And then we shall have a bit of cake!"

Elizabeth joined her in laughter.

An equerry came rushing out from the palace clutching a white paper note. He passed it, with a deep bow, to Madame Campan with a whispered explanation; she in turn came over to the bench and presented the note to Elizabeth with a curtesy. "From the embassy," she whispered.

Elizabeth read the note, and now it was her turn to sigh.

"My husband regrets he will not be dining at home to-night," she announced.

"Again!" the Queen said, smiling at her friend. "One might think Lord Gower has a mistress!" She saw Elizabeth's face darken and a frown form on her lips and quickly added, "Of course, we both know that such a thing would be impossible with your husband. Has he not told me himself many times how utterly devoted he is to you and his family?"

"Yes," Elizabeth said, "I am sure it is business. He has so much to do these days."

"Of course," the Queen nodded. She brightened. "Would you like to stay and dine with us? I am sure His Highness would not object. If he gets back from his hunting before the dinner is served."

"Thank you," Elizabeth said. "It is most gracious of you. But I must decline. I need to return home and see to Charlotte before her bedtime. Some other time, perhaps."

"You are welcome at any time," the Queen said. "I know there are hundreds of rules and traditions dictating when the wife of the British ambassador might dine with the Queen, but I am prepared to overturn all those rules. Perhaps I, too, am a revolutionary!"

The two women tittered with delight at the Queen's jest.

"Come, George," Elizabeth called to her son. "Bid Monsieur farewell for now. We must return home."

The little boy stood before the Dauphin, drew himself up formally and bowed deeply from the waist.

"Au revoir, Majesty," he said in his squeaky little voice. "I hope you remain well until we meet again."

The Dauphin inclined his head slightly at George, and smiled. "Good-bye," he said. "Please come again soon."

17

ower's carriage DROPPED him off at the Grande Taverne just before eight. A liveried servant opened the carriage door for him, and another bowed him into the well-lighted entrance hall where the maître d' was waiting to escort the ambassador to the first floor, and a private dining salon at the front of the building, with large windows overlooking the green park that lay in front of the Theatre Francaise. The evening was warm, yet the staff had laid a small fire in the grate, for effect, and opened the windows to try and catch the desultory breeze.

There were two red leather chairs in front of the carved fireplace, and in one of them sat Quentin Craufurd. Gower had met the man on several previous occasions; indeed, who in the diplomatic and aristocratic circles of Paris had not? He was quite an interesting man, this Craufurd, with connections that ran in several directions at once.

Gower had been to the man's home on the rue de Clichy and had in fact purchased several paintings and two fine marble pieces said to be of the Roman era from the man. Craufurd's home had been filled with wonderful art from all around the world. An avid collector, intent on filling his own home in London with the finest art treasures, Gower had been most impressed with the man's knowledge and taste.

The helpful dossier that Sir Jeremy had provided Gower before his departure from the embassy had reviewed Craufurd's known background. Born in Scotland, the third son of a wealthy landowner, Quentin Craufurd had made his way to the East Indies as had so many other "extra" sons of England's landed gentry. He had done quite well in commerce, first in India and then in Manila, where he spent nearly twenty years amassing a fortune said to be one of the largest in Europe. He had also acquired a mistress in Manila, the fabled Eleanore Sullivan. *Her* history was even more impressive than his own, according to Sir Jeremy's dossier. Born either in Ireland or Italy—the gossip was unsure of her origin—she had become one of the most well-traveled courtesans in Europe. Among her dalliances had been the Duke of Wurttemberg, the Emperor of Austria Franz Joseph (who happened to be the brother of Marie Antoinette), and several others until she had finally wed a wealthy Irishman, Frank Sullivan, who had made the mistake of taking his wife on a business trip to Asia. On that trip, in Manila, she and Craufurd had met, and fallen in love. Or so the gossip said: with Madame Eleanore, love was never a requirement for a relationship.

Nonetheless, once the inconvenient husband had been sent away, the couple had returned to Europe and settled in Paris, where such scandalous arrangements were merely sniffed at. Craufurd dabbled in his art business and also in private banking. He was well known among the aristocracy for being a reliable lender of hard capital to those who's gambling debts or bad decisions or excesses in consumption threatened the style of life to which they were accustomed. Craufurd's social connections and unconventional lifestyle endeared him to the upper classes; his shrewd eye for a deal and knowledge of which clients may not be able to repay his terms helped him, over time, to assemble a fine portfolio of property pledged as collateral: country houses, farms, pied-à-terre's and other valuable assets scattered throughout the whole of France and most of Europe as well.

Madame Eleanore, meanwhile, had also been busy working her way upwards through the social circles of the City of Light. Perhaps it had been her "friendship" with the Queen's late brother the Emperor, but it was not long before Madame and the Queen were the closest of friends. Naturally, the Queen's enemies, the pamphleteers and the pornographers, had soon produced reams of scurrilous tales of Sapphic love between the two. But of course, the Queen had for years been accused of sleeping with almost every conceivable person, male and female, in the entire Kingdom, so no one, other than the prurient, paid much attention to these latest whisperings. Indeed, on occasion, the two women had giggled together reading some of the worst accounts of their alleged love affair in one of the many hastily printed pamphlets that circulated regularly around the city.

Sir Jeremy's dossier had informed Gower that Craufurd maintained some important connections with bankers in Zurich, Vienna, Milan, Stockholm and Florence. This network of mostly anonymous gnomes were the men who actually controlled the vast fortunes that the various kings and queens, dukes and archdukes, counts and marquises thought they owned. They did not. They only owned the first right to ask for loans so they could equip armies, invade countries and vanquish enemies. The gnomes provided the liquid capital, and took it all back in the hard assets of land and property used as collateral.

Quentin Craufurd, Gower understood, was not quite at the same level as Europe's banking gnomes, despite his own impressive personal wealth. No, he was more a facilitator in this international financial game. He could propose certain transactions, the gnomes would agree to fund them or not, and Craufurd would take a small percentage of the deal as his fee. Quite lucrative and without the underlying risks of a war ending badly or a king suddenly dying of consumption.

Craufurd, who had been staring into the fire, started when he realized that Gower was standing next to him. He rose to greet his guest. Craufurd was elegantly outfitted in a suit of clothes of the finest silk, and a fine powdered wig with a black bow at the back. He was tall and fit, perhaps fifty years of age, but his face was unlined and ruddy with health. Gower thought he could see a bit of Scottish red in the man's eyebrows, and as they shook hands, he noted the fine gold rings that decorated several of the man's fingers.

"Lord Gower, thank you indeed for meeting me on short notice," Craufurd said, a very slight burr still noticeable in the man's voice.

"Not at all, Craufurd," Gower said with a short bow. "I am at your service."

Craufurd quickly called for champagne and the servant brought out two goblets on a polished silver tray. The elder man raised his glass at Gower.

"To profit," he said.

"And peace," returned Gower, and they clinked glasses and drank.

They swapped the latest gossip as they sat by the fire for some time. The Duc du Provence, the King's younger brother, was causing concern from his home base in Nice, well away from the chaotic politics of Paris. No one was quite sure which side the Duc was on: firmly behind his brother the King, on the side of those who would eliminate the monarchy altogether, or with those who favored ousting just the current occupant and perhaps installing another Bourbon on the throne instead, such as Provence himself.

Craufurd was doubtful. "Provence has no funds," he said. "He cannot raise an army of ten, much less ten thousand. Louis has nothing to worry about with him."

"What *does* the King have to worry about?" Gower asked.

Craufurd looked around to make sure the servants had left the room. It was dangerous to speak too candidly in Paris these days. The Assembly, the Jacobins, the other factions, and most of the countries of Europe all had eyes and ears everywhere.

"The King needs a change of locale," Craufurd said, his voice suddenly low and urgent. "The current situation is impossible. He is a virtual prisoner of the Assembly. He must wait for them to decide on a Constitution, on the future of the monarchy, on whether or not he and his Queen will live or die. Impossible! He must go."

"You mean…" Gower waited.

"He must leave France, and take his family with him," Craufurd said. "There is no other option left."

"Does the King agree?"

Craufurd stood up and began to pace.

"The King is unable to make a decision one way or the other," he said, shaking his head sadly. "It is most maddening. On Monday, he agrees that he must flee. On Tuesday, he says he must stay and fight for his rights. On Wednesday, he wants to go hunting. On Thursday, he stays in bed. On Friday, he must go to Mass. On Saturday, he agrees that he must flee. On Sunday … Oh, it is maddening! I thought we had finally convinced him of the need at Easter, when the mob refused to let him and the family journey to Saint Cloud for Mass. But the next week, he was back to his usual indecision."

"I can understand his hesitation," Gower said thoughtfully. "If the King decamps to another country, is that not a statement of resignation? Will his many enemies not take that act as a sign of abandonment, and eliminate the royal house once and for all?"

"They might ... until Louis can march back into Paris at the head of his own armies and restore his royal house to its rightful place," Craufurd said. "But he cannot convince his brother princes throughout Europe to stand at his side unless he takes forthright action to save his own throne. He must leave, and soon!"

Craufurd walked over to the open door and quietly shut it. He turned to look at Gower, eyes shiny with excitement.

"I will tell you, Lord Gower, that plans have been laid to accomplish this goal," Craufurd said. "I have paid some 5,000 livres to construct a new berlin coach for His Majesty and his family's use in their flight."

"Good God," Gower exclaimed. "That is an exceptional price for a coach!"

"It is an exceptional coach," the banker said with a proud smile. "I contracted with the finest *carrossier* in all of France to do the work. I told him it was for a wealthy client of mine who needed to make a journey to Moscow before the winter. It is large, it is sturdy, it has room enough for the King, Queen, their children and even the King's *tantes* if he insists on their going too."

"Do you know what will happen to you if the authorities learn of this plan?" Gower said.

"Of course," Craufurd shrugged. "All investments carry some degree of risk. I have judged this one to be worth it."

"Who else knows?"

"Other than the family and their most trusted servants, no one," Craufurd said. "Except for Count Fersen."

"The Swede?" Gower said. "Is it true what they say about him?"

"That he is the Queen's lover?" Craufurd chuckled. "Oh, I don't know. They may have had a dalliance a few years ago. It is of no importance; she is loyal always to the King. But Fersen is devoted to her, and wants desperately to see her free from the prison that is her life now in Paris."

"And what does the Queen think of this plan?"

"She is brave, that one," Craufurd said. "Eleanore says that she is ready to go tomorrow. She is adamant that the Dauphin be protected, no matter what happens. She understands that her future, and that of Louis, depends on the safety of their son. The people may hate her, and not be terribly pleased with Louis, but they love the boy. Or they love what they hope the boy may one day become: a King of whom France can be proud."

"Quite so," Gower said, nodding. "Where do they wish to go?"

"Ah, that is the first part of the problem, Sir," Craufurd said, and he began pacing back and forth again. "She cannot be seen to be running home to Austria, or the Austrian territories in the Low Countries. That would be seen as a direct insult to France and the monarchy, as you correctly surmised, would be over. They are thinking of staying within the borders of France, but in a district that is more friendly to the royals. And well fortified, of course."

"If there is such a thing as a friendly district," Gower said.

"Quite," Craufurd said, nodding. "Count Fersen has made arrangements for the family to journey to Montmedy, near Metz. There are troops in that region that are loyal, to her, and perhaps to him as well. Failing that, the Queen has expressed a desire for Switzerland, perhaps. They would probably allow the family to stay, at least until things calmed down."

"I suppose England is out of the question?"

"Oh, good God, yes!" Craufurd snorted. "Can you imagine what George would do with a French king hanging around London? He'd go quite mad again!"

Gower, not one for humor, let the irrepressible jibe pass without comment.

"But, Lord Gower, there is a second part of the problem, and that's why I asked you here tonight," Craufurd said. "Before the King leaves, he wants to make sure he has something to live on, once he gets wherever he's going."

"Ah," said Gower. Thinking: *now we will get down to it.*

"The Queen has asked me to assist her, and the King of course, in moving some of their assets out of Paris. Out of France, in fact. Out of reach, if you will."

Gower said nothing.

"Obviously, there is nothing we can do with the royal properties," the man continued. "Those will likely be confiscated by the National Assembly, if the royal family makes it out of the city. But I have been helping Louis quietly divest himself of certain property and become more, shall we say, liquid."

"And he has done so?" Gower asked.

"Yes, he has," Craufurd said. "It has been done very quietly, very secretly. If his enemies were to get wind of any of this, he would be in for trouble. I have been able to move some of this to various safe places; about half of the total. I need some help with the rest."

Gower said nothing, thinking. Finally, he looked up. "I am afraid His Majesty's government cannot be seen to be helping the King of France escape his country after having looted its vaults," he said. "That would be seen, and rightly so, of encompassing an act of war. I am quite certain that Lord Grenville, not to mention the Prime Minister, would agree with me on that."

"Milord, I cannot agree with you more," said Craufurd, somewhat to Gower's surprise. "I assure you, I am not asking the government of Great Britain to become involved in any such enterprise."

"Then what *are* you asking?" Gower said, his impatience with hidden meaning erupting.

Craufurd sat back down in the red leather chair and faced the ambassador.

"Do you know how much money France owes Great Britain?" he asked, eyebrows raised.

"No, I do not," Gower replied. "Is it a lot?"

"Oh, indeed it is, Sir!" Craufurd said with a wry smile. "I believe that the last time I checked, it was on the order of 500 million livres per year."

"Five hundred million?" Gower was stunned.

"That is correct, sir. The debts have been on the account books for years...decades in fact. Interest is accruing at its usual steady rate, as well. My contacts in Amsterdam, at the Wisselbank, have informed me that if the House of Bourbon is deposed from the throne of France, all of Europe will be cast into bankruptcy. It's all built on a house of cards, you see. France owes England, England owes Spain, Spain and the Germans owe the Austrians, and Russia...well, the Tsarina Catherine owes everybody! If one of the cards falls, the others will follow, as surely as night follows day."

"I...I had no idea," Gower stammered.

"No, few people do," Craufurd nodded. "But it is the truth. Each of these countries has invested in bonds issued by the other countries—it is how they continue to finance both war and peace. But poor Louis can no longer find anyone to purchase the bonds of France. It is easy to see why: no one is quite sure if France will survive, if Louis himself will survive, or what form of nation might emerge from the current upheavals. In short, France has become a bad risk, and thus threatens to cause the collapse the entire continent. Which is why I am hopeful that your government will provide the King of France some assistance to help him move himself and his funds, out of the danger that is Paris."

"What do you have in mind?" Gower said. The older man bent his head close to Gower's and began to tell him his plan.

SEVERAL HOURS LATER, after the men had concluded their discussion and enjoyed a fine dinner followed by an excellent bottle of Bordeaux, they bade each other good night. The staff summoned a hansom cab for each man and bowed them off into the darkness of the Parisian streets.

Neither man, each sated with fine food and ample drink, noticed the black coated figure lurking in one of the arched doorways of the Theatre across the street from the Taverne. The figure watched as the men's cabs sped off in opposite directions. Then, with a soft whistle, a horse was led out of the shadows of the nearby park, and the black coated man mounted and whirled the mount off in the direction of the Hotel de Ville, taking the broad passageway of the rue de Rivoli.

Though it was nearly midnight, the tall windows of the rococo edifice of Paris' city hall were brightly lit from within. People of all kinds streamed in and out of the doorways, engaged in official and scurrilous activities alike. The city may have been mostly asleep, but the work of the Revolution was endless.

The rider passed his horse off to one of the Guardsmen at the north entrance and strode rapidly inside. He took the steps two at a time to the first floor and continued down the marble hallway to the office of the Directoire of the National Guard. The soldiers at the entry waved him into the inner sanctum without delay.

Gilbert du Motier, the Marquis de Lafayette, was sprawled in a chair, his long, angular face creased with worry. As well it might, as Lafayette, one of the heroes of the American Revolution, was now the commander of the National Guard and the one man in all of France placed in charge of maintaining the public order. As such, he walked the seemingly impossible line of keeping the various revolutionary factions orderly, protecting the life of the besieged King and his family, yet allowing the slow-motion revolutionary proceeding of the still aborning French Republic find its way forward. The man in the black cloak studied the still young-looking General sitting exhausted in his chair and, not for the first time, pitied him his impossible task.

Lafayette looked up and waved the man forward.

"Henri," he said, his voice shaky with exhaustion. "What have we learned tonight?"

"Citizen Generale," Henri saluted and bowed. "The banker Craufurd dined this evening with Lord Gower, the British ambassador. They were together for some four hours at the Grande Taverne, after which they each returned to their home."

Lafayette nodded at this intelligence. "As we suspected," he said. "We must keep both of them under surveillance. There is something afoot. We must know what it is."

"I will add men to watch the banker," Henri said. "Shall I order a watch on the ambassador as well?"

Lafayette paused to consider. Money, as always, was in short supply. The Revolution had done many things, some good and some ill, but one thing it had yet to learn how to do was to make money appear and grow in the coffers of the government.

"We can afford a daytime watch only, Henri," he said reluctantly. "Put someone intelligent on it. If there are further indications, we will add men later."

Henri D'Anjou, Lafayette's most trusted undercover agent, bowed. "I shall handle the ambassador myself," he said. "Night and day, if that is required."

"I salute you, Citizen," the general said, smiling at the man standing before him. "Our country holds you in its debt. I know you will do your duty."

18

Lord Gower and his wife, as was their long standing habit, met for breakfast at eight o'clock. The servants brought him his usual plate of kippered herring, roasted potatoes, and eggs shirred with sherry. Elizabeth, by contrast, had a small plate of fruit, some cheese and toasted bread. The butler poured them each some coffee, an aromatic French roast.

"How was your dinner last night?" Elizabeth asked. She kept her voice level. Although she did not for a moment believe her husband was capable of having an affair with another woman, she had been unable to keep such thoughts at bay during the night. Her sleep had been restless.

"Most interesting," Gower said, as he scooped his food into his mouth. With his large, hooked nose, he often looked like a horse when he ate. Elizabeth kept her eyes elsewhere. "This man Craufurd seems to be highly connected with various factions around this city," Gower continued. "Even into the royal house."

"Oh?"

"Quite so," he said. "It appears that there may be an attempt to remove the King and his family from Paris."

"Really?" Elizabeth's attention was peaked. "Who wishes them to be removed? Where shall they go?"

"You misunderstand, m'dear," Gower said, patting his lips with his napkin and sipping from his coffee. "Craufurd is going to help the King escape from his captivity. He's had a new coach built for their use, and when it is all ready, they shall attempt to leave during the dark of night and make for Montmedy. There is a well-fortified castle there, and troops said to be loyal to the King. Count Fersen is helping. You know what they say about him and the Queen..."

He let the subject lie there, delicately.

"She is fond of him, I know," Elizabeth said. "But the Queen tells me she has ever been faithful to her King, in all things."

Gower waved his hand dismissively.

"Don't care, don't care," he said. "Gossip and women's tales. Not of interest."

"When is this ... this *adventure* supposed to occur?" Elizabeth asked.

"Not sure," Gower said. "Depends in part on me. Craufurd wants England to help arrange financing. Once that part is in place, they could go at any time."

"Is it dangerous?" Elizabeth was suddenly frightened for her friend, the Queen, and her children. "The family is already under close supervision. If they try to escape and are captured, will they be able to survive the scandal?"

"The King would likely be executed," Gower said flatly. He rose from the table and went to stare outside into the garden. "I do not know what they would do with the Queen or her children. But yes, Elizabeth, it is dangerous work."

He turned and looked his wife in the eyes.

"Which is why you must not breathe a word of this to anyone," he said, suddenly serious. "*Anyone.* Do you understand? Especially not the servants. There are eyes and ears everywhere these days. It could not only prove fatal to the King and Queen, but it could redound upon us as well. I intend to ask London what they wish me to do in this matter, but neither you nor I can be seen to participate in this matter in any way. That is absolute. Do you understand?"

Elizabeth had never seen her husband this way, ever. He was staring at her with what looked to her like fright writ large across his face.

"These are dangerous times, Elizabeth, and there are dangerous and desperate men all around us," he said. "My duties are clear, and I will fulfill them to the best of my abilities. But I will not allow you or the children to get caught up in this. I shall send you back to London instantly if I feel there is any danger. But this matter I have spoken of this morning must never leave this room. You must assure me that you understand this."

Elizabeth looked into her husband's eyes for a long moment. She could feel her heart pounding in her chest. She was afraid. Finally, she nodded.

"Yes, of course George," she said. "I understand. My lips are sealed."

LORD GOWER REPEATED his performance of the day before, and arrived at the embassy of the Hotel d'Angleterre just after ten o'clock in the morning. Sir Jeremy lumbered into the ambassador's office shortly thereafter and occupied his usual seat in front of the ambassador's desk.

"How was your meeting last evening with Mr. Craufurd?" he asked, cocking his head to the side.

"Most enlightening," Gower said with a small smile. "I learned quite a bit about governmental finance among and between the European nations. Among other matters."

Sir Jeremy lifted a finger. "Before you relate to me the details of your discussion, I must inform your Lordship that you were followed here this morning."

"Followed?"

"Yes, milord." Sir Jeremy seemed remarkably unperturbed. "A single horseman, dressed in black, followed your carriage between your home and this office. He disappeared soon after you came inside, but I expect he's still out there waiting."

"Who is he?" Gower suddenly felt nervous. "What the devil does he want? And how in the devil do you know this?"

"To answer your last question first," Sir Jeremy said calmly, "It has long been our assumption that each and every officer in this embassy has been or will be the subject of surveillance by the government of France, or by one, or all, of the various factions competing in the National Assembly. It is to be expected. I am sure that the government of Lord Pitt has most of the foreign consuls to London under steady surveillance. It is a common practice, so do not take it personally."

"I *do* take it personally," Gower said hotly. "And I plan on taking up the subject with His Majesty King Louis when next we meet."

"You may do so if you wish, milord, but I would recommend against that," Sir Jeremy said. "As I said, it is common practice in our world of diplomacy. In addition, I doubt if the King himself was responsible for your being followed. It is our assumption that it is General Lafayette who has asked to know the whereabouts and activities of your august person."

"Lafayette?" Gower was dumfounded. "But why?"

"His duty is to protect the King," Sir Jeremy patiently explained. "These days, that means both guarding the King from his more exuberant opponents as well as protecting the King from escaping the Kingdom. Your meeting with Mr. Craufurd, who is known to be a close financial advisor to the King, would raise suspicions in some quarters. Lafayette is only doing his job. But you must keep in mind that everything you do, every word you speak, every person with whom you meet, is likely to become known to General Lafayette and perhaps others in government or politics. It is the nature of the times in which we find ourselves, Sir."

Not for the first time, Gower realized that he was but a small cog in a massive machine that was churning away furiously throughout Paris, with vibrations coming and going from other machines in London, Amsterdam, Berlin, Vienna, Rome, Madrid and St. Petersburg.

"How did you know I was followed?" he asked.

Sir Jeremy smiled, an expression of self-satisfaction that spoke volumes. "I have people who watch your movements, to see if anyone else is watching," he said. "This morning, there was. My man followed the one who followed you, and has sent word to me. It is standard procedure, I assure you."

"I do not feel much assured," Gower said. "I take it that henceforth I shall be followed by two parties: the one who is watching me, and the person who is watching the watcher?"

Sir Jeremy shrugged, as if to say 'what else can I do?'

"Let us return to the subject of last evening's meeting," Sir Jeremy said. "Did Mr. Craufurd tell you about the plan for the royal escape from Paris?"

"How in the devil ..." Gower broke off his expostulation. "You already knew of these plans?"

"Of course," Sir Jeremy said. "We suspected something was up when the august gentleman you dined with last evening ordered a special coach to be built in a hurry. Did you know that there are seven secret compartments in that coach? Seven! It is quite extraordinary. One each to carry the personal jewels of the King and the Queen; while the others are for food and drink. Apparently His Majesty is worried that fleeing his captivity will be hungry work, and he wanted to make sure he could still enjoy a fine meal, even whilst being driven down a lonely country road."

Gower leaned back in his chair.

"What part of the plan *don't* you know?" he asked. "It would save us both a great deal of time if we get down to that."

"What does he want our government to do?" Sir Jeremy asked, his smile broadening some. "We have a general idea of what he has in mind, but we were hoping to learn some of the specifics."

"Craufurd says the King wants to ensure he has funding once he is out of Paris," Gower said. "He will need to raise an army loyal to himself, and will want to pay for a semblance of a government in exile. Politicians and soldiers are both expensive toys. He wants a bridge loan of one million pounds. Count Fersen is arranging a similar loan from the Swedish government. With those funds, and the impression of a working government they will provide, the King believes he can convince the other princes of Europe to back a campaign to recover France and restore the House of Bourbon to the throne and power."

"And how does His Majesty propose to secure this loan?" Sir Jeremy asked.

"Once his throne in France has been restored, the King proposes to pay down one-half of the total amount of the loan held at present by the Bank of England," Gower said. "At present, Craufurd says that would amount to ..."

"...two hundred and fifty million livres," Sir Jeremy said. "That is quite an impressive amount. Where, pray, does Louis plan to find this sum?"

"Craufurd believes he can raise it with a combination of new taxation on the aristocratic class, and a round of government bonds," Gower explained. "In addition, I believe the King plans on selling off properties owned by the royal family, as well as pledging as collateral some property currently owned by the church."

"The church?" Sir Jeremy, for once, sounded surprised. "I suspect the Holy Father in Rome will not look favorably on that idea."

Gower shrugged. "Craufurd says the King has lost patience with the priests. They have not been the most loyal backers of himself. Craufurd says the King will raise the money with ease."

"Yes," Sir Jeremy mused. "He would. Craufurd himself stands to gain a handsome profit if this deal works, doesn't he?"

"I am aware of that," Gower said. "But the question is: will our King agree? Does George want to help save Louis' skin?"

"I can think of two hundred and fifty million reasons why he might," Sir Jeremy said. "But I shall send a dispatch at once to London. Lord Grenville and Prime Minister Pitt should make the final decision on this."

Gower nodded his approval to this idea.

ELIZABETH WAS AT home that afternoon. Young Georgie and his little sister, Charlotte, just two years old, were playing quietly in the solarium, under the watchful eye of the nanny. Elizabeth was catching up on the paperwork of the household accounts. Lord Gower expected her to handle this part of the family budget, but he relentlessly double-checked and questioned all her expenditures, so she had learned to keep careful records on the whereabouts of every last sou.

One of her maids entered, carrying a silver tray upon which a calling card rested. Elizabeth took up the card, read the name, and nodded to the girl. "Show her in at once," she said. "And bring us some tea."

The maid scurried off, and soon ushered in the guest, dressed in a plain, modestly embroidered blue dress, her head almost entirely encased in a large hat of stiff felt and feathers that hid most of her features. She removed the hat to reveal Madame Campan, the Queen's chief *femme du Chambre*. She had a pleasant, round face with dark, sparkling eyes and thin lips. Unlike most of the women at Court, she did not use much of the rouge, and her natural complexion was pale and delicate. She moved with practiced elegance; as a longtime member of the royal court, with all its complex and confusing set of rules,

Madame Campan had the look of someone who knew what to do and how to properly do it at all times.

"You honor us with your presence, Madame," Elizabeth said, and waved her into a chair next to her desk, which was cluttered with bills from the household suppliers and pages of ledgers. "I have ordered some refreshments. How is Her Majesty?"

"Thank you, Madame," said the visitor. "The Queen is well. I cannot stay too long. The Queen requires me to assist her in dressing for this evening."

The children came running in to greet Madame Campan, whom they both had met and befriended before in visits to the Tuileries to play with young Louis-Charles. Madame hugged them both, bestowing plenty of kisses. Elizabeth nodded to the nanny who quickly escorted the children back to the nearby solarium.

"They are so lovely, Madame," Campan said, a wistful tone in her voice. "They grow up so fast."

"You do not have children, Madame?" asked Elizabeth.

Campan shook her head, looking down at her hands. "No," she said. "My life has been one of devotion to the Queen." Elizabeth knew that Madame's marriage to the son of one of the King's favorite courtiers was not a happy one; arranged marriages like hers seldom were. Monsieur Campan hunted with the King, which was often, and spent the rest of his time drunk or trying, often successfully, to seduce one of the many females connected to the court.

"To what do we owe the pleasure of this visit?" Elizabeth asked. She knew she was being somewhat abrupt, but she had learned from Lord Gower how to be direct, to get to the pith of the matter. Frankly, such directness was in her own nature, too. She never liked to beat around the bush.

"Her Majesty asked me to come to you with a request," Madame Campan said. "She is in need of some clothes."

"Clothes?" Elizabeth was surprised. "What manner of clothing does the Queen of France need from me that she cannot easily obtain on her own?"

"Some girls clothing, Madame," Campan said, her voice lowered to a whisper. "Something that might perhaps be the approximate size of your son George."

The two women looked at each other for a long moment. Each of them felt time stand still while the importance of what Campan had asked circulated in the room.

"You mean …" Elizabeth started.

"Oui, Madame," Madame Campan finished quickly.

Elizabeth understood at once what it was she was being asked to do. She felt a wave of anxiety and worry crash over her, but just for a moment. Then she knew that she would comply with the Queen's request. Elizabeth and Marie Antoinette had become close, as friends, and as mothers of like-age sons. They understood each other perfectly. They knew that each of them would do anything to protect their own son; they knew that the other would do anything to protect either of the boys. It was a pact unwritten, unspoken, but as real and as firm as an unbreakable law, like one of the Commandments.

"Of course," Elizabeth said after a moment, and she watched the relief flood over the countenance of the woman sitting across from her. "Charlotte's things would be much too small for … for the purpose," she said. "But one of my maids has a girl that is approximately George's size. I will make the arrangements. When, exactly, will you be needing this?"

Madame Campan reached over and grasped Elizabeth's hands in gratitude. "My Queen said by the end of next week, if that is possible," she said.

"Please tell her that I shall be honored to help," Elizabeth said. "Tell her that if she needs anything else … anything at all … she must only ask. I will do all that I can."

Madame Campan could not speak for a while. She tightened her grip until she could finally gasp out her thanks.

The girl came with the tea things, and the children came rushing back in, hoping for a biscuit or two. Elizabeth took up the pot and began to pour the tea.

19

Henri D'Anjou passed the long hours of the day waiting for the British ambassador to emerge from his embassy. But that does not mean he spent the day in one place. That would have been too obvious, and, as General Lafayette's most trusted intelligence operative, Henri knew how to blend in to his surroundings and become invisible, even when just waiting for something to happen.

Once the ambassador had emerged from his dusty, sagging old coach that morning and stepped quickly into the marble edifice of the embassy, Henri had quickly ridden to a nearby inn a few blocks away off the Boulevard de Saint Germain and handed his horse off to a stableboy, along with a few coins. "Feed him, water him, brush him and have him ready to go at all times," he had ordered the boy, who nodded and led the horse back to the stables. He had then walked quickly back to the rue Jacob.

He made his way around to the rear of the Hotel d'Angleterre and found one of the cleaning maids lounging in the alley. Henri had made it his business to know and befriend most of the girls hired by the English to work in their embassy. The smart ones he had taken under his wing, and by distributing a few francs, some extra bread or food, and even by means of some stolen kisses and caresses, he had enlisted their eyes and ears in the service of his master, the general. The girl, who smiled when she saw him, told Henri that the ambassador was in his office, conducting meetings with his staff, and seemed to be settled in for a full day's work, with nothing special, or so the girl had heard, on his schedule of events. Henri thanked the girl and promised to meet her in a popular bistro a few nights hence.

From there, Henri was off again, keeping within eyesight of the embassy, but never staying in one place long enough to attract attention from anyone who might be watching. He entered a wine bar across the street and spent an hour listening to the gossip of the others while watching the front entrance of the embassy, while his ordered glass of wine went mostly untouched.

After an hour or so, he moved four doors down the street, on the other side of the embassy's entrance, to a butcher shop owned by a former soldier in Lafayette's troop. Henri threw on a bloodstained apron, took up a cleaver, and loitered for a time near the shop's windows, where he could keep a sharp eye on the comings and goings of the embassy. The other butchers had been told by the proprietor, Monsieur Lescaux, that Henri was engaged in important work; they generally ignored him. The patrons of the shop, coming in to pick out their chops for the day's dinner, took one look at the hard-looking man near the window and left him alone. In the current conditions of the city, people had learned that being curious or overly talkative could be dangerous, and Henri d'Anjou was a dangerous looking man. He had an angular face with a sharp nose and pointed chin, and there was an ugly slash of a reddened scar over his left eye. His body was also lean and angular, his hands large and bony. And whenever one looked at his face, his cold black eyes stared back as if daring one to say something ... *anything* ... just to see what would happen. Instead, most people who encountered the hard-looking man holding a large meat cleaver looked away, suddenly nervous. At the noon hour, Monsieur Lescaux brought Henri slices of cold sausage, some bread and a goblet of wine. He nodded his thanks and ate, slowly, eyes never leaving the embassy or the activity of the street.

He was glad to have this work to do, gladder still that it was the English ambassador that he could keep under surveillance. Henri had long hated the English: His father, a poor shopkeeper from Marseille, had been killed in the Seven Years' War during the attack on Hanover. Henri himself had been wounded during the skirmishes of the Spanish-Portuguese War near Oporto at the hands of an English sword. He would gladly give his life, if it came to that, to defeat the hated English.

And, he was loyal to both his general, the Marquis de Lafayette, and to the Revolution. Henri had never cared much for politics, but he had seen and experienced the conditions of life under the Bourbon king, and he had great sympathy for those who wished to establish a republic in France and send Louis and all the aristocrats around him packing. He didn't care much whether Louis and his queen lived or died; if ordered to do so, he would gladly run a blade through the both of them without a moment's hesitation. He knew that General Lafayette was not unsympathetic to the royal cause, and Henri could not understand the reasons why. After all, Lafayette had fought bravely to establish a republic in far-off America; Henri did not understand why his general was not an enthusiastic supporter of ending the hated French monarchy once and for all. But Henri was not a soldier who questioned his general's decisions, nor one to argue politics with so important and lofty a man. Henri was a soldier who followed his orders, and did what he was told. He knew he was lucky to have come under the wing of such a great man as Lafayette and he knew that the general depended on him to ferret out the information the general needed. He would do what he was told, and let the politics sort themselves out.

In the afternoon, Henri changed his location again, this time taking a table outside the brasserie next to the embassy. But he first ducked into the back of the butcher's shop and changed into a coat of a different color that he had placed in Lescaux's cupboard, along with a different hat. If anyone in the Hotel d'Angleterre had been instructed to keep watch for a man dressed in black, they would not have glanced twice at the man in the maroon jacket and red cap, adorned at the top with the obligatory tricolor ribbon.

He ordered a tankard of beer, and nodded at the waiter in his short black waistcoat and long white apron, who brought it. The waiter was also an informant; Henri knew he could stay at his table as long as necessary without being subjected to the usual rudeness of a Parisian waiter intent on keeping the clientele, and the payments and tips, moving.

He purchased a newspaper from one of the hawkers passing by on the street and perused the latest headlines, still keeping an eye on the embassy entrance a few doors away. He skimmed over the reports of the latest speeches from the National Assembly on the endless debate over the form of government France should have. He read the list of names of the doomed, those destined to perish in the Place de la Revolution beneath the falling blade of La Guillotine, noting the handful of marquises, comtes and barons mixed in with the commoners and criminals. It would not be long, he surmised, before all of the aristocracy was eliminated, to be quickly followed, he hoped, by the priests and bishops. He wondered who would step in to fill those powerful positions in society, but pushed those thoughts out of his head. *We don't need them*, he thought. *The People will run things, and it will be better for all.*

At that moment, he saw the ambassador's old coach approaching from the west. He grabbed the coat of a nearby urchin, pushed a *sol* coin into the boy's hands and instructed him to run to the nearby stables and fetch his horse. "If you are back in two minutes or less, there is an *écu* with your name on it," he said. The boy's eyes widened and he took off like a rabbit.

Henri watched the coach pull up to the front of the embassy. It was still there, empty, when the boy came running back, holding the reins of the horse in his hand. Henri gave him the silver coin, left a few more on his table, and swung up into the saddle. He trotted down the street and stopped in the shade of a tree to wait.

It was a few minutes more before Lord Gower came striding out of his embassy and climbed into his carriage. The two Swiss bodyguards took their places on the rear running boards, the coachman cracked his whip, and the carriage creaked off down the rue Jacob. Henri watched silently as it passed him, waited until it was several hundred yards down the street, and then kicked his horse to follow.

Lord Gower's carriage pulled to a stop in front of the Hotel Dillon on the rue de Bac, perhaps a mile from the English embassy. The Hotel was the elegant home of the ambassador from the Kingdom of Sweden, the Baron Staël von Holstein. Gower climbed out of the carriage and mounted the marble steps to the entrance, where the servants bowed him in. Gower did not notice the man on horseback, dressed in a maroon coat, who dismounted yards away on the busy Boulevard Saint Germain and tied his horse to a nearby railing.

The Baron Staël, as Sir Jeremy had informed Lord Gower, had recently been recalled to Stockholm "for consultations."

"His wife the Baroness, on the other hand, remains in the city and is quite active among the revolutionaries," Sir Jeremy had said. "She is, as I'm sure you know, the daughter of Jacques Necker, who used to be Louis' financial director. Like many of the Swiss, she has a soft spot for intellectuals and revolutionaries. Her salon is full of them: Tallyrand, Delille, the Comte Clermont-Tonnere. The good news is that they are all mostly monarchists or republicans. None of her friends is baying for the King's head on a pike. On the other hand, if the mob of Paris awakens, they are all dead."

Lord Gower was escorted to the first floor, and shown into a sitting room of yellow walls covered in elaborate mirrors with crystal chandeliers hanging from the ceiling. Fine oriental carpets covered the parquet floor and groupings of chairs and chaises were carefully placed according to the latest fashion.

A side door opened and Quentin Craufurd came in, followed by a tall, distinguished man wearing the military uniform of the Swedish army: a blue coat festooned with gold epaulets and braid and pinned with colorful ribbons, striped breeches and tall polished boots. His face was friendly, his wig powdered and tailed, and his lace cravat tight against his neck.

"Ah, Lord Gower," Craufurd said, leading the other man to where the ambassador stood. "Allow me to introduce Count Axel von Fersen."

The men bowed to each other politely and Craufurd waved them both into a chair.

"Have you considered further on the matter we discusses last evening?" Craufurd asked.

"I have," Gower said. "I have written to London to ask for further instructions. I expect we will hear back from them tomorrow, if the mail packet sails on time."

"Excellent," Craufurd said. "I thought you might have some questions for Count Fersen."

Gower turned to look at the man.

"Just one," he said calmly. "And it is this: Have you completely lost your senses, Sir?"

Gower watched as the Swede's face fell, then turned red with anger.

"Sir," he managed to stutter out after a long moment trying to regain his self-control. "I must protest your impertinence."

"I may be impertinent, Count Fersen," Gower replied. "But I am deadly serious. You propose to kidnap the King and

Queen of France, smuggle them out of a city filled with two million rabid revolutionaries, most of whom are on the lookout for any kind of suspicious activity, and deliver them in safety to a city some two hundred miles away, passing unseen and unremarked by anyone throughout the length of that journey. I repeat, Sir, have you lost command of all of your senses?"

Fersen was shaking with anger and barely managed to keep himself from rising to his feet, striking the impudent diplomat across his face and stalking out of the room.

"I can assure you, Sir," he said between his tightly clenched teeth. "We have been working on this plan for more than a year, ever since the royal family was forcibly removed from Versailles and forced to take up residence at the Tuileries. Every step of the plan has been carefully considered. Resources have been expended to provide safety for the family during their journey to Metz. There will be heavily armed troops waiting for them at Montmédy, under the command of General De Bouille. Once they are in the control of the general, their safety will be assured."

"And you think a large carriage drawn by six horses will not be noticed in the countryside?" Gower said. "Why do you not send the family members in swifter, smaller coaches? Or even on horseback? They could get there faster and without drawing as much attention as the berline that Mr. Craufurd has generously provided."

"That was our recommendation as well," Craufurd answered. "But the King and Queen were adamant that they should not be separated from each other, nor from their children and family. The only way they would agree to the plan at all was if it was agreed that they would all be traveling together."

"And when some nosy official in some reeking village wants to know who it is traveling at high speeds across the country in this huge coach and six?" Gower said, shaking his head. "What will you tell them?"

Count Fersen leapt to his feet and began pacing back and forth. "We have let it be known that the berline was constructed for a Russian count and his family who are making the journey back to St. Petersburg," he said. "The family will be wearing clothing that comports with this ruse. Once they reach Montmédy, they will be safe."

"*If* they reach Montmédy," Gower said. "The chance of success is infinitesimal. If they are captured, it is likely they will be executed. All of France will be thrown into chaos. The bloodshed will not end with the royal family. Your plan, from what I have heard of it, seems ill considered. I do not have confidence in its successful conclusion, Sir."

"Well, I do!" the Count exclaimed. "We must do something to get Her Majesty…and the King, of course…safely away from the madness that now informs this pestilent city. Time grows short and the danger of staying here grows larger by the day. It is, Sir, now or never! The route we have selected was chosen after due consideration. His Majesty the King even instructed us to change our original plan, which was to journey to Montmédy through Mieux and Rheims. It is the straightest and fastest highway. But the King was afraid he would be recognized in Rheims; after all, he was crowned there and has many friends in the district who know him well. So we changed the plan, and now they will travel further south, to Sainte-Menehould, then north to Varennes on the River Aire, across the Dun at Meuse and on to Montmédy. It is longer, but far the safer itinerary."

Fersen stopped and faced Lord Gower. "There will be troops, Germans, waiting at Stenay to escort His Majesty and the family to safety," he said. "I wanted them to ride without escort all the way, thinking that to be safer and less obvious, but the King approved. He is thinking of his family's safety, of course."

"Of course," Gower muttered. "But I am afraid the King is not thinking *clearly*. Thinking is not his greatest attribute. For instance, who will be assigned to ride with the family and ensure that the correct route is followed? Who will make the decisions to change the plan in the event that something happens along the way?"

Count Fersen looked abashed.

"I had, of course, intended to ride with the coach alongside the driver," he said, his voice low. "But the Queen forbade me from doing so. She said she did not wish to endanger my own life by helping to save theirs."

Gower stared at the man, who fidgeted nervously.

"The coachman will know the way," Fersen continued, though he did not sound convinced of his own argument. "Even if an alarm is raised in Paris once it is learned that the family has left the city, no one will know where they are. No one will know in which direction they have fled. It will take time, perhaps several days, before they are discovered. By then, they will be safely under General de Bouille's troops in Montmédy."

Gower stroked his chin.

"I wish I was as confident that all will proceed as you foresee," he said finally. "I am not a military man. But I have heard many a general observe that the best-laid plans often go awry when the first bullets are fired."

"We must hope that no bullets at all are fired," Craufurd said.

The door to the salon opened and the Baroness de Staël entered, wearing a brilliant red dress and holding a long black shawl draped over her partially bared shoulders. A turban of twisted red and white silk sat atop her head of luxuriant black hair.

"Gentlemen," she said, sweeping in grandly. "I do hope I am not interrupting anything of importance."

"My dear Baroness," Craufurd said, leaping to his feet, grasping her hand and kissing it formally before escorting her to a nearby chair. "It is impossible for you to interrupt anything.

We are ever grateful that you grace us with your presence. How is your dear father?"

"He is well, thank you Quentin," the Baroness said, smiling fondly at him. "In fact, in his last letter to me, he asked me to send you his high regards."

The Baroness de Staël was the daughter of Jacques Necker, the well-known banker in Geneva who, for some time, had served as the financial advisor to King Louis XVI, and had been seen in many circles as the de facto head of the nation for a time before he had finally been forced to resign by the intrigues of the Court. She had been raised by her father in a Swiss home filled with philosophers, writers and men of accomplishment and had participated in conversations and debates with men like Voltaire and Rousseau. Her arranged marriage to the Swedish Baron had given her a solid position in society's upper circles, and the mutual disregard both spouses maintained toward that marriage had enabled her to move freely through those circles, adopting and discarding lovers as she wished. She had been a regular at Court, despite the enmity the Queen felt toward her father—as Director-General of France, Necker had been in control of the Queen's expenditures and that had inevitably led to conflict between the two. Marie Antoinette, however, had always enjoyed the company of the intelligent and ever-social Baroness Staël, and they had become good friends.

Now, she surveyed the three men in her salon. Craufurd, the crafty financier who had long known her father and participated in many of his international financing schemes, looked amused. Count Fersen seemed to be angry: his face was red and drawn. But he was often angry about something. After all, he was in love with the Queen of France, a relationship that seemed to have little chance of long-term success, for various reasons. The Baroness had learned, through the usual impeccable sources of gossip in and around the Court, that Fersen and the Queen had briefly been lovers, but years ago, when both were younger and carefree. In the current situation, with the royal family virtually under guard in the Tuileries, she suspected the opportunities for trysting, even if the Queen were still interested, were quite limited.

Lord Gower, the British ambassador, was a man she did not know well. She had seen him at Court at diplomatic events, and remembered meeting him and his Scottish wife at other parties, but only knew of him what she had learned from her other friends and sources. He looked like his reputation: he seemed serious, skeptical, perhaps a bit out of his depth. She noted his constant myopic blinking against the bright light of the day, which gave him the appearance of a man fumbling his way through life. Nobody in the diplomatic circles of Paris knew much about this man, save that he was quite wealthy and in line to inherit an even more substantial estate from his elderly uncle, the Duke of Bridgewater, the man who owned the network of shipping canals that crisscrossed the British Midlands. He looked like a man of great wealth: his suit was impeccably tailored and in the latest fashion; his shoes glistened with large, golden buckles. She liked that; she always liked a man who was not afraid to make a statement about himself. His buckles were like a beacon, informing the world that here was a man of substance.

"My husband has requested that I join him in Copenhagen," the Baroness said. "We have other family affairs to deal with in Stockholm as well. Do you think it a good idea to make the journey at this time?"

All three men understood instantly what she was asking: Should she, the wife of the Swedish ambassador and a known intimate of the King and Queen, make herself scarce for the next several months?

The banker Craufurd harrumphed. "I see no particular reason why you should stay here in Paris at this time," he said. "You might find the atmospherics a bit cooler and more relaxing in your home country."

"My home country, dear Quentin, is Geneva," she laughed. "But I take your point."

"You must go," said Fersen, speaking with his usual military directness. "Before a fortnight has passed."

The Baroness looked at the Swedish count with interest. They had known one another for years, but their relationship had never been anything but honorable. She found that interesting to think about. They both had engaged in numerous affairs of the heart, not to mention idle encounters of a more venal nature; they had certainly had ample opportunities over the years. Yet she had never fallen for the handsome count, and he had never once proposed feelings of a physical nature towards her. She recalled the words of Voltaire, a favorite of her mother's who had spent hours in her parents' salon trying out lines of his philosophy: "I know nothing of life, except that flies are born to be eaten by spiders, and man to be devoured by sadness."

The Baroness turned to Lord Gower, who sat silently, blinking furiously.

"And you, my Lord," she said, a brief smile playing upon her lips. "Do you, Sir, agree that it would be well for me to leave Paris at this time?"

"I have not the slightest opinion as to the propriety of your journey," he said, a bit gruffly. "But to observe that if your husband has requested your presence in some foreign city, it would be well to obey."

She looked at him for a moment or two.

"How very English," she said. It was not reproachful, although it might have sounded so.

"Perhaps that is because I *am* English," he said. He looked at her, unsmiling.

"Have the English come to a decision as to whether or not they will help in the financing of the project at hand?" she asked. "I know that the King, in particular, has been much vexed over the question and what it will mean for his future."

"My official answer to Milady's question is 'I do not know at present,'" Gower said. "My unofficial answer is that I do not discuss the official business of my government with those not authorized, especially with a woman."

The Baroness' face reddened slightly, but she did not respond, save for a slight nod in his direction, an acknowledgement that his point was well taken. They did not know one another well, and she had overstepped thinking that Lord Gower was an official co-conspirator in the plan to remove the royal family from its danger.

A rush of servants entered the salon, bearing silver trays carrying the tea service and heaping plates of food: cakes and biscuits, fruits and cheeses. The Baroness supervised the pouring and kept up an engaging and light-hearted banter until all had full plates and a fine china cup of tea. Fersen stood off by himself, tossing tidbits into his mouth without thought, his face dark and troubled. Craufurd and Lord Gower began to discuss a problem of customs duties and shipping fees that was being adjudicated in Calais, one of the usual transnational disputes that was the typical subject of the ambassador's attention.

20

It was late, past midnight. Henri found himself again in the spacious offices of the Marquis de Lafayette in the Hotel de Ville. As usual, the business of the revolution continued around the clock, with men bustling up and down the marbled halls, carrying papers and dispatches and holding whispered meetings in every corner of the mammoth building.

Henri watched as Lafayette poured them each some wine and dropped himself wearily into a chair set before the fire. His face was pale and etched with fatigue and Henri noticed a slight trembling in his hands. A solitary sentry stood at the door, face impassive, staring at nothing.

"What have you learned, Henri, about our friend the English ambassador?" the marquis asked.

Henri took a small sip of wine and carefully placed the goblet on the table next to him before removing some papers from his coat pocket.

"The Lord Gower has spent much of his time in the last week at his embassy," Henri said, looking over his notes. "He attended the Court on Tuesday for the investiture of the new legate from St. Petersburg. He called on the Baroness Staël at the Swedish embassy on Thursday, and was there for several hours."

"Anyone else there?" Lafayette asked.

Henri rustled his notes. "The banker Craufurd and the Swedish Count Fersen were seen leaving at the same time that evening," he said.

"Fersen, eh?" Lafayette drank some wine and looked thoughtfully at his spy. "He is the Queen's special friend, is he not? I have heard reports that he is encouraging the royal family to fly for the border. And the Necker woman … the Baroness. Despite the company she keeps, she has never truly been on the side of the Revolution. It would figure that they are conspiring together, probably with King Gustav's participation. The Swedes are brave everywhere except on the field of battle."

He stroked his chin. "But what are Craufurd and Lord Gower up to? That's the interesting thing. Craufurd does nothing unless he can make money doing it. And I hear the English ambassador is an extremely wealthy man. Why do you suppose they are meeting with the Swedes?"

"Perhaps the English gentleman intends to provide the money required to assist the King and Queen to decamp," Henri said. He didn't have much of a head for intrigue or politics, but some things were evident even to him.

"Perhaps, Henri, perhaps," Lafayette said, nodding to himself. "I can see King George putting up some livres to help Louis escape. Louis would then be very much in the English king's debt, would he not? There may not be much love between our two nations, but I can see how such a financial arrangement might come about. And with that Craufurd fellow, there is always a deal being struck, with himself the usual beneficiary."

"Shall I have someone follow Craufurd as well, Sir?" Henri asked.

Lafayette shook his head. "No, that would be a waste of resources," he said. "Craufurd meets and knows everyone in this city and does business with half of them. Stay with the ambassador for a while longer. He may yet lead us to someone we can use."

"What about the royal family?" the spy asked. "I can find men to keep them under surveillance."

Lafayette waved his hand in dismissal.

"I have two companies assigned to the Tuileries," he said. "I know what they do, whom they meet, and where they go before they do. Our King is a fool who could not plan an escape if his life depended on it, which it may well do. The Queen is a smart woman, but she has no power. She depends on him, and he would rather go hunting at St. Cloud than try to escape to Brussels."

He stood up and walked over to the windows, standing there looking down on the courtyard in front of the Hotel de Ville, where bonfires burned brightly in the night.

"Escape from Paris is their only hope," the marquis said. "If they stay in Paris, despite my orders to keep them safe and keep them here, they are doomed. The Assembly shall eventually fall into the hands of a violent faction and they will drum up some charge or another with which they can safely have them executed."

He turned away from the window with a sigh. He glanced at Henri with eyes that were haunted.

"It would be far better if they escaped from Paris," he said. "Once abroad, Louis can help muster an army from the other royal houses in Europe and come marching back to reclaim his throne."

"But that would mean war!" Henri said, his voice harsh with emotion. "War against the revolution!"

"Indeed it would," Lafayette agreed, nodding. "And we could then summon all patriots of France to defeat their cause. And *that*, my good man, would be the beginning of our glorious French republic. As I learned in America, there must first be a cause, and then the people will rally to it and the victory be well-won. What we have now are factions arguing endlessly among themselves, every day. Words, Henri! Mere words. Meanwhile the king and his family languish under lock and key awaiting their fate, which will be an ugly one. That is not the proper inspiration upon which to launch a new nation."

Henri stood silently for a moment, then smiled.

"Ahh, politics!" he said. "Too much for my poor head. It is good, *mon generale*, that you understand all that is going on. Should I continue to keep watch on the British ambassador?"

"Yes, continue to keep an eye on Lord Gower," Lafayette said, returning to his desk. "If money changes hands that would be a sign that something is about to happen with regard to our friend the King's location. I must be the first to hear. Do you understand, Henri?"

Henri saluted, bowed and disappeared into the night.

OUTSIDE, GROUPS OF people gathered around the fires, as they did every night. There were soldiers off duty for the evening, tradesmen, a few politicians, and some rough looking types. Prostitutes circled around at the edge of the light from the fire, trying to catch the eye of a customer, beckon him into a nearby alley. There were also children, despite the lateness of the evening, running freely across the square in front of the Hotel de Ville, and yapping dogs everywhere underfoot. For the citizens of Paris, the revolution was like an endless holiday. At the end of an evening, the people liked to gather, swap opinions, criticize either the King, the Queen, or the Assembly, or all of the above, and ask each other "what do you think will happen next?"

Henri D'Anjou stopped near one of the fires to watch after he left Lafayette. He accepted a skin of wine that was being passed around the group gathered at one of the fires and took a swallow before passing it on. *Liberte, Egalite, Fraternite ...* those were the code words that allowed entry into the brave new world of French politics; that and the tricolor ribbands affixed to one's cap, or collar, or coat. Red and blue were long the traditional colors of Paris and those colors had been worn by the militias and townspeople who had stormed the Bastille on that hot July day a year ago. White was added later, the color of the Bourbons, the royal family. Henri would have gladly removed the white band, but the rest of the people had adopted the tricolor, and he wanted to show his solidarity.

"Ooo, aren't you a big one?" cooed a painted whore, stepping out from the shadows and running her hands up Henri's arms and across his broad shoulders. "Fancy a little fun, ducky?"

He stared at her with his cold black eyes. She fell silent, pulled her hands away and disappeared silently back into the darkness. Henri knew that he could be a bit frightening when he wanted to. At the same time, a bit of fun hadn't sounded all that bad to him. He had been working hard, after all.

Henri hailed a cab and told the driver to take him to the Cours du Commerce on the Left Bank, near the Boulevard Saint-Germain. The cab moved quickly through the dark night. The streets were mostly empty as the city slept. Outside the Café Le Procope, he stopped the cab, paid the driver and looked up and down the street carefully. Seeing no one, he made his way to the familiar house nearby, the home of Georges Danton, knocked three times on the brightly painted red door and waited until someone inside came to let him in.

He was ushered into a room at the back of the house, away from the street. Two small candles were the only light in the room, as the curtains were drawn tightly. But they were enough for Henri to see Danton sitting behind a desk. There were three or four other men in the room, but when Henri arrived, the man behind the desk waved his hand, and the others quietly disappeared. A servant girl brought in some coffee for the two of them, and, after a quick glance around the room to see if anything was disordered, she, too, left the men alone.

They drank, silently. Henri looked over the rim of his cup at the man behind the desk. Danton was a large man, tall and stocky, with an especially large head. His forehead was strongly ridged, his thick black hair pulled back from his face and tied with a leather cord behind. Bushy eyebrows seemed to be fixed in a permanent scowl and even in the dimness of the light, Henri could see the terrible line of a long white scar running from ear to chin down the side of his face, a remnant, Henri knew, of a long-ago childhood incident with an angry bull near Danton's home of Arcis in northern France. The man's eyes were lost to view in the shadow of his deep eye sockets, but Henri could tell he was being scanned, analyzed, assayed. He waited patiently. One did not rush Georges Danton.

There was a force about Danton, not so easily dismissed as one related to his huge bodily frame and scary profile. His voice commanded attention, and, trained as a lawyer here at Paris' own Lycee Louis-le-Grand, he knew how to use it. But Henri could see ... *feel* ... that there was something about this man that made other men want to follow him, do what he commanded them to do. Henri felt that way himself. Danton was a leader. He had quickly assumed a leading position among the figures of the Revolution. He had become the de facto head of the Cordeliers, one of the main political factions in the city, and now commanded that group's small army of craftsmen, laborers, shopkeepers; all men who believed in a republic for France and freedom from the forces of the aristocracy, the church and especially the monarchy. His followers were many and all were deeply loyal to Danton. They would follow him through the gates of Hell.

"So, Henri," Danton said, finally, his deep, gruff tones cutting through the dim silent room like a knife. "What news do you bring me from the Hotel de Ville?"

"The King and Queen are preparing a plan to escape from Paris," Henri said. "Lafayette knows it is coming, but I think he secretly wants them to leave. He believes that they will escape to Austria, marshal an invasion force and march back into

France to seek the restoration of their throne, and the end of the Revolution. Lafayette wants this to happen so he can unite the country, fight the invaders, and, no doubt, assume control as the general of the armies and then the head of a new, republican, government."

"Is that so?" Danton chuckled softly, one large hand coming up to rub his nose. "I wonder where the general ever got such an idea in his head. Do you suppose it was when he was fighting for the revolution in America? He sees himself as our General-Washington, does he?"

"I think that is likely," Henri said. "He would like to lead his army, win a few battles and be acclaimed as the savior of France. But he does not like being the King's babysitter and protector."

"I think you are correct, Henri," Danton said, heaving his large frame out of his chair and grabbing a new candle from the mantle. He lit the wick with another candle and watched as the new source of light flickered to life. "Lafayette wants a nice clean revolution. He would prefer that we make the king a figurehead, but transfer the real power of the state to the people. Or the people's representatives, as they have done in America."

He found a candlestick and set the light down on the edge of his desk, blowing out the flame that had burned down to its last inch.

"I am not sure that the French people are the same as the Americans," Danton continued. "I think we must have a good bloodletting before we can begin to discuss what form our government should take. Lafayette is a bloodless general. He spends his time in his office, far from the battleground, surrounds himself with bodyguards and never himself gets his hands bloody with the business of war. To people like him, war is all about moving markers around on a map. He is wrong. War is about men dying, entrails being spilled on the ground, limbs being blown or severed from the body. It is about rivers of blood and oceans of tears. These are things he will never understand."

Henri stayed silent.

Danton sat down again, and yawned.

"I must try and get some sleep," he said. He reached into a drawer and pulled out a small velvet bag tied with a drawstring at the top. He tossed it across the desk where Henri caught it with one hand. Something metallic jingled inside the bag. "There are 100 livres in there," Danton said. "Let me know if you hear anything further on the King's activities. I suspect it will not be long."

Henri nodded his thanks, pocketed the bag and made his way back to the street. A light rain was falling and the city was silent and dark. There were no cabs about at this time of night. His own rooms were not far away, perhaps a half-hour walk. Henri turned the collar of his coat up against the misty rain and began to walk.

21

The Queen was furious. She felt trapped in her suite of rooms at the Tuileries. She *was* trapped: the squadrons of the National Guard, which answered to Lafayette, were posted at every entrance to the expansive palace; more soldiers paced the long hallways inside, admiring themselves in the floor-to-ceiling mirrors, and sitting in the gilt chairs whenever their sergeants weren't looking.

The situation had gotten progressively worse in the last few months. At Easter, the King had decided he would not accept a Holy Mass said by one of the priests who had sworn allegiance to the new state constitution, which subjugated the church to the state. So, he had gathered his family and prepared to spend the weekend at the Chateau de St. Cloud, the royal family's retreat across the River Seine west of the city, where they could find a non-juror priest to say Mass. But the King's two sisters, the Mesdames Tantes, had left for Geneva only a few days earlier, an event which had raised eyebrows among the people, and when the soldiers at the Tuileries and the ordinary citizens who came to gawk at the Royals on a daily basis saw the family enter their carriage, they feared an escape. Quickly, the soldiers and the citizens surrounded the carriage and refused to allow it to leave the palace grounds. The King's protective Swiss Guards had moved in to clear a way forward, fights had broken out and one of the Guards was severely injured by the mob. The family was forced to sit in their carriage for three hours while negotiations ensued. Lafayette had come running quickly from the Hotel de Ville, but could not get the commander of the forces assigned to the Tuileries to pull his men back. The King at one point had stuck his head out of his carriage and said to those nearby that he found it odd that he, a King who had granted his people liberty, was not able to enjoy the same. No matter, the howling crowd chased the family back to their suites.

Marie Antoinette understood what that day had meant. She immediately wrote desperate letters to her brother, now the Emperor of Austria, begging him for help. She implored him to contact the other heads of the countries of Europe and convince them to come to the aid of their French brother and sister. She told her brother that she did not know what the people of France might do next.

And now, her brother had finally written back. There was nothing he could do. Austria was heavily involved in its war with Turkey, and could neither afford, nor warrant, opening a new front to the West, with France. He didn't say such, but the implication was that France was on its own. He had written that the heads of Europe could hardly think of interfering with a sovereign neighbor while the King and Queen were not themselves in a place of safety, where they could help the effort. But he could not help them flee to that place either. His hands were, unfortunately, tied.

Re-reading that letter, the Queen grew angrier and threw it down in frustration. *We can't escape without help, and they won't give us help to escape*, she thought to herself. She recalled with frustration the hours of conversation she had with her husband, asking him to open negotiations with their neighboring monarchs to ask for their help. The King of Sardinia, she had told

Louis, wanted to claim Geneva as part of his kingdom: it would not affect France greatly, one way or another, so why not agree, in return for his troops? Louis had hemmed and hawed and his courtiers, always his many courtiers, had quickly changed the subject. She had mentioned the many feudal princes with their tiny kingdoms in Germany, all of whom had interests in territories in the Alsace region. Louis was uninterested. The King of Spain might be willing to help in return for some of the lands around Navarre. No, Louis said, such a thing had never been done before, it cannot be done now.

So there had been no efforts made to open negotiations. No efforts to ask for or obtain some outside help for his kingdom. Instead, Louis had gone hunting. And the soldiers of Lafayette prowled the hallways and gardens of the palace, while the citizens of Paris came to gawk outside its windows and hurl vicious insults against the Queen. Life had become nearly intolerable. After the incident at Easter, a mob had burned an effigy of the Pope in the Gardens of the Palace-Royale. The danger had become real. *I cannot understand it*, she thought to herself, *our very lives may be at stake, but all they can think about is politics.*

One of her courtiers approached the Queen, bowed low, and announced that the Lady Gower, wife of the English ambassador, had arrived for a visit. The Queen nodded her approval, and soon, Elizabeth was ushered into the royal presence.

"Majesty," Elizabeth curtsied. "Your face looks flushed. Are you well?"

"Hardly," the Queen said with a pout. "I am a prisoner in my own palace. My husband goes hunting six days a week. He will not approve of any action that might help us. We are told, by commoners and soldiers, what we can do, and what we cannot. It is intolerable. I fear for my children and what the future may hold for them."

Elizabeth reached out and grasped the Queen's hand. She heard several gasps from the dozen or more courtiers and servants who were always lingering in the room with the monarch. Touching the monarch was a violation of the rules of etiquette in the Court. Antoinette was never alone, ever. From the moment she awoke in the morning, until the time she crawled back into her bed late at night, there was always someone hovering nearby, watching, ready to perform whatever ablution or service she required. There were courtiers whose only job was to hand her the stockings she wished to wear, courtiers designated to remove her soup bowl, courtiers assigned to draw the drapes or open them to the sunlight, courtiers whose only job was the unobtrusive removal of the Queen's chamber pot. Each of these jobs and countless others were carefully inscribed in the traditions and the etiquette of the court, and the aristocratic men and women who held those jobs protected them carefully, indeed viciously, from encroachment from others. Even here in the Tuileries, with the National Guardsmen stationed at the doors and in the hallways, the elegant dance of the courtiers continued unchanged. Some continued to grow the fingernails of the smallest finger on their left hands to a certain length: etiquette called for one seeking permission to enter the King's chambers to gently scratch on the door with that one fingernail rather than knock.

Elizabeth ignored the quiet gasps of the outraged and held the Queen's hand. She could feel the sadness that enveloped her. The Queen cast her eyes down, but Elizabeth could see the tears that welled up nonetheless.

"You must not give in, Majesty," Elizabeth said. "You must continue to have faith in God that he will protect you and your children from harm."

The Queen nodded. "I do believe that," she said. "Despite the evidence that the Almighty, too, has abandoned my family."

Elizabeth withdrew her hand. "I have delivered the package that you requested, Majesty," she said, dropping her voice to a whisper. "I have left it just now with Madame Campan."

The Queen looked up and managed a brief smile. "We thank you," she said. She stood up suddenly. Two of her ladies in waiting materialized from the shadows against the nearby walls. "Madame l'ambassadeur and I wish to stroll in the garden," she said, raising her voice. "Make way."

The room burst into activity. Two liveried servants opened the doors that led to the courtyard, while two lines of courtiers formed a pathway to the door for the Queen and her guest to follow. Marie Antoinette was wearing a simple muslin dress, but her train-bearers fell into place behind her anyway. Her Swiss Guard bodyguards fell in behind the Queen and the train-bearers, and the rest of the Court assumed their hierarchical places behind that. When all were properly aligned, the Queen made for the door and the sunlight outside.

Elizabeth followed, and when they reached the manicured grounds of the royal gardens, the Queen motioned her to walk by her side. The collection of courtiers and servants melted away and regrouped under a nearby row of linden trees.

"It is best if we talk here," the Queen said, her voice low and quiet. "It is hard to know who I can trust."

"My husband has told me of your plans, your Majesty," Elizabeth said. "I understand the reasons why. But I am fearful for your safety."

The Queen smiled wanly. "No more than I," she said. "But once the decision has been made to go, I am expected to do what they tell me to do."

"Do you think the plan a good one?"

"What I think is of no importance," the Queen said. "I have asked a great many questions. I have a great many more I would like to ask. But Count Fersen and my husband assure me that their plan will work. There is nothing I can do but accept what they tell me. And to pray to Almighty God to watch over my children."

"When do you think …" Elizabeth let her question fade away uncompleted.

The Queen shrugged. "Soon," she said. "One night very soon. Or so they tell me."

"You are very brave," Elizabeth said. "You and the King."

"It is not bravery that propels us," the Queen answered. "It is the intolerant reality of our current condition. We are trapped here like animals in the zoo. There is no escape. They let the common people come and stare at us every day. We are not allowed to do anything, or go anywhere, without the approval of the National Assembly or General Lafayette. Sooner or later, they will tire of us, and then they will be rid of us."

She sighed. They had reached the rose garden, where the rows of bushes were exploding in colors: reds, yellows and whites. She leaned over one bush and sniffed deeply at a large red blossom, her eyes shut tightly.

"I have tried to get my husband to send for help from the other royal houses of Europe," the Queen continued. "They cannot, or they will not help us. So, we must go to them."

"The children…" Elizabeth said. "Your son, the Dauphin. He is so young…"

"He is doomed if we stay here," the Queen answered. "The only possible way to save him is to get out of this city. There are troops loyal to my husband in Montmédy. Or so they tell me. We shall find out soon enough."

"I wish there was another way," Elizabeth said, wringing her hands in anguish. "The danger seems so great."

"There is danger everywhere, Madame," the Queen said. "It is here, in this very palace. It is nearby, in the halls of the Assembly. And there is danger along the roads and in the towns where we wish to go. If danger is found everywhere one looks, it is not so frightening anywhere. One must merely select a path, and then follow it to the very end."

They walked silently through the gardens, watched by the courtiers, and the soldiers.

"I wish there was something I could do," Elizabeth said, fighting the teary wavering of her voice.

The Queen reached out her hand and grasped one of Elizabeth's. Her hand was warm and dry.

"You have done what I requested," the Queen said. "And I will forever be grateful to you for that. All that is left is to pray, and hope that our prayers are heard."

The women reached the end of the walkway and turned to begin walking back towards the courtiers waiting and watching in the shade of the tree at the far end of the lawn. They walked now in silence, each lost in her own thoughts.

22

Paris: June 20, 1791

The driver sitting atop the front of the plain-looking carriage looked bored. He was parked in the Petit Carrousel, on the rue de l'Echelle near the rue de Rivoli, outside the Tuileries Palace. His team of four horses waited patiently at the late hour, just past midnight, and indeed appeared to all be asleep on their feet. The driver wore a stained dark coat, wrinkled trousers, and a wide-brimmed hat that helped conceal most of his face. Like many a hired coach driver, he puffed away at a pipe, in part to have something to do, in part to help keep away the swarms of flies attracted by the ordure in the streets and the warm flanks of the team of horses.

The driver and his empty coach had been waiting for nearly two hours. Other coachmen, also waiting for their aristocratic clients to finish with the *coucher*, or the nightly bedding ceremony of the King, had wandered past to exchange greetings, spread some gossip or discuss the political occurrences of the day. The driver had nodded, laughed at their jokes and agreed with the general opinion that the King, being prepared for bed in his chambers in the nearby palace, deserved to suffer for his sins against the nation and its people.

Eventually, the other coachmen had disappeared, to drive their masters home to their own warm beds. But the driver continued to wait at his post, nodding once or twice when a night watchman or a guardsman strolled past. Finally, just before the clocks struck the hour of one, he saw a movement across the courtyard. A group of three women, one carrying a young girl in her arms and another holding the hand of a teenaged girl, approached the carriage. The driver leaped down and opened the door, helping the group to climb inside.

"Be as quiet as you can," the driver whispered. "When the others arrive, we shall depart. It won't be long now." *I hope*, he said to himself.

The little girl, who was the Dauphin of France, now wearing the plain dress of a commoner, crawled beneath one of the benches inside the coach and fell fast asleep. He had thought it a great adventure when, an hour or so earlier, his governess, Madame de Tourzel, had awakened him in his bed inside the Tuileries.

"Come at once, mon cher," she had whispered. "We have been ordered to take up a post!"

The boy, thinking he was being assigned to command a regiment of soldiers, had called for his boots and sabre. Instead, Madame de Tourzel had dressed him in a simple cotton dress and wrapped his head in an oversized bonnet. Half asleep, he was confused, but accepted this unusual behavior as part of some kind of new adventure. Madame de Tourzel told him they were all going to be part of a play and this was part of his costume. The Dauphin was excited and full of questions. His governess hushed him. Soon, they had joined with the Dauphin's older sister, Marie Therese, who was also sleepy and confused, although her mother, the Queen, had warned her a day earlier to be prepared for anything. Along with two servants, the group had made their way stealthily through the hallways of the Palace, now dark and quiet and deserted. Madame de Tourzel used a key she had been given to unlock the door to the apartments belonging to the Duc de Villequier, who had long since fled the country, and led the group out the side entrance to that suite, which was never guarded. They made their way around the Palace and into the Petit Carrousel courtyard, and saw the carriage waiting on the far side.

Once the children and Madame were safely inside, the two servants melted away into the night. The King had given them each a purse of money and instructions to leave Paris, and France, at once. Meanwhile, Count Fersen, for it was he sitting on the driver's bench of the carriage, puffed away at his pipe and awaited the arrival of his other passengers.

The first to appear out of the shadows was Madame Elisabeth, the sister of the King. She, too, was dressed plainly in the garb of a servant. Fersen jumped down, bowed, and helped her into the coach. She accidentally stepped on the arm of the young Dauphin, but he bravely stifled his cry of pain.

Not wanting to call attention to a coach suspiciously stationery for so long, Fersen climbed back onto the bench and cracked his whip, startling the horses awake. He guided the coach on a short trip around several blocks before returning it to its former place in the Petit Carrousel. While on this short journey, another coach-and-four rushed past, this one black with silver trim. It contained General Lafayette, who was heading to the Tuileries Palace to check the night guard and ensure that the King had been safely escorted to his bedchamber according to the nightly ritual.

Once back in place, Fersen and his carriage had to wait for another hour. Finally, a portly man dressed in valet's clothes, approached, in the company of another man. The valet was chuckling to himself as he flung open the coach's door and climbed inside.

"Oh, my word," the King said as he settled down onto the bench inside. "That was easier than we thought it might be. The guards thought I was the Chevalier de Coigny, leaving the palace as usual after the coucher. They waved at me! Waved! Oh, it was too easy. I even stopped and rebuckled my shoe when it came loose. They had no idea, no idea at all."

"It is so, Majesty," said the other man, who was the Comte de Valory, one of his most loyal vassals.

"Are we off then?" the King asked.

"We await her Majesty, the Queen," Fersen said. "She insisted on being the last to leave the palace, so that your Majesty could still escape in the event that she is captured."

"We shall not leave if she is not here," the King said gruffly. "That would be most unchivalrous. Unthinkable!" The coach fell silent as they waited.

The minutes crept past slowly and each of the persons inside the coach, with the exception of the Dauphin, who had quickly fallen back to sleep underneath the rear bench, strained to hear the sound of footsteps approaching, while each thought of the horrible possibilities that awaited if the Queen, or they themselves, were discovered by the authorities. Finally, after twenty long minutes, those inside the coach heard Fersen leap down again from his bench outside and heard him whisper: "Majesty! You are safe now."

The door opened and the Queen, dressed in the plain dress of a servant girl, with mantle and hat, climbed inside. "My dear," said the King with quavering emotion, "How happy I am to see you! How happy I am!" He embraced her and held her close for several long moments.

Fersen climbed back onto the front of the coach and cracked his whip again. The carriage jolted forward and soon was making its way down the rue de Rivoli, heading for the Porte Saint-Martin, one of the main gateways in and out of the city of Paris. In an abundance of caution, Fersen took a roundabout route to the gate, in case someone, somehow, might be following the royal party.

"I had to wait until General Lafayette left the Palace," the Queen told her husband, who still grasped her hand in his. "He was checking on the guard, making sure the King had retired for the evening. Once he left, I was able to make my way out. No one saw me. I am certain of it."

"Almighty God is watching over us," the King said.

They quickly rehearsed the roles they had assumed for their flight out of Paris. The King was now Monsieur Durand, a valet. His wife was Madame Rochet, a waiting-woman. Madame Elisabeth was now Rosalie, a children's nurse. Madame de Tourzel was the owner of the coach, the Baronne de Korff, a middle-aged German aristocrat, who was traveling to St. Petersburg with her two daughters, Aglaie and Amelie. They practiced saying their new names to each other as the coach sped through the empty Parisian streets.

Once they had passed through the Porte, the coach stopped at a roadhouse. There, the party exited the plain coach and climbed into the richly appointed new berline coach that Fersen had had constructed for the royal family's escape. He had told the coach builder that a wealthy German countess needed a strong, fortified coach and six to make her way to St. Petersburg for the fall session of the csarina's court. The wheels and axles were extra strong, the appointments inside the coach luxurious, the benches comfortable and soft, and there were compartments everywhere for luggage and food and drink.

Here, Count Fersen bid farewell to the royal family. He had wanted to continue on the journey to Montmédy, to be close to the Queen and her family as protector and guide, but had been overruled by the King. One of his usual horsemen climbed into the driver's bench, and Fersen bid them all a tearful farewell. He kissed the Queen's hand, and held it for perhaps a moment too long. The Queen remained impassive. The King thanked the Count for his service. "We must be off," he said. "Godspeed to you!"

The whip cracked. The new team of six leaped forward, and the yellow-and-green berline disappeared down the highway on the way towards Meaux. Fersen stood and watched until it was out of sight. Then, he mounted a horse made ready for him, and rode off to the north, in the direction of Brussels.

Elizabeth Gower and her husband were having a quiet breakfast on the balcony of their house the next morning, enjoying the warm sun and listening to the sounds of the city awakening and stirring around them. Their children were playing inside, occasionally running out to the balcony for a bit of toasted bread and jam, or to ask Maman a question about something.

The domestic tranquility was broken, around nine-thirty, by the sound of the *tocsin*, the alarm bells, which began ringing in every church tower and municipal building. The young family, like the rest of Paris, heard the bells, then noticed that their ringing was not stopping. Indeed, the insistent sound grew louder and louder.

"Something is amiss," Gower said, mostly to himself, as the noise increased as the minutes passed. "It sounds like the city is under attack."

At that moment, a servant came in with a sealed envelope, which he passed to the ambassador with a curt bow. Gower tore it open and read the note.

"Good Lord," he said. "They have left."

"They?" Elizabeth asked the question, although she knew immediately what had happened.

"The royal family. They escaped from the Tuileries sometime in the night. They have fled." Gower stood up and tossed his napkin to the ground. "I must go to the embassy at once." He rushed out. The children came out to the balcony to listen to the incessant clanging of the bells, the alarm ringing out across the rooftops of the city. Together, they watched as the streets below filled with people milling about, wondering what was going on.

Elizabeth pulled her children in and hugged them to her breast. *"Oh, Godspeed, Majesty,"* she thought. *"May you arrive safely at your destination."*

It was a full day and then some before Earl Gower returned to his home. He stumbled in just before noon the following day, haggard and slightly unkempt. His eyes were red with lack of sleep, his face unshaven. Elizabeth took one look at him and guided him gently into their bedchamber. She motioned at the governess to take the children elsewhere.

Gower sat down heavily on the bed and put his head in his hands.

"It is over," he said finally, his voice weak and wavering. "They have been captured."

Elizabeth came and sat down next to him, wrapping her arms around his shoulders. He sighed and leaned into her.

"What has happened?" she asked.

"They were apprehended in the village of Varennes," Gower said. "It is halfway between Reims and Metz. Someone, it is said it was the local postmaster, recognized the King when they stopped for a change of horses and a meal. They were arrested and held until one of Lafayette's cavalry squadrons could be summoned."

"Are they…still alive?" Elizabeth breathed.

"Oh, yes," he said. "For now, anyway. They are being returned to Paris. The monarchy in France is over. It is the end. I am sure there will now be a trial."

"What does this mean, for us?" she asked her husband.

He stood and walked to the window, peering out at the bright sunshine.

"My Lord Pitt has instructed me to continue at my post until such time as the King is formally deposed," he said. "My credentials were presented to his Majesty. King George and our government do not recognize the rebellious factions seeking revolutionary change. So we must wait and see. But you should be prepared to leave at a moment's notice. I do not know what will happen once the royal family returns to the city. No one knows."

"I will pack some things we can take if we need to leave quickly," Elizabeth said, thinking.

"And keep the children close at hand," Gower said. "Do not let them out of the house without one of the men to watch over them. That is vital. If things turn bad, and I believe they will, we are all at risk."

She went to him and held him closely again.

"Craufurd has left the city with his wife," Gower said. "I believe they're heading for Zurich. He has friends there. And money. He'll land on his feet. Those types of people always do. Fersen is said to be in Brussels, on his way back to Stockholm. It is likely he will never be allowed back in France."

"What about Sir Jeremy?" Elizabeth said. "And the others at the embassy? Are they in danger too?

Gower shook his head. "At the moment, no," he said. "Our nations are not at war. There is a strong tradition that foreign legates are to be protected by the host country. If that changes, they will have to leave Paris. But for now, they are safe."

"Oh, Gower, I am frightened," Elizabeth said. "Our lives, and those of our children, depend on the continued goodwill of other people. We are helpless. If they wish to do us harm, they will. What can we do?"

Gower stared at his wife. All that she said was true. If the mob milling about outside on the streets of Paris suddenly decided to storm their home and kill all the inhabitants, who would try to stop them? His two bodyguards? Against a furious and emotional riot? Not very likely. He had seen the mobs of Paris and what they could do to any unfortunate they decided was too close to the royalty or not strongly supportive of the revolution. He had seen the bloody heads carried through the streets at the end of pikes. He had seen men and women stripped naked and hung from lamp posts and trees. He had seen the ugliness of the mob, heard the bloodthirsty calls for justice. But he had never imagined that he himself, much less his innocent wife and small children, would possibly have to face that ugliness themselves. He would never admit it, to himself or to his wife, but he, too, was frightened.

What can we do? The most frightening thing of all was that he had no answer to her question. And so it hung in the air between them, unanswered, unanswerable.

23
Paris: April 1792

With the royal family returned to the Tuileries Palace, Paris began slipping towards total anarchy. There was the massacre in the Champs de Mars, about a month after the attempted escape. A meeting in that large public square, called by the assembly leaders Danton and Robespierre for the public to hear and discuss the new constitution of the republic, had degenerated into a riot, and the troops under the command of Lafayette had opened fire, killing dozens of citizens. That had been the last straw for Lafayette, already under some suspicion for allowing the royals to escape from Paris. He had resigned as general of the National Guard, taken an assignment with the Army on the eastern borders and soon escaped into Austrian territory, where he was arrested and imprisoned.

In October 1791, the Assembly passed the final language of the new constitution and the King, now known as Louis Capet, a citizen the same as any other, had been forced to sign the new law, which severely limited his powers as monarch. Worse, the members of the Assembly now refused to remove their hats in his presence; the disrespect caused the King to weep in frustration.

The Queen, now Madame Capet, was held in even lower esteem. Uniformly hated by the people, who blamed her foreign birth for most of the country's troubles, she was publicly berated and cursed during her now infrequent strolls through the gardens at the Tuileries. When she and her husband attended performances of the opera or the ballet, she was whistled at, and loudly cursed by the attendees. She learned to stay hidden in her box.

A new set of guards were installed in the Tuileries. Neither the King nor the Queen were allowed the privacy of their apartments: doors remained opened to all rooms so the guards could look in on the royals at any time of day or night. One guard was assigned to sit between the bedchambers of the King and the Queen throughout the night.

The Queen's normal retinue of servants were, for the first few months after their return from Varennes, dismissed. One woman servant from before the escape, uniformly acknowledged as a spy for the National Assembly, was assigned to serve the Queen: her portrait was placed at the entrance to the Queen's apartments so that the guards would admit no other person to her presence. The Queen's children were followed night and day by armed soldiers.

The threat of war loomed large. The National Assembly expected the nations of Europe to ratify its new constitutional government. Europe was slow to agree. King George of England quickly sent word through Lord Gower to agree to the new government, as long as Louis still had some monarchical power. Austria, Prussia and the other powers dithered, trying to decide whether to agree to the new French regime, or to invade and install the royals back on their throne. Emperor Leopold III, the brother of Marie Antoinette, died suddenly in Vienna, adding further confusion.

In the spring, Elizabeth of Sutherland received permission, after many previous requests had been denied, to bring her son George to the palace to visit with the Queen and the Dauphin, as they had many times before. Elizabeth was shocked to see the Queen's appearance: she was thin as a rail, her arms mere bones draped in skin, her face drawn and haggard. Elizabeth diplomatically did not mention the Queen's shocking appearance, but curtsied deeply and tried to ignore the tears that formed in her eyes.

"It is wonderful to see Your Majesty again," Elizabeth said, trying to smile. "And the Dauphin continues to grow more manly every day!"

The Queen smiled. "Yes, he requires new boots almost every week it seems," she said. "I am now forced to justify my requests for funding from the Assembly. It appears none of those gentlemen have ever had a growing boy in their households."

They walked outside in the Gardens, trailed closely now by two armed soldiers. As before, crowds of citizens also wandered at will through the vast gardens, gawking at the Queen and occasionally muttering some imprecation or other. The Queen ignored them completely.

"How have you been, Majesty, since …" Elizabeth was not sure how to refer to the attempted escape from Paris of the previous summer.

"Since we tried to escape and were captured?" The Queen was not afraid. She was resigned. "It has been difficult," she continued. "We are never alone. And the National Assembly…forgive me, it is now called the *Legislative* Assembly… controls everything. My husband has a veto, but it is highly recommended he not use it. We are mere figureheads, nothing more. And one day, they will tire of supporting figureheads and off our heads will come."

"Do not say that, Majesty," Elizabeth said imploringly. "The French people are civilized. All of Europe knows that. And God will protect you."

The Queen smiled at her friend. "And did God protect Charles I who once ruled over the kingdoms of England and Scotland?"

Elizabeth felt her face turn red. "B-but that was different," she said.

The Queen's smile deepened. She said nothing.

The Dauphin and young George Levenson-Gower were playing at war again, dueling with wooden sticks, laughing hysterically. The women watched, enjoying the boys at play. Enjoying the idea that the two boys had no idea of the life and death situation that swirled about them.

"What really happened?" Elizabeth asked, her voice low. "When you left, I mean. What happened?"

"Ah," the Queen waved her hand dismissively. "The usual. The best plans of the best men went awry, as they often do. General de Bouille was supposed to meet us in a certain place at a certain time: he did not. My husband did not know the country where we were—we had no one with us who knew the way. So we stumbled around as if in the dark until someone found us. I daresay you and I could have come up with a better plan. But, of course, no one asks us for advice. We are mere women."

Elizabeth did not know what to say, so said nothing.

The Queen looked around. The guards were ten paces distant and looked bored.

"Look," she said, whispering. She raised the corner of her bonnet. The Queen's once luxuriant hair, her pride and joy, had turned the color of a well-bleached sheet. Thin and snow white, the Queen's hair now resembled ragged, greasy strands. Elizabeth could not withhold a gasp of surprised horror.

"I show you so I may give you this," the Queen said. She reached out and placed a silver locket in Elizabeth's hand. She clicked it open. Inside was a lock of snow white hair, woven into a braid. Inscribed inside the locket were the words: *Blanchi par la tristesse.* "Whitened by sorrow."

"I am so grateful for the help you provided my family and myself, Madame Ambassador," the Queen said quietly, tears rolling down her cheeks. "I shall never forget your kindness. Please remember me, and my dear son, as we once were, and not as we will soon become."

Elizabeth, overcome with emotion, bowed her head and wept.

"Maman! What is wrong?" Little George came running over with his stick, concerned to see two adult women weeping together.

"It is nothing, dear boy," she said, wiping away her tears and caressing the unruly shock of hair on the boy's head. "Just women talking about the past. Come: say goodbye to Monsieur le Dauphin. It is time for us to go."

The boys embraced, the women curtsied to each other. They said their good-byes. Elizabeth, the 19th chief of Clan Sutherland and marchioness of Stafford, rode away from the palace in her husband's old and creaky coach. She never saw the Queen again.

LORD GOWER WAS meeting with Sir Jeremy at the English embassy.

"I have a letter from Craufurd," Gower said, tossing it across his desk at his assistant. "He is still in Zurich, although he has recently been in Geneva as well. He tells me that the bankers are betting on war between France and the rest of Europe."

"An excellent wager, Sir," Sir Jeremy said drily. "Milord Pitt has placed us, and all other embassies across Europe, on high alert. In the event of invasion, we must be prepared to evacuate. I have so instructed the staff and we have already sent the most important documents we have by courier back to London."

Gower paused. "Am I still being followed?" he asked.

Sir Jeremy rose and closed the door to the ambassador's office.

"You are, sir," he said. "And certain inquiries have been made about you."

"Inquiries?"

"Monsieur Danton and his faction appear to be in the ascendancy," Sir Jeremy said carefully. "The individual who was once assigned to shadow you now reports to him."

"Interesting," Gower said.

"Quite so," Sir Jeremy agreed. "This individual—his name is D'Anjou, by the way—continues to watch your movements around the city. He has also been seen asking questions of certain people close to your household."

"Questions? Questions about what?"

Sir Jeremy looked uncomfortable now. He stroked his chin nervously. It was quite unlike the usually unflappable *charges d'affaires*.

"I am told he is asking about your wife, Sir."

"My wife!" Gower stood up suddenly, launching his chair violently backward. "Elizabeth? What do they want of her?"

"Sir, there are rumors…little more than gossip as far as I can tell … that your wife has a close relationship with the Queen."

Gower was red-faced with anger, squinting furiously at his aide across the desk. Sir Jeremy let him fume for a moment, then continued.

"She and your son George have frequented the Tuileries Palace on several occasions," Sir Jeremy continued. "She has been seen deep in conversations with Her Majesty. Conversations which have included private whispering and occasional tearful discussions. This has raised questions."

"Questions?" Gower did not trust himself to say more.

"The exact reasons for this D'Anjou's inquiries are not known, Sir," Sir Jeremy said. "But my men have been told he is asking about her activities in the time just before the royals tried to escape Paris. We do not know why, just that those seem to be the direction his questions are taking."

"This is an abomination!" Gower exploded, finally. He began pacing back and forth in his office, hands clasped angrily behind his back, face red and angry. "My wife has been a friend to Her Majesty the Queen, but she is entirely innocent of any political or diplomatic intrigue of any kind. The boys—my son and the Dauphin—are of similar ages and interests and enjoy each other's company. I am told they like to play at soldiering. Has *that* become a crime in this godforsaken country now? My wife is the kindest, most understanding woman I know. She feels deeply for the Queen and the troubles she faces. But Elizabeth would never do or say anything to Her Majesty that would in any way affect our national policies toward the French nation. Never!"

Sir Jeremy waited and cleared his throat.

"Sir, I am in complete accord with your opinion in this matter," he said carefully. "Madame Gower is both intelligent and compassionate, and I agree that this insidious gossip is nothing more than that ... ugly gossip. Lord knows there is enough of that in this city. Unfortunately, we live at a time when even ugly gossip can be enough to cause one to be sent to prison or, worse, to the guillotine."

At the use of that word in regard to his own wife, Gower was struck into apoplectic silence. He sank back into his chair and his face turned from angry red to bloodless white. Sir Jeremy plunged ahead.

"Sir, I tell you this because both you and your wife need to know it. I think it very unlikely that this D'Anjou, or anyone else, will ever take any action against you or your wife. To do so would be a serious breach of diplomatic protocol and have serious repercussions. On the other hand, we live in a time of lawlessness and the usual rules of engagement are not always obeyed or enforced. Thus, you and your wife must be on guard at all times. I would strongly recommend that all contact between

Madame Gower and the Queen be halted at once. No need to provide anyone with fresh ammunition. I would further recommend that any records or gifts or other evidence of the friendship between the ladies in question be collected and destroyed. My men can help with this if you need them."

He waited, allowing Lord Gower to digest this information.

"The times are getting more dangerous by the day, Sir," he said. "Danton and his thugs in the Assembly are waiting for the opportunity to strike at the King and his Queen. It is coming. And if the Austrians come across the border with their armies, that will speed the demise of the royal family. Rightly or not, an invasion will be seen as an attempt to rescue the royal family and thus an attack on the new Republic. That will not be allowed to stand, and all friends of the royals could go down with them. Including your wife, if this D'Anjou is able to prove anything of the relationship she has had with the Queen."

Gower was still speechless. He could see what danger his wife was in, suddenly, and how she was there through no outward fault of her own.

"It may be time for my family and me to return to London," he said finally, his voice small and hollow. "For our safety."

"You may very well be correct in that assessment, Sir," Sir Jeremy returned. He bowed and left the ambassador to his thoughts.

24

Paris: June 1792

At the end of June 1792, events began to move. The city had become swollen with people from the countryside. Many were the families of the group of soldiers known as the *fedérés*, a large body of provincial troops that set up camp just outside the city gates. Others came to support the various political factions now fighting openly in the Legislative Assembly: the Girondists, the Jacobins, the Cordeliers. The city was on edge: rumors flew daily up and down the boulevards of the city. Soldiers fully armed marched back and forth. The news coming in from the front in Belgium were not good: the war was going badly for the Republic.

On June 20, ironically the one-year anniversary of their escape from Paris, an unruly crowd massed outside and then stormed the royal apartments in the Tuileries. Many carried pikes, hatchets and long knives, and they carried the effigy of a doll dangling from a noose and the bloody heart of a bull, labeled "the heart of Louis XVI." The National Guard, again assigned to keep the King and Queen safe, stood aside as the crowd surged into the old palace.

"Where is the bugger?" the crowd yelled as they burst into the King's chamber. He was there, with his sister, Madame Elisabeth, who whispered to her servants to let the crowd think she was Marie Antoinette, so to save the Queen from harm. The King showed bravery in the face of this new danger, donning an ill-fitting *bonnet rouge* and asking one of the attackers to feel his heart to see if it was beating wildly with fear. It was not, the man admitted.

The Queen, helped by her retinue, escaped into a secret compartment with her children: the Dauphin, now age seven, and his elder sister, thirteen. They listened to the crowd attacking doors with their hatchets looking for someone to chop into pieces. Order was eventually restored and the royal family reunited in the King's chamber. Trembling with fear and emotion, all they could do was gather together in a sad embrace.

More people from the provinces poured into the city to mark the new holiday honoring the fall of the Bastille on July 14. The King rode in a parade, but wore a thick, quilted waistcoat in the event of an assassination attempt. There was no violence that day, but the crowds were vocal in their disapproval of the monarch.

The summer heat and the tension in the city continued to climb day by day. A rumor crashed through the city about a manifesto allegedly written by the Prussian Duke of Brunswick which threatened retribution if the Tuileries were invaded again, or the royal family harmed in any way. The King was no longer allowed to go on his much loved daily rides through the city, much less escape to his estates in Saint Cloud for hunting. The royal family was kept cooped up in the palace, awaiting the next developments.

Those came on the hot humid morning of August 9. A large crowd began to gather in the Faubourg Saint-Antone. A body of reinforcements from the National Guard were dispatched to the Tuileries, reinforcing a volunteer group of some 300 aristocrats loyal to the King, who was also guarded by his faithful Swiss Guards, which had been sworn to protect the French king since the fifteenth century. All day long, these three bodies of protection for the King milled about the palace. The Swiss Guards maintained their order and discipline, while the aristocrats and the National Guardsmen wandered directionless around the grounds.

At midnight, the tocsins began to peal throughout the city, announcing the beginning of the assault on the palace and its royal inhabitants. The crowds surged forward, the troops fitfully pushed back. Shots rang out, the first of the guards died. The people pushed forward again. This time, the guards broke and ran. Except for the Swiss troops, professional to the end. They died by the hundreds at the hands of a bloodthirsty mob.

The King, the Queen, their children and relatives and some of their retinue escaped the madness by dashing across the courtyards and into the building which housed the Legislative Assembly. There, they huddled all day in one small antechamber while their former home was ransacked and thousands killed. That night, they were escorted into a nearby convent. After several days of debate, the royal family was then taken to the Temple in the Marais section of the city and ensconced in the prison-like section known as the Tower. A bloody sign was hung on one of the doors of the Tuileries: House to Let.

AGAIN, THE GOWER family was stirred from its morning repose by the sounds of the bells echoing across the city. They heard the roars of the crowds surging towards the Tuileries. They knew what was happening.

Gower received a hastily written note from his embassy just before noon. "Go!" was all it said. He looked at his wife, who was nervously wringing her hands. "It is time, Elizabeth," he said. "Gather the children."

They had practiced for the event. Gower ordered the servants to carry some suitcases which had long been packed and ready to the courtyard below. Elizabeth hurried the children into their clothing. Lord Gower spent a few minutes burning some official papers in the fireplace. Finally, they were ready.

In the courtyard, the coach was ready, with two fresh horses laced into the livery. The bags had been stowed and Elizabeth and the children climbed inside. Gower called his two bodyguards away from the coach.

"Hans, I want you to drive," he said to the first. "Peter—you ride on the back. Both of you need to look sharp. There is a chance we will be challenged. We shall do whatever they tell us unless there is danger to my wife and children. In that case, the three of us will fight to the death. Is that clear?"

The two Swiss guards, both experienced veterans of several European campaigns, nodded gravely. Gower climbed into the coach with his family and they set off.

The streets teemed with people of all kinds. The atmosphere appeared to be one of a holiday. Citizens greeted one another with hugs and kisses. But almost everyone had a weapon of some kind: an axe, a knife, a sharpened pike. As they made their way to the northern gate of the city, they passed many a streetlight from which dangled a bloody corpse. Most appeared to be well dressed. It seemed that anyone who appeared to be rich or connected or well known was fair game for quick trial and execution. Paris was celebrating a holiday: It was a holiday of death and it seemed to infect the entire city.

The coach crossed the Pont Neuf and made its way slowly down the Rue Montmartre heading north towards the city of Amiens and beyond that, to Calais. At the Porte Saint-Denis, with its triumphal arch replacing what had been one of the main entries to the city of Paris, two uniformed soldiers waved the coach to the side of the boulevard. The guard named Peter jumped down off the rear platform and waited near the door. He wore a sword in its scabbard and made sure that anyone looking at him would know that he was armed. Several minutes passed. The air inside the coach grew hotter and staler.

An officer strode out of a nearby building and approached the coach. He nodded at Peter and at Hans sitting on the driver's bench. The officer opened the door to the coach and peered inside.

"Your papers, please," he said, extending his gloved hand.

Gower passed over a sheaf of documents: the official seal of the embassy was on top, along with passports for himself, Elizabeth and the two children; there were ownership documents for the coach and employment letters covering the two Swiss bodyguards.

Several long minutes passed while the officer read through the documents, frowning as he read each one in turn. When he was finished, he peered up at Lord Gower again.

"Where are you headed, Monsieur Ambassador?" he asked.

"To Calais," Gower replied, squinting out into the hot summer sun. "I have been summoned back to London with my family."

"I see," the officer said, rifling quickly through the papers again, as if some new fact might come tumbling out. "The roads are dangerous. You do not have an armed escort."

It was not a question. Still, Gower responded. "My men are capable of seeing us safely to our destination. Is there anything else you require of us?"

The officer frowned again. He looked down at the papers once again. He then sighed, and looked up at the elaborate marble gate that Louis XV had constructed in the place where for hundreds of years, visitors to the City of Light had passed through old King Charles' wall. After studying the carvings on the face of the arch, the officer sighed again and looked back at Gower.

"Your papers are in very good order, Sir," the officer said, handing them back into the coach. "However, as you know, the situation of the country has changed. You will require an additional pass to safely move through the countryside in order to reach your destination."

"An additional pass," Gower echoed.

"Indeed, Sir."

"Where do I obtain such a pass?"

The officer shrugged. *How do I know? I'm just a guard at the Porte Saint-Denis.* "Perhaps at the Hotel d'Ville?" he suggested.

"That would take all day," Gower said. "We have no time to waste. Isn't there another way?"

The officer cocked his head to the side. "Perhaps," he said. "Perhaps I could construct a document for you that would do the trick. But, it is most unusual. I am not sure …"

"Done," Gower snapped. "How much?"

Thirty minutes later, the coach pulled back onto the dusty boulevard heading to the north. Gower placed the new, constructed and signed pass from the officer of the guard at the Porte Saint-Denis, on the top of his stack of documents. This new paper instructed all whom it may concern that the bearer, the ambassador of Great Britain and Ireland, should receive all courtesies and emoluments due to a nation that had demonstrated such respect and fealty to the new *Republique*, and that said ambassador's onward journey should not be restricted or delayed in any way. The officer's flourish of a signature was scrawled across the bottom of the document. It had cost Gower five livres. He suspected he would be required to purchase several more such passes before he strode, once again, on English soil.

25

The coach arrived on the outskirts of Calais late in the afternoon. The family could smell the briny ocean air and hear the gulls keening overhead as the horses drew up at an inn on the outskirts of the old city. Though not a large city, in terms of its population, Calais had long been the main shipping port in France that connected with the island of Great Britain, a mere 21 miles away across *La Manche*, or The Sleeve, as the French termed that part of the Channel. Groups of long, low warehouses spread out from the main pier in the center of the city, holding all kinds of goods which were either destined for shipment across the water, or that had recently arrived from England and were awaiting reshipment to various points across Europe.

Embarking from his coach, Lord Gower made arrangements for his horses and told his bodyguards to stay with the coach. He then escorted his family into the two-story inn. The old hag of a woman who managed the inn peered out at the travelers standing before her and, without a word, passed a room key across her desk and motioned them toward the stairs leading to the second floor.

"May we … is there a place for my daughter and I to bathe?" Elizabeth asked the woman. "We have been traveling all day."

The old hag rattled off a string of sentences that were, to Elizabeth at least, unintelligible, spoken in the argot of the region—her words sounded harsh and guttural. Gower, at least, understood most of what the woman said, and passed some money to the old woman. In turn, she rummaged around in a drawer and found two towels and a bar of gray soap which she passed over to the weary travelers. "I will send up some hot water," she said.

The family trooped up the stairs and found their one small room in the back, overlooking an alley next to the stables where their horses were being watered, fed and brushed. There was one bed in the room, beneath a small window. Elizabeth looked out and saw a sliver of sea in the distance. It made her think of her home at Dunrobin, where the sea was in view from almost every room in the castle. For almost the first time since she and her children had arrived in France, more than two years earlier, she felt herself relax a bit as she thought of home, where the rough mountains of the Highlands spilled down to the sea and the wind was always fresh.

"While you and Lady Charlotte freshen up, I will make arrangements for the first ferry in the morning," Gower told his wife. "Then we will find a place for dinner." Little George, their son, was eagerly exploring the small room, looking into the closet and opening all three drawers on the small dresser that stood opposite the bed.

Elizabeth smiled and nodded. There was a sharp rap on the door.

"That must be our hot water," she said and went to open the door.

Two men, dressed in the uniforms of the National Guard, burst in. They were both armed with muskets and wore scabbards at the side. The men took up positions on either side of the door and stood to attention. Little George scrambled to his mother, who grabbed both of her children and swept them into her arms. Following the soldiers into the room came a small man, not much taller than five feet in height, wearing a long black overcoat. His head was bare, hair greasy in unkempt strands, his face round, with a chin that arced sharply towards his narrow, pointed nose. His eyes were small and dark, behind a pair of spectacles with thin, round frames. He held a sheaf of papers in his hand.

"What is the meaning…" Gower started angrily towards the man, who held up a hand to cut him off.

"Monsieur le Ambassador," the man said, his voice thin and reedy, but carrying a distinctive edge of authority. "I regret to inform you that you and your family are to be considered under arrest."

"By whose order?" Gower was furious, blinking rapidly with his myopic eyes at the man. "I am the Ambassador to the Court of France, returning, with my family, to my home country as ordered by His Majesty King George of Great Britain. I have the right of free passage according to all the accepted protocols of Europe, and that passage cannot be denied or abridged by anyone for any reason whatsoever."

The man continued as if Gower had never spoken a word.

"You are charged with aiding and abetting the unlawful escape of Monsieur and Madame Capet of Paris, formerly known as King Louis XVI and Queen Marie Antoinette; and of unlawful espionage and attempts to undermine the lawful authority of the French Republic."

"This is preposterous!" Gower said, stamping his foot in frustration. "These charges are ridiculous. I demand to speak to the magistrate in charge at once!"

"You are hereby summoned to appear in Court at ten o'clock on the morrow to answer to these charges," the man said calmly. "Until that time, you will not leave these premises until you can be escorted to the Court. Arrangements will be made for your evening meal. Good evening, sir, madame…"

He nodded at each of them and withdrew from the room. The two soldiers snapped to attention again and left behind him, closing the door with finality. Gower stood motionless for a moment, then slumped onto the bed, head hanging down between his knees.

Elizabeth unwrapped her arms from her children and bent to her husband, laying her hand on his shoulder.

"Oh, my dear," she said, her voice breaking with emotion. "It is my fault. I brought those clothes to her Majesty. They must have been watching. How else would they know?"

Gower raised his head and blinked confusedly at his wife.

"Whatever are you talking about, Elizabeth?" he asked.

She began to sob. The children came to her side and hugged her. They had never seen their mother demonstrate such outward emotion. It frightened them, even more than the sight of the armed guards bursting into their room had frightened them.

"The Q-queen," she gasped. "She asked me to bring her some ordinary girls' clothes. She never said why she wanted them, but I knew. It was for the Dauphin, to dress him as a girl as a disguise. S-so they could escape!" She turned her head against Gower's chest and sobbed harder.

"But they caught them," she continued after a moment. "And now they have caught … they have caught me!"

Now, the two children were weeping piteously, along with their mother. Gower held his wife away from him, at arm's length and listened to the cries of his family. He not so gently guided her to sit on the nearby bed, the children following to sit beside their mother, one on each side. Gower then began to pace.

"It's nonsense," he said as he paced, talking as if to himself. "They cannot prove a thing, not a thing! " He paced back and forth across the small room. "You will deny everything, do you hear me? You did *not* bring the Queen any old clothes. Where is the proof of this? You are the wife of the British ambassador. They have no right to ask you such questions. If someone gave you old clothes, it was because you agreed to pass them on to a charitable body. To the church! That's it! You had clothes to donate to a church for the poor and indigent. Why, you barely know the Queen. You've only seen her once or twice at grand occasions. Where is the proof? Where, I ask you?"

Elizabeth gathered herself, only half listening to her husband blather on. She was thinking. She had asked one of her maidservants if she knew anyone with a daughter of about seven or eight years of age. Told yes, she had asked her servant to see if Elizabeth could perhaps purchase an old dress and bonnet, for which she, Elizabeth, would be happy to pay. It had all been quickly arranged. Elizabeth did not even know the name of the family from whom she had obtained the clothes. Now, she wondered if her maidservant had told the authorities, or perhaps the family of the girl whose dress she had bought. Or was it one of the Queen's courtesans? Someone had seen her passing the Queen that package containing the dress. Or had seen the Queen opening the package and had asked what that was. The Queen might have mentioned Elizabeth's name to someone. And that someone had remembered, and told the authorities. And now, here they were.

"Please do not worry, Gower," she said. "I am sure it will be fine. We must say our prayers and try to sleep. We must be rested and alert tomorrow. Rested and alert."

The two children had slept fitfully, sharing the one bed in the room. Elizabeth had tried to stay awake with her husband, but had finally succumbed, lying uncomfortably on the hard wooden floor, and had slept for a few hours before the dawn arrived. Lord Gower did not sleep. He continued pacing most of the night, thinking hard. He tried to remember what he had been told about the laws of diplomacy and safe passage during the brief time he had spent at Whitehall before leaving for Paris two years earlier.

He wished Sir Jeremy could be summoned to Calais, but knew there was no time. He alone would have to defend himself and his family; there was no one else.

During the long night, as he listened to the soft sighs of his children and wife as they slept, he planned what he might say. He rehearsed several versions of a speech to the court. One demanded their immediate release. One deflected the charges that might be laid against him or, worse, his wife. He devised several delaying techniques, thinking if he could buy some time, he could send a message back to Paris, or even across the Channel to reach London, and in that way obtain some official help for their plight. His mind raced along, words and ideas filling his head, being dismissed, more following behind.

By the time the light began to fill the room as dawn approached, he had organized his thoughts and felt he had done all he could to prepare for whatever ordeal awaited later that morning. He finally stopped pacing when he heard the cocks crow in the yard outside. He sat, finally, in the one wooden chair in the room, and, finally, closed his eyes.

Some time later, Elizabeth woke him gently, laying her hand on his arm.

"Gower?" she whispered. "Dear heart…it is time to wake."

He started, jumping to his feet. His wife and children stared at him with wide eyes, wondering, afraid. He stared back, and his resolve grew firm.

There was a sharp knock at the door. Gower opened it. A servant girl held a tray with plates of fruit, bread and cheeses, and some mugs of steaming chocolate. Gower thought that chocolate was something of a misplaced luxury to serve to a family held under arrest, but he gratefully accepted the tray and helped Elizabeth feed the children their breakfast.

The meal finished, the family waited patiently in the room. Gower sat in his wooden chair, Elizabeth and the children on the bed. Nobody spoke.

The sharp rap at the door made them all jump. Gower smiled at his wife. "Do not be afraid, my dear," he said. "It is not just you and I that go now to meet the magistrate. It is all of Great Britain. It is the King himself that is going to meet the magistrate. We are merely his loyal servants, doing our duty as we see fit to uphold our duty. And our King and his government is a power far, far greater than any court of law or French official can ever hope to be. So be of good cheer, and have faith."

Elizabeth grasped her husband's hand, brought it to her face, kissed it tenderly. Then, she stood, straightened her dress. Her children rose and stood next to her, standing straight. Lord Gower smiled at them all, then nodded. He turned and opened the door. The two soldiers came striding in, as they had the night before, and stood at attention, one to each side of the doorway. The little man with the hooked nose and the greasy hair came in behind and nodded.

"It is time," he said. "We go."

26

The family was driven to court in an open wagon, the four of them sitting on bales of hay. The two guards rode in the wagon with the family, redolent with the scent of body odor and garlic. Lord Gower thought about the tumbrels he had seen carrying the condemned to the guillotine in the Place de la Revolution in Paris, and shuddered. However, unlike in Paris, the townspeople of Calais, going about their normal workaday routines, paid the wagon and its cargo no heed.

As they left the yard of the inn, Gower looked for his two Swiss guards. He spotted Hans standing near the coach they had arrived in the previous day, but made no sign of recognition. Hans nodded at him. Peter was nowhere to be seen.

The ride from the inn to the Hall of Justice, a two-story stone structure next to the town hall, took no more than ten minutes. The family was escorted inside and shown to a courtroom on the second floor, where three long wooden benches faced a a table set upon a raised platform. They were told to sit in the first bench and await the arrival of the magistrate.

"Am I allowed an *avocat*, a lawyer?" Gower asked the man with the greasy hair. "I believe it is my right to have a representative."

"Be silent," he was told.

They sat there nearly an hour, listening to the sounds of life on the streets outside. Elizabeth held the hands of her two children, occasionally murmuring something softly to one or the other. A few people wandered into the courtroom to stare at them, but said nothing.

Finally, things began to happen. A clerk came in, straightened out some papers on the judge's desk, and then took a position at a smaller desk to one side, opening a sheaf of papers and preparing his quill pen and bottle of ink. The two soldiers, who had followed the wagon on foot to the courthouse, took up positions at the rear of the courtroom, muskets held upright at their sides. Spectators began coming in and sitting in the benches behind Gower and his family. He did not turn to look, but started straight ahead at the bench in front. Finally, there came a cry: *Attention! Ici le Juge*: Here is the Judge!

The Judge, a short, very round man with a red face walked into the courtroom, looking down curiously at the family in the front bench. He wore a black judicial robe, a fancy lace cravat, and the round velvet cap of his office, and carried some law books under his arm. His fleshy jowls were bright red, and his eyebrows were thick and bushy. He made his way around to his bench and sat down heavily, plopping the heavy tomes of the law down on the desk. He sighed once, and looked over at his clerk.

"We have today a case referred to this Court by the Committee for the General Security of the people of France," the clerk intoned, reading from a document he held close to his face.

"Is it a shipping case?" the judge asked.

"No, milord," the clerk said, shaking his head. "This case appears to be one of national security. It has been forwarded to your attention by the aforementioned Committee under the direction of Monsieur Georges Danton, the head of the Committee under the authority of the General Convention of Paris."

"Not a matter of shipping?" The judge sounded disappointed. "We usually hear cases about shipping."

"Yes, milord," the clerk said, patiently. "This is a special case that has been sent to us by Paris. They wish you to hear the matter."

The judge thought about that, stroking his chin. Then he nodded.

"Very well," he said. "We will hear the case. The particulars, if you please."

The clerk picked up another document, cleared his throat and began to read.

"The Committee for the General Security has charged His Excellency George Granville Levenson-Gower, ambassador extraordinary to the Court of the monarch now known as Louis Capet from His Royal Highness King George III of Great Britain and Ireland, with the offense of conspiring to promote the activities of said Louis Capet against the interests of the people of France …"

"Most extraordinary," said the Judge. "This is not a case about shipping, at all."

The clerk read on, undisturbed by the interruption.

"…and further charges Her Excellency the Countess of Sutherland in the country of Scotland and the wife of the heretofore mentioned defendant, the ambassador extraordinary, with acts of support and favor to Madame Capet, formerly known as Her Royal Highness the Queen of France, in contradiction to the orders of the National Assembly and General Convention of the Republic of France."

"The wife as well," the Judge said, shaking his head in amazement. "A most unusual case this morning. Are you sure there are no cases on shipping on the docket, clerk?"

"No, magistrate," said the clerk, bowing his head. "Just this one."

"I see, I see," the Judge said, drumming his fingers nervously on his desk. "Most unusual. Who is here to argue the case for the defendant?"

Lord Gower rose. "I have not been afforded access to an attorney," he said gravely, bowing to the Judge. "Therefore I assume that I will defend both myself and my wife against these scurrilous charges."

"Scurrilous," the Judge repeated, almost to himself. "I see, I see. And who is prosecuting the case, please?"

"That would be me, magistrate" said a voice from the back of the room. All heads turned around to look. A tall, angular man with sharp features and long black hair stood there, bowing to the Judge. He came forward and dropped a leather bag on the table before opening it and withdrawing a sheaf of papers. The man's sharp nose and pointed chin made him look somehow predatory, and an angry red scar above his left eye contributed to the affect he had.

"And you are …" the Judge prompted.

"Henri d'Anjou," the man said. "Special prosecutor for the Committee for the General Safety in Paris. I have been directed by his honor, the Chairman, to prosecute this case and seek justice on behalf of the French people."

"I see," said the Judge, who was looking more unhappy by the minute. "I don't suppose the Committee in Paris would be willing to give me some time, say a week or two, to read the particulars of this case and familiarize myself with the particular points of law that might be covered in this case?"

"They would not, Judge," said D'Anjou. "The Committee would agree to your decision to remand this case back to Paris, so that the people of the city most affected by the unscrupulous and illegal actions of these two people could witness and participate in the trial and thus receive a fuller measure of justice. Not that justice will not be served right here in Calais."

"I see, I see," the Judge rubbed his chin and looked up at the ceiling. He held this pose for some time, thinking. He looked over at his clerk, who merely shrugged his shoulders, as if to say *I have no idea what you should do.*

"No, Monsieur Prosecutor," the Judge said finally, "I will not so order. It is my deeply held belief that justice delayed is justice denied. I am here. You are here. The accused are here. And if I am not much mistaken, the accused wish to return as soon as possible to their native land. Is that not so?" He looked over at Lord Gower.

"That is so, Magistrate," Gower said. "My King has requested my return to London at the earliest convenience. I believe that I have the right of diplomatic passage free of encumbrance."

"Ah, yes, this is true, this is true," the Judge said, nodding and happy to find himself on firmer legal ground. "I am familiar with the laws of immigration and diplomacy. As an official representative of the Crown of Britain, you are generally free of any official encumbrances on your movements within our country, or in traveling to and from other countries, including your own. These precepts are generally accepted by all nations of Europe, including your own, is this not so?"

"It is, Magistrate," Lord Gower said, bowing again. "Credentialed diplomats in a host country may not be impeded in their movements among the people."

Henri D'Anjou cleared his throat loudly.

"Unless they have committed a serious offense against the laws of the host country," he said. "There is no diplomatic immunity in cases where serious crimes against the people of France have been committed."

"Quite so, quite so," the Judge said, nodding wisely. "Serious crimes will do it. You must not commit serious crimes, Sir," he said to Lord Gower. "That could certainly lead to the removal of any immunity you may have, in the eyes of the law."

"I have committed no such crime," Gower said gravely. "And neither has my wife. These charges are utter nonsense."

"Nonsense." The Judge was staring at the ceiling again. "Yes, I would think so. But there you have it, in a nutshell, the very thing we are here about. Monsieur D'Anjou, representing the citizens of France, charges that you have in fact committed a serious crime. You, Sir, the ambassador, maintain that you have not. It apparently has fallen to me to listen to the facts of this case and attempt to arrive at the truth. There, Justice dwells. Where there is truth, there is Justice."

He motioned for the first time at the two children sitting beside their mother in the front bench of the courtroom. "Do you hear that, children?" the Judge said, "Always look for the truth in a thing, and there you will find Justice. Remember that."

The children looked at the Judge blankly. He turned to the prosecutor. "Very well, Monsieur D'Anjou, let us hear your case. I warn you, Sir, please keep to the truth. There will be no Justice found in rumor, or falsehoods, or idle speculation. Only the truth, please, if you may." He nodded at the man to begin his case.

D'Anjou paused for a moment, as if he wanted to say something further. But he checked himself, glanced down quickly at his papers, cleared his throat, and began to speak.

"Milord," he began. "We began to investigate the activities of the Ambassador from Great Britain more than one year ago …"

"We?" the Judge interjected. "Who are the people you refer to as 'we,' Sir?" he asked. "Please be more precise. Precision is the pathway to the truth, Sir."

D'Anjou looked up at the Judge, annoyance etched across his face.

"The Committee for the General Security, milord, began to investigate the activities of the Ambassador from Great Britain more than one year ago," he continued. "It came to our attention that the Ambassador was coordinating activities with others for the purpose of assisting Monsieur Louis Capet, formerly known as King Louis XVI, to escape from Paris and flee to foreign nations for the purpose of fomenting a military invasion of France and overthrowing the duly elected government of the French people. That, Sir, is considered a treasonous act."

"Treason!" the Judge said, his voice squeaking with emotion. He wrote something down on the paper in front of him.

"This treasonous plan took place over several months during which time the defendant, Monsieur l'Ambassador, was observed having numerous meetings with others."

"How numerous?" the Judge asked.

"Sir?"

"You said he had numerous meetings. How many?"

D'Anjou leafed quickly through his sheaf of papers. I…I am not sure, Sir," he said finally.

"More than one?"

"Yes, sir," D'Anjou nodded. "Many more than one."

"More than ten?"

"I would have to review the notes of the investigation to obtain an accurate account, Sir," D'Anjou said.

"No need, no need," the judge said, scribbling again at his paper. "We will say more than one, probably less than ten. Acceptable?"

"Yes, Magistrate," D'Anjou said.

"Continue."

"As I said, the Ambassador was observed attending secret meetings with several foreign dignitaries who were all involved in planning or assisting the former King with his plans to escape," D'Anjou said.

"How can you say the meetings were secret?" the Judge interjected again.

"Sir?"

"You said he was observed attending secret meetings," the Judge said. "If he was observed attending a meeting, the meeting could not be said to be secret, could it? Someone saw the Defendant, the good Ambassador here, attending a meeting. Clearly, it was not secret. Who was the observer?"

"Sir?"

"Who saw the Ambassador attending these non-secret meetings?" the Judge asked.

"It was I, Sir," D'Anjou said, "Although I do not see how ..."

"*You* were the observer?" The Judge looked at D'Anjou with interest. "And you are also the prosecutor. Is that a standard practice in Paris? Because here in Calais, in the Pas du Calais prefecture, we generally assign a policeman or other duly authoritzed official to do the work of investigation of a case, and permit the prosecutor, such as yourself, to handle the legal procedures at trial. I find this circumstance to be most unusual."

"Again, Sir, I do not see how this could possibly affect the outcome of this trial," D'Anjou was beginning to get irritated at the constant interruptions of his presentation.

"It may, or it may not," the Judge said, nodding sagely. "That is why we are here today, Monsieur le Prosecutor, to find out the facts of this case and determine which facts may or may not be germane. Pray, continue."

"The investigation, by the Committee for the General Security, also obtained information concerning the wife of the English Ambassador, Madame Gower..." he nodded at Elizabeth, who stiffened and pulled her children in to her body. "...Which demonstrated that Madame, who had become a close acquaintance of Madame Capet, formerly known as the Queen of France, also provided assistance and advice to the Capet family to aid and abet the unconscionable attempt of the formerly royal family to flee France for foreign lands. To wit, it is charged that Madame Gower provided the Queen with a package containing children's clothing designed to disguise the Dauphin as a girl in order to evade detection during their unsuccessful flight. This act is also considered by the Committee to be one of high treason."

"Treason, again," the judge squeaked, writing furiously on his paper.

"Quite so," D'Anjou said. He held up a bulging stack of papers. "I have statements taken from more than a dozen witnesses attesting to all the things I have said," he said. "I would ask, Sir, that you accept these statements into the official court record and consider them evidence to support the charges I have made, on behalf of the Committee."

The Judge reached out and took the stack of papers handed to him by D'Anjou. He scanned some of the pages quickly, leafing through them.

"It is customary in a trial of this kind to have witnesses appear in the court to deliver their testimony," the Judge said. "It is also customary to allow the Defendant to cross examine the witnesses so that he may find contradictions and untruths, if any so exist."

"The witnesses in this case, Sir, are all in Paris," the prosecutor patiently explained. "Which is why the Committee for the General Security recommended that you, Sir, order this case to be remanded to Paris."

"And I have explained, Monsieur le Prosecutor, that I do not believe in delays in justice," the judge said, wagging his finger at the man across the table. He turned to look at Lord Gower and his family, sitting in the first bench.

"Do you have a response, Sir?" the judge asked him.

"I do, Sir," Lord Gower said, rising to his feet. "These charges are all lies. None of it is true. I did not conspire to help Louis escape from Paris; nor did my wife. These assertions are false. I did my job as ambassador honestly and to the best of my ability. Of course I held meetings with other diplomats…that is what I do. Yes, my wife was a friend to the Queen…our sons are of similar ages and they enjoyed each other's company. But she at no time ever tried to do anything beyond the bounds of friendship and comity between our two nations. And I don't care how many so-called statements this person has presented to you, Sir, but I denounce them all as falsehoods and damnable lies!"

His voice had risen in anger at the last, and his face reddened with his anger. The Judge stared at Gower for a moment, then he glanced at his clerk, standing against the wall at one side of the courtroom.

"Falsehoods and lies," he repeated, nodding his head. "Yes, I am sure that you do denounce these statements as falsehoods and lies. Most defendants would, of course. Do you have any proof that these are falsehoods and lies, Monsieur?"

"Proof?" Lord Gower raised his voice again. "You wish to see proof? To do so, I would need to call as witnesses all the diplomats and government officials I took meetings with over the last eighteen months, and ask them to recall the subjects we discussed during our meetings. That would be impossible, since circumstances have changed greatly in the country in recent months and many of the officials, the diplomats and foreign officers, have left the country and returned to their native lands, as I have been ordered to do by my sovereign."

Gower paused and looked down for a moment before he continued. "And I would hope, Sir, that the standards of decency in this country have not slipped so far that when a diplomat of a friendly nation, as England is to France, says that such a thing is so, that he would not be believed. To think otherwise is an outrage against common standards of decent behavior."

The Judge was silent this time, staring across his table at the English ambassador. Gower was momentarily afraid that he had gone too far, had insulted the national identity of the French as a civilized people in the brutal world. But he stared back at the judge nonetheless, and waited.

The Judge looked up at the ceiling again, pursing his lips as if in deep thought. He then motioned for his clerk to approach.

"What time is the next ferry for Dover scheduled to depart?" the Judge asked.

"I am not entirely certain, Milord," the clerk said. "But I believe the mail packet leaves on the outgoing tide, which is likely later this afternoon."

"Good," the Judge said. He straightened his back and looked at Prosecutor D'Anjou.

"Monsieur," he said. "I wish to officially thank the Committee for the General Security for bringing this case to trial. It is an important case, to be sure, one that conceivably involves matters of great importance to our Republic. I salute you, Sir, for your service to the country."

D'Anjou bowed in response.

"I am troubled, however," the Judge continued. "In our search for the Truth, I find it impossible to arrive at a conclusion that will fit the needs of Justice, which requires the truth in all things. Now, you have said you observed the defendant, the ambassador, attending meetings with other diplomats and officials. And you have provided statements supporting those observations from various servants and other citizens who also observed the ambassador attending meetings with these various officials.

"Yet, you have offered no proof...no *Truth*, Sir! . . . about what the defendant may or may not have discussed at those meetings. As he himself has stated, attending meetings with other diplomats is a large part of what his job as ambassador entails, is that not so?"

Henri D'Anjou stared at the judge, his face white, his eyes dark, his brow furrowed with concern.

"Absent any further testimony of what the defendant actually discussed in those meetings, I cannot rule that the ambassador committed any act against the Republic. There does not appear to be any Truth here, Sir, therefore there cannot be any final Justice."

The Judge next looked at Gower and his wife.

"As to the charges that Madame Ambassador might have committed some kind of treasonable act against the state by bringing old clothes to Her Majesty the Queen, or Madame Capet if that's what we call her now ...well, again, there is no proof. No proof, no Truth. No Truth, no Justice."

The Judge pointed at Lord Gower. "Please stand, Sir."

Gower did so.

"By the power of the courts of this country, which seek at all times to discern both Truth and Justice as they are known before Almighty God, I hereby find that you, Sir, are to be officially termed as a 'persona non grata' in the Republic of France. I further find that you and your family are to leave this country at the earliest possible time, which my clerk informs me is a few hours from now, when the tide is next ebbing, and that you not return to France again. Should you do so, you will be subject to arrest and further prosecution by the Committee for the General Security. Do you understand this ruling, Sir?"

"I do," Gower said, his face impassive. "And I thank your Honor for his careful consideration of this matter."

"Monsieur le Prosecutor?" The Judge looked at D'Anjou. "Do you have anything further to say in this matter?"

"I shall report this result to the Committee in Paris," D'Anjou said grimly. "I cannot predict what the response will be."

"Very well," the Judge said. "If the Committee has an objection, they will find me here in this court every day, hearing cases on shipping disputes, divorces and inheritances. If there is nothing further, I declare this case completed, and the orders shall be filed. Good day gentlemen, milady, and children. I wish you a safe journey home."

And with that, the Judge stood up, bowed to all the parties and left the courtroom.

THE MAIL PACKET for Dover did indeed sail on the outgoing tide at about three o'clock that same afternoon. Lord Gower, despite his high position, was not able to arrange the booking of a private cabin for his family, as all available had been previously reserved. The children did not care a whit, as that left them free to run about the decks, watching the sailors unfurl their canvas and tighten the stays, and laugh delightedly as the wooden ship felt the pull of the wind and began to labor through the choppy waters of Calais harbor on its way across the narrow Channel.

Gower and his wife found a spot in the stern salon, out of the weather at least, but a space shared with the common, everyday passengers heading back to Britain. No one else on board paid them much attention: from all outward appearances, they were just another English family heading home, perhaps after a summer holiday at the French beaches of Brittany.

The ship began to rock in a rhythmic pattern as it plowed its way through the larger waves of the Channel itself, once they left the harbor and headed for Dover. Neither Gower nor his wife spoke for many minutes, each lost in their own thoughts about what had happened to them that morning. Charlotte was watching her younger brother, making sure he didn't get in the way of the busy sailors, nor tumble over the side. From time to time, the children would come racing back into the salon, out of the wind, and report on the latest sight: a pod of dolphins had followed the ship out of the harbor, three or four of them playfully following the ship's hull as it pounded through the surf.

Finally, Elizabeth turned to her husband, reaching out to touch his arm with her hand.

"Gower," she said, her voice low and calm.

"My dearest?"

"It would be my fondest desire if we never had to leave our country again," she said.

He did not reply at first. Her words hung between them like a shimmery thing, a gossamer curtain. He knew he could either brush it away, make it disappear, with a wave of his hand or some well-chosen words; or he could face it and deal with it now, once and forever.

"I understand, Elizabeth, how you feel," he said. "I must confess that my own feelings are not at all dissimilar to your own."

"Can you resign?" she asked. "Can we just go back to London, and Edinburgh and Dunrobin? Back to the way our life used to be? Far away from the tumult of the crowds and the dangers of the world?"

He reached over and took his wife's hand in his.

"If that is what you want, my dear, I shall endeavor to make it happen," he said. "I do not know what Lord Pitt has in mind for me next, if anything, in the foreign service. Sir Jeremy told me last week that the government was looking for someone to take over as postmaster general. It might be a more suitable position for someone like me."

"I would like that," Elizabeth said, giving his hand a squeeze. They sat hand in hand for another long period of time.

"I do not think I like my fellow man," Elizabeth said, finally. "There is so much disputation in the world, so much hatred. I wish to live in peace for a change."

This time, Gower did not answer. He held his wife's hand and continued to hold it as the ship made its way back from the Continent, back to the sheltered island that was England, back to where Lady Elizabeth of Sutherland wished to find her peace.

BOOK III

27

Glencullen - May 1806

It had been just half a year, but already Anna Kenton's school in the old kirk at Glencullen had been a success. The first week, when the school had opened in January, she had welcomed a half dozen students. Six more came the second week, and by the third, she had more than twenty children, ranged from about six years to two girls of fifteen. She had quickly organized the children into rough groupings based on their ages and begun lessons in English grammar and vocabulary. Mary Ross often came down to the school to teach the rudiments of mathematics and even Mr. Fraser stopped in from time to time to relate a Biblical story and expound on the moral lesson told therein.

She had found the children eager to learn, and the older girls had even volunteered to help with the younger children in going over some of the lessons. Anna's favorite time was at the end of the morning, when the entire class often went outside to sit beneath the swaying, hissing evergreens in the churchyard for a bite of food. And Anna would talk with the children, not as a teacher, but as a friend. They would tell her things about their lives and families. Anna discovered that the children knew a great deal about the world around them: how the crops grew, the best places in which to trap rabbits, what the cows needed to produce milk, the natural rhythms of nature. They did not know much about current events, or the happenings in far-off places like Edinburgh and London: those kinds of things did not affect their daily lives here in the Glen, and so were ignored. The children had all heard of those places, the big cities where millions of people lived and worked, but seemed not to have much desire to go and see them. They had heard about the wars against Bonaparte, because many of their fathers were currently serving in the regiments in Portugal and Spain. They all wanted to stay here in Glencullen, raising their crops and livestock, marrying and having families of their own, just as families had done for hundreds, perhaps thousands, of years.

They all knew the stories of the glorious past of the men of Glencullen: the battles and wars that had been fought over territory and cattle. The battles and wars that had been fought, and lost, to the hated English. Many of the children had fathers who were absent at present from the Glen, fighting in new wars and battles in far off places they could not pronounce, nor knew where they were. The boys all swore they would one day take up their swords and fight again for family and for Glencullen. The young girls wondered why they, too, were not allowed to fight. Anna smiled and told the girls that they had more important work to do, other than fighting and bleeding for their country.

Near the end of May, one of the older girls had shyly raised her hand during one of these noonday sessions and asked, "Excuse me, Miss, but are ye coming with us to the shieling?"

"And what, Agatha, is the shieling?" Anna had said. "Use English, please."

"In the summer months, all but the men of the strath lead the cattle to the summer place, high in the mountains," Agatha said. "We live in the huts and cabins in the shieling, let our cattle graze on the grass and the heather, and stay for most of the summer months. The men who stay behind will tend the growing crops here in the strath, and do repairs on our houses and barns. We will return in the fall, when the cattle are fattened and the men are anxious to have us back again."

"I see," Anna said. "That sounds lovely!"

"Will ye come along then?"

"Are you all going to this shieling?" Anna asked, looking around. The children all nodded. It was something they all looked forward to in the warm months of the year.

"Well, then," the teacher said. "I suppose I will have to come along, if you are not going to miss any lessons."

Hearing this, the boys in the school groaned, while the girls grinned with delight.

It was just after the first of June, when the women of Glencullen set out for the summer shieling grounds. Oh, there were a few males along, but they were young: the Ross twins were fourteen and Harlan Grant a year older. Many of the older boys in the glen would stay in Glencullen for the summer to attend to the chores. The only adults were the women, and they ranged in age from the young twenties on up to Mute Meg, who insisted on being strapped onto the back of a mule, as she had done for most of her eighty years, rather than ride in the uncomfortable and jarring wagon piled high with supplies. Her housekeeper and ward, Catty Greer, walked by the old woman's side, keeping a close watch on Mute Meg's condition. Most of the women from the glen walked, and so did Anna and Mary Ross.

There were some thirty women in the group, and another thirty more of their children. Before them, they drove their cattle, which all seemed to know the way without much urging. Horses drew the several wagons which carried supplies and wooden cages full of irritated and squawking chickens. The path they all followed—if you could call a narrow grassless line winding through the bracken a 'path'—led northward towards the rocky peak of Ben Cullen. Soon, the pathway broke away from the winding path of the River Cullen and struck off to the north-west. Climbing a long treeless slope, they crested the top to see an endless rocky plain to the west, a rolling expanse of bogs and ponds nestled among hillocks; all in a barren environment of boulders, scraggy bushes and small trees bent almost in half by the relentless winds, and heathery ground scattered everywhere with stones and gravel. This horrific landscape stretched on as far as they could see.

But on ahead of them, to the north, the long ridges spilling down from the summit of Ben Cullen beckoned like welcoming arms. Thick forests of hardwoods and pine covered the lower slopes of the mountain before giving way to long rolling pastures of thick grass, ferns and wildflowers. On some of the higher reaches of the mountain, still covered with winter snow, they could see silver stripes of waterfalls pouring down the steepest slopes, crashing onto the rocks below. In the cloudless air of the sun-filled day, it was hard to tell how far away the peaks and valleys were: they looked close enough to touch with an out-stretched hand; but then one began to count the numbers of the peaks in the distance and realize how far apart the mountains were, and the mind could not grasp the vast distances. It made them all feel small and insignificant in comparison.

It was several hours more of walking across a rolling, heathery plain and through a thick pine forest before they ar-rived at their destination on the shores of two small lochans col-lected at the base of one of the mountain's ridges and fed by the freshets streaming down from the higher ground. These narrow bodies of water were called *Bán-loch Beag* and *Bán-loch Mor*: Small White Lake and Large White Lake.

The group had been quiet during the trek up from Gl-encullen, saving their strength for the walking, but once they arrived at the shieling grounds, the mood brightened and the children sped off in different directions with shouts of glee. Anna and Mary sank down on a boulder to enjoy the view and rest their weary feet, while the women of the strath made for the cliffs that formed an impenetrable wall along the eastern bank of the larger loch. A small burn, or stream, drained from that end of the loch, washing through a field of shingle, but collecting here and there in inviting pools of crystal clear water. A narrow strip of grass led to the base of the cliff, against which rocks had been laid untold centuries before to provide the base for a series of a dozen huts. Some had timbers set crosswise as supports for roofing, and within a few minutes, the children began bringing armloads of freshly cut heather and bracken from the nearby slopes, which were quickly draped across the timber supports to provide roofing against the elements. Embers from the home hearths had been carefully carried on the journey in metal containers, and these were now used to kindle fires in the newly roofed huts. The older women wielded brooms to sweep away the dust that had collected over the winter months and soon, the shieling huts were clean, warm and ready for occupancy.

"I can't believe how quickly they have made this place seem livable," Anna said to Mary Ross, who sat beside her watching all this activity.

"Och," the older woman said with a smile. "They've only been doing this same thing here in the same place for hundreds of years. I think they've got the knack of it by now."

"Why did they call it the White Lake?" Anna asked, looking out across the expanse of water. "It looks almost black to me."

"Och, you've never heard of the Scottish sense of humor, then?" Mary replied. "Or maybe it was the dead of winter when they first came here. "

At the end of the day, as the mountains cast their long shadows in the twilight, the group from Glencullen gathered together for the evening meal. Some of the boys had spent the afternoon fishing in the loch, and had returned with a number of plump *breac donn* or brown trout, which were quickly grilled on the fires and eaten with bannock, the unleavened oak bread, and some wild strawberries that the girls had gathered in a nearby meadow. After the meal, mugs of warm tea were passed around, as were the usual flasks containing the *uisge-beatha*, or water of life. The children played on the rocky banks of the *sruth* that washed down the hill below the lochan.

"It is so peaceful here," Anna said, sipping on her mug of honey-sweetened tea.

"Don't be saying that, now," said Jenny MacLeod, who was sitting on a woolen blanket nearby. "*Eiridh tonn air uisge balbh.*"

Anna looked at Jenny and raised an eyebrow in question.

Jenny smiled. "It means 'a wave will rise on quiet water,'" she said. "Like 'the calm before the storm,' as I think you English say. No need to tempt fate. There are some large waves rising out there, somewhere in the world, and they'll be breaking on us soon enough."

There were murmurs of agreement from the other women. They were all thinking of the great events of several months earlier, when Billy Hanks had led what was known throughout the Highlands as *Éirí amach na gcaorach*, the Revolt of the Sheep. Men from Glencullen and several other straths in the district had gathered the first flocks of black-faced sheep that had been brought into the straths and glens by the lairds, and had driven them back to the south, toward Inverness. They had made it as far as the plain at Rusdale before the soldiers and the lairds had intercepted them. Most of the Highlanders had disappeared into the untracked wilderness, chased but never captured by the government's troops led by Major Darnell. Four men had been arrested there in Strath Rusdale and were taken to the gaol at Dingwall. But someone had broken them out of their cells in the middle of the night, right under the noses of the guards assigned to the Tolbooth. That someone was widely suspected to be Billy Hanks, although no one in Dingwall nor anyplace else could say for sure.

The flocks of sheep, several thousand in number, had stayed for several weeks on that broad grassy plain in Strath Rusdale while the tenant farmers holding the leases for the new sheepwalks in Glencullen and the other straths had struggled to determine which sheep belonged to which farmer. That had taken a great deal of time and negotiation before it was sorted out. Eventually, the flocks had been driven back north again to their new homes. Mr. Knowles had finally taken occupancy of his new sheep farm at the entrance to the strath of Glencullen, but he was not happy at having to expend time, money and his energies getting his flock back in place. He had written several unhappy letters to Lord Stafford at Dunrobin demanding that his lordship provide security for his farm to prevent the local rebels from stealing his sheep again. Months later, the matter remained unresolved.

"Have you heard anything from His Lordship, Miss Kenton?" asked Jenny. "Are we still to be removed at Lammas?"

Anna felt the eyes of the group of women turn to stare. She felt her face turn red.

"Of course not," she snapped. "Why do you think I would hear of such a thing?"

"Well, there is only one of us sitting here who is related to the great mannie himself," Jenny said, a smile playing at the corners of her lips. "If anyone is to get fair warning of the arrival of the sheriff or the redcoats, it is sure to be you."

"I know just as much, or as little, as you or anyone else here," Anna said, with some heat. "Perhaps you should ask that man, Billy Hanks. He seems to know everything."

"Oh, I would ask him, if he were here," Jenny said, her

face breaking out into a grin. "But not afore he and I spent a wee bit of time getting to know each other better."

The other women tittered knowingly, and Anna felt her face reddening again.

"But Billy Hanks has gone to ground, it seems," Jenny continued. "Not a peep from him for weeks now. Have ye heard from him, Catty?" she called to Catty Ross, sitting beside the ancient Mute Meg.

"Nae," Catty said, shaking her head. "He's been on the run from the bastard Darnell. He sent word that he'd be in hiding for a wee while. But he'll be back, our Billy will. Not too long, I expect."

One of the women pulled out a *piobhorn*, or a stock-and-horn chanter, a simple instrument made of wood with a sheep's horn bell at the end, and began to play a lament. Soon, all the women were singing along, the words extolling the memories of a man lost to the wars and remembered for his strength and bravery. The thin sound of the notes cut through the air like a knife, and the emotions the song evoked brought tears to many of the women's eyes. Once finished, the player launched quickly into a more upbeat reel, which soon had toes tapping, and brought back to the fireside some of the children to listen and dance. Again, the song was taken up by singers, and others began to add harmonies and dissonances. Anna listened with amazement as the music swirled around them in this perfect, desolate place.

She felt, for the first time since she had arrived in Glencullen some months ago, that she had become part of the community. Yes, she was an outsider, and always would be. Yes, she was a distance relation to Lord Stafford, who was mistrusted and disliked. But she felt that she was accepted as one of them in many ways, and for that she was glad. It was a good feeling, to be part of the community, to care about these people, and to feel like they cared about her as well.

The music--the singing and the playing and the dancing children--went on long into the night, as the summer twilight deepened, the light clinging to life in the western sky as if it did not want to succumb to the night.

28

Dunrobin - June

"More claret, Major?" asked Lord Stafford. Darnell nodded, and the hovering form of Mr. Gunn was quickly at his side to fill his crystal goblet. As usual, the dining room at Dunrobin was bright with candlelight, even though the day outside was still bright, even at the hour of eight o'clock. Twilight lingers deep into the night at midsummer in the northern reaches of the British Isles. The table was full of guests tonight: Major Darnell of the Black Watch occupied the seat of honor to his Lordship's left; William Young, the estate manager, sat to the right of the head of table, with his wife beside him. Next came Robert MacCray and beside him was Captain Plessy, one of Darnell's aides. On the opposite side, next to the Major, sat Angus Monroe and James Graham and their ladies: both were large landowners in the county and distant relations of Lady Elizabeth, who as usual presided over the table from her seat at the far end.

When Darnell's glass was full, Lord Stafford raised his own. "To the King," he said.

Major Darnell quickly stood up, followed by Captain Plessy. "To the King," they replied in unison and drank.

"Standing is not required here, Major," Stafford said in a joking tone, as the two soldiers sat down again. "The King knows that all in our shire are loyal to him, and I'm sure he would understand our drinking his health from a seated position."

"I'm sure that he would, Sir," replied Darnell with a slight smile. "But it is such a rare pleasure to hear such good wishes for His Majesty in this country that I thought a further acknowledgment was in order."

"Quite so, quite so," said Stafford, nodding.

"Have you indeed found the people of Scotland to be disloyal to the King, Major?" asked Lady Stafford from her end of the table. "It has been my impression that most of us are quite happy with him, even as we hope that his health improves." George III had been plagued with recurrences of an illness that was said to render him confused and troubled—some whispered he had turned quite mad—although he always seemed to recover after a time.

"I would say that most people of your exalted station are happy with King George, madam," Darnell said. "But it is the lower classes that still seem to harbor some resentment towards the English nation and its people. I mean no disrespect, of course."

"I see," Lady Stafford said. "Is that the reason why you have had no success in locating the outlaw Billy Hanks and bringing him to justice? It has been some months since his little rebellion, has it not?"

Darnell felt his face reddening and fought to constrain his anger.

"We will find him, madam," he said between clenched teeth. "Of that I can assure your ladyship."

"Can you?" she said drolly. "I believe you said that to Lord Munro of Dingwall after Billy Hanks stole the sheep of our tenant and several more besides. I believe you said the same thing to Sheriff MacLeod after the men you arrested in Strath Rusdale somehow disappeared from the Tolbooth goal in Dingwall. It has been quite some time since those events, Sir, and here you are telling me the same thing. At what point, Major Darnell, are we expected to disabuse ourselves of the notion that you have any ability whatsoever to bring this man to justice?"

"Now, now, my dear lady," Lord Stafford blinked rapidly across the table at his wife. "I think you are being very unfair to Major Darnell, who is, I would remind you, not only a guest in our home, but is here because of an invitation that originated with yourself." Stafford was still somewhat put out that his wife had written General Cathcart at Fort George on her own initiative, asking for military intervention in the affairs of County Sutherland. He did not like being reminded that while he controlled the million square acres of the county, the land and the loyalty of its people belonged, in fact and in law, to his wife.

"Well, I certainly apologize if I am being either inhospitable or unfair, Major," Elizabeth said, looking at the Major, who nodded his acknowledgment. "However, it has been quite a long time since the actions that inspired my letter to the Viscount Cathcart. And I am just wondering when we might expect some results on your behalf."

All eyes at the table swung to the Major, who had to clench tightly his back teeth to quash the sudden impulse lash out in anger at this insufferable woman. Darnell, however, knew that Lady Stafford was a woman one could neither trifle with nor ignore. As the chief of her clan, she was not without some measure of power and status. Darnell was not used to dealing with women of power, but then, few men were. He wondered how Lord Stafford managed it in his marriage. As a man who had never married—a life in His Majesty's service did not allow for personal arrangements of that kind—Darnell was not used to dealing much with women at all. Except, of course, for his occasional visits to one of Inverness' brothels; and there the interaction between man and woman was simpler and more easily defined.

And so Darnell paused, briefly, before regaining his composure.

"Your question, Lady Stafford, is an apt one," he said carefully, staring down at his hands folded on the table in front of him. "We have not had much success, so far, in locating the trail of this man Hanks. He, the men from Glen Grudie, and others involved in the late unpleasantness, have all gone to ground. And as I'm sure you know, there is quite a lot of ground for him to hide in."

"God's truth," said William Young exuberantly. "This county is the largest in all of Britain. There are untold miles of empty bracken and dozens of mountains devoid of habitation. Talk about searching for a needle in a haystack … why, it would take a body a hundred years or more to search every corner of Sutherland. And I daresay this Billy Hanks is not exactly sitting under a tree waiting to be captured!"

The table tittered and some of the tension in the room was relieved.

"That is true, Mr. Young," Darnell said, nodding across the table at the large, florid gentleman seated opposite. "We have organized search parties in the straths of the River Cullen and Grudie," the major said, "And we have interviewed most of the residents of those places; all to no effect. Nobody will admit to having seen Hanks or his friends. Sheriff MacLeod has also searched and interviewed throughout the county."

"And?" Lady Stafford kept the pressure on.

"There have been reports that Hanks has left Sutherland, perhaps for good," Darnell continued as the servants began to serve the first course, a rich broth of fish and potatoes. "We have been told he has escaped to Caithness on his way north to Shetland. We have been told he has escaped to the south, to take up a new station in Glasgow or Edinburgh. We have been told he has decamped for France. And Holland. And Italy. And the Americas."

"Goodness," Lady Stafford exclaimed. "That certainly narrows things down, doesn't it?"

The table tittered again.

"And where do *you* think he is, Major?" Lady Stafford was implacable and unyielding.

Darnell paused again before answering. Not from anger this time, but to gather his thoughts.

"It is my belief that he is still right here, in Sutherlandshire," he said quietly.

This time some of the ladies at table gasped in disbelief.

"Do not be alarmed, ladies," the Major continued, nodding to the women seated at table. "I do not mean he is lurking anywhere near Dunrobin. No, Hanks is smarter than that. He is likely moving from place to place, never staying in one place long enough to be seen or reported. I don't even think he is wandering through the desolate places of which, as Mister Young has reminded us, Sutherlandshire has a great many. No, Hanks is with the people, the lower classes who are rebelling against the rightful laws of the King. He may be in Golspie tonight, Lairg tomorrow, Helmsdale the night after. He may travel to Ross … Assynt … Farr … Tongue. He will have sympathizers in all those places, people willing to find him a spare bed or a warm barn loft and a hot meal. He can continue in this way for many weeks or months, and there is naught one can do to find him."

"That is not very reassuring, Major," Lady Stafford said, picking up her soup spoon. "Do you need more men? Perhaps I should write Viscount Cathcart another letter and ask for more assistance so that we may bring this man to law and restore the tranquility and peace of the county."

Darnell was silent and did not respond. He did not trust himself to speak. Lord Stafford interceded.

"I do not think that a wise idea, my dear Lady," he said, frowning. "I understand your impatience. I share that impatience with you. We all do. We all wish heartily that this Hanks fellow is quickly found and hanged. But you must give the Major, and the Sheriff-Depute as well, time to do their duty, as I am sure they eventually will. If Hanks has left the county, well, all the better. Let him go and distress someone else in some other place. If he is still here, then he will be found, arrested and prosecuted. And that will be an end to it."

The others at the table murmured their agreement with Lord Stafford's sentiments. All except Lady Stafford, who fixed her husband with an icy glare.

"I hope your prediction comes to pass, Sir," she said. "In the meantime, I must tell you that I do not feel safe, and I don't think anyone in Sutherland should feel safe until this rebel is found."

"Do not worry yourself, Madam," said Captain Plessy, who had remained silent but watchful during the discussion. "You are well protected here tonight. In addition to myself and Major Darnell, there is a squadron of heavily armed men in the forecourt, and others patrolling the garden and the seafront beyond. If it will help m'Lady ease her mind, I can assign a permanent picket to keep watch at all hours here at Dunrobin, at least until the scoundrel is caught."

"Thank you, Captain," Lady Stafford said graciously, reaching over to pat his arm. "You are most kind. I would not want to reduce in any way the patrols you are conducting in searching for this Hanks." She paused, briefly. "You *are* conducting patrols, are you not?"

"Oh, indeed we are, Madam," the captain said, blushing slightly with the attention the Lady was bestowing upon him. "We are scheduled tomorrow to make a sweep through Skibo, Dornoch Ferry and on to Bonar."

Four servants entered the dining room bearing platters heaped with food. They were dressed alike in white wigs tied at the back with black ribbons, black liveried jackets and gold pantaloons. There were roasts of lamb and pig, heaps of stuffed pigeon, and bowls piled high with aubergines and carrots. Placing their trays on the sideboard, the servants began to clear the soup course and distribute fresh plates and utensils to the diners. Lady Stafford knew three of the liveried men working in her dining room, but the fourth, a slightly older, tall and sharp-angled man was unfamiliar to her. She watched him as he worked, following the lead of the other servers and glancing frequently at Mr. Gunn, the head of house, who gave him subtle clues with his eyes and cants of his head, to tell him what to do next.

She waited until this new man held the tray of vegetables for her to serve herself before she spoke to him, softly.

"You are new here, are you not?"

"Mum," the servant said with a barely noticeable nod of his head.

"This is Mr. Park, Madam," Mr. Gunn was quick to intercede. He missed nothing. "He is substituting tonight for Angus, who has a bit of the rheumatism this evening."

"I see," Lady Stafford said. "Thank you, Park."

"Mum."

The servants, once they had distributed the meal, retreated to the corners of the expansive dining room and became as statues against the wall. Elizabeth knew that Angus Pike, one of her gardeners, was getting on in years. He had been hired originally by her father, at least fifty years earlier. The conditions of his employment had been, as for most of the servants employed at Dunrobin Castle, to do what he was told, not steal anything, and be of good moral character including regular attendance at kirk. In return, he would have lifetime tenure at Dunrobin. Like other male servants on the estate, Angus was often drafted for additional duty as a server at her table; she asked Mr. Gunn only that he make sure they all washed their hands. She did not wish to be served by someone with garden compost or stable muck beneath their fingernails. She made a mental note to ask after

Angus and find out who this Park was tomorrow, when she and Mr. Gunn met to discuss the household's business.

"So you were saying, Captain, that tomorrow you intend to search Skibo, the Ferry and Bonar, is that correct?"

"Quite so, Madam," the young captain said, as he began to eat.

"And what will you do if you find this rebel, this Billy Hanks?"

"Why, we will arrest him at once," the captain said. "And if he resists, we will shoot him dead."

"How will you know if you've found him?" Lady Stafford asked.

"I beg your pardon?" Captain Plessy was nonplussed.

"Do you know what this man, this Billy Hanks, looks like?"

"Well, we have a description of him to be sure," the captain said, somewhat hesitatingly.

"A *description*?" Lady Stafford did not try to prevent the derision from her voice. "And what, pray, is the description that you have?"

Captain Plessy was turning red with embarrassment now. He looked across the table at Major Darnell, hoping for some assistance, but that gentleman was busily drinking from his goblet of claret and chatting quietly with Lord Stafford, having had quite enough of the cross examination from Lady Stafford.

"He is a man of about forty years," he said. "Black hair, long. Has a propensity for disappearing and appearing again somewhere else. He is said to have killed some fifty men, mostly with his bare hands, others with his knife. He lived with the red Indians in the Americas, you know..." Captain Plessy's voice trailed off.

"I see," Lady Stafford said. "It seems to me, Captain, that you have described his behavior and his history, but of his description, all I heard was that he is a man of some forty years with long black hair. I wonder how many men in my county answer to that description? What color are his eyes? What kind of knife does he carry with him? Clothing? Shoes?" Lady Stafford shook her head in frustration.

"I may have to write that letter to Viscount Cathcart after all," she said. "It is apparent to me that you, Captain Plessy, and you, Major Darnell, are gallivanting around the countryside looking for this Billy Hanks and you have no idea what he looks like, much less where he is. Why the description you give me could just as well describe my servant, Mr. Park over there, as Billy Hanks!"

All eyes in the room turned to look at the unfortunate servant standing motionless in the corner of the dining room. Park's face turned beet red and he suddenly burst out in a high-pitched giggle, as if he had suddenly taken leave of his senses. Mr. Gunn quickly snapped his fingers and the man fled the room.

"I can assure you madam, that our search for this renegade is well under control," Major Darnell spoke through clenched jaws. "I myself have seen this man. I knew him when we both served His Majesty in the Canadian provinces. I would know him again if I laid eyes upon him."

"Is that so, Major?" the Countess snapped. "You have not seen him since thirty years ago, when he was naught but a boy, from what I have heard. Yet you think you will know him upon sight, now that he has become a man? I am afraid, Sir, that I have grave doubts as to your abilities."

"My dear woman," Lord Stafford started to speak.

"Enough, Gower!" she snapped at her husband. She glared across the table at him, then her lip began to tremble and tears started in her eyes. "Enough," she said again. "I have lived before in a country where I did not feel safe, where my children were not safe. I vowed that never again would I live in a place like that. And now..." her voice quavered and she ducked her head to regain her composure. When her head came back up, she looked around the table, eyes blazing with emotion. "And now, I find myself living in a place where one man can encourage others to act with lawlessness and disrespect toward the natural order. I will not allow this to happen. Be assured, I will not allow this to happen in my own country, or on my own estates."

Then she rose, Mr. Gunn leaping to hold her chair, bowed at the company, and she, too, fled the room.

29

When the dinner was over and the guests had been escorted into the lounge for after-dinner drinks and conversation, Mr. Gunn was able to return to the kitchens, located in a connected outbuilding on the eastern side of the castle. There he found Mr. Park, his new servant, chatting away with Mrs. Murray, his head cook, both seated at the long pine servant's table in the anteroom. They were laughing aloud as one or the other of them had apparently just finishing telling a joke. Mr. Park sat before a nearly empty plate of food and was nursing a goblet of His Lordship's finest wine.

"By all the saints in heaven, *that* is a scene I never wish to observe in this house again," Mr. Gunn said, pulling out a handkerchief to wipe his brow. "Her Ladyship has retired for the evening and required a sleeping draught to calm her nerves. And the others have retired to the Music Room, where they cannot stop talking about what just happened."

"She's a feisty one, the Countess, isn't she?" said Mr. Park with a grin. "The marks she left on Captain Plessy's hide will leave scars. I've always liked a feisty woman, I have."

"Och, she's much too old for you, Billy," said Mrs. Murray with a laugh. "Much too old to become the next Mrs. Han…"

"*Wsssst!*" Billy Hanks hissed her into silence. "Darnell's men are all about us, Morag," he said in a whisper. "My name is Willie Park, from Leith. Visiting my old uncle Angus, who is not well."

"Aye, aye, Billy," the cook said, "I mean, Willie. I told those bloody redcoats to keep their muddy boots away from my kitchen and I showed them my biggest cleaver when I told them. They'll not be coming down here any time soon."

Mr. Gunn went into the kitchen and made himself a plate from the platters that had been returned from the dining room upstairs. He had perhaps an hour of respite from his duties upstairs while the guests sipped whiskey and coffee in the Music Room, attended by the servants. Mr. Gunn would then begin to arrange the transportation to send the guests away, turn Lord Stafford over to the nightly ministrations of his valet and, finally, begin to close down the castle the for night and take himself off to bed.

He came back into the dining hall and sat down heavily at the head of the table.

"Were you not afraid that Darnell would recognize you, Bil…er, Willie?" asked Mrs. Murray. "I thought he knew you back when you served in the Colonies."

"Nae, Morag," Billy said. "He might have seen me once or twice around the barracks, but he never had cause to speak to me nor learn my name. I only became known to the officers after I went into the woods. And I was just a lad then. My countenance has changed since those days. We all knew who Darnell was, though…and we all knew to keep well clear of him. He was a nasty one, that Darnell."

"So what did ye learn, Billy?" Mr. Gunn asked his erstwhile servant. "Sounds like the redcoats will be searching along the Firth tomorrow. Are ye intending to follow along and wreak your particular brand of havoc upon them?"

"Nae, nae, Jimmy," Billy said. "I'll let them have their fun. Other than affrighting an old woman or two along the way, sticking their heads into the odd chicken coop, there's not much trouble they can get into. I suspect they'll soon be heading back south to Fort George. Either because they miss the comforts of Inverness, or because General Cathcart may need them for other duty. In any case, they won't be finding me nor the lads from Glen Grudie. Won't be too long before we see the back of them."

"Where have the Rosses of Grudie gone, then?"

"I dunno," Billy Hanks said with a laugh. "I know they were planning to visit some of their cousins on Harris for a time. They could still be there, or any of the isles for all I know. We agreed to stay low for at least three months and let the redcoats wear themselves out searching for us."

"So where are ye off to next, then?" Mr. Gunn asked.

Billy took a long draught from his cup of wine and thought a moment.

"I've been thinking about the shieling," he said finally.

"At Bán-loch Beag?" Mr. Gunn was surprised. "I've not been there since I was a wee lad."

"Aye," Billy said. "Nor I. But I still remember the place."

"Oh, aye," Mr. Gunn said. "Who can forget the smell of the heather on the mountain, or the cold of that first swim? The way the mountains come right down to the water's edge and when the day is clear, you think you can see all the way to Dunnet Head."

"Aye," Billy nodded in agreement. "We boys would set our traps in the morning, and by noontime they'd be full of plump hares, enough to feed the village for three days."

Morag Murray pushed her chair back and rose creakily to her feet.

"'Tis said you men of Glencullen are hopeless romantics," she said with a smile at both. "And I believe it. But neither of you are wee bairns any longer, and even the shieling ground must change with the years. Go, Billy … go to the mountains. The redcoats will not follow you there, where there are no roads. Soak up the sunshine and the clean mountain air. But as sure as day follows night, the redcoats will be back, and they'll be looking for ye, lad. So take care. I will not be happy to attend to your funeral, Billy Hanks, or whatever name you wish me to call ye!"

She stomped back into the kitchen to finish the evening duties there, and prepare for breakfast, for which preparations would begin in a few short hours, before the sun was seen again in the eastern sky.

When she was gone, Mr. Gunn rose and went to the sideboard, where he took up a bottle of spirits from one of the cupboards. He came back and poured a dram for himself and one for Billy.

"Slainte," he said as they clinked and drank. He fixed the younger man with his eyes, hard and level-headed and clear, the same eyes he used to observe everything going on in the household.

"Can you do it, Billy?" he asked now. "Can you save the strath? Young and MacCray want the people gone, sooner rather than later. They've got the sheep men lined up from here to Inverness ready to put deposits down on the land. Money is like water, Billy: it will find its way. You can redirect it, or dam it up for a time, but sooner or later the money will out. I don't know how you can stop it."

Billy Hanks took up the whiskey and poured them each another healthy glass. He sipped from his own, slowly, while he thought about what to say.

"Sometimes," he said slowly, "sometimes the money, like water, backs up, slips its banks and cascades away down the hill, washing all afore it away. I dunno if I can stop them, Jimmy. But I think I can back them up for a wee while. After that, we'll see what happens next. We'll see where the water goes from there. But I do ken one thing, and I ken it very well."

Mr. Gunn drank some of his whiskey. "And what is that?" he asked.

"I know I have to try," Billy Hanks said, his face hard.

Mr. Gunn sat motionless. Then he drained his glass, heaved himself out of his chair and prepared to return to his duties.

"*Am fear dan dàn a'chroich, cha tèid gu bràth a bhàthadh,*" he intoned.

Billy Hanks looked up at the man and laughed. "'He who is born to be hanged will never be drowned,'" he said, repeating the old Gaelic proverb. "I'll try my best, Jimmy, to do naught but to die quietly in my own bed at a very ancient age."

"All the saints in heaven protect ye and keep ye," Mr. Gunn said. "And if I can do aught to help, you just need to ask."

30

Glencullen - July

The Reverend Fraser was working on a sermon in his study. He had the window open to take advantage of a cooling breeze wafting down the river valley, and he was half-listening as he worked to the beck-and-call of the birds outside enjoying the early summer season in his orchard. It was a quiet time of year in Glencullen: most of the people of the strath had left for the summer shieling, leaving behind only a few of the older men with some of the older boys of the strath to tend the growing fields of grain and potatoes. Fraser took advantage of the good weather at this time of year to schedule more visits to neighboring parishes where his ministry was required: there were christenings in the summer months, as well as weddings to perform. The need for funeral services declined at this time of year, although there were always one or two.

Of course, Fraser also took advantage of the season to collect more specimens for his collection of indigenous fauna. Whenever he could, he headed out to explore the fields and open mountain meadows in search of unusual insects, reptiles or mammals to capture, bring back to his study and carefully gut, mount or preserve for posterity. And there was the never-ending correspondence with his network of fellow collectors all across the British Isles and into Europe. Fraser was in the habit of regularly sharing his finds with his fellows, and they with him: creating a constant flow of letters back and forth.

He was somewhat lost in the contemplation of a particularly tricky passage from II Corinthians when he was startled out of his reverie with the sound of a sharp rapping at his door. He looked up, surprised, to see the countenance of Robert MacCray grinning at him from the doorway.

"Morning, reverend," the man said, striding into the room unbidden and commandeering a chair in front of Fraser's small desk. "Save any souls today?"

Fraser was insulted by the man's impertinence, but even more by the interruption of his work. He wondered where Mary or Katherine had got to: they were supposed to be his gatekeepers and they knew he was not to be disturbed when working in his study. He decided not to respond to the factor's insult, but merely sat back and with a level gaze, waited.

MacCray grinned at the older man. "No small talk today, Fraser?" he said. "Fine, then." He rummaged around in the leather bag slung over his shoulder and pulled out a handful of papers. He glanced down at them, and then handed them across the desk.

"This is your official notice of relocation," he said. "Her Ladyship has found you a new parish to serve. You will be translated to Durness, taking up your duties there immediately."

"D-D-Durness?" Fraser was stunned by the news. "That is Lord Reay's parish, is it not? Do they even have a kirk in Durness?"

"I know not and care less," replied MacCray. "Her Ladyship's orders are quite clear. You and your wife, one horse and one cow, are to remove to Durness in a month's time."

"But my glebe...my orchard ...my collection ..."

"Yes, yes, all of that belongs to this parish, which is to say, it belongs to Lady Stafford," MacCray said. "She will dispose of it as she sees fit."

"But who is to preach the word of God to the people here?"

MacCray laughed. "People?" he said. "Soon there will be no people here in Glencullen, only the sheep. And they do not require the ministrations of such a learned man as yourself. Better to get thee to Durness and look for some human souls to save."

Fraser tried to read the document MacCray had given to him, but the words dissolved before his eyes and he could not make himself focus. What was he going to do? He was an old man, not suited for moving his household a hundred miles to the north. He had come to think of Glencullen as his home, the place where he would die. He loved his work, he loved wandering through the hills and valleys looking for and collecting specimens. He even loved the people to whom he ministered. They all had become part of his life. And his wife! She would be violently angry with him at this news.

"I must speak to the Lady Stafford about this," Fraser stammered. "She will listen to reason."

"The Staffords have left for London," MacCray said, smirking. "If you wish to write to her, I will certainly see that your letter is posted at once. Although I would not plan on waiting around for a reply. Her Ladyship told me that her mind is quite made up on this matter. Furthermore, your letter of assignment is from the moderator of the presbytery. You should properly take up any complaints with him."

Fraser fixed his gaze on the younger man. "'Whoever sows injustice will reap calamity, saith the Lord my God,'" he thundered.

MacCray stood up. "Careful, old man," he said. "One could understand you to be threatening Lord Stafford and his wife. That would have repercussions of a more serious kind."

"I am quoting Holy Scripture," Fraser said. "I am not afraid to rely on the word of the Lord."

"And I would never try to convince you to do otherwise," MacCray said. "But if I were you, I would put more reliance onto the Writ of Transference, since that is the operable document here."

"You are a vile person, Robert MacCray, and I shall pray for your eternal soul," Fraser said sadly, shaking his head.

"Thank you, Sir," MacCray said. "I hope the Lord can hear your prayers when they are uttered from the wasteland that is Durness. I wish you good day and good riddance."

He turned to walk from the room, but at the doorway, there was a high-pitched scream and a black wraith hurled itself against MacCray, causing him to stumble backwards into Fraser's study. Martha Fraser, the minister's wife, had been listening outside his door and, convulsed with raw anger, was now beating her fists against MacCray's chest, spittle flying from her lips as she screamed imprecations and curses upon his name.

Regaining his balance, MacCray pushed the woman away and reached for her swinging, punching arms. He managed to grab one, but her free hand dropped to her apron and emerged holding a pair of sewing shears, with which she raked madly at his face and eyes.

"Bloody hell," MacCray shouted and a thin stream of blood appeared on his cheek, just beneath his right eye. He dropped the woman's arm and brought his hand to his face, then took it away to look at the crimson drops. "You'll pay for this, woman, mark my words!"

The Reverend Fraser jumped forward and grabbed his wife, holding her tightly, where she struggled once, twice, her face red and tearful, before she collapsed, chest heaving. Fraser managed to lower her form to the floor, where she lay. A low keening sound filled the room. The two men stood there for a long moment, staring at the form of the woman who just seconds ago had been a powerful, uncontrolled engine of hatred and revenge.

MacCray pulled out a handkerchief and dabbed at his face, where the slash of Martha Fraser's scissors had cut his flesh.

"You and your wife will be gone from this parish in a fortnight, or I will speak to the Sheriff-Depute about pressing charges for assault," MacCray said, his voice a low and angry growl. "Do not doubt me on this, preacher."

Mary and Elizabeth, the servant girls, came running into the study, their faces red and sweaty from having been out in the sun. Mary held an armful of wildflowers they had been cutting in the meadows near the manse.

"What has happened?" Elizabeth said, excited and concerned. "We heard shouting as we were returning from the garden. Is madam ill?" She bent down to minister to Mrs. Fraser, who continued to whimper and moan on the floor, her legs drawn up in a ball tight against her chest.

MacCray pushed angrily out of the room, making both the servant girls step back out of his way, and left the house. The Reverend Fraser collapsed onto his chair and put his head in his hands.

"All is lost," he said, his voice a hoarse whisper. "All is lost."

MAJOR DARNELL HAD changed his plans. Initially planning to have his troops beat the bushes along the Dornoch Firth between Lonemore and Spinningdale, he had instead halted at the Meikle Ferry and commandeered an aged boat to take his men south across the Firth to the promontory on the shore near Tain. The two dozen men of the troop, along with their nervous horses, crowded into the open deck of the old vessel, which slowly made its way through the fast-running tides, the cold waves from the North Sea slapping against the hull and threatening to swamp the entire vessel, before making landing on the far shore. The ferryman mentioned a number he thought suitable for the fare, but Darden simply stared at the man until he turned away, deciding that his life was far more valuable than any coin he might be able to extract from His Majesty's troops.

"Prepare the men," Darden ordered once they were off the boat. "We ride for Fort George."

Darden ducked into the local inn, which doubled as the ferry station, hoping for a bit of refreshment before the long ride. He was surprised to encounter there William MacLeod, the Sheriff-Depute for Ross and Sutherland.

"Major," the sheriff said, bowing in greeting. "I thought you were hunting the fugitive Billy Hanks deep in the wilds of Sutherland."

"We were," Darnell replied. "I have decided to return to our post and wait for further intelligence. What have you heard?"

"About the same as you, I fear," MacLeod said with a wry smile. "He has disappeared. I heard whispers that the Rosses of Grudie had been seen on the Isle of Harris, and I sent a man out there to look. But they were not there. As for Hanks, there is nary a trace. He may indeed have left the country."

"He is here," Darnell said. "I can feel him. He is not the type of man to run away from trouble. Or trouble-making."

"Hanks does not strike me as a fool," MacLeod said. "He knows that he is being hunted. He is either holed up in the vastness of the wilderness, or he has decided to run. I have men checking the manifests of all ships leaving for the Colonies, and for Europe. No one of his description has been seen departing. He could, of course, find passage on some fisherman's vessel, and make his way out of the country in that way, and we would never know."

"He will not leave his people behind," the major said. "Lord Stafford plans to remove all the people of Glencullen before the end of the year. Billy Hanks will try to stop him. He will come out of hiding to do that. And that is when we shall capture and hang the brute."

The Sheriff stared at Darnell. Then he shook his head.

"I fear you continue to underestimate the man, Major," he said. "He does not seem to operate the way other men would. That much is obvious. His background is quite unique. A native of Glencullen, he is sure to know every inch of land around these parts. As a former soldier in the Colonies, he is wise to the ways of you in the military, and will use that knowledge to his own benefit. And finally, he has lived with the wild savages in the New Lands and knows all their ways. Put all that together, Sir, and I do not think you will find Billy Hanks acting as any other man would do. Nay, Sir: to catch this man, you will have to out-think him, and that might prove to be very difficult indeed."

Major Darnell's face turned red with anger. "It sounds, Sheriff, that you have some admiration for this criminal," he said.

MacLeod laughed. "I do admire his abilities, Sir," he said. "Any man would. I do not admire his actions, and will see to it that he is brought to the bar of justice to answer for them, if I am able. Those are two different things, Sir."

"Excuses!" snapped Darnell. "You civilians are always making excuses. Hanks is an outlaw and has been one for most of his sorry life. The only remedy for the likes of him is to be found at the end of a sword, or from the drop of a rope. That is a job best left to the professionals like us."

"The professionals like you did not have very good success against the likes of men like Billy Hanks in the late war in the Colonies, did you?" MacLeod said. "Perhaps a different kind of thinking would be of more benefit, Sir."

"Bah!" Darnell spat the word as he stood. "Do not blame the soldier for the betrayal of the politicians above him," he said as he turned to leave. "We could have beaten the Colonists if they had let us fight as we saw fit. And we may yet defeat them, if another war occurs, as it seems it will. This time, they will let us carry the fight to them, instead of tying our hands."

MacLeod bowed. "I wish you every success, then, Major," he said. "Please let me know if there is anything I can do to assist you."

"There is," Darnell said with a snarl as he strode from the room. "Stay out of my way."

31.

The Shieling

Anna had taken to spending her mornings accompanying Catty and old Mute Meg on wanderings near the shieling hunting for herbs and medicinal plants. Although the older lady was well into her eighties, she could still make her sprightly way through the meadows and forests, always under the watchful eyes of her housemate and assistant, and her sharp eye never failed to spot a patch of flowers or plants that she could use.

On this bright sunny day, the three of them wandered down an ancient pathway beside the burn that flowed out of the loch and away towards the waters of the River Cullen. In an open meadow bathed in sun, Mute Meg spotted a mass of white flowers, like clouds growing out of the tall natural grasses, and motioned at them.

"Ah, Cuchulainn's Belt," Catty exclaimed, and began to cut armfuls of the stalks, gathering the flowers in a basket she had carried along. "You English call it meadowsweet."

"It smells not unlike almonds," Anna said, wading in to help cut some of the waist-high plants.

"Aye, that it does," Catty agreed. "In the olden days, we would spread the leaves on the floor in the summertime to give the home a pleasant odor. But Meg likes to use the flowers to make a tincture that is good for calming the nerves and reducing pain. It is very helpful for that purpose."

Once they had cut and gathered a basket of the plants, they walked on. Anna was irritated by the clouds of insects—the midges—that collected around her face and head. Catty noticed Anna's constant fanning and laughed.

"The midges are bad this time of year," she said. "Having had no humans to suckle for the long winter months, they can be vicious. Here—" she walked over to a bush growing near the water's edge and plucked off a handful of leaves. "This is sweet gale," she said. "Crush the leaves and put some in your bonnet or the pocket of your dress. The midgies will soon leave you in peace."

Anna did as she was told and, sure enough, the clouds of swarming insects soon disappeared. Mute Meg, watching, smiled and nodded her approval.

"How did you learn all these things about the plants?" Anna asked Meg. "It seems almost every growing thing here has a purpose and a usefulness that is unknown to those of us who are outlanders."

Meg smiled. Catty spoke up. "The wisdom comes from generations of women like Meg who have studied the land and its bounties," she said. "Some plants are good for healing, some are good for food. Some have roots with healing properties, some have leaves and flowers that will sustain a man in battle. These things have been known to us for hundreds, if not thousands, of years now. It is good that we know these things, and good to pass the knowledge on to others to keep for the future. Meg learned the knowledge as a girl, from her grandfather, who was a bard and a healer."

"Who will know these things once Meg is …" Anna paused. "When she is no longer with us."

Catty laughed. "Oh, she has taught these things to many people," she said. "You see, there is no way to know who will possess the ability to heal. That is a special skill that comes from God alone. So Meg has helped many, like me, to know things. But there is no way to know who will carry on her work. Perhaps it will be you." She smiled as she said this.

"Oh, I don't think I can possibly learn all there is to know," Anna said, shaking her head in disbelief.

Mute Meg's face brightened as she smiled and nodded.

"Meg says that she felt exactly the same way, when she was just a wee girl and her grandfather took her on a walk quite like that which we do this morning," Catty said, translating the unspoken message from the old woman. "The knowledge can be learned by anyone. But the ability to foresee and prescribe comes from the Father, and He alone. That is the mystery of it."

The women continued on their walk, venturing into a dark pine wood before emerging into a clearing overlooking the loch. Catty pointed out the *tri bhilean*, or bog bean which she said was used to create a tonic good for easing aches and pains; and a patch filled with a plant she called *Bramasag*, or burdock. "Soon, the burrs will be in full bloom and ready to harvest," she told Anna. "The seeds, along with some of the root, makes a tonic that will reduce fevers and infection."

The women stopped to rest near the bank of the loch, sitting in the shade of a willow, and shared some bannock cakes. Mute Meg suddenly raised her head, listening to some unheard sound, then turned to look at Catty, who nodded back at her.

"I know," Catty said. "He's here."

"Who?" Anna asked, perplexed, looking around and seeing no other person. "*Who* is here?"

The two other women just looked at one another and giggled.

Mute Meg soon nodded off, her head falling forward onto her chest. Anna got up and wandered off, looking now with new interest at the plants and bushes that were bright green with the growth of early summer, wondering what magical, healthful property each one held. She strolled for some time along the shore of the placid lake, admiring the views of the distant mountains reflected in the still black water. A skylark flittered madly overhead as if it had suddenly forgotten how to fly and was trying furiously to beat its wings to stay aloft. Anna knew, however, that the bird was probably just gulping down some of the same insects that had recently been harassing her own face, and smiled.

She was facing the water, lost in thought.

"Good morning to you, Schoolteacher," said a deep male voice, making her start. She spun around. A man was sitting atop a boulder set back a few yards from the water, one leg dangling down, the other drawn up beneath his body. He wore a woolen kilt, with one end of the cloth draped across his left shoulder. His long flowing black hair hung loosely down his back, strands caught in the gentle breezes coming off the loch. He gestured at the distant mountains. "Tis a bonny sight, is it not?"

Anna took a step back, more in amazement than in fright. The man was the outlaw, Billy Hanks, smiling down at her from his rocky perch.

"Don't be alarmed, Madam," he said. "I mean no harm."

"I am not alarmed, Sir," Anna said. "I was just wondering where the soldiers of the Black Watch, which I understand have been searching for you for some weeks now, might be."

Billy Hanks laughed. "A very good question, Madam," he said. "My understanding is that the Black Watch have returned to their base at Fort William. Since I am here and not there, I suspect they are unsuccessful in their efforts to find me."

"You seem unconcerned that you are so hunted, Sir," she said.

He stretched his long limbs. "Oh, I am concerned," he said. "But I am not concerned that the soldiers will be coming to this lochside any time in the near future. I do not think they know this place exists, nor do I think they could manage to find their way here even if they did."

"And is that why you have come here?"

He laughed again. "Another very good question, Madam," he said. "I am here in part because I know they will never come here."

"In part?"

"And I am here because it is such a bonny place," he said. "And a place I remember coming to when I was a wee bairn. It is a place full of memories, all of them good. I hope that this visit will provide me with more memories, and I hope that they continue to be good ones."

He smiled at her. She smiled back.

"You are well spoken, Sir, for someone who once lived with the wild savages in the Colonies," she said.

"And you are well spoken, madam, for someone who has lived among the savage Highlanders now for several months," he responded. "I am sure many of your Lowland friends and acquaintances believed that you would not escape Glencullen with your life, or your intelligence, intact. Why, didn't Mr. Young himself predict that you would go running back to Dunrobin Castle within a fortnight?"

Anna looked at Billy with amazement. "How do you know that, Sir?" she asked. "Do you have spies everywhere?"

Billy Hanks eased himself off the boulder he had been sitting on and came to stand next to Anna. He smiled at her. "Madam, I make it my business to know things," he said. "Knowledge can be a useful tool, as you, a schoolteacher, should well understand."

There was a rustling and Catty came into the clearing where the two were standing.

"Ach, then, you've found our Billy," she said, nodding at them. "Good, good. I'm going to take Meg back to the shieling. It's almost time for tea. Would you two like to come along?"

Billy Hanks bowed, elegantly, and swept a hand out to indicate the women should proceed. The women went first down the ancient path, and he followed. But Anna could not help casting repeated glances over her shoulder from time to time to make sure that Billy was still walking behind them. He had the habit, she now knew, of disappearing all of a sudden.

Later that night, as the sun dipped below the rocky peaks of Ben Cullen and the sky gradually darkened, the people of the shieling gathered around a roaring fire. Food and drink were passed around while the children, engrossed in their play, boundless in their energy, darted in and out of the clearing where the firelight danced with the shadows of the day. Some of the women worked on their knitting and sewing while the older boys smoked their pipes and stared into the flames. Someone brought out a fiddle and someone else a hornpipe and soon they were all singing some of the hymns, psalms and sacred tunes they all knew by heart: *Be Thou My Vision, Na Hu o Ho, The Cave of Gold*. They sang in harmony, they sang in the *sean nos*, or old way, letting first one voice carry the melody, with others chiming in during subsequent verses, and with the men providing a steady droning bass, much like the pipes. When one song ended, they would all sit quietly, letting the final notes drift out over the loch, where the wind collected them and carried them up to the rocky cliffs far above. They all would feel the peace of the moment, and then, someone would begin another song and the rest would join in.

Anna sat quietly, hugging her knees to her chest, listening quietly to the music. She did not know many of the words, especially the ones sung in Gaelic, but she was able to pick up the melody and hum along to herself. On the far side of the fire, she saw Mary Ross approach Billy Hanks, who had been sitting on his own, also enraptured by the sounds of the night. Anna watched as Mary sat down and began to talk to Billy. Mary talked for some minutes—Anna noticed two songs sung and completed—and then she saw Billy Hanks reach out and envelop Mary in his strong arms in a long embrace.

She felt a movement as Catty came to sit next to her. Catty, too, was watching the two figures on the far side of the flickering fire.

"It appears that a family has been reunited on this blessed night," Catty said. "I am glad of it. It is good for Billy to know that he is still connected to someone."

"I hope it is good for Mary, too," Anna said. "She has never said anything to me, but I fear she has long been lonely."

"Aye," Catty said, nodding her agreement. "It is good for her, too. We all need to feel connected, and family is the best place for that. Loneliness is something we all must overcome, in one way or another. Billy will look out for his sister, and protect her. He is a good one, that Billy Hanks."

Anna continued to watch across the flames as the two siblings continued to talk earnestly, hand-in-hand.

"Yes," she said finally. "I think he is."

32

In the morning, Mary Ross found Anna helping some of the women with the washing, down by the loch. The clothes were soaked in the lake water, a bit of soap was judiciously applied where necessary and the piece of clothing was slapped vigorously against a rock before being rinsed again and laid out on the grass to dry. Like most of the activities of the shieling, the laundry was a shared exercise, usually performed by the women, and accompanied by rhythmic singing and much talk, gossip and laughter.

"Come, Anna!" Mary exclaimed when she found her. "My brother and I are going to the *Loch an Uaimh* … the Lake of the Cave. Mute Meg says that the evrons should be ripe."

"What is an evron?" Anna asked.

"The *oidhreag*" Mary said, pulling Anna's arm and leading her away from the lakefront. "They are also called cloudberries. They only grow in the high boggy places, like at the Lake of the Cave, which means a good long hike up Beinn Klibreck. Bit of a climb, but well worth it. They are delicious and Meg knows how to make a fine brandy with them."

At the shieling, the women dressed in warm clothes and donned sturdy shoes for the walk up the mountain. Billy Hanks was waiting, a pack strapped to his back, filled with bowls and baskets to be filled with the cloudberries.

"Ach, schoolteacher, you are in for a rare treat" he said to Anna, "The oidhreag only bear fruit when the conditions are right. Meg has foreseen that they are many this year. So we shall go and collect them. Tis a long walk uphill, but Meg is never wrong, so our labors will be useful."

They set off on their journey, circling around to the far side of the loch, opposite where the shieling camp was, and, after traversing a dark pine forest, began to climb the largely treeless slopes of Klibreck Hill. While walking through the forest, Billy Hanks had found three stout pine limbs and he passed two of them to the women to use as walking sticks as they began to climb. The path up the heathery mountainside was not steep, but the ascent was steady, and Anna found the stick useful as they climbed.

They hiked through the morning, stopping occasionally where a freshet crossed the pathway to cup the cold clear water and drink. The higher they climbed, the more dramatic the views came into sight, as the mountains continued to roll in every direction ever upwards to the commanding heights that was Ben Cullen, the tallest of the hills in the region. There were still some areas covered with snow atop Ben Cullen, mostly in the shady crooks and crevices where the rocky cliffs fell away.

The day was mostly dry, although gray clouds crowded the sky, and while the temperature was moderate, the higher they climbed, the more the wind began to increase and they could all feel the cooling chill of the altitude.

"That wind is coming from the East," Billy Hanks said at one point. "Sure to be some weather coming with it."

"Will we be all right?" asked Mary Ross, whose face was red with the effort of climbing.

"Oh, aye," Billy replied with a reassuring smile. "Once we get to the loch, there'll be shelter in the caves there. Tis a grand place to ride out a storm."

They continued climbing for the rest of the morning, and shortly after the noon hour, Anna estimated, they cleared one of the last ledges and looked down on an empty plain spread out before them. At the far end was a small, black loch nestled between some rocky outcroppings, and the loch drained into a long boggy stretch that filled this high mountain valley. Beyond the loch, the mountain swelled upwards again, in another treeless slope leading onwards to Ben Cullen.

"Loch an Uaimh," Billy Hanks said as they paused to take in the view. "The caves are there, where the mountain meets the loch. But we'll find the evron growing wild yonder in the bogs below."

They began to descend now, following the narrow, worn path through the heather and grass as it switchbacked several times down the long treeless hillside to the valley floor. Now sheltered somewhat from the growing wind, they all felt warmer as they made their way down to the lochside.

Billy Hanks was right: a series of dark caves had been carved out of the mountain by the millenniums of springtime melting of the snows and the constant etching of the wind; and these dark empty chambers gaped like open mouths over the rippling surface of the loch. Billy Hanks led the two women to the entrance of one of these caves, where they could sit out of the wind. He passed out some bannock cakes and cheese, and they all ate in silence while the wind blowing past the caves created a haunting moaning sound, almost harmonic.

After they ate and rested a bit from their climb, Billy Hanks pulled some buckets and bowls from his backpack and handed them to the two women. He untied and shed his sturdy shoes and removed his knee-high woolen stockings and smiled at them.

"I recommend that you also go bare-legged," he said. "The berry plants are in the boggy ground which is almost always wet and muddy. Please do not fear for your modesty. I have seen a woman's legs before today, and I promise I won't look at yours." He paused, and Anna and Mary Ross looked at each other questioningly. "Well, I might take an occasional peek. But I promise to pretend that I don't notice."

The women laughed, and shucked off their own shoes and stockings. They then followed Billy down past the end of the loch and into the boggy ground that stretched out for several acres beyond. Billy led them into the bogs, and sure enough, the ground was soft and squishy, with hummocks of grass and heather surrounded by ankle-deep dark water into which their feet and legs sank in several inches of muck and mire.

Mary Ross could not help but squeal. "Och, I have never liked the squishy feel of the mud on my feet," she said, holding her dress high to her knees.

Anna, too, took some time to get used to the feeling of moving through the bog, and finally figured out a way to tie her skirts up so they didn't trail in the muddy water. She was then able to move with more certainty, although she could not help but blush when she considered that Billy Hanks, *a man!*, was looking at her white and delicate calves and ankles. It was slightly scandalous, but she reassured herself that here in the wildness of the Scottish mountains, a certain reduction in one's standards of personal modesty was probably not the worst thing in the world. Indeed, she felt quite comfortable in the company of Billy Hanks, for reasons she could not possibly explain to herself. And so she relaxed.

"Now then," Billy said as they slowly moved deeper into the bog. "We are looking for berries that have turned bright orange in color. If they are red, or mostly red, they aren't quite ripe for the picking as yet. Look only for the orange ones…like here!"

He reached over and pointed at a plant growing amid the woody branches of the heather which covered most of the bog. It had variegated leaves shaped in lobes that resembled a cupped hand, dotted with spots and colors, ranging in color from green to a deep burgundy shade. From the midst of the plant a tender and naked stalk protruded, atop which grew a smallish fruit that looked something like a raspberry, save for its bright orange color. He plucked it and passed it to the two women.

"They are quite delicate," he said, "so try not to handle them too severely. Go ahead, schoolteacher," he said to Anna with a smile. "Taste it!"

She popped the fruit in her mouth. The taste was sweet like an apple bathed in honey, yet with a certain underlying tartness that made her mouth pucker a bit. Billy saw that and laughed.

"Mute Meg will mix the berries with sugar, either to boil them to make a fine jam, or to crush them and turn the juices into a wine or a brandy," he said.

They spread out over the boggy ground and began searching for and picking the cloudberries, which, as Mute Meg had prophesied, were indeed growing prolifically. After an hour or two of work, all three had filled their buckets with the berries. Anna's hands were stained orange from the juices and her back was suddenly sore from being bent over at the waist for so long. She stretched and yawned.

None of them had noticed the weather had been changing. The sky that had been almost free of clouds in the morning had become an ominous sheet of slate gray, and the wind had begun to pick up, even in the protected vale of the loch and bog. They all heard a faint rumbling of thunder.

"Looks like the rain is coming," Billy Hanks said, sniffing at the wind. "Best we find some shelter and let it pass us by."

He led them back to the loch and they found one of the caves that was tall enough and deep enough to provide good shelter for the three of them. Billy left the women in the cave and went out to gather some firewood, mostly old dead branches from the gorse as there were not any trees of size to be seen here in the high desolate wastes of the mountains. Still, he managed to collect a good supply of tinder, which he carefully stowed under the lip of the cave and, pulling out his flint, soon had a cheerful fire burning in a shallow pit ringed with rocks near the cave's entrance.

"You are quite proficient, Sir, at creating comforts," Anna said as the air in the cave began to warm around them.

Billy Hanks shrugged. "One learns how to survive on one's wits," he said. "Fire and water are important. If we needed food, I noticed a few graylags out on the loch. And one can always catch a few dotterels if need be. They are quite easily captured, as they seem to have little fear of a man. And there are plenty of wild hare in these mountains, if one knows how to set a trap. It was not that long ago when any Scotsman worthy of the name could survive alone for weeks in these lands. Now, I'm afeard, there are very few who could last more than a day or two."

"Perhaps we should hire you to teach our children some of these techniques," Anna said. Mary Ross nodded her approval. "It might prove useful to them at some future date."

Billy tossed a few more sticks on his fire, which sparked and stirred and glowed. "It would be a sensible thing," he agreed. "But I daresay the bloody priests and Her Ladyship in Dornoch would disapprove. They don't even understand why you should be teaching the wee ones to read and cipher, especially the girls. Tell them you wish to teach the bairns how to catch and spit a nice plump dotterel and they might have a seizure."

Mary Ross laughed and twiddled her bare toes closer to the fire. "You are right as rain about that, dear brother," she said. "We've become a nation of indoorsmen."

Within a few minutes, the rain began to fall, gently at first and then gushing down in huge gouts, driven nearly horizontal by a ferocious wind. In their cave, they were protected from wind and rain, and the fire offset the sudden chill in the air as the storm blew across the bare and open slopes.

Billy Hanks rose and stepped outside the cave for a few moments, sniffing into the wind and looking up at the sky. When he ducked back inside, his long hair was soaked, silvery globes of rainwater clinging to the strands, winking red and gold as they reflected the fire. For a moment, Anna was mesmerized at the vision of this tall and, she had to admit, quite handsome man, standing there tall and sturdy, strong and sinewy. Her breathing stopped, and then started up again, shallow and tense.

If Billy Hanks noticed anything, he ignored it.

"Looks like this storm may have settled in," he said. "We might have to stay here until morning."

Oh, yes Anna heard herself say, and was thankful to realize she had not said it aloud.

"Well then," Mary Ross said, rising to her feet. "We'd best set about it then. Billy, we're going to need more fuel for the fire if we're here for the night. I'll not be sleeping in some dark cave without a bright fire to keep the animals away."

"Aye, sister," Billy said, smiling at her with amusement. "What else?"

"We will need food," Mary continued. "I suppose we could eat all the cloudberries and pick more in the morning."

"No need," Billy Hanks said. "I've got enough food with me for a couple of days. And some whiskey. Mute Meg would not be pleased if we came back empty handed."

"Good," Mary said, folding her arms across her chest. "Anna? Can you think of anything?"

Anna was silent, thinking. She turned her head to look deeper into the cave.

"Ah, right," Mary Ross said, following her gaze. "We will determine who sleeps where later. As for now, Billy: more wood. And give us what food you have. I don't know about Anna, but I'm starving."

Billy Hanks rummaged in his pack and came out with a bag of oats. "When I get back with more wood, we'll boil some water and make brose. Not quite the same as a roasted, stuffed goose, but it will keep us alive for a day. And if we all agree not to tell Meg, we might throw a handful of the wee berries into the cup. Make for a right rare treat, it will."

He disappeared into the rain, pulling his woolen tartan up around his head to stave off the weather.

Mary Ross watched him go, and smiled at Anna. "I cannot believe that Billy Hanks is my own brother," she said. "It has made me very happy."

Anna reached out and patted her friend and companion on the arm. "It is good that you two are connected again, after all the years when you each believed you were alone in the world." she said. "But I'm sure you must worry, as do I, about what the future holds for him. He seems to have many enemies."

"Aye, that he does," Mary said. "But that only means that I have many enemies as well. He does not have to face them all alone. I will stand by my brother, come what may."

Anna smiled at her friend and nodded. But she was worried. Mary Ross was a lovely person, but she was somewhat naïve about people and about the world. Anna feared for her. And for him.

33

The rain continued to pour down all through the afternoon and into the evening. Billy Hanks ranged far enough afield to find some firewood, enough to keep the fire burning throughout the night. Mary Ross boiled a pot of water and mixed it with the oats to form a broth called brose, into which she stirred a handful of the cloudberries, which disappeared into the broth, save for the orange color. The three of them sipped the warm brose, nibbled on more of the oat cakes and pieces of cheese, and found it a filling meal.

Sated, they sat in the warm dry cave, listening to the pattering of the rain falling outside. The long twilight of the summer night lingered outside, and the gusty wind chilled the mountain air. They were all glad of the comfort of their shelter and the cheerfulness of their small fire.

"Tell us a story, Billy," Mary Ross said, finally, breaking the introspective silence they had fallen into. "Tell us what it was like living among the red men of the Colonies."

Billy Hanks sat quietly for a long time, staring into the fire. He shifted uncomfortably.

"I do not like to talk about those times," he said. "The memories are not all good ones."

Mary Ross persisted.

"Well, then, don't tell us of your memories," she said. "Tell us a story that was told to you. We do not mean to make you feel sadness, we just want to understand what life was like in a place we have never been."

He was silent for another long time. Anna felt her heart breaking for him. But then he stirred himself, and smiled at the two women.

"I will tell you a story that the women of my village often told the children at bedtime," he said. "It is a pleasant story."

"Oh, yes," Mary said, nodding. "Tell us a happy story."

Billy Hanks sat up, pulling his woolen tartan closer around his shoulders. And then he began to speak.

Many moons ago, he began, *there was a young girl who was alone in the world. The World Creator had reclaimed her mother and her father and she had been taken to live in a different longhouse in a different village where her relatives lived. But they did not want this girl to live with them, and they treated her badly. They made her work all the day long in the fields, with the corn and the squash and the beans, weeding and hoeing from dawn until dusk. And at night, she was always the last one allowed to reach into the food bowl, when only scraps were left. Many nights she went to sleep still hungry, with just a bit of an old blanket, in the farthest corner of the longhouse, far from the warming fire.*

Now one day, the hunters of this village returned with a fine deer they had killed in the forest, and the people made ready to hold a great feast. But not the girl. They chased her from the longhouse, saying there was neither room in the lodge, nor enough meat to share with her.

The girl ran into the fields of corn, deep among the rows where she could not be seen or found, and, heart-broken and hungry and alone, she cried and cried until she slept. When she woke, she was surrounded by a strange band of little people,

men and women both, who were staring at her with wide eyes as they walked out of the green growing stalks of corn and gathered around her. Though none was taller than her own knees, they gave her comfort, stroking her hair, wiping her tears and washing her face and hands.

"Don't cry, Pretty Child," they said. "Come with us. We will care for you, and feed you and nurture you. We will make a feast in your honor. We know why you are sad, for we can understand the thoughts of earth children. Come with us and we will show you many wonderful things!"

"You are so kind to me!" the girl replied. "But I do not recognize you and I have never seen your like before."

"We are the Jo-gah-oh," their leader said. "The Little People you have heard about in your stories and tales. Come with us and you will learn about our world."

The women slipped some winged moccasins upon her bare feet and wrapped her in an invisible blanket, and they wove a magic plume of corn stalks and placed it in her hair. Then, with a wink, they were all flying high through the air, high above the treetops of the forest and away from the girl's own village. The girl was thrilled to be flying as if she was a bird, and her heart was overcome with joy.

They approached a high mountain ridge with a ledge of great rocks and, at the touch of the leader of the Little People, the rocks opened and they all flew inside. Suddenly, they were in a beautiful wooden lodge, with thick beams overhead and many warm blankets and skins strewn upon the ground. There was a huge hearth around which the kind Jo-gah-oh mothers were roasting delicious smelling meat, simmering pots of vegetables and baking aromatic bread. They welcomed the girl and soon a feast was spread in her honor and they all ate until their stomachs were full.

The heart of the girl was bursting with happiness, and she almost danced with the joy she felt.

"I cannot thank you enough," she cried. *"What wonderful, generous folk you are! Can you go anywhere and do anything?"*

"Of course," said the chief of the Jo-gah-oh. *"We are small, but we are also great. Come with us and see what we can do."*

And with a nod of his head, they were again flying high in the air, across the high mountains and over the deep forests and vast expanses of lakes and rivers. Soon, they came to the village where the girl had been living with her relatives. It was night and all the people were asleep in the longhouses, but they could see the stag hanging in the tree outside the main lodge, dressed and ready for the next day's great feast.

"Watch!" the chief said to the girl. "We will call the wolves out from the forest and put an end to the selfish feast of these people."

And sure enough, although none had been seen in this forest for many moons, at the call of the Little People a pack of hungry wolves came running out of the forest, ran to the lodge, seized the deer and tore it into shreds as they ate it all up. Then they silently disappeared, melting back into the forest.

The girl's eyes were wide with wonder as they flew back to the lodge in the rocks. But she was not afraid of these Little People. She instead felt happy and wished she could live with them forever.

The next morning, after a good night's sleep, when they had given her the thickest blanket and the spot nearest the fire, and after eating a delicious breakfast of wild berries and dried venison, the chief said "Come! Today we shall see more wonders."

He led the girl outside the lodge where a birch bark canoe was waiting. They helped the girl climb into the canoe and the others piled in after her, and they were soon skimming along down a broad river, not touching the waves, but flying in the air at a rapid speed.

Soon, they came to a great tree on the riverbank, with limbs that reached almost to the sun, and thick roots that burrowed into the muddy banks. The canoe stopped beside the great tree.

"In that tree lives a great black bear," the chief told the girl. "Every day, he comes out the door high up in the tree to wander and hunt in the forest. Now watch."

The chief threw three stones through the open door in the tree, and each time a blanket of flame covered the doorway. They could hear a growling and scratching from inside. Then, all became still. "The door is now closed fast. He cannot come out. A deep sleep has come over the bear and he will sleep for many moons. I will come to awaken the bear again in the spring. But for now, he is locked up for the winter. Let us continue our journey."

The girl pulled her invisible blanket closer around her shoulders as the canoe began to sail through the clouds above, along with the birds. "Faster!" the girl screamed, and the chief spread wide the invisible sails of his canoe and the canoe flew past the birds like a bolt of lightning. Even the great eagle could not keep pace.

The girl clapped her hands in delight. What fun it was to fly fast like the birds! She could have sailed thus forever, but the chief turned to look at her with his kind smile.

"It is time for you to return to your people," he told her. "But fear not, for we have softened their hearts and enlightened their minds. They have been searching and calling for you throughout the woods and fields. They will be glad to see you now."

And sure enough, when the canoe returned to her village and the girl walked through the doorway of her longhouse, her relatives greeted her with great joy, for they had feared she was dead, killed by the wild animals of the forest, or abducted by a war party of their enemies. The girl turned to bid farewell to her new friends, but the canoe and the Little People inside had vanished. Her family welcomed her inside her longhouse, spread a soft skin near the fire for her to sit upon and gave her the best of the food they had.

And the girl was happy, and she lived among them for many happy years.

There was silence inside the cave for several minutes after Billy Hanks finished his story. The fire crackled and the wind gusted outside on the mountain.

"The red Indians have the faeries too?" Mary Ross finally said.

"They do," said Billy Hanks.

"Are they the same *daoine sìdh* that we have here in Scotland?"

"I don't know. I am not an expert in The Folk."

"If they are the same, how did they cross the vast seas?"

"I do not know."

"Perhaps they built a special currach, like the one the Blessed Saint Columba used to sail from Ireland to the Holy Isle to bring to us the words of the Holy Scripture, and then used their magic to fly it across the waves to the New Lands."

"Perhaps they did," Billy said, smiling fondly at his sister's imagination. "Or perhaps it is just a bedtime story for the children."

"O, don't say that, brother," Mary sat up, her voice stern, her eyebrows knitted. "It is ill fortune to speak against the *sidh*. They can hear us when we speak. If they are nearby, they can read our thoughts. Am I not right, Anna?"

Anna smiled, but was silent. As a girl growing up in the home of a country squire in Shropshire, she had not heard the stories of the Folk and the other superstitions and tall tales. She had been raised on Biblical stories and, of course, the old folk tales of witches and goblins, ogres and enchanted forests. In the years since Mary Ross had become her servant and companion, she had watched with amusement as the woman had performed certain rituals and rites to assuage the *sidh,* the faerie folk: pouring a cup of warm milk on the doorstep at night, or nailing a piece of iron to the wall to ward off an unpleasant visit.

"I'm afraid that I, too, am no expert on the subject of the faeries," Anna said. "But if you tell me not to speak ill of them, then I will not."

"Well answered, schoolteacher," Billy Hanks said. "The world would be more peaceful if we all allowed each other to believe what we will. But I'm afraid the priests and the masters will never permit such a thing."

Anna stifled a yawn. It had been a long day. Billy noticed and gestured to the far side of the crackling fire.

"You and Mary can lie there," he said. "I will stay awake a bit longer and make sure there are no creatures about to bother your sleep."

The women made themselves comfortable and soon fell fast asleep. Billy Hanks sat by the fire, occasionally feeding it more bits of wood and stirring the red glowing coals. Outside, the rain fell more gently now, and the wind died down. The storm appeared to be over.

Anna awoke early in the morning. Outside the cave, the light was gloomy in the pre-dawn, but bright enough that she could see the loch below and the rising slopes of the mountains beyond. The fire was still crackling gently, and Billy Hanks was sitting beside it, as he had been when she fell asleep the night before. He was awake.

"Did you not sleep?" she asked.

He stirred and turned to look at her. "Nae," he said. "Sleep did not come to me. I had things to turn over in my mind."

"Things?"

He stretched and smiled. "The people of Glencullen depend on me to tell them what to do," he said. "Lord and Lady Stafford wish the people to leave the glen. The people do not wish to. That is a problem which I am trying to solve."

"Will there be trouble?" Anna asked.

"Oh, aye, I expect so," he replied. "There usually is when the ruler of a place wants one thing, and the people want quite another. Sometimes one can see a pathway to satisfy both parties in such a dispute."

"But you see no such pathway here?"

He shrugged. "You ask too many questions, schoolteacher, and my brain is too weary to think of good answers."

Anna rose and came around the fire to sit next to Billy Hanks. She put her arms around him, and he leaned his head onto her shoulder.

"I will ask no more," she said. "Try to sleep."

And very shortly, he was asleep. She held him while the world outside the cave went from dark gray to light, and then the first rays of the morning sun broke onto the dark water of the Loch of the Caves. It was a new day.

34

Billy, Anna and Mary Ross returned to the shieling early in the afternoon. After the persistent rain, the day dawned bright and clear, and sunshine sparkled on the wind-driven ripples of the loch's black surface. The people of Glencullen were all busy with their chores and duties: the children had driven the cattle to one of the nearby meadows to graze; the women were busy at their mending, sewing, knitting and cooking; the few old men who had come to the shieling had collected the day's firewood and were now sitting by the fire smoking their pipes and swapping stories.

Billy Hanks dropped off the buckets filled with cloudberries to the stone hut of Mute Meg and Catty, who immediately set to work crushing most of the delicate fruits into juice, the first step in the fermenting process that would eventually result in a delicious, tart liqueur. Anna and Mary went to help with the work, and were soon enough elbow deep in the orange juice.

Billy Hanks found some cool water and drank a cup or two, and grabbed two apples from a bowl set just outside Mute Meg's hut. He was still feeling the effects from his long night without sleep, and so decided the afternoon could best be spent in resting. And he knew just the place.

Pocketing his apples, he climbed atop one of the rocky cliffs that rose above the stone huts of the shieling, and continued climbing a short way up the grass and heather-filled slopes above. He continued until he found the place he had first discovered as a young lad, trying to avoid doing the daily chores he had been assigned. It was a cleft in the hillside, about six feet wide, narrowing down on the inside. And, thanks to the melting snows, or the shade provided by the walls of the cleft, the bottom was covered by a blanket of soft moss, which over the years had thickened to create a natural and soft mattress. As he had learned in his youth, this cleft hid him from discovery and provided a comfortable and private place to stretch out and sleep, shaded from the brightest sun and protected from the wind.

He sat for a time, munching on an apple, and thinking of the woman in whose arms he had awakened just a few hours before. She had managed to maneuver him, once he had gone to sleep, into a prone position, holding his head in her lap, and he had but the faintest memory of her soft hands stroking his temples while she sang an old lullaby from her childhood. He had been unaware when Mary Ross had awakened, unaware when she had prepared more brose for the breakfast, along with cups of hot tea. He had been unaware when the two women talked, in soft whispers, while he slept.

But he remembered, now, the feeling of her hands, and her scent, and the smile she had given him when he had finally awakened, looking down at him resting in her lap. He had jumped up, embarrassed, but Anna had continued to smile, and the three of them had quickly packed their things and begun the long hike back to the shieling. A hike that had been mostly wordless among them.

He finished his apple and lay back on his mossy bed, arranging his tartan behind his head, and he thought of Anna's hands stroking his temples and hair, and he fell fast asleep again.

It was a rough boot in his ribs that brought him awake again. He sat up, all senses screamingly awake and on alert. There was a man standing at the entrance of his cleft, the shadows hiding the man's face. Billy's first thought was anger at himself for not arranging a lookout—one of the wee boys—to protect himself while he slept. But then he began to calculate how to escape from his predicament.

"Easy, Billy," the man said, his voice deep and gruff. "I mean ye no harm." The man squatted down, and his face came out of the shadows and into view. It was Robert MacLeod, the sheriff-depute. MacLeod was short, stocky in build, dressed in trousers and a long leather coat. A man of some forty years, his face was creased and weathered, but his eyes were sharp and they were focused on Billy with care. Billy Hanks noticed the pistols MacLeod carried on either hip. He took it as a good sign that neither one was in the sheriff's hands, pointed at himself.

"How did you find me?" Billy asked, pulling himself slowly to a seated position. He wanted to stand, the better for it if it came to a fight with MacLeod, but decided to wait and see how the situation would unfold.

MacLeod shrugged. "Not that hard," he said. "Captain Gordon in Glencullen told me where the glen's shieling was. I came out to look around, see if anyone might have heard from you at all. Twas a wee lass who told me she had seen you climbing up here. You snore when you sleep. The sound was easy to follow." He looked around at the cleft. "Tis a nice place for a sleep, I'll grant you."

"Found it when I was a wee bairn," Billy said, smiling. "Good place to hide from the others, when they have chores for you."

MacLeod nodded. He understood. He had been a youth once, at a summer shieling, looking to escape the chores for a time.

"So, what is the plan?" Billy asked. "Ye plan to take me back to Inverness to face the law? All the way to Edinburgh, perhaps? Ye'd best not plan on sleeping yourself. I have been known to disappear at night. Tis said I have a connection with the Wee Folk who come to release me from bondage."

MacLeod chuckled, and sat down across from Billy, his back to the other wall of the cleft.

"Nae, nae," he said, shaking his head. "I told ye that I mean no harm. I wouldna try to carry you back anywhere, Billy Hanks, for as you say, I couldna do it on my own. I came to find you so we could parlay a bit."

"Parlay is it?" Billy Hanks laughed aloud, his voice dripping with sarcasm. "That's rich. Ye hunt and find the most wanted man in Sutherlandshire, if not all of Scotland, and all ye want is to parlay? Do ye not know how much of a bounty there is for the man who brings me back, dead or alive, to Lord Stafford?"

"Oh, I am keenly aware of the price on your head, Billy Hanks," MacLeod said, smiling. "And my wife in Tain wouldna ken why I haven't yet shot you dead. But I did not come here to arrest ye today, nor to enrich my own coffers."

"Then, why?"

"My job is to keep the peace in the shire," MacLeod said. "And I fear that peace will be sorely disturbed if I canna find a way to convince the people of Glencullen to obey Lord and Lady Stafford and remove themselves to the coast at Golspie. His Lordship has made it very clear that he intends to turn Glencullen into a sheepwalk. Now, that may be something the people of Glencullen disagree with, it may be something that you disagree with, and it may be something I disagree with, God's truth, but that does not change the fact that Glencullen is the legal property of Lord and Lady Stafford of Dunrobin, and, as such, it is within their rights to do with that property as they wish. And even though we might all disagree with the mannie's decision, there's not shite-all we can do about it. The law is on his side. The dragoons from Fort William are on his side. As the sheriff-depute, God help me, *I* am on his side. I dunna wish to be so, but there it is. Tis his land. He wants the people to go and the sheep to come. And so it will be, Billy Hanks, so it will be."

MacLeod stood up and went to the opening of the cleft, looking out on the valley, the loch below and the rising purple slopes of the mountains that rolled onward and upwards to the distant summit of Ben Cullen.

"Tis a bonnie place, Billy," he said.

"Aye, it is that," Billy said.

"I would much prefer that ye remain alive to enjoy it," MacLeod said. "And the people down there, who have been coming here for generations now. We all would like things to remain the same, as they have done for centuries of time. But you yourself know that life is made up of changes, some for the good, and many for the ill. Is it worth your life, Billy Hanks, to fight against something that canna be changed? Is it worth endangering the lives of the good folk down there?"

"What are you suggesting?" Billy Hanks kept his voice low and controlled.

MacLeod turned and looked at Billy, face on. He stared into the man's eyes.

"Give it up, Billy," he said. "Ye canna win this fight. They will kill ye. They will send Darnell against ye. He will have cannons and muskets and soldiers with horses and bayonets and swords. More soldiers than you can count, if need be. You will come to a violent end of it. Others may be killed, as well. I do not wish to see that happen."

"And what would ye have me do?"

MacLeod shrugged. "Leave," he said. "I don't have to tell you, Billy Hanks, that the world is a large place. Ye have seen a good bit of it in your own lifetime. Go, go somewhere else. Go back to the Colonies. Start a new life there. Go to Europe. Ye have many talents and many skills that can be put to good use. It may not be what you want, but you must choose life. The people of Glencullen will do what you tell them. Tell them to choose life, not injury and death. Tell them to go to Golspie and start life afresh. It will not be easy, it will not be perfect. It will not be anything they wish to do. But it will be life. The other way leads only to death. I do not wish that, upon you, or upon them."

The sheriff turned back to face Billy Hanks.

"I will help you," he said, spreading his hands wide in supplication. "I have relations in Shetland, cattle farmers and fishermen. I know the men who seek workers for their holdings in Canada, far to the west where the mountains soar and the plains stretch onward past the horizon. I can make arrangements. But only if you choose to go."

Billy listened to the sheriff's argument. He wanted to believe it was possible to pull up his roots and start anew somewhere else. He understood that MacLeod was trying to negotiate an end to the conflict. He wanted to believe it was possible. He had not come back to Scotland in order to become a hunted outlaw. He had come back because it was his home. Glencullen, the shieling, the mountains, the lochs, the fast-running streams, the sounds of the birds, the wind … all of it. He had not asked to be the leader of Glencullen, it had just fallen to him. He thought of the old people, near the ends of their lives, and the children, just beginning theirs, and he only wanted them to be able to live in peace, as the people of the glen had done for many hundreds of years. Here, in the glens and valleys and mountains where they had lived, and worked, and loved and fought for so long. How could it all be coming to an end, an inglorious end, all for the prospect of herds of sheep and short-term profit for one of the richest men in the world?

"I am grateful for your words," Billy said. "You are a brave and good man to come here and find me as ye have. Your arguments are most persuasive. But I canna leave again. I am Billy Hanks of Glencullen. Not of America. Not of Europe. Not of Shetland. Not of Canada. Nor even of Golspie. This—" he waved his hand to indicate all around him, "This is who I am and who I shall be until I die. I am Billy Hanks of Glencullen."

"But Billy…" The sheriff began again to remonstrate. But there suddenly came a high-pitched shriek, and someone wielding a wooden club stepped into the narrow space of the cleft's entrance and delivered a blow to the back of MacLeod's head, a blow which landed with a dull but resonant thud. The sheriff sank to his knees and then keeled over face down onto the mossy floor and lay still.

A red faced Mary Ross came into the cleft, holding her club high above her head, ready to deliver another blow. Behind her, Anna Kenton stepped forward, cupping a good-sized rock in each of her hands. Seeing the sheriff lying on the ground motionless, Mary Ross's eyes grew wide and her hands began to tremble.

"H-h-have I kilt him?" she asked with a shaky voice. "I said I would not let you come to harm, brother. I meant it. And Anna agreed to help. But I dinna mean to kill him."

Billy Hanks took in the scene and began to laugh. It started with a few chuckles and soon, in a gushing release of tension, became an uncontrollable spasm of deep laughter that caused him to bend over at the waist while tears rolled down his cheeks.

Mary Ross and Anna stared at the man, uncomprehending, thinking that Billy Hanks might have lost his senses. But soon, they too could not help but smile, then giggle, then chuckle until they too were convulsed with laughter, holding onto each other for support.

"Nae, sister," Billy was finally able to speak. "Ye have not killed the man. But perhaps you should go ahead and finish him off, for I'm afeard the sheriff-depute may have to arrest you for assault and carry you off to the Tolbooth in Dornoch."

At that, they all three began again to laugh uncontrollably and it was some time before any of them could speak again.

"Dear God in Heaven," Anna said finally, wiping away her own tears and bending down to attend to the sheriff. "You have assaulted the sheriff-depute, Mary Ross. I hope you can come up with a good excuse for that."

"Excuse?" Mary Ross was outraged, even as her chest continued to heave with waves of mirth. "I was defending my own brother from a stranger who meant him harm. I need no other excuse for that."

Anna managed to roll MacLeod over onto his back and gently tended to the man until his eyes opened with a start, and he groaned.

"Wha the bloody hell…" he started to sit up, but Anna put a restraining hand on his chest and he sank gratefully back down onto the mossy bed.

"Miss Ross wishes to apologize, Sir," Anna said. "She did not recognize you and was defending her brother from what she thought was a highwayman."

"Except," Billy Hanks said, "There isn't a highway to be found within three days walk."

With that, the three of them were sent off on another convulsion of laughter. They only began to stop this time when MacLeod began to groan as he reached for the back of his head.

"I've got a knot the size of a tuppence," he said. "But I will forego arresting you, Madam, if you can help me back to the shieling and find me some good whiskey."

"It would be my honor, Sir," Mary Ross said politely, and she helped the man to his feet.

THE THREE OF THEM helped Sheriff MacLeod back down the hillside to the shieling community. Anna brought him a cold compress for his aching head, Billy Hanks a flask of good local whiskey and Mary Ross a heaping bowl of rabbit stew and a chunk of freshly baked bread. They all watched as he ate and drank, finally sitting back with a groan of satisfaction. His head was still sore from Mary's fervent blow, so he acceded to their recommendation that he spend the night and rest, and Billy Hanks went off to order some of the lads to feed, brush and make MacLeod's horse comfortable for the night.

In the morning, feeling better save for the still sore place on his head where Mary Ross had felled him, MacLeod saddled his horse and prepared to ride off. Billy Hanks helped him with his saddle, drawing the cinches tight, and pulling the reins over the horse's ears.

MacLeod tied his bag onto the back of the saddle. He looked over at Billy, his eyes questioning.

"What happened, back there in Canada, Billy?" he asked, his voice low and quiet. "With the boy?"

Billy Hanks finished straightening a strap of the bridle, and gave the horse a bit of apple. "That is something I dunna like to talk about, Sheriff," he said. "And it was a long, long time ago."

"Darnell tells his story about it," MacLeod pressed on. "He said the boy stole a bucket of milk."

"Johnny Dunn was a good lad," Billy said. "He never stole a thing in all his short life."

"So what happened? You were there, I take it."

"Aye, I was," Billy said, staring off into the distance. "And I will always regret not running that bastard Darnell through with my bayonet when I had the chance."

"They would have hanged you for that."

Billy Hanks shrugged. "At least it would have been warranted," he said. "Unlike the fate of poor little Johnny. He did nought wrong. It was Darnell that did the wrong. He tried to entice Johnny into his bed, for unnatural purposes. Johnny told me about it. He was a good lad, always cheerful, always helping the men in our squadron. I told him the men and I would not let Darnell harm him. I was wrong. I wasna much beyond a wee boy myself. I could not help him. I could not stop Darnell from what he did to Johnny. First, he defiled the lad, and then he had him killed. Johnny never stole a drop of milk from anyone. It was all just a tale Darnell told to get the boy out of his way, once he'd had his pleasure with him."

MacLeod was silent. "So you walked away," he said.

"Aye," Billy said. "I swore to the other men I would kill Darnell, sure as the sun rises in the east. They convinced me to go, said there was no way I could ever get close enough to kill the man. So I left my uniform, my musket, everything that belonged to the Army and I walked into the woods. I did not expect to live long there. There are wild animals in the woods, and there are the red men. Both tend to be lethal. I welcomed death, I sought for death. The world of men had no more appeal to me, after that."

"Yet here you are," MacLeod said. "Alive yet."

"Aye," Billy Hanks said. "And here I am."

The men shook hands and Billy helped him mount his horse.

"Think on what I said, Billy Hanks," MacLeod said when he was mounted. "Choose life, for yourself and those you love and care for. But mark this well: if ye don't and we meet again, it will not go easily. I have my job and I am sworn to do it. So think hard, Billy."

Billy Hanks nodded up at the sheriff and released the reins. MacLeod rode away, down the slopes toward the south, back toward Glencullen and the world which awaited there.

35.

London - July

It was a glorious night of dancing at Cleveland House. Elizabeth, the Lady Stafford, had presided over a delicious, seven-course supper for about a hundred guests, and after suitable time had been spent for the gentlemen, all dressed appropriately in their knee breeches, white cravats and soft *chapeau-bras* hats, to smoke cigars and guzzle down some of Lord Stafford's fine French brandy; and for the ladies, in their elegant and flowing silk gowns, to refresh their make-up and gossip delightedly (His Highness the Prince Regent, better known to most as Prinny, who was in attendance at the ball, was the usual topic of delighted and scandalous conversation), the orchestra in the Grand Ballroom struck some introductory notes. That was the signal for the guests to arrange themselves in preordained lines, men on one side, women on the other, and await the beginning of the Grand March.

It was Elizabeth herself, as hostess of the evening and holder of the position of doyenne of London society, who led the Grand March, on the arm of her husband Gower. She was the very picture of grace and elegance, while Lord Stafford, blinking rapidly in the bright light, red-faced, his powdered wig flopping about on his misshapen head, did his utmost to keep up. Luckily for him, all eyes were on his wife, tall, raven-haired, her blue eyes sparkling with pleasure as she paraded with her husband past the line of the other dancers. At the end, once the leading couple had completed their promenade, nodding and smiling at their friends, the entire company all began the elegant back-and-forth of the steps in the favored Country Dance. The music filled the ballroom while the ladies gowns swept majestically across the floor, and the muffled steps of the dancers beat in rhythm to the tune.

Servants carrying trays of champagne and whiskey scurried about the ballroom refreshing the dancers, and the tables set up on the room's periphery groaned with cakes, sweetmeats, pickled vegetables and other culinary delights. And then Elizabeth called for a Scotch Reel, which everyone, knowing that she was the Chieftess of Clan Sutherland, expected and approved. The guests now arranged themselves in groups of eight and when the fiddle began its quick-paced jig, the dancers launched into the elaborate quick-step routine, weaving in and around each other, turning left and right before returning to their original partner. This dance did not last as long as the first, as the pace was quicker and the dancers were soon panting for breath.

After the reel, Elizabeth gave her husband a smile and a nod to inform him that he was officially excused, for the time being, and he scurried off to join a group of uniformed generals and well-dressed businessmen standing near the elaborately carved marble fireplace, where he grabbed a glass of champagne and visibly relaxed, out of the public eye and among men of his own kind who much preferred talking and drinking to dancing. The orchestra launched into a slower tune for a cotillion, and the guests again arranged themselves into groups to perform the steps.

Elizabeth looked around the ballroom happily. The party was a great success, as always. Her guests, her friends, her acquaintances from society, were all present, having a wonderful time. She paused and took it all in. *I have done this*, she thought to herself. *I have provided the home, the music, the food and the drink for all these people's entertainment. They shall talk of this party for the next week, and nothing else, and they shall all talk of me.* She was content.

"My dear Lady, a wonderful evening, is it not?" She turned to face the speaker, and found herself looking into the face of the Prince Regent himself. He was a small man, rotund, with a full and florid face. This night he was elegantly dressed in militaristic raiment, complete with gold epaulets at the shoulders of his sky-blue coat, various medals and ribbons affixed to his red waistcoat, shiny knee-high boots and a long sword in a sweeping polished black scabbard at his side. Elizabeth curtsied, and the Prince kissed her hand. She thought he might have held her hand for several moments longer than necessary, and blushed, thinking of the man's somewhat roguish reputation. Prinny, as Elizabeth knew from the gossip of the other ladies in society, was often in debt, often said to be in someone's bed (other than his distant wife, the Lady Caroline of Brunswick), and often in trouble with his father, King George III for these and other failings. Luckily for the Prince Regent, the king fluctuated in and out of the states of madness that came over him, and so Prinny's many foibles were often left unchecked.

"The glory of the evening is enhanced immeasurably by your presence, Your Royal Highness," she said. "For you are the shiniest star in our constellation."

He laughed, throwing his head back and showing his two rows of somewhat discolored teeth. "Ah, my dear Lady, you are too kind. And too modest, methinks. From what I understand, your husband, Lord Stafford, has far more stars in his heavens than a modest Prince such as myself. And that does not even begin to include the treasure that is represented by yourself, my dear lady."

Elizabeth smiled coquettishly at the Prince Regent and with a snap of her wrist, unfurled her lace fan, giving herself a brief cooling breeze. They both knew that he spoke the truth: the net worth of the Staffords far exceeded that of the Prince; indeed, it was likely greater than the combined assets of all the Hanovers. But it would be inelegant to discuss, much less compare, their finances.

"How is your dear wife, the Lady Caroline?" Elizabeth said, hoping she wasn't broaching a sore subject. "I am so sorry she could not be with us this evening."

The Prince nodded, glancing around to make sure no wayward ears were nearby. "She is well, thank you Madam," he said. "She is at Sandringham with Lady Charlotte for the nonce. She prefers the country air at this time of year."

"I quite understand," Elizabeth said. "I am always sorry to leave the brisk air of Dunrobin to come to London for the season. And yet, I always find myself sorry to leave this house to return to Dornoch as well. Though I think my feelings may be more directed toward the difficulties of the sea journey in either direction."

"Oh, quite," the Prince said, nodding vigorously. "I am not a good sailor either, Madam. A beastly business, that."

They paused and looked around at the dancers. Elizabeth could not help but notice the Prince's eye lingering on the form of Lady Carstairs, whose red velvet gown was cut quite low in the front. She remembered hearing something about the Prince Regent having invited Lord and Lady Carstairs to weekend hunting parties at his estates in Norfolk; and knowing full well what went on at such affairs, she wondered if the Prince had bagged another mistress. But she put such thoughts out of her mind.

"I have been hearing some disturbing things about conditions in Scotland, my dear Lady," the Prince turned back to her.

"Oh, dear," Elizabeth said. "Whatever have you heard to cause you distress?"

"Oh, it is mostly the usual news from that uncivilized place," the Prince Regent said, sniffing the air. "Lawlessness and rebellion."

Elizabeth felt herself growing pale. "Oh?" she said.

"Yes," the Prince continued. "I have heard that some months ago a rough band of ruffians kidnapped some farmers and drove several herds of sheep off their lands. A brazen display, if you ask me. In fact, now that I think about it, I believe some of the farms in question under such attack were located in your shire. Is that correct?"

"Oh, of course," Elizabeth said. "Yes, that incident occurred quite some time ago. The farmer was released unharmed and the livestock have all been returned to their rightful owners."

"And have the criminals been captured and executed?"

The Prince peered at Lady Stafford, his eyes now narrowed, his face red. She felt the danger rising.

"I believe the authorities are still searching for the miscreants," she said finally. "General Cathcart has dispatched some squadrons of the Black Watch to assist our local sheriff-depute. I am sure they will soon find the perpetrators and bring them to justice."

"Hmmm." The Prince said nothing for a while. "I am always concerned about lawlessness in the Scottish provinces," he said finally. "You know, my great-uncle once had to clean out that viper's nest, fifty or sixty years ago. Perhaps it is time we did it again."

Now Elizabeth felt her anger rising, and fought to keep it under control. "Your Highness, I can assure you that the people of Scotland are, to the utmost extent, both peaceful and loyal to your family. I can certainly assure you that the people of Sutherlandshire, who were, as you will recall, loyal to the King during the unpleasantness of the Rising of '45, continue in their loyalty to this very day. There is certainly no need for a military expedition or invasion on the scale of what occurred in the now distant past." *Especially*, she thought, *led by someone as horrible as the Butcher of Cumberland, brother to the old King and uncle to this one.*

"I certainly hope that is true, Madam," the Prince Regent said. He brought his head close to hers and spoke in low, intimate tones.

"My father, in his more lucid moments, has talked about creating a duchy for your husband," he said. "It would be an honor certainly well-deserved for a family that has contributed so much to the nation. However, I think there would be great opposition to such an appointment in Government if Sutherland continues to be a den of thieves and a factory of rebellion." He paused and stared into Elizabeth's deep blue eyes. "Do I make myself clear?"

"Quite clear, Your Royal Highness," she said, bowing her head. But then she raised it again, and looked straight back at him. They stayed that way, staring one at the other, for several long moments.

Y-y-Your Highness," came a high-pitched voice, which made both the Prince Regent and Elizabeth jump back, startled. They turned to see Lord Stafford, blinking rapidly at the two of them. "Major General Williamson is entertaining us greatly with his tales from the front lines," said Stafford. "I think you would enjoy hearing it."

"Old Pogey telling lies again, is he?" the Prince said, clapping Lord Stafford on the back, causing him to flinch. "Very well, then, let's go listen to them. Can I get another glass of champagne?"

The men tottered off, leaving Elizabeth alone and slightly sweaty and nauseous. A Dukedom! For her husband! She would be the Duchess of Sutherland! It would be the highest and most prestigious honor of her life. Her husband would be counted among the highest ranking men in all of Great Britain. Their children would live in the finest houses, obtain the richest spouses, be accorded all the honors and respect worthy of their name.

And yet…the Prince Regent had made it abundantly clear that no such royal honor would be forthcoming until the outlaw Billy Hanks was first captured and hanged. And the rest of Lord Stafford's plans to remove people from the glens and straths of her county had to proceed without further problems or trouble. The stakes had just been raised, and raised immeasurably higher than ever before. It was no longer a parochial question of making more money in rents. Now, the prize was a lifelong, hereditary title to be passed on to countless generations of her family. She would become Elizabeth, Duchess of Sutherland. Her eldest son George would be the second Duke of Sutherland, once his father died.

She was almost breathless with the weight of this news. She looked around at the brightly lit ballroom, where hundreds of her friends were still dancing and laughing and eating and drinking. Suddenly, she wished them all gone. She wanted to be alone. She needed to talk to Gower, her husband. They had plans to make. The future was suddenly waiting right in front of their noses, and they needed to take hold of it. And soon.

36

Despite Elizabeth's wishes, the party at Cleveland House lasted well into the early hours of the morning. It was approaching three o'clock when Lord Stafford knocked and entered his wife's bedchamber. She had changed from her spectacular gown into a comfortable dressing robe and was seated at her table, worrying her hair with a brush and staring, sightlessly, into her mirror.

"It is late, wife, and I am in need of my bed," he said, a bit grumpily, when he entered. He sat down in an upholstered chair next to his wife's bed with a sigh. "What is it you wished to discuss?"

Elizabeth had asked Mr. Gunn to request Gower visit her boudoir before he retired, saying she had something important she needed to talk about. She had sent her servants to bed so they could be alone and talk freely. Now, she told her husband what the Prince Regent had said to her hours earlier.

"W-w-what?" He was taken aback at the news. "Tell me exactly what he said. Word for word."

She did so. He sat there, blinking rapidly and shaking his head back and forth.

"I am to be made Duke?" he said. "Did he say when?"

"No, Gower, he did not," his wife said. "But he left little doubt that it would not occur until this Billy Hanks fellow is captured and sent to trial. That part was very clear."

Lord Stafford thought about that for some time.

"Prinny would love nothing better than to raise an army of his own and take it to Scotland to pillage and rape the countryside," he said finally. "I've heard him talk such nonsense many a time at the club, usually when he is deep into his cups. He thinks such a thing is his inherited right as the scion of the Duke of Cumberland."

"They won't let him actually *do* that, will they?" Elizabeth asked. She could not imagine British troops riding in force through Scotland. While the mad passions that had afflicted her country during The '45 had long since cooled, and the executions and title and land forfeitures of the clan chiefs that had rebelled against the English crown had sharply focused the attention and loyalty of those who remained in power, Elizabeth knew that any impression that the English King was once again trying to repress and subjugate his Scottish subjects by way of arms would awaken afresh the passions and enmity of the people. It was unthinkable.

"No, of course not." Hands clasped at the small of his back, Lord Stafford began pacing back and forth in front of his wife's fireplace, which was laid but not lit in the sultry summer heat of London. "The Prime Minister wouldn't let the Prince Regent within a mile of commanding his own battalions, never mind letting him loose in Scotland. The man's a vainglorious fool, a drunkard and a whoremaster and everyone knows it."

"But what about the Duchy?" Elizabeth said. "Do you believe what he said is true? That the King has been thinking about creating it for you?"

Stafford could not help but smile, something he did not normally do. It stretched his face in an unusual way, making him look like he was smelling something most unpleasant in the way his nose and lips stretched and rearranged his face.

"I will confess, Elizabeth, I have heard other talk of this," Stafford said, nodding at his wife. "Mostly whispers, to be sure. But I have had intimations of it from people close to the King. People I trust."

"But is the King well enough to make such a decision?"

Stafford frowned. "I do not know," he admitted. "He is reported to be the picture of health at present, but no one is quite sure how long that condition will last. He has been this way before, only to relapse again into …"

He trailed off. Elizabeth finished his sentence.

"…madness."

Stafford shrugged. It was true. The King was well until he wasn't. And then he was quite literally insane. The doctors were helpless; they had no idea what caused these sessions of insanity, nor what to do to treat them. Which is why the Prime Minister, Pitt the Younger, had wrangled with Parliament to create the Regency. George's son was named the Prince Regent, but full authority over the government was withheld from him. No one wished to see Prinny handed carte blanche to rule over the army, or the exchequer. Pitt, along with others in Parliament, closely guarded national policy and the Prince Regent was carefully permitted to play only a ceremonial role in the governance of the country.

"So it may not happen after all." Elizabeth was thinking aloud now. "The King may relapse into his illness, and forget all about his plan to make you Duke of Sutherland."

"Quite so," Stafford said. "Or he may die and we are at the mercy of Prinny."

"I believe he is an ally," Elizabeth said, remembering his lingering kiss of her hand. "He seems to enjoy coming to our parties. But can we count on him to follow through?"

Stafford continued his pacing.

"We need to begin a courtship," he said finally. "We will need to woo Prinny to our side."

"And how…?"

"First, we will invite him to Dunrobin," Lord Stafford said, beginning to count on his fingers. "He loves to hunt. We shall arrange for him to bag our best stags. My gamekeepers can arrange that. Next, I shall talk with my bankers at Drummonds: Prinny is always in debt to someone. Perhaps I can do some things towards the retirement of some of those debts. And he is always spending money on his palaces. I can introduce him to some of my builders. Those things all might help us rise in his favor."

Stafford continued his pacing. Elizabeth wished he would sit still and just talk to her.

"His other love, of course, is women," Stafford said. "I don't suppose you…"

Elizabeth jumped to her feet. "Are you asking me to become his mistress, husband?" she snapped, her eyes furious. "Because if you are …" She snatched up her hairbrush, the heavy silver-backed one, and looked for a moment as if she was going to hurl it at her husband's head.

Stafford looked at her in amazement.

"My dear woman," he said. "That you should even think that I would consider making such a request is most distressing to me. I was merely wondering if you knew of someone who, well, might be a candidate for such a thing. We need to place ourselves in His Royal Highness' good graces. You must know of the type of woman the Prince prefers…"

She thought. And then could not help smiling. "Thinking of the women who have submitted to him, I would say the salient characteristics are 'female and breathing,'" she said with a giggle. "He does not appear to have many other standards beyond those."

Lord Stafford could not help himself. He guffawed, loudly. His wife joined in, and they embraced, laughing together.

When they broke apart, Elizabeth looked into her husband's eyes. "I will think on it," she told him. "Perhaps I can find a candidate or two that might be encouraged to find their way to his bed. But I think we must also discuss the other thing that Prinny mentioned."

Stafford began his infernal back-and-forth pacing.

"Ah, yes," he said. "Glencullen."

"Quite," she said. "We must take care of this problem, and quickly. There must be no further uprisings. The time has come to move ahead, and quickly."

"I quite agree," Stafford said. "I will write to Young and tell him to make the necessary arrangements. We will remove the people of Glencullen at once."

"Tell him to do it at Michaelmas," Lady Stafford said. "It is the customary time for collecting rents at the end of the harvest season. The new tenants can move in by All Souls' Day. Golspie is ready. It is time, Gower."

"Agreed," he said.

"But what about that outlaw, that Billy Hanks?" Elizabeth said. "He is still at large. Prinny seemed quite upset about that."

"I will inform the sheriff-depute and General Cavendish that the outlaw must be accounted for before Michaelmas," he said. "I suspect that this Hanks fellow will show his hand once the people are moved out of the strath. When he comes out of hiding, we shall grab him and put an end to it."

"I think you are correct, Gower," Elizabeth said. "Good. Let it be done. And now it is time for bed, at long last." The first rays of the morning were beginning to lighten the night sky to the east of London.

Lord Stafford bowed to his wife, kissed her hand and retired to his own chambers.

THE NEXT MORNING, two letters were sent out from Cleveland House, both posted for Scotland. The first was addressed to William

Young, factor of the Sutherland estates in Dornoch. Written in the hand of Lord Stafford himself, it formally assigned him to begin all procedures necessary to enact the removal of all the population currently living within the environs of Glencullen, along with such livestock and housing timbers as belonged to said population, to be accommodated in the newly created housing district outside the village of Golspie on the coast of the North Sea. Further, the letter told Young to begin the process of removal on or about the date of Michaelmas, September 29, one of the quarter days of the calendar.

The second letter was hurriedly scribbled by Mr. Gunn, and addressed to his cousin, the wife of a shopkeeper in Dornoch. This letter was much briefer and to the point than Lord Stafford's dictated legalese. It said:

"Michaelmas. Tell Billy."

37

Fort George - Inverness

Major Darnell was shown into his commanding officer's billet within the imposing edifice of Fort George in the early afternoon. The Viscount Cathcart was seated at a small round table near the window of his personal quarters, looking out across the thick stone battlements of the fort, with views of the Moray Firth and, on the far shore, the low, cloud-studded hills of the Black Isle. The Fort, built in the twenty years after the Rising of '45, had been placed on a shingled promontory extending into the waters of the Firth to the northeast of Inverness, designed to hold several thousand troops in the garrison to pacify the Highlands. The broad stone walls had been built in a star shape, but many Scots saw it as a sword-point extending out into the firth and pointing straight at the heart of the Highlands.

Cathcart was heavily involved in eating his dinner, which Darnell could see consisted of two guinea hens, a large baked turbot, neeps and tatties, a healthy wedge of aromatic and blue-veined Stilton, and a large bowl of apples and pears. Two bottles of claret had been opened and, Darnell noted, one was empty. The general had removed both his outer coat and his wig for his midday meal, which he was attacking with gusto. He was a large man, with rounded, ruddy jowls, and his unwigged head was mostly hairless, save for a brief ring of silvered hair that ran from ear to ear. Cathcart motioned with his knife, greasy from the labors of slicing up one of the hens, for Darnell to take a seat. The general poured Darnell a glass of the port, and refilled his own glass.

"Your health, Sir," the general said, pausing in his gustatory labors to offer a brief toast. Darnell took but a sip and waited.

Cathcart resumed his all-out attack on his dinner.

"I have received two letters this morning from London, Major," the general said, pointing with his knife at some papers at the edge of his table. "One is from the Home Secretary, Mister Dundas, and the other is from Lord Stafford of Dunrobin. Do you know what these letters concern, Sir?"

"I do not, Sir," Darnell said.

The general sliced off another piece of the guinea hen and dispatched it into his mouth. Outside, a flock of gulls were sitting, face into the wind, atop the broad battlement of the fort's walls. One began to beat his wings and uttered a screaming cry.

"You do not," the general echoed. "Well, I did not know, Major Darnell, that you had been requested by Lord Stafford to use His Majesty's troops to find the gentlemen from Sutherlandshire and Wester Ross who liberated some sheep from their farms a few months ago and drove them to Rusdale before disappearing into the gloaming. I do not like surprises, Major, especially when they come from the likes of Lord Stafford or Secretary Dundas of London. I would like a report, Sir."

"Begging the general's pardon," Darnell said, "But you ordered me to take two regiments to Dingwall when the reports came in, suggesting a general rebellion among the people was underway. In fact, I believe that you were in receipt of a letter from the Lady Stafford at that time, asking for your support."

The general waved his knife in the air dismissively. "All that is true, Sir, but I expected that you would have dealt with the miscreants then and there," he said. "I had no idea that the search was still ongoing. What has it been…four months now? Five? I had expected some results before now, Major."

"But, General…"

"Don't but-General me, Major," the general thundered, pointing his knife at the major's chest. "I expect to be informed of all operations under my command. And I expect my subordinates to keep me informed of their operations. What I do *not* expect is to have my superiors in London question me about what is going on in my own district. Now then, Major, I would like a report."

Darnell sat up straight. He knew he'd better get this right.

"Sergeant-Major Williams has just returned from Portree with his squadron," he said. "They were unsuccessful in their search for the men from Glen Grudie, who had been reported to be among the rebels who stole the sheep from their laird. We had intelligence that they had been seen on the Isle of Skye. Williams found no trace of the men, and could not obtain any further intelligence from the people of the town there."

General Cathcart grunted as he continue to eat. "I suppose they roughed up a few of the local lads," he said. "And no one talked, is that right?"

"I believe that is so, Sir," Darnell said. "I was not present at the interrogations. I have personally led expeditions into Glen Grudie and Glencullen, as well as other straths in the region, also to search for the men involved, and especially the alleged ringleader, this man they call Billy Hanks," he said. "Again, we have been unsuccessful to date in locating the fugitives."

"Of course you are," the general snapped, as he sawed angrily at the baked fish on the platter in front of him.

"Sir?"

"Unsuccessful, Major," the general said. "Of course you've been unsuccessful. You go riding into these straths with full squadrons of troops, probably doing everything but blowing trumpets and shooting muskets to announce your arrival, and the miscreants see you coming from miles away and melt into the wilderness. Am I correct, Sir?"

"Well, yes, general, but..."

"And none of the regular folk in the straths will admit to ever having seen the rebels you seek," the general continued. "Am I still correct, Sir?"

"That has been the general reaction to our searching, yes, general," Darnell said. "I have not pressed my inquiries to the point of violence, Sir, as I am mindful that the population of these districts may yet retain some animosity towards the Crown of England. I know the last rebellion here in Scotland took place many decades ago, yet we both know that the Scottish people, although outwardly loyal, still have an ingrained resistance to British troops."

"Hmmm," the general's grunt was noncommittal, although he knew the truth of what Darnell said. "And what, if I may ask, is your plan going forward?"

Darnell hesitated. He knew his answer would be seen as inadequate. But it was the only answer he had.

"I am awaiting further developments, Sir," he said. "I have made certain inquiries to certain gentlemen in both straths in question. Let us call them *congenial* gentlemen, who appreciate the efforts of the Crown in these matters. We all expect that the rebels from both locations will eventually reappear. Once they do, my men and I are ready to set forth at once to apprehend them."

Cathcart was silent as he carefully peeled one of the apples he plucked from the bowl. He concentrated on slicing off the red skin in one piece, going round and round the apple held against his sharp knife. When he was finished, he sliced the white fruit in quarters, removed the inner core and stuffed a piece in his mouth, along with a good-sized chunk of the Stilton. He then washed it down with a swallow of the claret.

"Wait and see, wait and see," the general muttered, almost to himself. He looked up at Darnell, eyebrows raised. "And what if there is no further word of the men in question? What will you do then?"

"I-I suppose that will mean they have left the country," Darnell said. "There are already rumors that this Hanks has sailed for France."

"So: out of sight, out of mind. Is that right, Major?"

"Yes, Sir, I suppose that is correct."

Cathcart's fist pounded the tabletop with a resounding crash.

"*No*, Sir," he shouted. "That is *not* correct. There has been a challenge to the primacy of law and order in these shires. That cannot be allowed to stand, and will not be allowed to stand as long as I am commander of His Majesty's army in the country, Sir. *I will not have it.*"

Darnell was shocked into silence. He had not been expecting this from the general.

Cathcart reached over to the corner of his table and flipped the stack of letters there with the blade of his knife.

"The Home Secretary informs me that the people of Glencullen are to be removed on or about Michaelmas, which is just a few weeks away," he said. "This rich idiot Stafford tells me the same thing. Says he fears for the orderly execution of his writs of removal. Not that I give a bloody damn what he wants. But both of these gentlemen expect us to find this Billy Hanks before then. Is that clear, major?"

"Yes, sir," Darnell said.

"Good. There will be no more half measures, Major. I want you to take three companies. You are to set up temporary bivouac in Lairg. That town lies an easy day's ride from both Glencullen to the north and Glen Grudie to the west. You will send scouting parties into both straths on a daily basis until these men are found. Is that clear, Major?"

"Yes, sir," Darnell said, trying to keep his elation from showing itself outwardly on his face.

"I want no more half measures with the people, either," the general continued, waving his knife around for emphasis as he spoke. "If someone has information but refuses to divulge it, burn their barn to the ground. We will lollygaggle with these people no more. The reason the King has entrusted us with the power of military force is so that we will use it to further his interests. And his interests, as described in the pages of these letters, include finding the men responsible for the theft of property and the disruption of the civil order of his Kingdom, and bringing those men to immediate justice. Is *that* clear, Major?"

"Yes, sir," Darnell leaped to his feet and snapped off a salute. "Exquisitely clear, Sir."

"Good." The general refilled his glass one more time, and took a healthy swallow with a satisfied look on his face. "Dismissed."

38

The Shieling

The weather had been poor for four days straight, and everyone at the shieling was sick of the cold rain, sick of the grey clouds that covered the sky, sick of being stuck inside the rocky bothys whose thatched roofs did not do the best job of keeping out the rain. The children were grumpy and at each other's throats; mothers and grandmothers were tired of having to constantly discipline them and of not being able to send them outside to gain a bit of peace and quiet.

So when the fifth day dawned bright and sunny, with an achingly blue sky above and just a bit of a cooling wind, the mood of the entire village rose. The livestock were led out to the grazing fields by the boys who were suddenly full of energy and mischief. Some of the older girls went down the loch to do some fishing, and to talk about what the boys must be up to. The older women started in on a long list of neglected chores. There was butter to be churned and cheese to be made, clothes to be mended, winter things to be knitted, but since the day was so bright and happy, they set about their work with a smile on their faces, and a good word for their neighbors.

Two people in the village were still preoccupied with darker thoughts, however. One was Billy Hanks, who kept thinking of his talk with the sheriff, and the things the sheriff had said. The other was Mute Meg, who was strangely ill at ease during the morning. She could not sit still, but kept getting up and walking, looking back down the valley as if she expected someone to come riding up.

"There's some bad news on the way," Catty confided to Anna and Mary Ross as they swept a few days' collection of dust out of the cabins. "She awoke with the feeling of it. And then, just before dawn, she heard the call of a corbie far overhead. Bad news always arrives after the corbie's call. Tis known by all."

Anna and Mary did not respond to that. They knew nothing of the signs and omens. But they had long since learned not to discount anything that Mute Meg said. She had always been right. So they accepted that some kind of bad news was on the way, and since there was nothing they could do about it, they went about the business of the day.

Anna kept an eye on Billy Hanks throughout the morning, something she caught herself doing more and more. Ever since they had returned from the expedition to gather the cloudberries on the mountain, and the unforced intimacy they had there, they seemed to spend more and more time together, enjoying each other's company. Catty and Mute Meg had noticed, and smiled knowingly at each other. Mary Ross, still excited at finding a long-lost kin, felt inwardly happy that her longtime companion and her newly discovered brother appeared to have a close relationship. It made her feel, even more, that she had suddenly discovered she was part of a new family, and she was content.

But on this morning, Anna could tell that something was troubling Billy and found an excuse to bring him a cup of tea late in the morning as he sat looking out at the loch, sparkling in the day's bright sun. He accepted the steaming mug with a nod of thanks.

"You look like the weight of the world is resting on your shoulders, Billy Hanks," she said gently.

"Aye," Billy said, smiling at her. "It feels like it, too, schoolteacher."

"Is there anything I can do?"

"Nay, lass," he said. "The sheriff said some things when he was here a few days ago. I've just been thinking on what he said."

"What did he say to you?"

Billy was about to tell her when they heard a sniffling sound, and a small boy, little Davie Gordon, wandered up to them. His eyes were red from weeping, and he brushed at his drippy nose with the sleeve of his shirt.

"Och, Davie," Billy said to the boy, "What's got into you to bring the waterworks? The older boys teasing you again?"

"It's me kine," Davie said, fighting to keep his voice from wavering. "I canna find her anywhere. She dinna come home last night, nor this day. D'ye think the wolves have got her, Billy?"

"Nay, lad," Billy said, a small smile playing at the corners of his mouth. "The cows are good at wandering off in search of tender grasses. And we've not seen wolves in these parts for near a hundred years now. Dry your eyes boy. We'll go and find yer wee beastie."

He looked at Anna. "Would the schoolteacher like to come along and aid in the search?" he said.

Anna stood up. "The schoolteacher wants to know if the outlaw has a plan," she said. "She is not the least bit interested in wandering high and low over the mountainside looking for a wee cow that is certain to come wandering back when it gets hungry or wants to come in out of the rain."

Billy clapped a strong hand on little Davie's back. "Och, y'see, Davie? The womenfolk are always afraid of adventure. We menfolk do not shirk from our duty. If the cow is lost, the cow must be found. But to answer the lady's question, yes, I do have an idea where the beastie has gone. There is some particularly tasty clover growing in a meadow just downstream from here a bit. I remember finding my own lost kine there when I was a boy about Davie's age. Shall we go take a look?"

Anna smiled and nodded her assent. Truthfully, she was glad to be in Billy's company, and, she thought, he was glad to be in hers. To both, it just felt right. And, it was a beautiful morning on a glorious day.

The three of them followed the gushing stream as it flowed out of the loch and snaked its way down the gentle slope to the south. After a mile or so, another freshet came spilling down the mountain slope and joined the first stream. Billy pointed upstream.

"Few hundred yards up yonder stream," he said. "Ye'll find a lovely meadow full of wild flowers and thick with clover. To a cow, tis like a publican's house to a thirsty man. Once they find it, they'll never forget where it is. Must be like having a meal of naught but sweets."

Billy helped Anna make her way across the stones to the far side, then picked up Davie and swung him across the stream. They began to climb, following the freshet that cascaded down through a collection of boulders and rocky outcroppings. And Billy was right: in a few hundred yards, they came upon a broad, open meadow of bright green grass and clover, dotted with pink and white flowers. The stream here flowed deep and quiet at one edge of the meadow, which buzzed with bees collecting pollen from the wildflowers, and songbirds swooped overhead singing their daylight songs, or perched in the branches of a stand of pines that bordered the edges of the meadow. And there, standing in the shade of those trees, looking very pleased with itself, was the small brown and shaggy haired cow.

Davie Gordon squeaked with pleasure, and ran across the field to embrace his cow, before launching into a stern, finger-wagging lecture about her aberrant behavior. For her part, the cow seemed happy to see Davie as well, as it lowed happily and lowered her head to butt the boy gently in the chest. Billy and Anna listened, watched, and managed, barely, to staunch their laughter.

Anna had brought along some bannock cakes, cheese and an empty jar, which Billy filled with the clear, cold water from the stream. Davie and his cow lay down in the shade and both were soon fast asleep. Anna gathered a handful of daisy-like flowers and came to sit next to Billy Hanks in the warm sunshine. He watched as her fingers deftly wove the flowers and stems into a crown, and he felt as contented as he had felt in many months.

"So, what was it the sheriff said to you last week that has your countenance full of gloom and doom, Billy Hanks?" Anna asked.

"Och, a woman never forgets to remember when there is a subject to be discussed," Billy said, smiling at Anna.

"And a man never likes to talk about things that are bothering him, at least to a woman," she returned. "But you need to talk about it, and here I am to listen to you."

He thought about that, and eventually nodded.

"Ye are right," he said. "I keep turning things over and over in my mind. MacLeod, who is a good man, I think, wants me to give up."

"He wants you to surrender? Why didn't he just arrest you and take you back to Dornoch?"

"Nay, schoolteacher, he wants me to tell the people of Glencullen to give up their homes and go to Golspie. Go to the plots of bare ground his Lordship has prepared there, ground that will yield no crops, no fodder for our livestock, no hope for our future. He wants me to convince the people that they should abandon the strath, abandon the mountains, abandon the river and the fields and go to the sea to become fishers of herring. He wants me to tell the people to go and turn themselves into beggars, not the proud men and women who have lived in these mountains for hundreds of years. He says there is no hope. He says his Lord and Ladyship own this land and will do with it what they want. What these people want is of no concern to them. They want to make more money letting out our land to the sheepmen. He says they will do it, the law will let them do it, and there is nothing that I, nor any man, can do to stop it."

"Is he right?" Anna asked, quietly.

Billy Hanks was silent for some time. Then he spoke.

"Aye, he probably is, schoolteacher," he said. "The times have changed from the old days, when the chief of the clan would listen to his people and try to do what they wished. MacLeod said he does not want to see people hurt. He says if they do not go, they will be hurt. He thinks I should just leave the county. He even offered to help me go."

"Will you?" Anna could not help but keep her voice from quavering with emotion.

"No lass," Billy said. "I canna leave. This is my home. I have left before, and the world was not right with my leaving. Bad things happened. I will no leave it again, unless I leave the world as well."

"But you aren't sure if you are right," she said. "That's why your heart is heavy."

"I am right about myself," he said. "I will not leave this place again. But MacLeod is right about the others. What right do I have to tell these folk they should stay and fight? How can I tell them to disobey their rightful Lord? What if Darnell and his men come with swords and muskets and someone gets hurt? What if someone hurts little Davie?" He pointed across the meadow, where Davie Gordon was snuggled next to the shaggy brown fur of his calf, both sound asleep in the warm sunshine. "I do not like to think of what may happen."

"The people know what they want, Billy," she told him. "They want what you want: to be able to continue to live here as they have for hundreds of years. No one wants to live at Golspie and fish for herring, or work in his Lordship's colliery. These are simple, decent people who just want to be left alone. And they believe in you, Billy Hanks. You are not asking them to do anything they don't want to do. They want to fight, and you are the one to lead them. So do it."

She had been weaving the strands of the flowers together while they talked. When she finished, she tried to place the flower tiara on Billy's head, but he stopped her, and, taking the flowers from her hands, instead placed it on her own head.

"I dub thee Anna, Queen of the Meadow," he said. And then he kissed her.

Time froze in place, the bees stopped buzzing and the songbirds became mute as they kissed, slowly and hesitantly at first, and then with growing and unstoppable passion. He reached up and stroked her face and ran his fingers through her hair, and she groaned faintly and wrapped her arms around him. Together, they sank back onto the warm, fragrant grass and were suddenly enveloped in the sweet aroma of the sunkissed meadow.

Eventually, the kiss ended, as all kisses must. They lay there, both slightly out of breath, and looked in each other's eyes.

"I believe that is the first time you have spoken my name," Anna whispered happily, reaching up to trace the line of his jaw with the tips of her fingers.

"You mean, you really *are* the Queen of the Meadow?" he said. They laughed, she poked him gently in the chest, and they kissed again. This time, they did not stop for a long, long time.

When little Davie awoke, some time later, Anna and Billy were sitting and talking. They shared with the boy the bannock and cheese, and Anna gave the cow the woven chain of flowers, which were now wilted and partially crushed. Both the boy and the cow seemed happy with their snacks, and Anna and Billy smiled at each other knowingly.

Billy Hanks produced a length of sturdy rope and, with Davie's cow in tow, they retraced their way back to the shieling community by the loch. It was a glorious afternoon and both their hearts were full of happiness. It seemed as though the world had been recreated and remade solely for the pleasure of the two of them. The songs the birds sang were songs of love, directed only at them. The flowers they came across blooming in sunny spots along the streambanks had been placed there just for their eyes to see and admire.

But when they reached the shores of Bán-loch Beag, they saw the entire community gathered outside one of the shelters, surrounding a man and his horse. Obviously, someone had arrived with some news.

"Come, Billy," cried Catty when she saw them approaching. "Duncan Grant has news from the strath!"

The news was not good. Major Darnell, Duncan told Billy, had arrived in Lairg two weeks ago with three platoons of heavily armed and mounted troops. He had basically taken over the town and placed it under military law. Worse, he had launched an attack against the people of Glen Grudie, the strath that lay to the southwest of Lairg. The redcoats had ridden into the strath, demanding news of where the brothers Grant had gone. When the folk had refused to tell them—because they did not know— the soldiers had put many buildings in the glen to the fire. Barns, outbuildings and several houses had been destroyed. Crops had been uprooted and hayfields mown down and trampled under the hooves of the garrison's horses.

"They said they're coming next to Glencullen," Duncan Grant said, his face stern. "Unless we tell them where ye are, Billy Hanks. We have a week."

Billy Hank's face was red from the sun, but all the fullness of his heart was pushed aside. The time he had been long expecting was now at hand. It was time for action.

"Ride for home, Duncan," he told the man. "Tell the others not to worry. Darnell will not be coming to Glencullen with his horses and his fire."

"How in the bloody hell do you know this, Billy?" Duncan asked. "Darnell already has five men locked up in Lairg, and says he will begin flogging them in public if no one tells him where you be."

Billy nodded. "He will not come to Glencullen, and no one will be flogged," he said. "Darnell will soon ride off."

"Why would he do that?"

"Because he will find out where I am," Billy said.

"And how will be know that?" Duncan Grant said. "Not a man in the strath will so much as hint at your location, or he'll have to answer to me."

"He will know where I am, because I will tell him," Billy said with a smile. "I will be in Durness."

"Durness!" Grant was taken aback. "That bastard Mac-Cray sent the Reverend Fraser and his lady off to Durness two months ago."

"Aye," Billy Hanks said with a smile. "And it will be Fraser who tells Darnell where I am. Now listen, all of you: the time is coming when we must defend our homes. This attempt by Darnell to scare you all is just the first move. There will be more. We need to be ready, we need to be prepared. So gather round and pay attention. I will tell you what we must do."

The people came in closer to hear as Billy Hanks began to speak. Even the children stopped their play and came to sit and listen. They listened closely, carefully, and they all began to smile as Billy laid out his plans. All except Anna. She listened with the heaviest of hearts, because she knew what this new development meant, and she was not happy.

39

Durness - One week later

Durness, a town clinging to the rocky cliffs along the rugged coast of northwest Scotland, contained less than 200 souls, and the population of the other handful of townships and crofts for miles in either direction added just a few dozen more. So when the tall lanky stranger arrived in town with no apparent reason or business to conduct, and instead began spending much of his time at the Goat and Thistle public house, people took notice. And gossiped.

It was inevitable that someone would soon mention the new stranger's appearance in town to the new minister, Reverend Fraser. The reverend was living temporarily at Balnakeil House, one of the manors owned by Lord Reay, whose ancestors had been chiefs of Clan MacKay for hundreds of years. The two-story masonry and plaster house stood near the ancient Balnakeil church overlooking the beach and protected waters of Balnakeil Bay. The church, built on the site of a fifth century monastery, had seen better days: the roof leaked during bad rains, the nave was dark, cold and drafty, and the current Lord Reay had given notice that he was not prepared to furnish the funds necessary to restore the church to modern standards. Even the tilted, weathered headstones in the kirk yard, pushed over by centuries of cold wind off the North Atlantic, seemed to be symbols of decline.

It was the housekeeper at Balnakeil House, Edna Buchanan, who first told Mr. Fraser about the strange man who had just arrived in town. But she was not sure that he understood, for Mr. Fraser, like his church, was also in an advanced state of decline. Shortly after he and his wife had arrived in Durness two months ago, Mrs. Fraser had hailed the first mail coach making the biweekly Thurso to Lairg run and left the area. Nobody knew where she went or why, or if she was planning to return. Mr. Fraser had seemed to shrink before his congregation's eyes when she left him there alone. The gossip that accompanied Fraser's arrival in town was soon passed around to all: Fraser had run afoul of Lord and Lady Stafford of Dornoch, and his appointment to his former parish had been revoked. And now, his wife appeared to have abandoned him as well.

He seemed to all to be a broken man. He went through the motions of pastoring to his flock, but his heart was clearly not in his job. He spent most of his days locked in his bedchamber in Balnakeil House, staring out the window at the sea. His first month of sermons had been desultory. He had postponed baptism. He had neglected any kind of religious instruction. He had not even tried to ride his parish and get to know the people. He was a stranger to most, and they to him.

So when Edna Buchanan told him that a stranger had taken up residence at the Goat and Thistle, he showed no reaction. A day later, taking an afternoon walk along the strand near the church on a warm and sunny day—something of a rarity in Durness—he stopped to exchange pleasantries with old Jamie MacKay, a fisherman repairing his nets on the shore. MacKay told him about the stranger, too.

"He's an odd duck, Reverend," old Jamie said, running his needle back and forth. "Says his name is Hanks. Billy Hanks."

"W-w-what did you say?" Fraser stuttered. "What did you say his name was?"

"I dunno for sure, o'course," the old fisherman said, "But he's told the publican that his name is Billy Hanks and he is from Glencullen. Do ye know of him?"

Fraser did not answer, but stood silently staring out at the placid water of the bay and thinking.

"Reverend? Are ye ill?"

Fraser snapped back to attention. "Nay, nay, thank ye sir," he said. "Please excuse me, I have an important letter to write." He turned on his heel and went striding back up the beach toward the church, his limbs suddenly infused with energy.

Old Jamie MacKay watched him go, and shook his head.

"Mad as a mink, that man," he said to himself. "Like most of them what gets into the preachin' business. Mad as a mink."

FRASER'S LETTER, WHICH had been addressed to Robert MacCray, was placed into the hands of Major Darnell two days later. The timing was fortuitous: Darnell and MacCray had been making their plans for a raid on Glencullen, set to occur in two days from Darnell's new base in the town of Lairg, overlooking the dark waters of Loch Shin. The platoon of troops from Fort George had taken up residence in the town: the enlisted men bivouacked in a farmer's field, Darnell comfortably lodged in a room at the Loch Shin Inn in the center of the town.

MacCray, sent by the Staffords to help with the search for the outlaws, had provided the officer with a detailed map of Glencullen, and had helpfully circled the houses of the men he considered to be the most oppositional to the planned removals. "Burn these six men out, and the strath will calm down to a great extent," MacCray had told Darnell.

Now, MacCray quickly scanned the letter that had just arrived. A young man from Durness, given half a crown by Fraser for his troubles, had ridden almost nonstop all the way to Lairg. MacCray's face lit up in a broad smile as he read. "We've got him!" he said, pumping his fist in exaltation. "He's in Durness, Sir! Billy Hanks is in Durness."

"Durness?" Darnell jumped to his feet and began rummaging through the papers on his desk. He found a sheet and quickly scanned it. "Yes! I had a report from a local fellow a week ago that said Hanks had been seen near Durness. I didn't think it was real—you know how some of these layabouts tell you things just for the sport of it. But now we have another report. Who is your correspondent, Sir? Is he reliable?"

"Oh, yes," MacCray said with a laugh. "It is the former minister in Glencullen, Robert Fraser. Her Ladyship removed him to Durness a month or so ago. He states that he is hopeful this cooperation with Her Ladyship will convince her that he is a loyal servant. He wants a new assignment. He did not want to go to his new parish, and who can blame him? Have you ever been to Durness? "

"No," Darnell said, "I can't say that I have."

"Bloody desolate place, Durness," MacCray said. "If it's not raining, it's blowin' fair. Almost impossible to raise any crops there; the people there either fish or collect the kelp along the shores. But the price of kelp has been falling for four years now, and we hear Lord Reay is losing money with his holdings every year. Lord Stafford is about to make Reay an offer to purchase the entire district. Lord Reay will jump on it. He lives in Edinburgh most of the time, when he's not in Holland, and will be glad to be rid of the pestilence that is Durness."

"I'm not interested in your business dealings," Darnell said. "We must ride at once, or this Hanks fellow will disappear again. What is the lay of the land?" He began to search for a map of northwest Scotland.

"Durness lies between Loch Eriboll and Cape Wrath," MacCray said. "The main road from the south passes by the peak of Cranstackie and skirts the edge of the Kyle of Durness. It continues on to the east and circles around Loch Eriboll. You'll want to make sure you trap him inside Durness else he'll flee into Cape Wrath, and there'll be no finding him there. Tis wild, wild ground, fit for no man but perfect for a savage like Billy Hanks."

Darnell was studying the map. "I see," he said. "We'll ride with twenty men. I'll leave half on the west side of the town and have the others circle around to the east. If we arrive at night, all the better. Then we can move in, pinch him and we'll have him at last."

"Good, good," MacCray said, nodding his approval. "Do you want me to come along?"

Darnell looked at the man with barely disguised contempt. "I believe His Majesty's Black Watch can capture one unarmed man in a Scottish village, Sir," he said.

MacCray shrugged. "As you wish," he said. "Of course, this man, unarmed or no, is unlike any other."

Darnell sniffed. "I am quite familiar with this Hanks," he said. "I am not afraid of him. And I shall prove to you and any other that he will die like any man must."

DARNELL RODE OFF at the head of his troops a few hours later, heading northwest from Lairg along the northern shore of Loch Shin. By nightfall, they reached Laxford Bridge, at the head of Loch Laxford, and after the spending the night, they set off on a northeasterly route, crossing the River Naver at midmorning and continuing on all day until they reached the River Dionard, which flowed northerly into the Kyle of Durness. They made camp again near the hamlet of Keoldale, and while his men cared for their tired horses and refreshed themselves, Darnell continued on alone to reconnoiter the town of Durness.

It did not take long. The main road turned to the east and passed the waterfront, where three wooden docks extended into the waters of a shallow harbor formed by three rocky outcroppings extending from the shore. There were no ships to be seen. Darnell could see four or five buildings clustered near the docks, and a handful of others huddled miserably against the westerly wind on a few side streets. To the south were farmlands, showing crops of potatoes and grain bent nearly horizontal by the constant winds, and a few grassy fields occupied by thin-looking cows.

Only one of the buildings near the waterfront had smoke trickling sickly from its chimney and that one's windows seemed to show candlelight from within. It was, Darnell surmised, the local public house and inn. There were no signs of people anywhere he could see in the waning light of the day.

Darnell returned to his men. They would commence the operation at first light. *We'll take him early*, he thought. *He won't be expecting us before breakfast. If he is expecting us at all.*

Darnell's men had pitched his tent for him near all the others, and had a fire burning in the open area around which the others had been erected. The soldiers had requisitioned a young goat from the farmer, and it was roasting aromatically on the fire. Darnell ate and gave his men their orders for the morning. "We'll go in quick and hard," he told them. "If the man resists, run him through. Though I'd prefer to take him alive. I'd like to talk to Hanks before we hang him." The men nodded. It was a standard operation. None believed it would be hard.

Darnell posted the night's watch and retired to his tent and bedroll, looking forward to a few hours of sleep before dawn arrived. He poured himself a glass of claret, removed his boots and stretched out under his blanket. He was looking forward to the next day's operation.

DARNELL AWOKE TO the uncomfortable feeling of a sharp knife held to his throat. He blinked awake and was about to sit up.

"*Wisshtt*, man" said a voice, low and hissing in a whisper. "I wouldna make any sudden moves, were I you. Nor would I make any sounds at all."

The tent was dark in the dead of the night. Darnell could only make out the shadowy figure of the man who was holding the knife to his throat.

"Is that you, Hanks?" Darnell said, keeping his own voice low.

"The very same, Major," Billy Hanks said. "It was courteous of you to build a nice fire last night. Made it easy to find you. Of course, stealing Angus Mackay's goat for your dinner was also helpful. He was complainin' about it all night in the pub."

"Billy Hanks," said Darnell, "I arrest you in the name of the King and charge you with the crime of desertion. And that's just the start ..."

"That's a good one, Major, a good one indeed," Billy Hanks said, chuckling softly. "It appears to me that, as I have a knife ready to dispatch you at the time of my choosing, you are not arresting anyone."

"If you put down your weapon and surrender at once, I will recommend leniency," Darnell continued, as if Hanks had not spoken. "Of course, the penalty for your crime is hanging, but perhaps the judge will allow you to see your loved ones before you die."

"Umm, perhaps," Billy said. "Assuming that ye can figure out a way to disarm me. *Wissshtt!*" Darnell made a sudden move to sit upright, and in so doing, the sharp edge of Billy Hanks' knife sliced thinly into the skin of his neck. "Now you've done it, Major ... I told you to move carefully. Blood is so hard to remove from one's shirt."

"And now you have attacked an officer of His Majesty's Army," Darnell said grimly, through clenched teeth. "That crime, too, is punishable by death."

"Well, that may be true as well, Major," Billy said. "But you have neglected to consider, Sir, that you first have to arrest me. Then transport me across the country. Then find a court to try me. If you can do all that, ye might…I say *might*… be able to have the pleasure of putting your rope round my neck. But I would not wager a day's pay that you can do all that. Not so long as I hold this knife."

"What do you want, Hanks?"

"Ach, a good question, Major," Billy said. "I could say that I wanted the people of Glencullen to be left alone to live their lives as they have for five hundred years and more. But that most fervent wish of mine is not within your power to grant, is it Major?"

Darnell was silent.

"I could say that I want my life back," Billy continued, "Beginning from the moment soldiers of your Army, those you paid well for their troubles, kidnapped me when I was just a boy and sent me, against my will, across the seas to Canada and the Colonies. But that, too, is not within your power."

Darnell was silent.

"But there is one thing that is within your power. And that is justice for Johnny Dunn. He was an innocent lad, Major, and you had him killed to protect your own perverse nature. That is a debt that needs paying for, Major, and the time has come to settle the debt."

Darnell made his move. With one motion, he swept the arm holding the knife against his throat up and away and leapt to his feet. Billy Hanks was ready, and with his other arm, he drove a fist into Darnell's belly. The major bent over and gasped for breath. Hanks chopped down on the back of his neck and Darnell slumped onto the floor of the tent. He began writhing and gasping for air.

"So that is what I want, Darnell," Billy bent over and whispered in the other man's ear. "I want justice for a long-dead boy. And I shall have it. And now, I have a question for you: Do you believe in the faeries, Major? They are said to have a powerful magic. Do you believe?"

Darnell could only groan in response.

IN THE EARLY hours of the morning, as the eastern skies above the rounded peak of Cranstackie began to glow with the coming dawn, the camp of troopers stirred. The men who had been assigned to the overnight watch saw the skies brightening and went to wake the others. The men crawled from beneath their blankets, the fire was fed and was soon burning cheerily, and water boiled for tea. Soon, all were dressed and assembled. All except for Major Darnell. The men looked at each other and wondered, and, finally, Captain Plessy, Darnell's aide de camp, went and stood outside Darnell's tent. He listened and heard nothing inside.

He coughed. "Major? Major Darnell? Are you awake? The men are ready."

He heard no response, so he finally pulled the canvas to one side and ducked into the entrance. The tent was empty, save for Darnell's bedroll on the ground. A stud of a candle lay next to a half-filled bottle of claret, and a goblet that was on its side, a few dregs of the drink remaining in the glass.

Plessy came out of the tent and quickly organized a search. The men began by forming a perimeter around their camp and searching on foot in ever expanding circles. There was no trace of the major, and no indication that anyone had entered or left the camp. After an hour of searching on foot, Plessy and his men returned to the camp, saddled their horses and began searching the surrounding area. Dawn broke and the sun was high in the sky when the searchers returned to the camp, where a handful of men had been ordered to remain, in case the major returned from wherever he had disappeared to.

Plessy saw to the watering and feeding of the horses as he tried to decide his next move. It was then that the farmer, Angus

Mackay, approached on the back of an ancient donkey. Mackay's legs stuck out comically to each side to keep from dragging on the ground, but he deftly dismounted and bowed courteously at Plessy, tugging at his bonnet.

"A very good morning to you, Sir," Angus said. "Is there something I can do for you gentlemen, in addition to providing you with good land upon which to sleep, and a tender goat for your dinner? For which I have not been paid, as your Lordship is aware."

"Have you seen an officer of His Majesty's Black Watch wandering anywhere in the country?" Plessy asked the man.

"One's gone missing, has he?" Angus asked. "Well, nay, I canna say I have seen the like o' that. But I also canna say I am surprised to learn one is missing."

"Why do you say that?" Plessy demanded. "Officers of the Black Watch do not go missing for no good reason."

"Och, no, I daresay they do not, Sir," the farmer said, his bushy red eyebrows dancing up and down his broad forehead. "On t'other hand, officers of the Black Watch dunna often sleep in the Field o' the Tangies. The wee folk dunna like humans truckin' aboot in their lands. Tis why there are no crops planted here."

"Fairies?" Plessy laughed. "You expect me to believe that Major Darnell has been carried off by fairies? My good man, have you been at the whiskey already today?"

Angus Mackay removed a handkerchief from the pocket of his coat and wiped his brow. He looked around at the soldiers who were staring fascinated at the man. He shrugged his broad shoulders and spat, twice, on the ground.

"Sober as a judge, Your Honor," he said. "Ye may ask any-one in the town aboot the Tangies. They all know better than to set foot on this place. No good will come o' this, mark my words."

"Mount up," Plessy ordered the men. "We've wasted enough time with this crazy old man. Harkens—take your squad and search the shoreline of the Kyle. Billingsley: you ride with me. We'll do a house to house in the town."

Angus Mackay nodded as the soldiers made ready to leave. "Aye, the Kyle is the place to look," he said. "The Tangies will often bring their captives to the kelpies. And the kelpies are known to trade with the bluemen of the Minch. Like as not, your major is living now in a cave deep beneath the sea, and his blood is bein' drunk like whiskey. They say the bluemen need fresh human blood at least once ever' seven years to live."

"Utter nonsense," Plessy said. "Riders, away. Let's find him."

He spurred his horse on, away towards the town, while the others galloped off to the west, where the tidal flow of the Kyle cut deeply into the terrain, leaving a broad sandy gash in the hills and heather.

Angus Mackay watched them go, shaking his head. "They dunna ken," he told his donkey with sadness. "They dunna ken their man has gone, likely for seven long years, until the bluemen of the Minch are done w'him. But they'll learn the truth."

It was late in the afternoon when Plessy and his squad finally finished their search of the town. There was no sign of Major Darnell, and no one could say they had seen the man. Plessy asked the publican where the man calling himself Billy Hanks had gone.

"He was here for several days," the man told Plessy. "But he left here yesterday at noon. Said he was going east, to Thurso. I believe he was riding in a wagon with a tinker who was passing through."

Plessy was trying to decide if he should press on toward Thurso, a good day's ride along the rocky coast to the east, when Harkens and his squad came riding into town after their search of the shoreline of the Kyle. The sergeant dismounted and approached Plessy. Silently, he handed the corporal a white shirt. It was that of Major Darnell. It was soaking wet but Plessy could see bloodstains on the neck and front.

"We found this on the shore, about two miles from last night's camp," Harkens reported. It was lying near some rocks. There was a bar of soap there, too."

The townsfolk who had gathered around the soldiers heard this, and gasped. Several of the women crossed themselves in the Roman way, although almost all were now steadfast members of the Protestant Church of Scotland.

"I-I don't understand," Plessy said.

The publican stepped forward.

"The legend is that the *baobhan sith*, the white women, lure the unsuspecting to their doom, Sir," he said. "They are known to kill their victims, but then launder their clothing so that we humans can use it again."

"Enough!" Captain Plessy practically shouted. "Major Darnell has not been captured or killed or sent to live in the briny deep by faeries or kelpies or white women or bluemen or anything else. He has gone missing and we will find him. Mount up men…we'll ride for Thurso and find this Hanks fellow. I suspect he will know what happened to our major."

The soldiers mounted their horses and galloped away on the road to the east. The townfolk watched them go.

"We'll not be seeing that major in this lifetime again," said one old woman. The others murmured their agreement.

40

Two weeks later

The official inquiry into the disappearance of Major Charles Darnell of the 42nd Regiment of Foot and the Black Watch convened in a large room at Fort George often used as a mess hall. The commanding officer, the Viscount Cathcart, was in attendance in his full dress uniform, and the Inquiry Commission of three senior officers from Fort William, a hundred miles down the Great Glen, called the session into order promptly at ten o'clock in the morning.

Captain Plessy was the first witness, and he described the events of the evening and early morning when Major Darnell was reported missing.

"Is the Captain certain that Major Darnell did not leave the encampment of his own volition?" one of the Lieutenant-Colonels from Fort William asked.

"Yes, sir," the captain replied.

"What is the basis for this certainty?"

"He left the camp without his own horse," Plessy said. "And without his boots. The latter were left behind in his tent."

Plessy went on to describe the search he had ordered, and the resulting discovery of Darnell's bloodstained shirt by the shore of the Kyle of Durness.

"Have the waters where the shirt was discovered been searched?" the colonel asked. "I assume these are tidal waters that open to the sea?"

"Yes, sir," the captain said. "Interviews with local fishermen have informed us that the tides in this area are rapid and quite dangerous for those unfamiliar with their pattern. The local farmers are quite familiar with livestock getting swept into the current and out to sea. Happens all the time, they say."

"This outlaw that your regiment was sent to apprehend, this …" the colonel rustled through some pages in the report in front of him …"this William Hanks. Has he been apprehended?"

"Nay, sir," Plessy said. "We rode on to Thurso after the major disappeared, as the publican said Billy Hanks had announced he was going there. There was no trace of him anywhere, either on the road to Thurso, or in the town itself. We could find no one who admitted that they had seen such a person."

Plessy's story continued: the regiment had returned to Durness and continued to scour the countryside for several miles in all directions, looking for evidence that either Major Darnell or Billy Hanks had been seen. The search turned up nothing.

One of the other colonels from Fort William spoke up next.

"Is there any indication that Darnell was not alone in his tent that night?" he asked. "Did the watch see anything out of the ordinary?"

"No, sir," Plessy said. "The night's watch saw nothing unusual, heard nothing. There were no signs of anyone either entering or leaving the encampment. The men on the evening watch remember when Major Darnell went to his tent, because they saw he had a bottle of claret and a goblet with him when he turned in for the night. The watch changed at two in the morning, and neither man on that watch reported any unusual activity at all."

"Was the wine still in Darnell's tent?"

"Yes, sir," Plessy said. "The bottle was half empty and the goblet was on its side, with some wine left in it. This was found next to the major's bedroll."

"Turned on its side, the goblet?" the colonel pressed.

"Yes, sir," Plessy replied. "But the ground is uneven in that field and it would not be unusual for a goblet to fall over in the course of an evening, if the major tossed and turned in his sleep."

"No violent cause, then?"

"No, sir."

The commission then called Sheriff-Depute Robert Macleod of Sutherland Parish to report on the criminal investigation he had pursued in the matter.

MacLeod repeated most of what Plessy had already related, and said he had talked to most, if not all, of the citizens of Durness and the surrounding hamlets. He said he had located ten men from the immediate area who had talked with the man called Billy Hanks during the week he had been seen in Durness. All of them had conversed with Billy at the pub, where he had spent most of his time. The publican himself had told MacLeod that, unaware of the existing warrants for his arrest, he had given permission for Billy to sleep in his stable at the rear of his establishment, in the hayloft.

All who had talked with Billy Hanks said his story was the same: he was a resident of Glencullen in the Lairg district to the south. The Marquiss of Stafford had announced that all the people of Glencullen would soon be removed from their homes to make room for the sheepwalks, so Billy Hanks was looking for a new place to begin anew. He had hoped to find a new home and farm near Glencullen, but had so far found nothing suitable, and so was headed north into Caithness. He had mentioned that, if unsuccessful, he might be forced to emigrate to the Colonies. The men from Durness who talked with him had agreed that it would be difficult to find a new steading anywhere in the

Highlands, as many of the lairds were also turning farmland into sheepwalks; and they discussed the stories of people they knew from Durness and other areas nearby who had already emigrated to Canada.

"None of the folk of the town thought that Billy Hanks and the story he was telling them was unusual in any instance," MacLeod told the commission. "There are thousands of men and families who are looking for new situations. Lord Selkirk, to mention just one gentleman, has already sent a dozen ships across the ocean with men and families bound for his lands in the Red River area of western Canada. The situation described by Billy Hanks was not an unfamiliar one."

"Did any of them know he was a wanted outlaw?" the colonel asked.

"No," MacLeod said. "Hanks might be infamous in his part of the county, but word of his deeds has not been told in Durness parish."

"What about the minister?" the third colonel jumped in to the conversation. "This Fraser fellow lived and worked in Glencullen for many years. *He* certainly recognized the name, and the reputation attached to it, enough to send the letter to Mister MacCray, the estate under-factor."

"Yes, sir," MacLeod said, nodding in agreement. "But Fraser never met nor saw Hanks when he was the minister of Glencullen parish. At least, not that he knew. He simply informed MacCray that Hanks had been seen in the town. It was the right thing to do on Mr. Fraser's part. This Hanks is known to be dangerous, and it would be foolhardy for a minister of the kirk to attempt to apprehend a known criminal."

"Did any one in the town see or speak with Major Darnell?" The first colonel chimed back in.

"Nay, sir, they did not." MacLeod said.

"Do they have any idea where the man went?"

MacLeod paused, looking at the three colonels sitting behind a long table, papers spread before them. He glanced as well at the General, Viscount Cathcart, who sat in a chair beside the court of inquiry members, drumming his fingers impatiently on his thigh, one of his legs, encompassed in an elegantly shined black boot, crossed over the other.

"The people of the town, Sir, are nearly unanimous in their belief that Major Darnell has been taken by the faeries and passed along as ransom to the bluemen of the Minch."

There was dead silence in the room.

"I beg your pardon?" The presiding colonel cocked his head to one side in disbelief at what he had just heard.

"The people of the countryside have their particular beliefs, Sir," MacLeod explained. "They are all good Christians in every important sense of the word. But they maintain an allegiance to certain age-old myths and legends. When something cannot be explained by ordinary reasons, whether it is the untimely death of an infant, the failure of a season's crops or, in this case, the disappearance of a man who should not have disappeared ... well, they have ways to explain the unexplainable. And that is the reason for their belief in faeries and kelpies and bluemen. It may be hard for men like yourselves to comprehend, but for these people, it is the most logical explanation."

"You sound like you believe in these faeries as well, Sheriff," said the colonel. "Is it your official conclusion that Major Charles Darnell was spirited away in the middle of the night by fairies and delivered to some hobgoblins said to haunt the waters of the Minch?"

"No, sir," MacLeod said, his voice firm. "It is my official conclusion, based on the evidence we have at hand, that Major Darnell drowned in the Kyle of Durness and his body was swept away out to sea."

"How did he get *into* the Kyle, sir? In the middle of the night, unseen by two watchmen."

"At present, that is unknown, Sir," MacLeod said.

"What about the bloody shirt?" another colonel jumped in. "Where did the blood come from?"

"At present, that is unknown, Sir," was the reply.

"Where is this Hanks fellow?" said the third colonel. "He seems to be the key to this mystery. Find him, find Darnell's killer."

"Billy Hanks remains at large," MacLeod said. "We are looking for him."

"I have a question, Sheriff-Depute." The voice was that of Viscount Cathcart.

"Sir?"

"Have there been any ships departing for the Colonies since Major Darnell disappeared?"

"Yes, sir," MacLeod nodded. "Two in fact. One embarked from Thurso three days after Darnell went missing. Another sailed from Ullapool a week after that. I have checked the passenger logs for both vessels. The name of Billy Hanks is not listed on either. Of course, he could have used another name: this gentleman is noted for his ability to evade arrest."

Cathcart slapped the table in front of him with his hand. The sound made all in the room jump. "That's it, then," he thundered. "Hanks has fled the country. Whether or not he is guilty of murder, he has fled. Darnell is dead, not sleeping with some blue persons under the sea. Hanks likely killed him. We'll never know. But he has gone and good riddance to him. I would say there is little more that can be determined here. Gentlemen?"

The three colonels put their heads together and whispered to each other for a moment or two. Then, after each resumed his position of rectitude behind the table, the colonel in the middle rapped his knuckles on the table.

"This Commission of Inquiry into the disappearance of Major Charles Darnell of the 42nd Regiment of Foot is hereby concluded, full report to follow. Our finding is that, absent any further evidence to the contrary, that said Major Darnell likely drowned in the Kyle of Durness. It cannot be determined by this Commission if the outlaw known as Billy Hanks had any responsibility in Major Darnell's disappearance, but this Commission recommends that General the Viscount Cathcart send, posthaste and without delay, notice to the authorities in His Majesty's Colony of Greater Canada to find and detain said William or Billy Hanks for further questioning in this matter. Hearing no objection, this Commission is adjourned."

41

Glencullen - September 1

Jamie Campbell was the constable at Lairg, and as such, had the unwanted duty of delivering the writs of removal to the people of Glencullen. His duty was unwanted, because he personally knew most of the people who would be receiving the duly processed and signed legal orders he carried; he did not look forward in the least to telling them they had but a month to leave their homes with as much of their possessions as they could carry to go to the prearranged new housing lots in Golspie. Not only would these people, many of them friends and not a few relations of Jamie himself, have to leave behind their ancestral lands in the strath, the only home they had ever known, but most would also be forced to sell or leave behind their livestock, the main source of their income.

Jamie was thinking about all this from the moment he left Lairg riding on his little pony and for the four hours his journey took him along the River Cullen on its twisting pathway up the floor of the strath. Delivering these writs, which he carried in a satchel attached to his saddle, was the last thing Jamie Campbell wanted to do. But he knew it was his duty. The landlord, Lady Stafford, legally held title to the land. She had petitioned the Court of Session to obtain the writs to remove her tenants from

Glencullen, claiming nonpayment of rent for many years, and the writs had been duly granted. So the removal was legal and authorized. But that did not make the action right, or easier to carry out. But someone had to do it, and that someone was Jamie Campbell, Constable at Law in the Parish of Lairg.

The weather was cool and threatened to rain. Jamie could feel the first tangs of autumn in the air. All around him, he could see Nature changing from summer to fall: the leaves on the trees he passed had changed color from the bright green of spring to the deep dark green of summer, and now were gray-green, as if weary and aged. Soon, he knew, the leaves would turn golden before falling from their limbs. Jamie passed several farms in the lowlands along the river, before the road began to climb upwards into the heart of the glen, and he saw the farmers and their families out harvesting the golden stalks of grain in the fields, stacking them in round mountains before the threshing began. Nature was changing. The times were changing. Jamie could feel it in his very bones.

Jamie had received strict orders from Robert MacCray, her ladyship's factor on this part of her estate. He was to proceed first to the home and farm of Robert Gordon, long the blood relation and tacksman of Lady Stafford in Glencullen. There, Gordon would, along with a half-dozen of his strongest servants, accompany Jamie as he made the rounds. There were eighteen writs in his satchel, and all had to be delivered by hand to the person named in the writ. Lady Stafford said she did not want any trouble, and Captain Gordon and his men would be present to prevent it.

But Jamie Campbell never made it to Captain Gordon's farm. He approached the twin rocky monoliths that bracketed the road at the entrance to the upper glen, the place the locals called the *Geata Diabhail*, or the Devil's Gate. No sooner than his pony had passed between the rocks then a dozen women appeared at his side. They seemed to materialize out of the ether, for Jamie never saw nor heard their presence before they were there, standing all around him, his pony's reins in their hands.

The women had their bonnets pulled down low on their foreheads, and had wrapped woolen scarfs around their faces, so Jamie could not make out exactly who they were. But he knew instantly that he was in trouble.

"State your business in Glencullen, stranger," one of the women said.

"Stranger?" Jamie said, trying to keep his voice from squeaking in fear. "I am no stranger to Glencullen, Madam. I am Jamie Campbell, constable of the law. I come from Lairg with business to attend with Captain Robert Gordon, tacksman to Her Ladyship. Let me pass at once."

"What is your business with Gordon?" the woman said.

"That, Madam, is between myself and him," Campbell said. "Again, I demand you let me pass on."

One of the other women circled around behind Campbell and removed the leather satchel from the saddle where it had been tied. It was quickly opened and the papers inside passed to the one who had spoken. She stood there and riffled through them, reading the page headings. The glen was quiet enough at the noon hour so all could hear the papers as they were read and shuffled.

"Writs of removal," the woman said. "Eighteen of them. Is that all you have?"

"Aye," Jamie said. "That's the lot."

The woman holding the papers began tearing them into bits. Because there were so many, each containing many pages of legal verbiage, she worked on just a few at a time. But she stood there folding and ripping until each of the writs had been thoroughly destroyed. She then let the shards of paper drift through her fingers and they all watched the papers drop onto the dusty road and float off into the surrounding rocks and bushes, dancing in a sudden gust of wind.

"Now you have none," the woman said. "So ye may return to Lairg. When you get there, please tell the Lady Stafford that the people of Glencullen reject removal. We do not wish to go, and we shall not. Instead, tell her that we have demands. Three, to be exact. One: she will negotiate new leases with the people of Glencullen, leases that will be less dear than they are now, for the people here are poor and cannot afford her high rents any longer. Two: the people of Glencullen will not be removed from our ancestral homes. We have lived here in peace for the last five hundred years and more, and we intend to continue to live here for the next five hundred years or more. And Three: we will not allow our lands to be enclosed for the purposes of raising sheep in this glen. Sheep do not mix with cattle, and fences do not mix with cattle, and we are cattlemen as we have been for hundreds of years. Do you understand, constable?"

Jamie shifted uncomfortably in his saddle.

"I understand, Madam," he said, "But I must warn you that Lady Stafford will not accept your conditions. Those papers that you just destroyed were approved by the Court of Session, and the law, Madam, will not be denied. You can send me away, but others will come in my place. And the next to come may not be a peaceful constable such as I, but a regiment of His Majesty's troops, armed with guns and swords. This will not end well with you."

"Thank you, Jamie," the woman said. "Well spoken. This does not have to end with violence, if Lady Stafford decides to be more reasonable. But until then, we will demonstrate how determined we are that she gets our message."

She turned and made a motion with her hand. The women stepped forward as a group. Jamie was pulled from his pony, and his coat and shirt quickly stripped off his back. Next, his hands were tied tied behind his back. Then, to Jamie's utter horror, his trews were pulled down and yanked off his legs. Only his boots remained. Jamie struggled, but his hands were tightly bound.

"In the name of God!" Jamie shouted, embarrassed and furious at once. "Have none of you any decency left?"

The women were silent, except for one whispered titter Jamie thought he heard, as they lifted him back onto his pony. The creature was turned around and sent back down the road to Lairg with a loud and enthusiastic swat on its flanks. The pony started to trot, but Jamie quickly called out and it resumed its usual, languid pace down the road. With his hands still tied behind his back, Jamie struggled to find a position where he could sit comfortably and not lose his balance. But there was little else he could do.

It was a long time before Jamie came upon one of those farms in the lower strath, and, though embarrassed at his nakedness, he was finally able to get the attention of a farmer, and put an end his ordeal. Wearing borrowed pants and coat, Jamie also begged use of the farmer's best horse and was soon galloping toward Lairg.

The group of women who had stopped Constable Campbell began walking up the road that led to the smithy and gristmill, but soon, without knowing why, they began to trot and then to run, helter-skelter. When they reached the small bridge that crossed the millrace, they instead turned off the road and ran, as a group, down to the banks of the River Cullen. By now, they were all giggling and tittering as they ran until they finally collapsed in a laughing heap on the sandy bank on the river. The river was wider here, near the curve where the millrace entered; and here where the sand bank had been created, the water was shallow and warm and the current slow. It was a place to gather, to swim and to gossip that they all had known since they were girls. And their nervous and exultant laughter now made them all sound like they were teenaged girls again.

They unwrapped their scarves: Mary Ross had been the leader. Among the others, who had held the pony and helped strip poor Jamie of his clothes, were Catty Greer, Mary Gordon and Katherine Ross from the parsonage, Mhairie McKinnon, Agatha Ross, Betty Gordon, Elizabeth McKay, Rosie Murray and a number of women whose children had attended the new school at the church.

"Och, did ye see?" Mary Ross said, her face red and shining. "Poor Jamie's willie was no bigger than me thumb!"

This set the women off on another gale of helpless laughter, clinging onto each other to stay upright.

"D'ye think he can ride like that all the way to Lairg?" asked Betty Gordon. "His poor bum may ne'er recover."

"Good," said Mary Ross, crossing her arms defiantly. "He was coming here to remove us from our homes and send us all away. I hope his bum aches for a week!"

"Oh, I'm sure it will."

The voice came from behind the bushes beyond the sand bank, and out from behind stepped Billy Hanks, his face wreathed in a wide smile.

The women ran to greet him, each of them relating the tale of the capture and return of the enemy Jamie. Billy laughed as the various versions came rushing out of each of them, and he allowed himself to be led, or pulled, to the sand bank, where the women finally sat down in a heap, exhausted.

Billy put his hands on his hips and studied them all. "Well done, my little *bandittis*," he said. "You have sent them a message and I believe it will be heard in the town, loud and clear. And in Dunrobin."

"What will they do next, Billy?" asked Catty Greer. "Will the soldiers come?"

"Och, I hope so," said Hannah Gunn. "I hope their willies are a bit bigger!"

The women giggled and then laughed aloud, casting slightly embarrassed looks over at Billy, who just shook his head.

"I dunna 'no who will come next," Billy said. "But we'll be ready for them."

"Oh, how I wish Anna could have been here," said Mary Ross, a bit wistfully. "She would have enjoyed today."

"Aye, she would have," Billy Hanks said, nodding. "But 'tis best that she's not getting involved in this. It's likely to get uglier, next time. It's a good thing Her Ladyship called her back to Dornoch, to Dunrobin Castle. It's where she belongs."

"You don't believe that for an instant, Billy Hanks," Mary Ross said hotly, hands on hips. "My Anna is part of this community and she wanted to be here, and you know it. It's just, well, she had to obey her uncle. But her heart is here. I know it and you do too, Billy Hanks."

I do, he thought to himself. *I do, indeed.*

In fact, Anna Kenton had been, and was still, furious at being summoned back to Dunrobin Castle by her uncle, Lord Stafford. Shortly after the word had come to the shieling that the Black Watch troops had attacked Glen Grudie and were planning the same on Glencullen, and after Billy Hanks had left for Durness in his attempt to draw the troops there, buying some time, the people of the strath gathered their livestock and possessions and made the day-long trek home from the shieling in the mountains.

The menfolk that had stayed behind at Glencullen to tend the crops, replace the roof thatch, and repair the outbuildings for the coming winter had been glad to see the women and children return. But the news that greeted the women when they returned to the strath was not all good. The potato crop had been sorely affected by the mildew, and about half the anticipated yield was ruined. The fields of oats and barley had survived, but the old-timers, looking at the size of the harvest, knew that the coming winter was going to be a hungry one for many. And, of course, most expected that the armed soldiers of the Black Watch would soon be descending upon the strath looking for Billy Hanks. And following that, the sheriff would arrive ordering them to leave the strath forever. It was a tense and troubling time for them all.

Not long after the people returned, the under-factor, Robert MacCray appeared in the strath and found Anna sweeping out the old church, preparing once again to begin holding classes there, once the grain had been gathered from the fields, something that required all: men, women and children working together from dawn to dusk.

"Good day, Madam," MacCray said. "Your uncle has requested your presence at Dunrobin. You are to accompany me to Dornoch at once."

"It sounds like you are arresting me, Sir," Anna said. "Is that so?"

"Not at all, Mrs. Kenton," MacCray said, his face impassive. "Your uncle…really, it is your aunt, I must confess … they are both worried about your safety. Certain events are…well, all I can say is that Glencullen may not be a suitable place for someone like you in the weeks ahead."

"Someone like me," Anna repeated.

"Indeed, Madam," MacCray said. "A woman of your breeding and culture. The native residents of this place are to be removed to the seaside, or to the Americas. There may be trouble. Your aunt wishes you to return to the safety of Dunrobin for a time."

"And my school?" Anna gestured at the small church building. "Am I to abandon the children of the strath. Simply disappear and leave them wondering where I have gone?"

"Her Ladyship said that, once things have calmed down and the people have taken up their new allotments in Golspie, that perhaps then you may re-establish your school. In fact," he said, "She is of the opinion that such a thing might well be very helpful in assisting the people of this strath in reconciling to their new circumstances in Golspie."

"I see," Anna said. "So I have no choice but to accompany you away from here."

"Afraid not, Madam," he said, bowing low. She could see his smirking smile, although he tried to conceal it. "If you would like to organize your possessions, I have a brief appointment with Captain Gordon. I shall call for you at the parsonage in an hour's time."

And with that, he left her standing there, broom in hand, her heart fallen.

But she had gone. She did not know what else she could do. Billy Hanks was away at Durness, trying to lure the soldiers from Lairg there. She trudged back up the hill to the parsonage where Mary Ross and the three former servants of the Reverend Fraser hugged her and cried while helping her pack away her few items of clothing, toiletries and books. She was waiting in the parlor when MacCray arrived in his carriage and horse.

The journey back to Dunrobin had been one of the longest in her life. McCray had tried to engage her in conversation: she refused. He had tried singing ditties and familiar tunes: she remained silent. Eventually, he gave up and they rode in stony silence all the way to Lairg, where she waited in the carriage while McCray stopped in at the roadside inn to learn the latest news from the military men stationed there. He returned to the carriage in a good mood.

"The troops under Major Darnell have likely arrived in Durness," he said, climbing back in and switching the horse off down the road with a jolt. "They'll have this Hanks fellow in irons shortly and return him to Inverness for trial and execution."

It took most of Anna's self-control not to scream and try to scratch the man's eyeballs out of his head with her fingernails. But she forced herself to sit still and counted to herself silently until the wave of her anger passed. The ride from Lairg to Dornoch was as silent as had been the journey from Glencullen to Lairg.

When she arrived at Dunrobin, she discovered that Lord and Lady Stafford were away, spending some time with relatives in Edinburgh. For several days, she was alone with only her thoughts. Mr. Gunn brought her meals to her room on a tray. She found some volumes in Lord Stafford's extensive library to read, and she took daily walks in the formal gardens below the castle, a walled-in expanse overlooking the sea. She was desperate to hear the news from Durness, or Lairg, or even Glencullen, but there was no one she could ask, and no one who could tell her anything. The days that passed were long and tedious.

But the Staffords had finally returned to Dunrobin late the previous evening, and tonight, Mr. Gunn had informed her at breakfast, she was expected for dinner at seven o'clock.

THE GUEST LIST at dinner that night was smaller than usual, and Anna discovered that she and Lady Stafford were the only women at table. The stern-looking Reverend Kirkwell from Dornoch Cathedral was there, sans his wife, and there was another man, whom Anna did not know. He was of small frame, thin and angular, and he wore pince-nez spectacles over a pair of sharp, gray eyes that peered out, seeing everything. He had a pointy chin, thin lips and a severe wig tied with a small black bow at the rear. He was introduced to Anna: James Loch, the business superintendent for Lord Stafford's commercial empire.

Elizabeth, the Lady Stafford, greeted Anna with a hug.

"It is good to see you again, m'dear," she said. "I am so happy that you are safe and well removed from the dangers of Glencullen."

"I am not sure what dangers you reference, Aunt," said Anna. "I found the strath to be a peaceful and pleasing place to live. I hope to rejoin the populace of that place as soon as possible to resume my teaching of the children."

"Oh, yes," Lady Stafford said. "You must tell us all that you learned in attempting to education the children there. I can only imagine how difficult it must have been for you, what with the language and the illiteracy."

"The language was not a problem," Anna said calmly. "Between the Gaelic that I knew and the English that the children knew, we were able to communicate perfectly well. And I discovered that, except for the youngest children, all were quite able to read. In fact, one of the boys in my class, a lad of about twelve years, is remarkably adept in the poems of Wordsworth and Coleridge. Listening to him declaiming that wonderful poetry brings tears to one's eyes."

Lady Stafford stared at Anna for a moment, trying to decide if she was joshing. Unable to make up her mind, she led them into dinner.

The conversation for most of the meal was between Loch and his employer. The topics were mundane: conversations about rents, the latest tonnage figures from the busy canal properties, and negotiations that were ongoing concerning Lord Stafford's London properties, which were apparently numerous.

It was only when the dinner had arrived at its final course—bowls of nuts, platters of fruits, some sweetmeats and several varieties of cheese—that the topic of Glencullen was broached.

"It is my understanding, Mrs. Kenton, that you are lately arrived from a term of living among the people at Glencullen," Loch said, turning with interest to face her. "I wonder if you could inform all of us what the attitude of the people there might be towards their impending relocation to the new allotments which have been graciously provided for them by Her Ladyship at the muirlands in Golspie?"

"I can indeed, Mr. Loch," said Anna. "The people are quite aghast at the prospect of being forcibly ejected from their ancestral homeland. They simply cannot believe that their landlord, who is also the head of a family which has cared for and protected them for nearly nine hundred years, is ready to abandon them to a future of penury and abject misery."

Mr. Loch had been chewing on a filbert as Anna spoke, and when he heard her, he began coughing and choking, his face turning bright red in the process. Mr. Gunn stepped forward and raised his hand as if to pound the man on the back, but Loch raised his own hand as a signal that such a drastic action was not required, and soon regained his composure. He sipped some wine and looked at Anna again, this time with narrowed and suspicious eyes.

"So I take it that we cannot depend upon a lady such as yourself to convince the people of the strath in question that the prospect of their moving to the new location would be of great benefit to them and their future prospects?"

"I cannot tell them such a thing if I do not believe it to be the case," Anna said, her face impassive. "I do not believe such a change would be to the people's advantage, although it is quite evident how it would provide a benefit to my aunt and uncle."

"I believe, Madam, that you have not considered this situation from all sides, especially the side of your relations here," Loch said. He nodded at Lord and Lady Stafford. "They have expended hundreds of pounds over the years to provide needed grain and foodstocks to the people of Glencullen when they proved unable to sustain themselves. They have forgiven debts and rents in arrears. To maintain the people living in Glencullen, and, to be fair, those living in many other straths around their estate, has been a most costly prospect."

Loch took some sliced fruit and some cheese from the platter on the table in front of him, and took up a knife. "And now, for the first time, the Sutherland estates have an opportunity to generate income and profit from a part of the land which heretofore has provided naught but debt and expense. As a member of the Stafford family, I would think that you would be glad to hear this, and would support your relations in their endeavors."

"And the people?" Anna raised an eyebrow. "Do they have an opportunity to generate income and profit? Or are they inconvenient and must therefore be shoved out of the way?"

"My dear niece," Lady Stafford protested. "My husband has provided the people with generous allotments in which they can prosper and benefit, if they wish to work at it. He has offered them an opportunity to live there rent-free for the first year, and to provide timber and nails for those at no cost who seek to build new homes. We are not shoving them anywhere, dear girl. We are offering them a chance to start over and prosper."

"Prosper?" Anna turned to address her aunt. "I am told the land in Golspie is poor, and rocky. It is said to be unsuitable for any kind of agriculture. There is no room for their livestock, which has long been the sole source of the people's income. I do not see how they can prosper in such a situation."

"There are the fisheries," Loch said. "They can hire out with the herring men."

"These men are farmers, not fishermen," Anna snapped. "If you put them on boats, they will drown. And besides, many of the men are now serving with Wellington's Army in the Peninsula. The strath is left with old men and young boys. Unless you think the women can fish for herring."

Anna did not mean this as a jibe, yet the others at the table laughed at the idea of women manning the rickety fleet of herring boats.

"Nay, Sir, I believe you have miscalculated," she continued. "I do not believe the people of Glencullen can prosper upon the muirs of Golspie, and I will predict right now that within a year, two at the most, the people you remove will find themselves even more destitute and despairing than they are now, yet you will have taken them away from the land which they have always depended on, in good years and bad, to see them through; you will have taken away from them their livestock, cattle and goat, which provided them with the basics of food and sustenance; and you will find yourself expending even greater sums to keep them fed and housed than you have ever spent before."

There was silence around the great table as Anna's words were heard and understood. Loch helped himself to more cheese before he finally spoke again.

"Your words are heartfelt, Mrs. Kenton," he said finally. "And perhaps understandable from an emotional being who has spent some months living with these people. As such, your words are forgivable in their harshness. But in any case, our decision has been taken after careful and deliberate consideration. And you are wrong, Madam. The people will be removed as planned, and I am certain, as certain as a man of my professional abilities can be, that the people will thrive in their new location. You will see, dear woman, that I am right and you are wrong."

Anna once again felt an upwelling of anger and emotion sweep through her body. She felt her face redden. Her anger came not so much from Loch's rejection of her opinions as from his utter disregard of their validity. Because they came from a woman. She bit back the impulse to shout at the man. Instead, she clenched her teeth together until it hurt, bowed her head to stare at the hands she kept folded in her lap. And she was silent.

42

Glencullen

Billy Hanks spent a few days organizing the people of Glencullen to defend their homes. Rather than call everyone together at once—calling a community meeting at the kirk, for instance—Billy traveled the length and breadth of the strath, talking with the people a few at a time. He would arrive at a croft after dark and, with one or two neighbors in attendance, outline his plan and hand out assignments. The next night, he'd be somewhere else, meeting with another small handful of people. In this way, he made sure he was attracting no interest from anyone who might be watching.

The plan was simple. First, watchers were assigned to keep an eye on the road leading north into the Glen from Lairg. That road basically followed the twists and turns of the River Cullen as it flowed down towards Loch Shin and eventually into the Dornoch Firth. As the road approached the *Geata Diabhail*, or Devil's Gate, the terrain on each side rose sharply as a series of rounded, mostly treeless hills gave way to steeper and higher mountains with their rocky cliff faces and deep defiles carved by millennia of water streaming down from the heights.

There were plenty of places along the summit line of these hills and mountains where one could see any traffic making its way up the winding road into the valley; plenty of places where signals could be sent from one hilltop to the next. From dawn until dusk, the people of the strath volunteered to have someone—man, woman or child—perched atop these aeries, keeping watch. After generations of herding cattle and goats to and from the upper pastures, everyone knew where the overlooks were, and these were quickly stocked with braziers and dry timber, ready to signal the approach of any forces.

Once the watch was in place, everyone in the strath was assigned a role to play in the plan to confront the invaders that all expected would soon be coming. There were no weapons, save for the scythes and axes and sharpened hoes used by the men in their work. Since a great many of the men who usually resided in Glencullen had been called away to duty in the armies in Europe, these few implements were to be taken up by the old men and teen-aged boys. The women of the strath began collecting strong wooden branches from the hardwood trees along the riverbank, cutting and whittling them down to comfortable size and shapes for a woman's hand. The younger children spent hours wandering up and down the river with baskets, looking for smooth round stones that could fit easily in a hand, to be used as projectiles. Billy also roughed out, and explained to them all, a battle plan. He kept it simple so all could remember: women in the front, men and boys behind.

"But Billy," he was asked, "Shouldn't the men go in front, the better to protect the womenfolk?"

"Nay," Billy responded. "Put the women in the front and let the bastards know they'll have to wade through them first to get to our homes. They will hesitate, and that gives us the advantage."

In just a few days' time, the people of Glencullen felt themselves armed, to a degree, and as ready as they ever would be to defend their strath and their homes from the removers.

"I dun'no know when they'll come," Billy told one and all. "But come they will. And soon. We must be vigilant. And ready."

There was still some weeks until the Martinmas deadline. But Billy Hanks had warned the people that Lord Stafford's factors would likely jump the announced deadline, try to surprise the people and upend any resistance they might show. He urged one and all to prepare as if each day was the day when the removers would come into the strath.

But the days slowly went by, one after the next, and the teams of watchers saw nothing on the roadway. The last of the harvesting was finally finished, the grains and produce carefully winnowed and stored away. The cattle, especially the ones who had fattened themselves all summer long in the high mountain meadows of the shieling, were ready to be driven to the autumn markets in Inverness, awaiting only the arrival of the drovers who would take them there to sell for hard cash. The people waited, nervous, unsettled, wondering what would happen next. Billy Hanks strode from place to place, trying to keep them calm, alert, focused.

And then Agatha Grant went into labor. Her husband had been among the last of the Glencullen volunteers to march off to the Peninsular War in Spain, but before he had departed, he left a new life growing in her womb. She had known her time was close, having already given birth to three bairns, but her calculations led her to believe she still had half a month or more to go.

Billy Hanks had been sitting and waiting in Mute Meg's cottage when two of Agatha's neighbors had carried the young woman in the doorway and laid her on a bed against the far wall. She was pale and drenched in sweat, her eyes wide with alarm at what was happening to her body.

Meg and Catty drew a curtain and went behind it to examine the girl. Billy heard soft murmurings and once, he flinched when Agatha cried out in pain. The two were behind the curtain for a long time, and when they finally emerged into the main room of the cottage again, they both wore anxious, worried looks.

"She'll be needin' a doctor," said Catty, frowning. "Looks like a breech birth, and a bad one at that. Meg has birthed many a child that way, but it's a difficult procedure. Meg is worried that Agatha may not have the strength to do what is required."

Billy jumped to his feet. "Shall I fetch the doctor from Lairg?" he asked. "I can leave at once."

Catty shook her head. "By the time you could get back with him, the girl will be dead," she said. "The only hope is to take her to Lairg and hope ye can get there in time."

"Right," Billy said. "I'll fetch Angus's wagon. We'll put extra straw in it and some blankets. Tell Agatha not to worry. I'll get her to Lairg as fast as I can."

Mute Meg waved her hand in the air.

"Nae, Billy, ye can't do that," Catty said. "They'll be looking for you in Lairg. There are soldiers everywhere. It's too dangerous."

"Can't be helped," he said, shrugging. "We've got to get help for Agatha and the wee bairn. I'll be back in a few minutes. Have her ready to go."

He disappeared and Catty went back to her patient. Half an hour later, Billy was back with the wagon and horse, and he carried the moaning girl outside and laid her carefully in the wagon bed among the fresh straw he had placed there. Catty came along with an armload of blankets and placed them around the girl to help make her as comfortable as possible for the jouncing ride to come. Billy then climbed up onto the front seat. Catty leaped up to sit next to him.

"What are you doing?" he asked.

"I am coming with my patient," she said. "She may need me before we get there."

Billy shrugged, but applied the whip to the horse, who leapt forward. Agatha moaned aloud as they began to make their way south out of the strath, but after that, she was silent.

Billy went as fast as he dared, but the road was rutted and rocky and the going was slow, even once they passed through the *Geata Diabhail* and both the road and the river straightened out somewhat in the broader lower valley. Even on a good horse, the trip to Lairg was a good half-day's journey. In a wagon, with a pregnant woman in the bed, it was all of that and a bit more.

So it was late in the afternoon when they finally arrived in Lairg. It was not much of a town, really. The road passed by a half dozen farms on the outskirts, and the High Road was a dusty stretch that passed perhaps a dozen shopworn buildings that contained the inn, a granary, a store, the school and a small gray church with steeple and belfry.

Doctor Ramsey had a surgery above the all-purpose store, and Billy Hanks carried Agatha, now almost senseless with pain, upstairs. Catty followed close behind and she and the doctor set to work on the patient at once. Billy decided that this was no place for a man, and went back outside to take care of the horse and wagon. He led the horse to the stables behind the inn and, having unhitched it from the harness, began washing it down and brushing its shiny mane.

"Bold of you to show up here, Billy," said a voice behind him. Billy kept brushing and did not turn around. The horse's ears pricked upwards. Billy finished brushing down the left flank and walked behind the horse to begin on the other side. He looked up and saw Robert MacLeod, sheriff-depute of Sutherlandshire, leaning against the jamb, smiling at him. MacLeod, he could not help but notice, was holding a pistol in one hand, cocked and ready to fire.

"Agatha Grant is in childbirth," Billy said. "She needed a doctor."

"Well, that was good of you to bring her here," MacLeod said. "Good of you to save me a trip up the strath to find you. But here you are, and here I am, so I'm afraid you are under arrest, charged with larceny of property, creating a riotous situation in the county as well as suspicion of causing the unnatural death of Major Charles Darnell of His Majesty's 42nd Regiment of Foot."

Billy chortled as he continued to brush the horse.

"Unnatural?" he said with a laugh. "How is death unnatural? Seems to me the most natural thing there is."

"You know what I mean, Billy," MacLeod said. "Darnell led a squadron to Durness to apprehend you, and then he mysteriously disappeared in the middle of the night. I daresay that sounds exactly like something you would do."

"And do you have any witnesses to this unnatural death, MacLeod?" Billy said as he continued to brush the horse. "For that matter, do ye even have a body? How do you even know the man is dead? He could have gone wandering off and fallen into a bog. There are a number of those around Durness. Dangerous things for a man who knows not where he's going. Or maybe he caught a ship back to the Americas. I hear there are some in the Army who miss that place. I'm not one, but I hear there are those who do."

"Och, Billy, I dunna care to listen to your patter," MacLeod said. "It will be up to the courts to decide who did what to whom. My job is simply to bring you in and let the procurator fiscal argue the case." He sighed. "I told you to leave. I warned you this would happen if you did not. I'm sorry, Billy, but my duty is to bring you to the Tolbooth in Dornoch, and then down to Inverness for a trial."

"I know it is, Robert," Billy said. He finished brushing and returned the brush to the shelf next to the stall. "I'll not resist. Let's go."

Robert MacLeod was surprised. He had expected Billy Hanks to put up more of a fight. But he quickly placed irons on the wrists of his prisoner, and they rode that night to Dornoch.

ANNA KENTON HAD been moping about the castle since the night of the dinner with James Loch. She tried to find things to do to help occupy her mind and keep herself from worrying so much about events in Glencullen. At the request of Lady Stafford, she spent some time providing lessons in Gaelic to the three younger Stafford children.

But the children, as well as all the other staff in the castle, could tell her mind was not engaged in teaching the rudiments of Gaelic grammar. One afternoon, after a particularly trying hour, she snapped her book shut and told the children to go outside and enjoy the last bit of a lovely September afternoon. It was warm and sunny, with high thin clouds scudding across a deep blue sky, and only a gentle breeze to ruffle the leaves on the boulevard of elms that led up the main drive to the castle.

Anna went into the library, dark and cool and quiet, and threw herself into a chair and gave herself up to her emotions. Tears came, and she cried silently, wishing she could do something, and wishing she knew what it was she could do.

She did not hear Mr. Gunn come into the room. He always moved silently, so even if she had not been consumed with her worries and her sadness she might not have heard his entrance. But he coughed quietly, and she looked up through teary eyes.

"Oh," she said, reaching for a handkerchief in her dress cuff, "I am sorry Mr. Gunn. I did not hear you. I am sorry that I am ..."

"Tis alright, miss," the old servant said. "No apologies necessary. I understand. I thought you might be interested in some news from the county."

"Oh, yes," Anna said, smiling as she dried her tears. "I feel as though Glencullen is located on the moon, so little have I heard from there since I arrived."

"Of course, madam," Gunn said. "First, Billy...I should say Mr. Hanks...is safe and well."

"Oh, thanks be to God," Anna breathed, feeling as though a weight of a thousand pounds had been lifted from her soul.

"However, he is currently residing in the Tolbooth gaol in Dornoch," Gunn went on. "He was arrested two days ago in Lairg when he brought Mrs. Agatha Grant to the doctor in an emergency situation."

"Agatha's had her bairn?" Anna sat up with interest. "We didn't think she was due for another three weeks. Is she well?"

"Happily, yes," Gunn said. "Doctor Ramsey delivered her of a healthy baby boy. I believe he is to be christened as Billy Hanks Grant."

Anna laughed happily. Then she frowned, and the tonnage returned to her slender shoulders.

"But wait," she said, "You said he was in gaol? How can that be?"

"The Sheriff apprehended him in Lairg," Gunn said, "And he is awaiting transport to Inverness where the Court of the Justiciary will soon be seated to try his case."

"What are the charges?" Anna asked.

"In addition to the riotous behavior and the stealing of Mr. Knowles's sheep, he is to be charged in the death of Major Darnell in Durness," Gunn said, watching Anna closely and hoping this bit of news would not result in an hysteric reaction.

"Did…did he really kill the Major?" Anna asked the question in a tone that said she dreaded the answer to come.

"That, madam, is a question yet to be determined," Gunn said. He explained the strange events of the night when Major Darnell disappeared from his tent, and the assumption of the populace that Darnell had been taken by the wee people of the district and sold to the bluemen of the sea; a reading of the case, Gunn noted, that was not shared by the authorities.

Anna listened without speaking, without outward reaction.

"I see," she said. "That is quite odd, is it not?"

"Odd, indeed, madam," Gunn agreed.

"Can I see him? Is he allowed visitors?"

Mr. Gunn frowned, although he had anticipated this request.

"That would be difficult indeed, madam, even if it were possible," he said. "I am told that the prisoner is not allowed visitors. Only family members and his solicitor, and he does not yet have a solicitor, I am told."

Anna was silent. Gunn let her ponder this news. She looked up at him, cocking her head to one side.

"Family?" she said. "He has no family. Except of course for his sister, Mary Ross from Glencullen." She thought some more. "And nobody knows that Mary Ross is his sister. That was only discovered some few weeks ago."

"Indeed, madam," Gunn said.

Anna's face brightened. "Is there a way to get me to Dornoch, Mr. Gunn?" she asked. "Perhaps they would allow Billy's long-lost sister a few minutes with the prisoner."

"It is very possible that the authorities might do just that, madam," Gunn said. "I believe I heard Mrs. Murray is planning a trip into town tomorrow morning to visit the greengrocer and the fishmonger. Perhaps tomorrow she will need the assistance of a scullery maid whilst on her shopping errands."

"Oh, Mr. Gunn, I would forever be in your debt!" Anna leaped to her feet and smothered Gunn in hugs and kisses. Her heart was once again inflamed.

He pushed her away, embarrassed although he could not help smiling. "Now, now, enough of all that," he said. "Mrs. Murray will be leaving at ten o'clock."

He bowed and edged his way out of the room.

43

Dornoch

The Tolbooth and gaol in the center of Dornoch were located in the impressive, crenelated edifice known as the Dornoch Castle. Originally used as the residence of the Bishop of the Dornoch Cathedral that rose across Castle Street; and later, as the in-town home of the Earls of Sutherland, the yellow sandstone structure had been repurposed as offices for the town officials, including the sheriff and courts, and the three dungeons in the building's basement were used for prisoners being held for local trial or for transport to Inverness.

Anna Kenton, wearing the rough clothing of a kitchen's maid and carrying a wicker basket, applied for permission to visit the only prisoner currently being held at the gaol, the renegade known as Billy Hanks. She told the constable on duty that she was Billy's sister, and, after some hemming and hawing, he agreed to allow her a few minutes with the prisoner.

He led her down the stairs into the dank space underneath the building, and jammed a large metal key into the lock on one of the doors. The hinges squeaked in loud protest as he opened the door and waved Anna inside.

"Be quick about it," he said.

The cell was dark: only a small window set high in the far wall allowed light from the outside world into the space. Anna made out the slightly arched ceiling and the walls and floor of thick dark stone. She turned to ask the constable for a torch, but he had gone back up the stairs. Anna waited for her eyes to adjust to the dimness of the cell, and she finally spotted the prostrate form of a man lying on the floor, with a chain affixed to one foot and bolted to the wall.

"Is that you, Billy?" she called out, softly.

"Schoolteacher," a voice came back. "Have you come to give me some lessons?" He chuckled and struggled to sit upright, moving his manacled leg with its clanking length of chain out of the way.

"I came … I'm here … I want …" Anna's voice quavered as she sought for the words her heart wanted to utter. "Oh, Billy," she finally said. "Are you well? I have been so worried about you." She knelt by his side and reached for his hand. He flinched at her touch, but she did not pull away, and he finally let her touch him. And then they were embracing, wordless. And they were no longer crouched in a damp basement dungeon, at least in their minds, but were again in the high mountain meadow, surrounded by wildflowers and singing birds.

"I've missed ye, lass," Billy said, his voice gruff and full of emotion. "But ye should not have come here. It could be dangerous for you."

"I came dressed as a kitchen maid at Dunrobin and I told them I'm your sister," she said. "I don't care if they find me. I had to see you. Are you well? Have they mistreated you?"

"Och, one of the police lads who works at night thought it his duty to apply some of His Majesty's justice with his fists," Billy said. "But I've been beaten worse many a time. The food is nae very good, but my friend the rat seems to like it fine, so I'll not complain."

"Have they told you what is to happen?"

"MacLeod, the sheriff, tells me I'm to be shipped off to Inverness in a week's time," he said. "There'll be a trial. If I'm lucky, I'll be sent off to Australia. If not …" He let the thought drift out into the darkness.

"Oh, Billy," she whispered, and hugged him tightly again.

"Enough about me," he said after a time. "What is the word from the strath?"

"I have not heard," she said. "They tell me nothing in Dunrobin. It's almost as though I'm being held prisoner myself, although in much nicer conditions than this."

"I expect Mrs. Murray feeds you a wee bit better than the stale bannocks they give me," Billy said. "And ye don't have to fend off the rats to eat your dinner. But I ken what ye mean, lass."

"I brought you some fresh bread and some cheese and some fruit," Anna said, digging into her basket. "Eat…you must be starving."

"Aye," he said, "I could use a right good meal. Thank you, Anna." He began wolfing down the victuals she had brought. While he ate, she studied his face, his body. She could see the bruising where he had been beaten, and reached out to touch it as if she could somehow erase it. He flinched and pulled his head away.

"What's going to happen, Billy, when they come to evict the people of Glencullen?" Anna asked, stroking his hand again. He let her do that. "How will they be able to resist if you are not there to help them?"

He was silent for a time. "They must do this for themselves," he said. "I canna do it for them."

"They think you can," she said. "They think you can do anything."

"Well, if anything includes being locked up in a dungeon before being taken away for a trial and execution, they are correct," Billy Hanks said. "But I'm no miracle worker, lass."

"They think you are, Billy," she said. "And so do I."

They both heard the footsteps of the constable coming back down the stairs. Anna reached into the pocket of her coat, grabbed something and slipped it quickly into Billy's hands. Then she stood up. The constable came into the cell.

"Time's up, miss," he said. "Let's go, now."

"Be well, brother," Anna said. "I'll try and return to see you again tomorrow."

"Thanks for the food, sister," Billy said and smiled up at her. Her heart nearly broke, but she maintained her demeanor and meekly followed the constable out of the cell. He closed and locked the heavy door, the tumblers of the lock clanging noisily into place.

Going up the stairs, Anna berated the man.

"How dare you beat a helpless prisoner like that," she said angrily. "And he should get better food than a stale bannock. And he should get some fresh air every day. These conditions are a disgrace."

"Now, missy," the constable said wearily. "Take all that up with the sheriff. I do what I'm told. He'll be out of here in a few days anyway. Nothing can be done, miss, nothing at all."

"We'll just see about that, we will," Anna huffed and stalked out of the gaol. She went to find Mrs. Murray at the market and return to Dunrobin.

Down in the cell, Billy waited until the constable had locked the door and the sound of his footsteps died away. Only then did he look at his hand to see what Anna had slipped him. He smiled. It was a short and sturdy dagger, most likely a *sgian dubh*, the small dagger many Highlanders wore tucked in their knee socks. He hefted it in his hand, thinking. Then he turned to the lock on his ankle and began to pry into it with his dagger.

THAT AFTERNOON, THE four o'clock ferry at the Meikle Landing on the Firth of Dornoch arrived with a full load, its hull grinding heavily into the wet sand at the northern landing. Off the boat came two dozen men: hard-looking men with scruffy beards, long greasy hair and old, dirty coats. The ferry captain turned to the only passenger he knew: the under-factor Robert MacCray, who was also watching the men embark and gather in a group on the shore.

"Who be that group of ruffians, MacCray?" he asked. "Have not seen them in Sutherlandshire before."

"Aye," MacCray said with a smile, looking at the ferry captain. "I dare say not a one of 'em has ever been this far north before. I recruited them myself, from Edinburgh and Leith. They're mostly coal miners and dock workers."

"And in which mine and upon which dock are ye thinking of employing such gentlemen?" the captain asked.

MacCray laughed and clapped the captain on the back.

"Nae, my good man," he said. "I have need of these gentlemen for a rougher purpose. We have some evictions to accomplish, and these are just the men to do it."

The captain understood at once what MacCray was talking about, and he did not approve. Like most people in Sutherland, he knew of the plans to remove people from the straths in favor of sheep farms, and like most people in Sutherland, he knew or was related to some of those people. But he kept his mouth shut. It was not, after all, his concern. But he watched the men, led by Robert MacCray, set off to the west, in the direction of Bonor and Lairg, and he sent a silent prayer after them, wishing them ill luck and failure in their task.

44

MacCray had hired two wagons to carry his crew of evictors from the ferry landing all the way to Lairg, a half-day's journey. He had arranged for one hogshead of beer to be carried in each wagon, and hoped the supply would last until they reached their destination. It seemed to work: the men passed around cups of the warm beer during the early stages of the trip, and by the time the wagons rolled into the dusty High Street of Lairg, the two dozen men were singing bawdy songs about a fair lady from Scilly. Except for the few who were already sound asleep.

When they arrived, MacCray, who had been following on horseback, dismounted and clapped his hands for attention.

"Right lads," he said, "We'll overnight here and leave before dawn. The innkeeper has kindly consented to allow you gents to sleep in his stables. Please do not interfere with the animals. A supper will be provided: I need to go check on that right now. And there will be more beer as well. But I expect you to be ready to go to work at first light, so don't overdo things, if you please. Remember: if the work is not done correctly, there will be no payment, and you can find your own bloody way back to Edinburgh and the Devil help ye. Am I understood?"

There was the usual grumbling assent from the men, save for one who called out "Awww, go fuck yerself, governor!" which caused some of the others to laugh. But the group staggered away towards the stables, so MacCray believed his message had been heard and, for the nonce anyway, accepted. MacCray remembered his last conversation with James Loch a few days ago in Dornoch, as this operation was reviewed for the final time. Loch had been adamant that the evictions of Glencullen were to be accomplished with as little confrontation and violence as possible. "And whatever you do," Loch had told him, wagging a finger for emphasis, "Do not use fire on the houses of the people. Tear down the timbers, scatter the thatch, confiscate the livestock, but do not set fire to anything. Lady Stafford does not want it known, especially in certain circles in London, that she has burnt out her tenants. Removing them for being in arrears of their rent is of course perfectly legal, but using fire to do so will reflect badly upon her."

MacCray understood Her Ladyship's hesitancy, but he was somewhat doubtful that he would be able to control his band of ruffians on the morrow. Like any mob, it often had a mind of its own, and could not easily be controlled once it had been let off its lead.

He went into the inn to check on the meal he had promised his men with the innkeeper, and came face to face with Sheriff MacLeod. The sheriff was hurriedly packing up some papers as if he was getting ready to leave.

"MacLeod," the under-factor said, "Are ye going somewhere? Our appointment in Glencullen is scheduled for the morning, bright and early."

MacLeod waved him off. "You'll have to make do on your own," he said. "I have just had news from Dornoch. Billy Hanks has escaped."

"*Escaped*?" MacCray was gobsmacked. "How did that happen? I thought you had the man shackled to the wall."

"Aye, we did," MacLeod said. "He got free somehow. I need to get back there and find out what happened."

"Check the pockets of your gaolers," MacCray said. "I'll bet you'll find there a bit of gilt placed there by whoever paid to get him out."

MacLeod stared at the young man while several hot retorts sprang to his mind. But he let them pass unspoken.

"My men are honest," he said quietly. "I'll stake my life on that. The constable says that Hanks was visited yesterday by a young woman from Dunrobin's kitchens, who said she was the man's sister. No one else has been allowed into the cell."

"His *sister*?" MacCray was incredulous. "Wait. His sister … I have heard talk that Billy Hanks discovered he had a sister just a few months ago. It is the servant and companion of that schoolteacher woman, Mrs. Kenton. She was originally from the strath and they only put two and two together when Mrs. Kenton arrived in Glencullen. Mrs. Kenton is now residing at Dunrobin. Where is her servant?"

"That is something I intend to find out," said MacLeod, who finished stowing away his papers and made ready to leave.

"Wait," MacCray said, holding out a hand to stop the sheriff. "What about tomorrow? You were supposed to be there to oversee the operation, make sure everything was done legally and on the up and up. What do I do now?"

"You may take Constable Campbell with you," MacLeod said. "He's fully capable of handling the situation."

"Fine," MacCray said. "He'll be in the mood to wreak some revenge upon the women who so ill treated him recently."

Sheriff MacLeod stared at MacCray. "Remember, Mac-Cray," he said, "No violence, no rioting, and above all, no burning. I've given Campbell those orders. I expect both of you to follow them. Am I understood?"

"Of course, sheriff," MacCray said. "Of course."

ANNA KENTON AWOKE that morning feeling that she was about to fall to pieces. She had tossed and turned in her bed all the night before, thinking of Billy Hanks locked away in his cell in Dornoch, and thinking of the people of Glencullen who depended on him for his leadership and his skills. She felt a desperate need to do something … *anything* … but could not seize upon any possible action that she might take.

Until she awoke, after a few hours of sleep just before the dawn. And then she knew. Quickly dressing, she went downstairs to find Mr. Gunn. It was still too early for breakfast, so she hurried back to the kitchens. Mrs. Murray and her crew of cooks and maids were busily preparing the morning meal for the Staffords and the other guests in the castle, and Mr. Gunn was supervising the waiters and butlers, making sure their uniforms were neat and clean and that each understood his assignment for the next few hours.

"Good morning, Mrs. Kenton," Gunn said when Anna came into the kitchen nook. "You are up early this morning. Is there anything I can do for you?"

Anna hesitated in responding. She did not necessarily want the others in the kitchens to hear what she had to say. Gunn, ever attenuated to silent expressions of wishes and needs, gently took her by the elbow and led her into the Long Hall that connected the kitchens with the main castle. He found a nook where a window opened onto the back gardens and provided a bit of privacy for a conversation.

"C-can you get me a horse?" Anna said when they were finally alone. "I need to ride to Glencullen. I need to be there. I need to go right now."

Mr. Gunn looked at Anna with kindness and understanding. "I would not advise that course of action, Madam," he said, gently. "I am quite certain that you would regret the circumstances that would follow. It would, first of all, put you in grave danger. There are events going on in Glencullen that could be harmful to a lady such as yourself. Additionally, I am quite certain Lady Stafford would be most upset if you were to attempt such a journey."

"I am going, Mr. Gunn," Anna said, her eyes locked into his. "I am leaving right away. If you can't get me a horse, I will walk. I will find a tradesman going to Lairg and ride with him. I'll steal a horse, if need be. I am going to Glencullen today, sir. I am asking for your help."

Gunn turned and stared out the window. He knew that something like this would happen one day. It was inevitable, once he had decided to throw in with Billy Hanks and the people from his native strath. He considered himself a loyal servant of Lord and Lady Stafford, whom he had served unwaveringly for nearly forty years. He was grateful for all they had done for him, grateful that he had been able to see parts of the world that a lad from Glencullen would never expect to see. He had been in the presence of the King. He had served the King his dinner. He had seen gracious ladies in their finest habiliment. He had been to the racing at Ascot, had dressed his gentleman for the shooting at any number of the finest houses in Britain. He had seen and done things unimaginable for a young boy who grew up in a dank croft near the River Cullen, who often had to sleep among the cows to keep warm on the coldest winter nights. He was certainly grateful for all of that.

But he was a Gunn. His father, his grandfather, his great-grandfather and all the Gunns before as long as anyone could remember were the Gunns of Glencullen. It was that place that had defined the kind of men they had become. They had lived in the same place, farmed the same stingy soil, enjoyed and endured the same summer rains and winter storms, for many hundreds of years. He was not, and never would be, Gunn of Dunrobin Castle. That was merely his job, a description of his employment. No, when he slipped into bed each night and rested his head upon the pillow, or when he kneeled in the kirk and opened his heart to his God, he was a Gunn of Glencullen the same as his ancestors had been, and that would never change. And that's why he helped Billy Hanks—with information, advice, and assistance—when he was asked. Because Billy was also of Glencullen and because Billy Hanks, of all people, *believed* in Glencullen and thought of it the same way. Gunn had been to many fine palaces and homes and estates. He had seen and served some of the most famous people in the world. But he would not exchange one of them for the chance to live again in the strath, beside the dark rushing water of the River Cullen, beside the golden fields of oats and barleycorn, and in the shadows of the purple hills and snow-dusted mountains. And that is why, Gunn suddenly realized, why he would help this woman find her way there. To Glencullen.

He turned away from the window. Anna was waiting, her face hopeful but determined.

"Meet me at the stables," he said. "One hour."

She laid a hand softly on his forearm. "Oh, thank you, Mr. Gunn," she whispered. "Thank you."

Robert MacCray began waking the men in the stables behind the inn at Lairg well before dawn. He found them scattered throughout the stalls, lying in the hay. He noted the dominant scent of spilled beer, urine and vomit, along with the usual odor of unwashed men, and knew it had been a long and rough night for the toughs from Edinburgh. He kicked and prodded them all awake, and announced the wagons were leaving in exactly thirty minutes, and any man who was not ready to leave at that time would forfeit his promised pay and would have to find his own way back home.

There was grumbling and many groans, but the men slowly rose, visited the privy, washed their faces in the water trough, and grabbed a hunk of bread from the loaves MacCray laid out for them. The men began to show a bit more life when they noticed the two new hogsheads of ale that MacCray had stored and secured in the two wagons that were ready to leave.

Still, the factor was amazed when, fully loaded, the wagons set off for the journey to Glencullen roughly on time. The men were unusually quiet at this time of day, bereft of sleep and still hungover from the night before, but they were there. And MacCray figured that the four-hour journey and the new supply of ale would have them ready for duty once they arrived at their destination.

MacCray looked around but did not see the figure of Constable Campbell. "Can't wait," he told the stableman as he swung up onto the saddle of his horse. "Tell the Constable we've left. He can catch up."

And he rode off to follow the wagons on the northern road, heading up into the valley of the River Cullen and whatever fate awaited them there.

45

Glencullen

Little Johnnie Gordon was the first one to spy the two wagons slowly making their way up the river road. He had arrived at his watch station atop the hill known as *A'Chailleach*, or The Old Woman, well before dawn, to replace the overnight watch, Mhairie Ross. He rubbed his eyes to get all the sleepiness out, and looked again. Yes! He saw the two wagons and a single man on horseback trailing behind. Billy Hanks had told them all what to look for: the wagons filled with men were one of the things Billy had said would be coming.

Quickly, Johnnie turned and bent to the pile of dried leaves and old thatch and struck his flint. A spark landed in the pile, and soon a fire was blazing away among the logs that had been soaked in pine tar and oil so they'd burn even if it were raining. The stack of wood was at least eight feet tall, and when the fire had completely enveloped the stack, the flames reached even higher.

Three miles away, on the far side of the glen across the river, perched atop *Sgurr Choinneach*, or the Mossy Mount, Agatha Mackay saw the flames rising atop the Old Woman. She could not yet see the wagons coming up the road, but she immediately ignited her own pile of logs and soon had the fire blazing, sending its signal of fire and smoke high into the sky that was just beginning to lighten to the east.

Further up the glen, atop *Sgairneach Mor*, or the Big Stony Hillside, the old man known as *Sean Dearg*, or Old Red, was busy sharpening his long dagger on a whetstone. With his head down, concentrating on his task, Red did not see the signal fire from Agatha right away. But *Sean Dearg*'s dog did, and began to bark with excitement. The old man looked up and finally noticed the smoky flames from down the strath. He laid his knife down in the dirt and bent to his task, and the third signal fire was soon burning brightly.

It was high above the village, which is what the locals called the old millrace and smithy, on a high rocky crag on the mountain they called *Stob Diamh*, or Peak of the Stag, that Willie Stewart, another young lad of fifteen years, spotted Old Red's signal fire, And he could see the one beyond that, just as Billy Hanks had told him he would, so he knew that this was real.

Instead of lighting a fire of his own, Willie set off down the rocky hillside at nearly a run. He had been selected for this last outpost because he had grown up climbing in these heights, tending his cattle and hunting for the deer that loved to graze on the tender plants that grew in the crevasses and slopes. He was surefooted as he descended rapidly to the floor of the glen, running to the old whitewashed church above the river. There, next to the door of the kirk, he grabbed the rope of the church bell and began yanking on it, up and down, remembering to do as Billy had told him: stay calm, pull with a slow rhythm, let the bell do the work.

Up and down the strath, the people, just beginning to awaken, save for those up early to milk the cows, heard the peals of the kirk's bell and knew what was coming. All of them—men, women and children—quickly dressed, grabbed their tools, their sticks, the piles of rocks they had gathered, and set out for the bridge at the entrance to the village.

In less than an hour, a group of more than a hundred residents of Glencullen had assembled in the clearing in front of the old grist mill and smithy house. There was an air of excitement mixed with dread among them. The day they had all feared had arrived. It was time.

Mary Ross arrived with the other three girls from The Manse and began to take control. She clapped her hands. "Now, people," she cried, "Let's get ourselves organized and in position, please. Ladies, gather here, next to the bridge. Men, fall in behind. Let's go, we might not have much time!"

Quickly the people took up their positions. Those whose children had come with them, sent them up a nearby hillock, well out of the way, with teen aged girls set in charge to watch over them. Soon, the people of the strath were all in position, looking down the valley, waiting.

"I wish Billy were here," said one woman, talking mostly to herself. "We might stand a chance if he were."

"We have just as much of a chance with him as without," Mary Ross growled. "This is our home. No one else can defend it as well as we can."

There was murmurs of agreement from the women. They were ready.

Suddenly, the men, standing in the background, back away from the bridge and near the two old wooden buildings, began to cheer raucously. The women, gathered in the front, surprised, turned around to look. The men had gathered together in a tight scrum, yelling and pounding at one in their midst. The crowd parted and out came Billy Hanks, gaunt and pale, but smiling broadly.

"Yer a noisy bunch," he said as the men continued to pound him on the back, shouting and raising their fists in triumph. "I was tryin' to get some sleep after walkin' all the night long. Tis a long gadabout from the Dornoch gaol."

Mary Ross ran to embrace her brother, as the other women also began cheering loudly at the arrival of their hero. The spirits in the clearing rose, and the people again took up their positions, ready for the confrontation to come.

BILLY HANKS HAD sent two young lads down to the *Geata Diabhail* to watch for the coming men, and it was not long before they came dashing up the dusty road, waving their arms wildly. "They're coming," the boys cried, "They're here!"

The crowd from Glencullen snapped to attention. The women gathered to block the road at the small wooden bridge—nothing more than some wooden planks set across the millrace—while the men formed behind them, near the smithy's doorway. Half the women held their wooden cudgels and sticks, while others carried baskets filled with stones. The men held hoes, scythes, pitchforks and other farm implements. Away on the hillock, a small girl began to cry.

"Hush, Becka," her mother called from the line at the bridge. "Yer Mam has some work to do."

And then they saw them. Two lines of rough looking men, many holding their own cudgels and clubs, walking slowly up the road. Behind them, the hated figure of the under-factor, Mac-Cray, riding his horse and smiling as he saw the scene in front of him.

"Steady all," Billy called out softly. "Wait on it."

MacCray dismounted, handing the reins to one of the street toughs, and came to the front of his men. He put his hands on his hips and shook his head at the people standing across the rude bridge who stared back at him.

"There are two ways we can do this," MacCray said, speaking loudly to send his voice all the way back to where the men were standing. "The easy way is for you to disperse and let us through. I have signed writs of eviction for all of you. Approved by the Courts in Inverness. You must obey the law and the orders of your chief, Lady Stafford of Dunrobin. Stand aside now, and I will ignore this show of contempt for the law. The harder way is entirely your choice. My men and I are coming through to enforce the law, and come though we will, no matter who is standing in our way."

"The law?" Billy Hanks shouted out. "I dunna see the law here today. Where is it?"

MacCray sighed, and turned around to look at the men behind him.

"Where is that constable, Campbell?" he said. "He was right behind us just a minute ago."

Suddenly, they all heard the sound of a horse galloping loudly up the road. In seconds, a large black stallion came into view, ridden by a hooded figure in a flowing cloak. The horse came at full speed up the road, scattering the lines of MacCray's toughs and pulling to a stop just before the bridge. The rider pulled the hood back and the long auburn tresses of Anna Kenton came tumbling down on her shoulders.

The crowd across the bridge erupted in cheers as Anna dismounted, slapped the horse away and strode defiantly across the rude planks and into the midst of the women standing on the far side. She disappeared in a mass of welcoming hugs. The women quickly reorganized and took up their positions blocking the bridge again, Anna beaming proudly in their midst.

Mary Ross stepped forward and shook her fist.

"There, damn ye, MacCray," she called. "Even Stafford's own niece is on our side. Ye'll not tear down our homes this day. *Awa'n bile yer heid, ya bloody bampot!*" The people standing around her roared their approval.

The cruel smirk on MacCray's face never wavered.

"So," he said. "The hard way it is." He turned to the first man standing beside him, a tall, gaunt bearded man, slapping a wooden cudgel loudly into his palm. "You may proceed," he said. "Take them down."

The man hesitated. "Begging your pardon, guv'nor," he said, tugging at his cap, "But those are womenfolk. We don't fancy knockin' the heads o' the lasses, now. That were not part of the agreement, Sir. Beggin' yer pardon an' all."

MacCray turned and looked at the man. "Double the pay," he said. "Two guineas a man. Take them out, *now*."

The man shrugged and turned to look at his fellows. Most of them shrugged too, although a few smiled as though they were looking forward to what was to come. He slapped the cudgel he held into the palm of his other hand.

"C'mon then, lads," he said. "Let's make short work o' it."

With a roar, the men from the city rushed across the bridge and wedged deeply into the line of women on the other side. They were met with a hailstorm of rocks and stones, and while those women in the center of the formation were pushed backwards by the sheer force of the charge, those on either flank moved in and began beating the men with their sticks or throwing their stones with full force. Shouts and shrieks rent the air and a thick cloud of dust arose over the scene, blocking much of the battle from view.

Mary Ross had been standing in the front row, in the center of the group, and she was among the first to go down. She was clubbed in the head in the first rush, and those coming up behind stomped on her as she fell to the ground, and bashed her on the arms, shoulders and her head again. Blood gushed from her nose as she fell lifeless into the dusty road. Catty Greer, who had been standing on one side of Mary, was pushed back and fell backwards. One of the toughs kicked her in the stomach and again on her breasts, and she groaned, gasped for breath and curled herself into a ball. Anna, standing on Mary Ross' other side, held up her arm to fend off a blow from another cudgel-wielding tough, and heard the sound of her forearm breaking before she began to feel the excruciating pain. She screamed and tried to turn away, but the onrushing crowd of toughs and the other women pushing back against them had her pinned, and there was nothing she could do but try to keep her feet and try to protect her arm from any further movement.

The first rush of the toughs had managed to clear the women back from the bridge a few yards. Now, the second wave came storming across, the men shouting and clubbing with abandon, and woman after woman began to drop with heads bleeding and limbs broken. Another volley of rocks thrown by other women did some damage, as one or two of the toughs dropped to the dust, grabbing their heads in pain.

The battle raged as the group of toughs finally began to clear out a space on the far side of the bridge, stepping over the bodies of the women they had beaten senseless and forming a rough circle. It was then that Billy Hanks shouted his command, and the men of Glencullen, lacking in numbers but filled with anger, charged headlong into the melee.

Though the men of the strath were mostly older they fought with abandon against the younger and stronger toughs from the city. The blows from their farm tools, as well as their own fists, found their marks, and MacCray's men suffered several casualties. One man was thrown into the millrace, two were knocked unconscious and several others sustained serious injuries that took them out of the fight.

Billy Hanks fought his way into the center of the scrum, looking for Anna. He finally saw her, her face drawn in pain, crouched down low, trying to protect her injured arm and at the same time fending off kicks and blows aimed at her head and shoulders. Next to her, Catty was lying on her back and moaning in pain. Billy picked up one of the toughs, grabbing him bodily by the belt and collar, and tossed the man into a group of four others that were charging at him: they all went down in a heap of groans and shouts.

Finally, Billy made it to Anna's side. She looked at him, her pale face etched in pain.

"Help them, Billy," she called. "Catty is hurt, and I don't know where Mary is."

"Your arm," he said, reaching for her.

"It's broken," Anna said. "But help them, Billy, please!"

He turned and picked up the prostrate form of Catty Greer as if she were made of feathers and carried her off to the side, away from the donnybrook that continued all around him. He laid her down gently and turned to peer again through the cloud of dust that had risen around and above the screaming mass of the fighters. There! He saw the form of Mary Ross, unmoving amid the riot, lying on her side, her face covered in blood. He fought his way to her, pushing and shoving bodies out of the way, and finally managed to reach her side. He bent down and touched the side of her neck.

Coming up from behind, one of the toughs planted a boot in Billy's back and with a half-kick, half-push, sent him sprawling in the dirt. Billy jumped to his feet as the man came charging at him, his cudgel beginning its lethal swing toward Billy's head. He stepped forward, parried the blow with his forearm and brought his knee sharply upwards into the man's groin. The tough collapsed in a heap, the air expelled in a rush from his lungs.

"*Stop … stop …* stop this at once, in the name of the law!" Constable Campbell had finally arrived and was now trying to restore order to the chaotic scene. He waded into the fight, pulling people apart, shouting all the while. It took several minutes, but eventually the two sides separated and retreated some distance apart. And then, the blood lust of the fight spent, they all began to tend to the wounded.

Billy saw that Anna had gone to the side of Catty and was trying to attend to her, despite her own pain from her broken arm. He joined her, and saw Catty's eyes flutter open. Catty tried to rise, but Billy and Anna made her lie still.

"Mary," Catty gasped. "Mary Ross. I saw her hit. I saw her blood. Is she all right?"

Anna looked at Billy, who shook his head.

"She's dead," he said. "They've killed her."

Hearing the dreadful news, Catty sank back onto the ground and began to keen.

"We must take her to Meg's," Anna said. "She is in need of Meg's knowledge."

"As are you," Billy said. He bent and picked Catty up in his arms again and the three of them set off for the river.

Behind them, the men from the city who had managed to survive the fighting began to tear down the walls of the old wooden smithy. They knocked out the posts on one side that held up the roof, which fell with a crash raising another cloud of dust. The glass of the windows were smashed and from inside came the sound of broken timbers. The destruction of Glencullen had begun.

46

Mute Meg was waiting inside her cottage by the river, rocking in her chair by the hearth. When Billy Hanks walked in carrying the groaning figure of Catty and trailed by Anna, still holding her injured arm close to her side, Meg took one look and motioned toward the bed. Billy carried Catty there and laid her down gently. Meg went to Anna and quickly felt her arm. Anna stiffened once, lips drawn back in a grimace, but Meg patted her good arm and helped her sit on a stool.

On a table, Meg had laid out a number of bottles and packets of her medicines and cures, as well as a dozen rolls of bandages: old sheets she had ripped into strips in readiness. She took up several and went to Catty to begin ministering to her injuries.

Billy Hanks strode to the door, as if to leave and return to the fray. But Anna stopped him.

"Nay, Billy," she said, holding out her good hand. "It's over. They have won the day, as we knew they must. If you go back, they'll kill you this time."

"I must go and find my sister," he said. "I am her only family."

"You cannot help her now," Anna said. "She will be honored for what she did here today. She will be remembered forever by the people of Glencullen. But her fight is over, and yours must be as well."

"The fight is never over, lass," he said. "No matter what they and their bloody law says, this is our land, our home."

"Aye, Billy," she said, rising to her feet and unsteadily making her way to his side. "It will always be your home. But you cannot live here now. You must leave. You must live. For I cannot bear to think of the world without you in it."

He stopped, then and looked at her. She stared at him, eyes imploring. He moved toward her and she to him, and they embraced.

"That may be the sweetest thing I've seen today," said a voice from the door. Robert MacCray came inside as Billy and Anna sprang apart. Billy made a motion as if he was about to launch himself at the other man, but then he noticed that Mac-Cray was holding a cocked pistol in his hand. And it was pointed directly at Anna.

"Let's all be nice and calm, here, shall we?" MacCray said. He motioned with the pistol for Billy and Anna to move away, towards the hearth. They did, standing next to each other. MacCray glanced over at Meg, who was holding Catty's head in one hand as she encouraged her to drink from a potion she had mixed. "I see the old witch is at her tricks," he continued. "But not for long. I shall take great pleasure in seeing this house burned to the ground, and all its evil magick with it."

"And what has this old woman ever done to you, Mac-Cray?" asked Billy Hanks, his voice low and dangerous.

"Nothing I can think of," MacCray said, "But that is of no importance. She's spent years fooling the people with her tinc-tures and creams, her stories and wicked incantations. Well, now she can go with the rest of these vagabonds to Golspie."

Against the wall, Catty suddenly sat upright, holding her head in her hands. She rubbed her forehead, then looked up at MacCray.

"Forgive us, Sir," she said weakly. "But we have forgotten our manners. May we offer you a glass of port? You must be fearfully thirsty after such hard work as you've done this day."

MacCray looked at the woman as if she were daft. But then he thought for a moment, and finally nodded his assent. "Aye, woman, a wee taste would help with the dust in my throat," he said. "I am obliged."

Catty struggled to her feet, with the help of Mute Meg, who held one arm until Catty's balance was in place. Then, she walked unsteadily to the table where a leather bottle and two glasses had been placed on a silver tray. She carefully poured out a glass of the dark red wine the color of blood and handed it to MacCray, who downed it with one gulp.

"I've always been amazed at how you people hold true to the traditions of hospitality," he said, almost as if to himself. "Here I am about to throw you out of your home, but because I'm a visitor, I must first be served a wee refreshment. It's remarkable. If unutterably stupid." He laughed and threw his glass against the wall, where it shattered into a thousand pieces.

Billy, incensed, again started forward with his fists clenched. But MacCray quickly brought his pistol around to point at Billy's heart, and he stopped.

"Nice and easy, Hanks," MacCray said, a smile playing at the edges of his lips. "I have plans for you. Not only will I have accomplished Lady Stafford's goals here today in removing this lot of useless dreck, but I will have captured and returned the escaped fugitive and murderer of Major Darnell. That ought to be worth some kind of reward from His Lordship, eh? Heaven knows he's got enough gold in his vaults."

"Thirty pieces of silver, right Mr. MacCray?" Anna said.

He looked at her and laughed. "A very good analogy, Madam," he said, "Very good indeed. You know, I had once thought that you and I would make a good pair. You with your connections to Lord Stafford, and me with my abilities and talents. It would have been a most productive marriage, don't you think?"

"I would rather die than be wed to the likes of you," Anna said between clenched teeth.

MacCray raised his pistol as if to strike her across the face with it. Billy again started forward to stop him. But then a strange look came into MacCray's eyes. He took a deep breath, staggered slightly, the arm holding the pistol dropped to his side and, with a dull clatter, the firearm dropped to the floor. MacCray, his eyes now glassy and sightless, stood there weaving from side to side.

Billy stepped forward and drove his fist onto the point of MacCray's chin, and the man toppled over backwards.

Catty exhaled, and sat back down heavily on the bed.

"Tincture of club moss," she said, "Meg put it in the wine. I think she knew he would come here. You didn't need to hit him, Billy. He would have been mostly paralyzed in a few minutes."

"With my apologies, Catty, but rarely has there been a man more deserving of being struck than that lot," Billy said.

Meg began waving her hands. Catty watched and waited. Tears came to her eyes.

"Are you sure?" she asked the old woman, voice quavering. "There is no other way?"

Meg continued to communicate her thoughts in the ways that no other man or woman could understand. She reached beneath the small bed and pulled out an old leather satchel. She handed it to Catty.

"This belonged to her grandfather," Catty said. "She wants me to have it now."

"But why?" Anna asked.

Meg came over to Anna and pushed her down onto the stool.

"First we need to attend to your arm," Catty said. "Billy, put the man onto the bed, will you please?"

Meg bent over her table while Billy heaved MacCray, now basically comatose, onto the narrow straw mattress. Meg came over to Anna with a small bottle.

"She says to drink this," Catty told her. "It will hurt a bit when she sets the arm, and this will help dull the pain."

Anna did as she was told and almost immediately began to feel the room spinning around her. She barely noticed when Meg and Catty firmly slid her broken bone into place, then tightly bound a length of wood against her forearm to hold it in place, and used some of the torn sheets to fashion a sling. The entire thing took just a few minutes.

When she was done, Meg turned and waved Billy to come close. She took his left hand and placed it around Anna's right, and, taking from her pocket a linen cloth upon which several colorful and unusual symbols had been embroidered, she bound their two hands together with a few deft wraps. She then bowed her head, spread her own hands wide, and Billy could see her lips moving as she mouthed her silent words. She then looked up at Billy and smiled, and patted his hand.

"Congratulations," Catty said.

"Thank ye," Billy replied. "For what?"

"You are now husband and wife," Catty said with a broad smile. "May you be healthy all your days, blessed with long life and peace, may your children be many and may you grow old with goodness and riches. You may kiss the bride, although I'm afraid she won't remember it later."

"She won't remember that I asked her to be my wife," Billy said with a laugh, "Since I never did."

"It will not matter," Catty said. "It is done, and a good thing."

Billy Hanks kissed Anna, who smiled fondly at him. Meg gave Billy a hug, and kissed him on the cheek. She looked at Anna, who sat on her stool, looking around the room with a half-smile. Her eyes were still mostly unfocused.

"And now we must leave," Catty said. "The men will come here soon, and there is one thing left to do."

"And what is that?" Billy asked.

But Catty merely shook her head. She looked around the cottage one last time, then grabbed the leather bag Meg had just given her. Billy helped Anna to her feet and led her to the door. Catty went to Meg and hugged her.

"*Beannachd dhuit*," she said in a whisper. Blessings be upon you.

"*Chì mi thu san ath bheatha.*" The words were spoken so softly, that neither Billy Hanks nor Catty Greer was sure they had actually heard them. But Anna Keaton, despite her half-conscious state, or perhaps because of it, heard the old woman speak the first words she had spoken in more than eighty years.

"Yes," Anna said, "We *will* see you in the next life. Goodbye, then."

She then walked slowly out the door, followed by Catty and Billy, and the three of them began walking up the road that followed the river, walking north, towards the wild lands and the mountains. Billy held tightly to Anna's arm, as she was still unsteady in her drugged state, and Catty walked behind. They ascended the hill beyond the old white kirk, where people from the strath were now beginning to gather, and turned to look back down the valley.

At the bend of the river where Mute Meg's cottage stood, smoke was billowing up into the sky, in clouds black and dark as death. Within minutes, the red scar of the flames leapt high into the air as the cottage was completely enveloped in fire.

The three stood there for several minutes watching the fire. They were wordless, for there was nothing to say. A puff of white smoke emerged from the midst of the blackness, twisted around the trees and then vanished in an instant.

"She is free," Catty said then.

They turned and began to walk north again.

47

Epilogue

Life as the people of Glencullen had lived it for more than seven hundred years came to an end that day. MacCray's gang of toughs and the handful of deputies that Campbell had brought with him from Lairg pulled down the cottages and crofts of more than twenty families. They stripped the thatch off the roofs and dislodged the central timbers that formed those roofs. The threw the rude furniture—the tables, the chairs, the stools, the beds of straw—out into the yards. They smashed the implements of cooking and eating and doused the hearthfires. They drove the livestock down the strath to Captain Gordon's farm, scattered the chickens and geese, pulled down the rickety constructions of the barns and out buildings.

The people of Glencullen, grabbing what possessions they could before the rough men began tearing apart their homes, made their way to the kirkyard by the river. For some reason, they did not go inside the church, feeling that would be trespassing against God himself, but constructed some rude tents with blankets out among the headstones of the honored dead beneath the sighing boughs of the evergreens. The rough men and the police would later come and tear down even these small protections against the elements, but for a time, they gave the people some shelter.

The day after the clearance of Glencullen the people held a funeral for Mary Ross, the brave woman who stood at the bridge and died there defending her home. No clergyman was present to preside, so the people buried her themselves, in the kirkyard of the sighing boughs. They spoke the words of their faith and they placed a wooden cross at her grave. And they pledged to never forget Mary's bravery.

Soon, the people left the strath. Some traveled to Golspie on the coast and took up Lord Stafford's offer of building anew on the small lots on a muir. Others went north, where a landlord in Caithness offered them a chance to start again with their cattle and their crops. Others emigrated to the new colonies in Canada, while still others went south to the newly industrializing cities of Edinburgh and Glasgow where there was said to be work and wages.

By the next spring, the people were gone from Glencullen, and the sheep came in, by the tens of thousands. The sheep grazed placidly among the ruins of the crofts, and in the high mountain meadows where the cattle had once roamed. Instead of crops, the strath was now returned to Nature, and instead of a community of people, Glencullen was now home to a few shepherds and their barking dogs, herding the black-faced sheep up and down the valley.

Nobody knew what became of Billy Hanks, his wife the English niece of Lord Stafford, or the woman who had inherited the skills and knowledge of Mute Meg. Nobody *knew* what happened to them, but everyone had an opinion. Some said that they had all three gone to Canada on the first available ship, but there was no record of their passage in any ship's log. Some said they had gone to Orkney or the Shetlands, but people who came back from those northern islands said there was no trace of three strangers there. Some said they went into the wilderness, into the million square miles of Sutherlandshire, and lived off the land in the mountains and the muirs and the broad empty spaces of wetlands and hills.

But no one knew, for sure.

Lord Stafford considered the clearing of Glencullen to be a success, for the most part, despite the death of his under-factor MacCray in the fire. "I specifically instructed the man not to use fire in the removals," he told his friends and associates in London. "But in his zeal to burn the house of a reputed witch in the district, he seems to have managed to kill himself. A tragedy, to be sure, but there you are …"

In due course, Lord Stafford was elevated by the King to the hereditary honor of being the first Duke of Sutherland, and his wife took the title of the Duchess Countess. Their wealth continued to grow, even as the Duke's vast network of canals were supplanted by the coming of the new invention of the steam railroad. His superintendant, James Loch, made sure that the Duke invested a goodly sum of his wealth into the new railroad companies, investments that paid off handsomely.

And he continued to clear the people off his land in Sutherland, and replace them with sheep. It continued to be highly profitable. Vast tracts of the inner reaches of the county were depopulated. It was a quiet kind of genocide, where the people were not directly killed, but pushed away from their homelands, never to return again.

In 1815, the coalition of European nations began tightening the noose that had been placed around the neck of Bonaparte after his disastrous campaign in Russia a few years earlier. Thanks to the command of the Duke of Wellington, the French were pushed out of Spain, and soon, the Austrians chased the French army out of German lands. To bolster his troops for the final push against the French tyrant, King George asked his Scottish lairds to launch an all-out effort to raise new recruits for the British armies.

The 93rd Regiment of Foot, also known as the Sutherland Highlanders, had long been made up of the young men from the straths and glens throughout the county. The last time, in the

1790s, the clan chief, Lady Stafford, had put out a call for volunteers, more than a thousand men flocked to enroll. The new Duke of Sutherland had no doubts that he could easily surpass that number.

And so the word went out. Posters went up in every village and town; the ministers in every kirk inveighed both patriotic and religious fervor to encourage their parishioners to turn out in support. The Duke of Sutherland himself, now elderly and somewhat hard of hearing, nevertheless sent word to Scotland that he would arrive from London in a month's time to appear at a grand patriotic rally and enlistment event on the grounds of Dunrobin Castle.

Major General Weymss, who had commanded the 93rd for some twenty years, traveled with the Duke and Duchess-Countess to Dornoch, and the three enjoyed an elegant repast in the castle the night before the event. With a number of both active and retired military figures at the table, the stories of war and glory continued long into the night, well fueled by the contents of the Duke's ample cellars.

The Duchess-Countess Sutherland did not appear for breakfast the next morning. She had learned the night before that her eldest son, George, was expected to accompany the Highlanders to the Low Country. To be sure, he would be safely attached to the general's staff, well away from the actual fighting, but she was still upset. Mr. Murray, the head of household who had replaced Mr. Gunn some years earlier—that gentleman had suddenly resigned his post one day and left Scotland to live in retirement in the south of France—brought the Duchess her morning chocolate.

"I do not like talk of war," the Duchess said. "For you men, it's all about the glory of battle and the honor of fighting. For women, it is about our family members getting killed or maimed. I fail to see the glory in that."

"Mum," said Mr. Murray. He was still learning the ways of his employers, and usually pursued a path of strict neutrality in all matters.

"What time does the meeting begin?" she asked.

"I believe at noon, Mum," he said, and bowed his way out of her chambers.

It was a glorious spring morning at Dunrobin. A morning shower had moved away and the air was fresh and clear in the burst of sunlight. The gates to the castle were opened at eleven, but the gatekeeper was somewhat surprised to see that there was no one waiting to come in. Indeed, over the next hour, perhaps a hundred people, men and women alike, strolled down the avenue beneath the towering rows of elms and gathered in the front bailey.

When the Duke was informed of that number just before noon, he smiled and said "My adopted countrymen are living up to their reputation for tardiness. We will postpone the beginning of the ceremony for an hour, until they drag themselves in."

But at one o'clock, there were no more than three hundred gathered outside the castle, and almost half that number were women. Nevertheless, the Duke gave the order to begin, and the pipers he had hired for the occasion began to fill their bags and play the march, *Caber Feidh*, and the skirling sound of the pipes soon filled the air.

Finally, the Duke led a procession out the door of the castle, accompanied by the Major General and his staff, all resplendent in their red military coats, decorated with brass buttons, glittering medals and bright colored ribbons, their high boots gleaming with fresh polish in the bright spring sunshine.

There was some polite applause as the Duke mounted a dais set just behind a long table on which was spread the enlistment forms, and a tall pile of pound notes. Two sergeants from the 93rd sat at the table, ready to take the signatures and pass out the banknotes to the new enlistees.

"My fellow countrymen," the Duke began, his squeaky, high-pitched voice struggling to reach the back of the crowd of people, who shuffled in closer in order to hear. "It is my honor to be here today to welcome all of you who will be answering the call of your King and volunteering to do his service in the war against Bonaparte. You men of Sutherland have fought bravely and with distinction in many of our country's wars. The valor and bravery of the 93rd Regiment of Sutherland Highlanders are unparalleled around the world. Your country needs you now and I am certain you will respond as you always have when your country has called.

"I want you all to know that any man who signs the form today and enters His Majesty's service will receive an immediate bonus of six pounds. It is my honor to tell you that this comes from my own personal funds. And that my own son, George Sutherland-Leveson-Gower, will go with you to the Low Country to serve as aide-de-camp to our great Major General Weymss."

The Duke turned and nodded at the general, who was scanning the crowd with a practiced eye, looking over the men assembled there and mentally gauging the regimental positions he would be able to fill.

"So without further ado, I encourage you now to come forward and sign the register," the Duke continued. He signaled to the musicians at one side and they launched into a fast-paced march, designed to stir the blood of any Scotsman within hearing.

And yet, no one came forward. The crowd stood silently, watching the Duke and the General talking to each other. Halfway through the march, the Duke noticed that nobody—not a one—had stepped forward. He stood and blinked furiously out at the crowd, a frown building on his face. Finally, he raised a hand, and the music died away and then suddenly stopped.

"Did you not hear?" the Duke said tremulously. "Please come forward to join the ranks of the Sutherland Highlanders. We need all hands in order to defeat that French bastard."

If the Duke thought a mild vulgarity would break the spell, he was wrong. Again, the crowd stood silently, unmoving. Three hundred pairs of eyes stared at the Duke, who began to feel that something had gone terribly wrong. His face reddened in anger.

"Well, then," he said finally. "I hope there is someone here who can tell me what is the matter. The men of Sutherland have always answered the call of the King for service. I demand to know the reason for this abrogation of your duty."

Standing at the back of the crowd, a man removed his cap and cleared his throat. Those around him edged away to give him some room. He began to speak.

"Begging your pardon, your Grace," he began, "I am sorry for the response to your offer here today, but there is a good reason for it. Most of us here believe that if Bonaparte himself were to sail across the sea and capture Dunrobin Castle on the morrow, the people of our shire could not be treated worse than we have suffered at the hands of you and your family over the last many years.

"You came here expecting men to enlist in your army. But where are the men? They are no longer here because you have removed them all long ago, sending them to Canada or Glasgow. You have put them out of their homes, you have caused their children to weep, you have taken away the lands that they faithfully farmed for many hundreds of years.

"You want us to fight for our country? We have no country. You have taken it away from us in return for gold and silver. You robbed us of our country and you have given it to the sheep. Once, the glens of Sutherland were filled with men, brave men, strong men, who would have gladly served their King in battle. They would have gone to their deaths happily, singing songs of praise and glory. But you replaced those men, replaced them with sheep. So let the sheep defend you! Let the sheep fight your battles. For we, the men of Sutherland … we will not."

The crowd erupted in cheers. The applause, the shouting, the fists raised in the air …it went on for many minutes. The sound carried deep into the rooms of the castle, and found the Duchess-Countess sipping at her tea in the Drawing Room. She heard the sound, which reminded her of nothing else but the sounds she still remembered from Paris, all those years ago, and she blanched with fear. She clutched at the locket that hung around her neck, a locket she wore almost every day of her life. Now, hearing the noise arising from the throats of the people gathered outside her home, she felt for that locket, pulled it free from her clothing and opened it, to look again at that clipping of snow-white hair and the portrait of the poor dead Queen, Marie Antoinette, who had once been the Duchess-Countess' friend, to read again the sorrowful words: *bleached in sadness*. For reasons she did not quite understand, Elizabeth Gordon, the 19th chief of clan Sutherland and the Duchess-Countess, began to weep.

Outside, the Duke turned and left the dais, trailed by the Major General, and then by the officers. The sound of the cheers, the calls, the applause, followed them inside the heavy wooden doors of the castle. The sound continued long afterwards, even as the crowd began to disperse, walking down the broad avenue. But slowly, the cheers changed, and the people began chanting.

"Bill-ee, Bill-ee, Bill-ee…"

Afterword

There are no happy endings in any stories about the Highland Clearances of Scotland. In the end, the people of the glens were forcibly removed to make way for the sheep (and later, for the deer runs and fishing beats that landowners offered to wealthy clients from the big cities; and later still for the tourists who come to enjoy the empty spaces and beautiful views, devoid of humanity.).

So it may be hard, at first, to understand why a storyteller would grab on to this subject, and spend a good thirty years of his life researching and reading and trying to understand what happened and why.

Most of my career was spent as a travel writer, with a specialty in golf. As a result, I made numerous visits to Scotland, and the rest of the British Isles, to play the famous courses and stay in the lovely nearby resorts, inns and hotels. Yes, it was a dirty job, but *somebody* had to do it!

On one of my first visits to Scotland, I needed something to read for the long flight back home, so I stopped in the airport bookstore, and in the Scottish History section I found, and purchased, a copy of John Prebble's *The Highland Clearances*. I had heard about the Clearances, of course, but really knew next to nothing about that period of history.

That book got me started on what became a lifelong interest in the Clearances, and while I have since learned that Prebble's work was and is controversial among academic historians (he was a lifelong communist and a journalist, and is accused of letting his political views shade his historical storytelling), that book was massively influential on me. A great many of the stories Prebble told of incidents at the various removals over the fifty-plus years of the Clearances made their way into my novel, although I moved them around in both time and space to better fit my own fictional story.

I should quickly add that Prebble was not my only source material: I have read numerous other histories and studies of the Clearances, including those of more academic historians who have been more willing than Prebble to at least give some consideration to the economic and societal forces that led the Scottish landlords of that time to try to do something about the seemingly endless poverty of life in the glens and straths. The late Eric Richards wrote a seminal two-volume history of the Clearances and also wrote a book-length biography of the first Duke of Sutherland, titled *The Leviathan of Wealth: The Sutherland Fortune in the Industrial Revolution*.

It was Prebble's chapter on the Massacre at Greenyards, also known as the Massacre of the Ross Women, which took place in Strathcarron in 1854, which was the first brick in the foundation of what became *Year of the Sheep*. I have been to Strathcarron (which is a doppelgänger for Glencullen), and walked through the kirkyard at Croick Church, where removed people lived for weeks outdoors in tents.

But the images from that incident, where the women of Strathcarron made a stand against the forces of the laird (in this case, Ross of Balnagowan), and were savagely beaten for it, stuck in my head.

Most stories of the Clearances begin, and sometimes end, with the infamous one at Strathnaver, where the odious Patrick

Sellar threw the people out into the cold and rain, burned their crofts and killed their cattle. He was rightly charged with manslaughter and wrongly acquitted by a court of law in Inverness.

That story did not make it into my novel, other than in a passing mention, because it's both too infamous and has become, in my view anyway, a caricature of good versus evil and stripped of deeper meaning. Instead, reading about Sellar and visiting the still almost empty land along the River Naver, I began to wonder about the people who sent Sellar to do his dastardly deed: the lairds of Dunrobin Castle in Dornoch.

And there I found the motherlode of material that made my story into what I hope is a more interesting novel. For the landlord who removed the people from the glens of Sutherland was a woman. How did Elizabeth Gordon become the chief of Clan Sutherland? *That's* a pretty good story. How did she end up marrying the richest man in probably all of Europe, that "Leviathan of Wealth?" *That's* a pretty good story. What happened early in their lives together that might have had an impact on why they acted like they did in the Clearances? *That's* a pretty good story, even if I might have stretched the historical truth just a wee bit to make my story better.

Even Eric Richard's biography, which is numbingly detailed on most aspects of George Granville Levenson-Gore's life, is practically silent on the two-plus years he served as England's ambassador to the Court of Louis XVI during the French Revolution. Nor does he appear in Thomas Carlyle's rambling but entertaining history of the French Revolution. That could mean he was woefully ineffective as an ambassador, or that his duties were important, but secretive. As a novelist, I went with the latter interpretation.

I picked up other biographical material about the Duke and Duchess-Countess of Sutherland at Dunrobin Castle's gift shop after touring that wonderful old house. From those pamphlets and books, I learned that it is family legend that Elizabeth Gordon was a close friend to the doomed Marie Antoinette and that she indeed provided the girl's clothing for the Dauphin's disguise prior to the ill-fated Flight to Varennes. True or not, it makes for a good story.

This would be a good time to instruct my American readers on the proper pronunciation of the man's name. "Levenson" is pronounced "Lew-son," and "Gower" is pronounced "Gore." I don't know why: I am from the Colonies.

Most of the major events in the novel actually happened. The people of the Black Isle and Cromarty responded to the first invasion of the sheep men by herding up the flocks and physically driving them back out of the county. Several police officers attempting to serve writs of removal were physically attacked, the writs destroyed, and at least one, I think on the Isle of Skye, was de-pantsed for his effort. Several of the removals used city toughs imported from Edinburgh and Glasgow. Again, I took actual events from history and moved them into my fictional framework to tell my story. I don't feel guilty about that—I'm a novelist and storyteller, not a historian.

But Prebble and most historians agree that a significant part of the resistance to the Clearances came from the women of the glens. Partly because their men were indeed off fighting wars on the Continent, but I think also because the women were strongly defensive about giving up their homes. And thus I came upon my central theme of woman against woman as well as class against class, bourgeoisie against proletariat.

Personally, I do not subscribe to the current fad of revising, revisiting and reforming history to meet our modern, politically correct beliefs. I do not believe that the first Duke of Sutherland was an "evil" man, per se. His wife owned a million square acres of land in Scotland's Far North, and as a highly successful land reformer in his time, he was trying to do something to alleviate the poverty of the people on his estates. That poverty existed long before he came along, had been exacerbated by the changes in the clan system and with the coming of the Industrial Revolution, and his decisions were in line with generally accepted legal and moral standards of his age. His solution was ham-handed, unfair, destructive and calamitous, to be sure, but I don't believe for a minute that he removed the people of the glens because he enjoyed throwing people out of their homes.

After the Duke's death, a collection was taken up in Sutherlandshire, and a large statue of the man was erected on the summit of *Beinn a'Bhragaidh* near Golspie. As John Prebble poignantly points out, the statue faces out to sea, and his back is turned to the Highland glens that he emptied. There is still, to this day, a movement in Scotland to take that statue down.

I can understand that feeling; indeed, who cannot? But even if that monument is taken down, there will still be no happy ending to the story. For history is implacable in its unchangeable facts, and it is only those of us who spin our fanciful tales who can at least try to add some meaning and understanding and perhaps some inspiration to what will always be a very sad chapter in mankind's ongoing story.

--James Y. Bartlett

ABOUT THE AUTHOR

James Y. Bartlett is an American journalist, writer, editor and author.

He turned his interest in the game of golf into a forty-year career as one of the most-published golf and travel writers of his generation. His articles and columns on the Royal & Ancient game appeared in hundreds of publications ranging from *Bon Appetit* to *Esquire*, *Men's Journal* to *Golf for Women*.

Bartlett was the golf columnist for *Forbes FYI* magazine for the first fifteen years of that publication's history and wrote a similar column on the golf lifestyle for *Hemispheres*, the in-flight magazine of United Airlines for nearly twenty years under the pseudonym of "A.G. Pollard, Jr."

Bartlett also worked as a staff editor for a number of national publications, including *Golfweek*, *Caribbean Travel & Life*, and *Luxury Golf*.

He began writing his popular Hacker Golf Mystery series in 1991, with the publication of *Death is a Two-Stroke Penalty* (St. Martin's Press). That series now includes seven titles. Bartlett is also the author of five nonfiction books.

He lives with his wife Susan in Rhode Island.

For more information about the author and his books, please visit his website at

http://www.jamesybartlett.com

The Hacker Golf Mystery series

DEATH IS A TWO-STROKE PENALTY
DEATH FROM THE LADIES TEE
DEATH AT THE MEMBER-GUEST
DEATH IN A GREEN JACKET
DEATH FROM THE CLARET JUG
AN OPEN CASE OF DEATH
P.G.A. SPELLS DEATH

Other titles by the author:

CADDIEWAMPUS: LOOPING FOR GOLF'S GREATS
SERPENT POINT: A POLITICAL THRILLER[*]
THINK LIKE A CADDIE, PLAY LIKE A PRO
MASTERING GOLF'S TOUGHEST SHOTS

* written under the pseudonym Caleb Clarke

www.ingramcontent.com/pod-product-compliance
Lightning Source LLC
Chambersburg PA
CBHW020539120726
47903CB00001B/42